I0819903

WRATH OF DRAGONS

 ELDEREALM BOOK ONE 

SCOTT KING

This book is a work of fiction.

Wrath of Dragons is Published by Majestic Arts

Cover Art by Jason Nguyen

Cover Design by Scott King

Chapter Headers by Kevin Cromwell

Edited by Leslie Watts

Manufactured in the United States of America

Paperback ISBN-13: 978-1548433048

Paperback ISBN-10: 1548433047

Hardcover ISBN: 9780692063354

First Edition: Published March 2018

BOOKS BY SCOTT KING

Elderealm

The Wrath of Dragons

Unchained Shadows coming soon

Queen of Flames coming soon

Tales of Elderealm Series

Other Books

The Zimmah Chronicles

National Cthulhu Eats Spaghetti Day

The Eye of Hastur

Ameriguns

Resist Them

The 5 Day Novel

Story Pitch

Outline Your Novel

Finish the Script!

DAD! A Documentary Graphic Novel

Holiday Wars

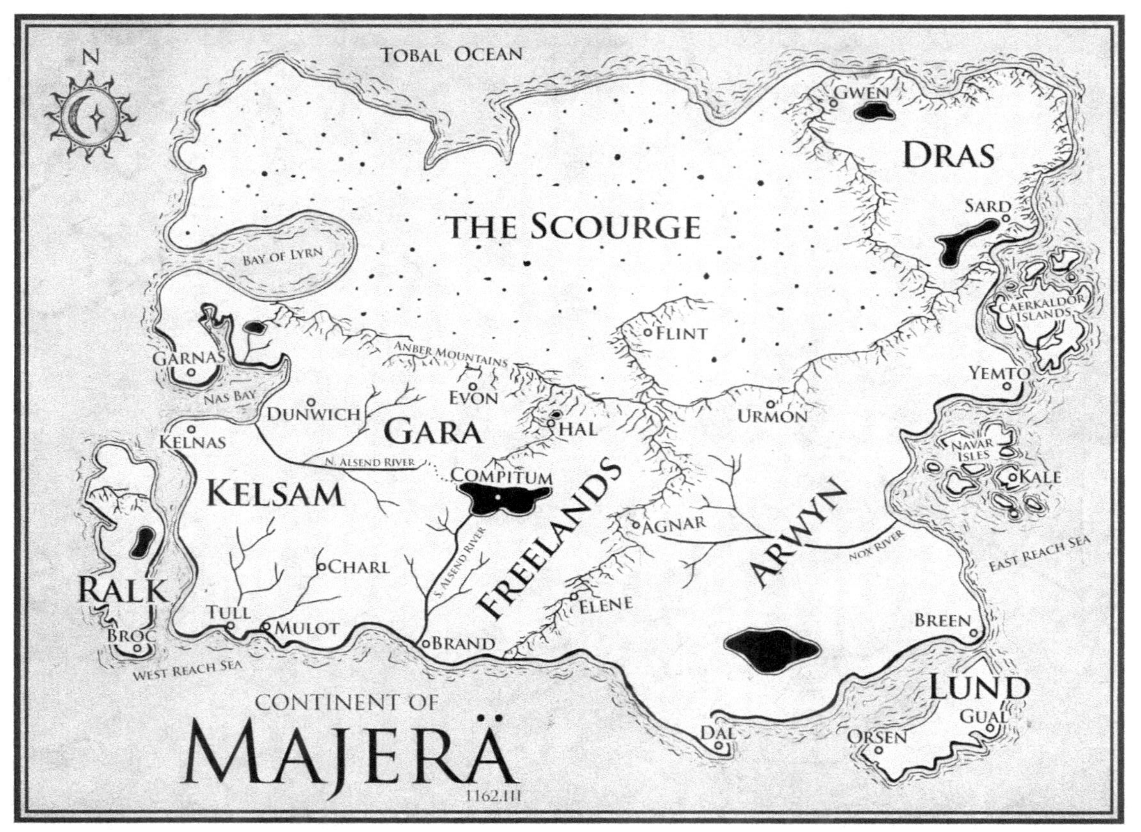
N
TOBAL OCEAN
THE SCOURGE
DRAS
GWEN
SARD
CAERKALDOR ISLANDS
YEMTO
NAVAR ISLES
KALE
EAST REACH SEA
BAY OF LYRN
GARNAS
NAS BAY
ANBER MOUNTAINS
FLINT
EVON
DUNWICH
GARA
HAL
URMON
KELNAS
N. ALSEND RIVER
COMPITUM
KELSAM
FREELANDS
AGNAR
ARWYN
NOX RIVER
CHARL
S. ALSEND RIVER
RALK
TULL
MULOT
ELENE
BREEN
BROC
BRAND
WEST REACH SEA
LUND
GUAL
DAL
ORSEN
CONTINENT OF
MAJERÄ
1162.III

"...and the sun sank below the horizon, marking the end of the age of races. The night brought upon the dawning of the age of man."

— Hemmingwell's History of The World Vol. III

PROLOGUE

"He has chosen the wrong path."

"Good thing we have the contingency."

"Good thing."

"Will they be able to handle it?"

"We thought he could, and he didn't. Why should these do better?"

"He can still get us what we want."

"Too risky. It was too much of a burden for one, but the shoulders of three..."

"Let us watch and see."

1

DRAGON ATTACK

ISLESDAY, 45TH OF WEOD, 1162.111

"Don't be alarmed." Owen shook Carter awake.

Groggy eyed, Carter sat up, knowing when Master Owen said he shouldn't be alarmed, it meant he should be. "What's wrong?"

The cottage shuddered as a blinding orange flash surged past the bedroom window. It illuminated Owen's wrinkled face. In the bright light, the folds of skin on his cheeks and brow looked like deep canyons that faded into the smooth dome of his hairless scalp. Owen tried to hide it, but Carter detected the traces of fear hidden in the corners of Owen's eyes.

"It's a dragon," Owen said.

Carter held his breath. There hadn't been a dragon sighting in five years, and the rumors back then had been less believable than the size of the catfish Mr. Kohley claimed to have caught in the Alsend River.

Dashing to the window, Carter looked to the night sky. A

shadow dipped below the clouds, and fire erupted from it, striking the lake that surrounded Owen's cottage. The water boiled, and thick clouds of steam rose into the sky, hiding the dragon.

"Do you see it?" Carter craned his neck out the window and looked directly up. He saw soft flashes of fire behind the clouds, but he didn't spot the dragon.

"Stay inside." Owen looked frail, but was far from it. With a single jerk of Carter's nightshirt, he pulled the teen backwards. "The dragon cannot harm us here. Stay calm, stay inside, and we will be safe. I don't want to see any brashness or fool hardy actions."

"Brashness? A dragon is attacking us!" Carter pointed out the window. "We can't sit here and do nothing."

"Look again."

The pine trees along the shore of the lake burned, lighting up the night sky. The dragon dove, blasting another stream of fire east, away from the cottage.

Carter caught a glimpse of the monster. It had a slender form, two carts wide, and its length was four times its width. A powerful tail curved and twisted as the dragon broke through the clouds. Dark colored scales covered the dragon's entire body including its wings, though in the dim light Carter couldn't be sure of their color.

"It isn't attacking," Owen muttered under his breath, and a gentle yellow orb, no larger than the old man's thumb, sprung to life over his right shoulder. Its surface shifted and moved, like running water, and it shone, illuminating the entire room. "It moves forward with no real purpose."

"The dragon fire–"

"The cottage is protected. We are safe inside."

The dragon roared and made another pass, this time scorching the grove of hemlocks where Carter and Owen spent most of their time doing lessons. The dragon somersaulted and continued east, heading directly for Hal.

"The town," Carter whispered. His eyes went wide, and he looked at Owen with concern. "What about everyone in Hal?"

"There is nothing we can do."

"Sure there is. You know hundreds of spells. There has to be one strong enough to stop a dragon."

"I cannot."

"Why?"

"There are things in play you do not understand. This dragon is bait. If not for me, then for something else, and if I took action, more people would end up harmed."

"What does that mean?" Carter groaned and pinched the bridge of his nose. "No. Doesn't matter. We can't to let people die."

"My hands are tied."

"Fine." Carter climbed out of bed and tore his faded azure cloak from a hook on the wall. "If you won't stop the dragon, I will."

"I thought you were over this hero nonsense." Owen rose and stood between Carter and the door. "Haven't you learned a damned thing these past few years?"

"It's not about being a hero. It's about right and wrong. What if Dale or Allison are in town? What if their parents are there or Mr. Kohley is at his shop restocking supplies? How could I live with myself knowing something bad happened to them and I did nothing?"

"And what is your grand plan? You are hardly eighteen, and you have little control over your magic. The best you could do is tickle it with a summer breeze."

"I know more than you realize."

"You will get yourself killed."

"Maybe, but I don't think I could live with myself if I didn't try."

"If you chose to leave... that is your right, but I highly advise against it."

"You won't stop me?"

Owen stepped sideways, motioning to the door. "Free will, the ability to choose one's own fate, is more important than most realize. If this is the path you choose, I will not stand in your way."

"Do you have any advice for dealing with a dragon?"

"Magic isn't always the answer."

"So what? You expect me to talk a dragon out of attacking?"

"Don't mess with the dragon. Let it be. Take plenty of cream and poultices and focus on helping any who may have been burned or badly hurt."

Carter lifted the lid of the wooden chest under his window. He removed a travel satchel packed with herbs and emergency medical supplies. He expected Owen to say more, to try to convince him to stay, but Owen said nothing, and his silence was more condescending and hurtful than if he had spoken.

The sorghum fields along the main road to Hal blazed, filling the air with a heavy, black smoke. The closer Carter got to town, the thicker the smoke became, and the more bits of flaky ash drifted from the sky. With every breath, the flecks of ashes crept into his mouth and left a burning sensation against the back of his throat while the smoke caused his eyes to water.

Carter considered casting a spell to bend the air around him and keep the ashes away from his face, but if he caught up with the dragon, he would need all his energy. He decided to go with a more practical solution.

He opened his satchel and removed a washcloth and a vial of distilled water. He poured the water over the rag and used it to cover his mouth and nose. The damp fabric wasn't perfect, but it managed to filter enough of the soot so he could breathe without choking.

Less than a league from Hal, Carter saw the dragon again. This time, Carter stood close enough to see the boney ridges surrounding the dragon's yellow eyes and the flax-colored markings streaking across its triangular face. The leading edge of its wings grew from a space between its shoulder blades, and the muscles there were equal to those on its hindquarters.

The dragon flew in erratic zigzags with no apparent direction.

The aimless meanderings and abrupt loops caused it to backtrack on itself and allowed Carter to follow the dragon with ease.

Passing a bend in the road, Carter stopped.

Marta, the metalsmith's apprentice, crouched behind a handcart loaded with ore. Most likely, she was heading into town to start her day. The firelight of the burning fields backlit her, highlighting her long, dark hair. Beside her was Jonathan, her husband.

The dragon roared. There was a blur.

Quicker than Carter could track, the dragon had Jonathan and lifted the man into the sky.

Thirty parses up, the dragon dropped him.

Jonathan screamed.

Carter averted his gaze, but still heard a wet, crunching sound, like a melon bursting.

"No!" Marta darted to the limp form of her husband.

"Stop!" Carter yelled too late.

The dragon whipped over the sorghum field and lashed out with its tail.

Marta flew sideways, slamming into the ore cart.

"Ahh gorph!" Carter took a deep breath. He needed to focus.

Aware of his quickly beating heart, Carter concentrated on slowing his breathing. He purged his mind of all extraneous thoughts, and reached into himself for his magic. It was there, ready. He had to time it right. He would have only one chance.

Carter watched the sky. He listened.

From the corner of his eye, he caught a flicker of movement. To the northwest, away from town, the dragon drenched the forest in fire.

The dragon looped and flew farther away.

"Coward!" Carter released his magic and turned his attention to Marta and Jonathan. Jonathan was a pile of sludge and broken bone. There was no doubt he was dead.

Marta lay next to the cart. Her body was twisted, and her legs bent in the wrong direction. Blood that looked black in the dim light matted her hair. A laceration from the dragon's tail stretched across her chest and abdomen, gushing. A gurgling sound from the back of her neck made Carter realize she still lived.

She wouldn't live long. No magic or medicine could save her.

A part of Carter felt guilty. He had never liked Marta much. She was one of the few locals who had gone to school to study agyls, and she always rubbed it in his face that she had formal training. It always came off unpoxed. Now she lay dying before his eyes, and he thought he should care more, for as much as he didn't like her, she did know her agyls. It was a waste to see someone so talented die so young.

Carter couldn't save her, but he could ease her transition to death.

He knelt beside her. She blinked at the movement, but no recognition showed on her twisted face. Removing a glass bottle from his satchel, he popped the stopper. The rancid stench of the zewik juice was so strong he could smell it through the smoke and washcloth. Two years ago, he had spilled a single drop of it onto the back of his hand, and it took more than three days for it to wear off. The whole time, Master Owen had made him sleep outside in a tent.

Pressing the bottle against Marta's lips, Carter poured. Bubbles of blood frothed out of her mouth, and she spit the juice back out. Her shaking subsided, but didn't stop. Carter needed to get a larger dose into her system. All it would take is half a quarter port, but to be safe, he used it all.

Carter poured the teal liquid over Marta's mashed chest. The juice reacted with the oozing blood to create tiny, violet bubbles. Carter gagged, tasting a mix of soured meat and swamp clay.

Marta made no final gasp or jerking motion. The sick or injured rarely did such things when dying. The death was quiet. One moment there remained a flicker of movement in her eye, and in the next her gaze became a blank stare.

To the north, the dragon continued to dip in and out of the clouds as it flew toward the Anber Mountains. That was good. It meant the dragon was avoiding Hal, and others wouldn't suffer like Marta had.

It also meant that Carter had a choice to make. His instincts told him to listen to Master Owen. He should head into Hal and be there in case the dragon changed direction.

His heart told him otherwise. To the abyss with playing this defensively. He wanted to hunt down the dragon and kill it. Not out of revenge or a wrong sense of justice. He wanted it gone so it couldn't hurt anyone else.

2

THE DRAGON'S DEN

ORNSDAY, 1ST OF HEARFEST, 1162.111

When dawn came, Carter was two valleys past Hal. Once he was into the thick of the woods, tracking the dragon became difficult because the creature soared over the foothills and ridges. It left Carter racing up steep inclines and along the rocky banks of fast rushing mountain streams.

By midmorning, he had lost the dragon. One moment it flew, leaving a trail of fire, and in the blink of an eye, it was gone. Thin, glassy clouds filled the sky and were too high for the dragon to hide in. The only thing that made sense was that the dragon had landed.

The Anber Mountains ran east to west and possessed some of the highest peaks in all of Majerä. Even now, he could see snow-capped tips reflecting the morning sun. Fractured crags and shears of rock with deep nooks made the mountains impassable, not that anyone had a reason to pass it. Nothing lay beyond the mountains, making it an ideal location for the dragon to hide.

Hal was the northern most settlement in the Freelands, and all the major towns in Arwyn or Gara lay farther south. If Carter were a dragon, somewhere around here is where he would make his home. The dragon's den had to be near.

Carter picked the tallest tree around, a blue pine whose needles were golden as it prepared to shed for winter. As he climbed, the tree's sticky sap clung to his cloak and fingers.

Little vegetation grew among the cliffs, and although there were plenty of nooks and crannies that could be caves, none were big enough for a dragon. He clambered higher up the tree, stopping at the point where he thought the branches might no longer support his weight.

Carter's lips curved into a smile.

Near the top of one of the closest cliffs was a flat bluff, and tucked into its back was a wide opening the size of a barn. It had to be where the dragon had gone.

Getting to the bluff took the rest of the morning. The climb was slow, and more than once, he was tempted to use magic to lift himself up the side, but ultimately he decided he should not expend his energies if he didn't have to.

Carter's fingers clenched a jagged piece of limestone, and he pulled himself onto a narrow ledge. From there, he shuffled up the final five parses and stepped onto the bluff. The stone, smooth to the touch, felt as if it had been polished.

Sweat ran down Carter's temples, and he took in deep breaths of the cool mountain air. He needed to calm down before entering the dragon's den. Trying to call upon his magic now wouldn't work.

To the southeast, past two low ridges, he saw smoke, but in the daylight he couldn't see any flames, and he didn't know if it was the forest or fields burning. Last winter had been a hard one, and losing crops right before harvest might break families that had no other way to survive. He hoped for the residents of Hal that it was the trees and not precious produce.

The bluff shook, and Carter's attention shifted back to the cave. The entrance curved to the right, so he couldn't see more than a few parses into it. The constant drumming he felt through the rocks suggested something big was moving on the other side. That was good. It meant the dragon was inside.

Some movement caught Carter's eye. Squinting, he saw a three-horned bullfrog squatting in the shadows of the cave. The frog hopped into the light and uncoiled its back legs from underneath rolls of fat. It let out a deep croak and sprawled on the polished rock, sunning itself.

Considering how the cliff would be impossible for a frog to climb, Carter figured the cave must lead to an underground river. This meant there might be an easier way down, and he wouldn't have to scale the treacherous cliff again. Calmed and centered, Carter made sure to step around the bullfrog and entered the cave.

A small antechamber lay past the curved entrance. He expected it to be filled with rough rock and dirt, but a vibrant mural greeted him. The painting wrapped around the cave, depicting strange creatures and unfamiliar landscapes. The largest portion of the mural was of a mighty plateau that disappeared into cloud banks.

Carter had no trouble seeing the mural. Crystalline columns flowed from the ceiling, and they shone with a sparkling ivory light.

"How?" Carter muttered to himself. He didn't see a single agyl powering it.

"I hollowed them out and filled them with a special algae," a deep voice said.

The antechamber opened into a natural cavern. Carter was sure the voice had come from there, but he saw no one. More glowing columns and murals occupied the room, but his eyes had yet to adjust to the darkness, and there were plenty of shadows for the dragon to hide in.

"Dragon?"

"Go away." The voice echoed off a wall to Carter's right.

"You speak?"

"Better than you."

This was odd. In all of the books Carter had read, he had never heard of a speaking dragon. Master Owen had never mentioned such a thing. Of course, he could count on one hand the number of dragon sightings that had happened in the past fifteen years. Maybe all dragons could talk? "Why did you kill those people and burn the fields?"

"Go away!" The voice came from both the right and left, leaving Carter unsure of where the dragon was.

"Show yourself," Carter said.

"Get out of my home."

"Remove your tail from between your legs and face me!"

When the dragon didn't respond, Carter decided he had had enough. With his right index finger, he traced kölprufta in the air by extending his arm in a sweeping motion to make the agyl as large as he could. The moment he finished, the lines flared and emitted a bright light.

He blinked as his eyes adjusted and was shocked to discover that less than ten parses away sat the dragon. It was not the dragon he had seen flying earlier. This one's scales were shades of red with darker patches along its belly and light-bronze-colored strips extending off the ridges of its back. More distinct was its body. It wasn't lean and muscly in the way dragons should be. It was chubby. Its girth dwarfed its head, making it out of proportion with the rest of its body.

"For gorph's sake." Carter's mouth fell open. "You're fat!"

"Who are you to talk?" The dragon said. "You're scrawnier than a plucked crenzel." The dragon lurched forward, and the scales on its stomach made a shrill scraping sound as they brushed the cavern's floor.

"I'm a great magician. I don't need muscles to slay you."

"Slay me?" The dragon's lips curled back as if it were laughing. "What did I do to you?"

"Your cohort attacked Hal and the surrounding farms."

"I know nothing about that." The dragon continued to close the distance between them. "However, I will eat you in self-defense, so save my intestines the trouble of having to digest your bony body and leave."

Carter stood his ground.

"Die!" The dragon roared.

It was so close Carter could smell the stench of its breath, like garlic mixed with sour wine.

Carter had seen how quickly the other dragon had attacked. He dared not turn his back to this one. It was kill or be killed. He would end this beast and then track down the other. Hal would be safe.

He pushed away any sense of fear and cleared his mind. Then he filled it with an image of the dragon, focusing on its robust curves and the plumpness of his body.

A warm sensation, like that produced by Kelsam-spiced coffee, filled Carter's gut. His instincts told him to call upon it. Already the power was more than he usually handled, but he didn't want to take a chance of underestimating what he needed, so he allowed the warmth to grow and surge through his entire body. When it got so hot that it started to hurt, he spoke. "Zultonætto mika ty brumälalo zo choven waltorski."

Instantly, the heat was purged from his system, leaving him much colder than he had been. His vision blurred, but he could still see the dragon coming toward him. The spell seemed to have done nothing.

"What's with the gibberish?" the dragon asked. "You daft in the head?"

Carter tried to respond, but the moisture in his mouth was gone, and his words came out as an incomprehensible drunken slur. His head felt wobbly, and if it weren't for a nearby column he had latched onto, he would have fallen over.

"Answer me, boy–"

A golden ball of energy sprouted from the dragon's chest.

The light radiated across the beast's body as if it were caught in a net of lightning.

The air filled with the smell of burning metal.

"I don't know what you think you've done," the dragon said, "but I've been hurt worse by tine berry thorns."

Carter wanted to say something snarky, but the room spun so badly he could barely keep his eyes open, let alone form a coherent thought.

The dragon lunged for Carter with an outstretched claw, but before it made contact, the rippling light popped, dissipating.

Where the dragon once had been now stood a fat, naked man. His hair was dark and shaggy, covering most of his body, and his skin was much lighter than Carter's. The man ran his hands over his chunky frame. He had a look of horror in his eyes. "What did you do?"

Carter's last thought before falling into blackness was that he had no idea what he had done.

3

THE FROG

ORNSDAY, 1ST OF HEARFEST, 1162.111

From the shadows, the bullfrog watched as Carter's eyes rolled backwards. The boy crashed to the ground, and the naked man stood stupefied. This was the perfect opportunity to make the kill, but the frog didn't take it. It hopped out of the cave and back into daylight, making its way farther up the cliff and finally stopping when confident it was out of hearing range.

The frog extended its left back leg, bringing its webbed toes to its nose. The muddy skin shifted, and a translucent, indigo pebble emerged from its flesh. The frog licked the pebble, and it turned a dark navy color.

"Did you find the dragon?" a voice emanated from the pebble.

"Easier than we thought. Your pet didn't lure him out, but I spotted a hidden garden while flying over its cave."

"Good then, that should do it. The last free dragon is dead."

"I didn't kill him."

"Since when do you hesitate?"

"Since the dragon got turned into a human."

"How?"

"As I was about to enter the cave, a boy appeared."

"How old was the boy?"

"Late teens. I don't think over twenty." The frog's face expanded. It had seen Carter for only a brief moment, which was more than enough time for it to mimic Carter's face. The slits of the frog's nostrils stretched into a human nose, and its skin turned a tawny-beige, as it shape shifted to resemble Carter. "I would have killed the boy and the target except I believe the boy to be Owen's ward."

"He used high magic?"

"Yes."

"You did the right thing. The boy is Owen's ward. As of now, Owen isn't a player, and we don't want to provoke him into becoming one. Keep watch and report in if anything changes."

"You are making a mistake."

"Then it will be my mistake."

"I don't work for you." The frog's human face deflated, resorting to a mushy, black goo that snapped into the shape of a frog. "I'll do as I see fit."

"Remember who it is that can get you what you want."

The frog was tempted to argue, but words were meaningless. Instead, the frog reabsorbed the pebble into its skin, cutting off communications. It would watch, for now. The frog knew when to stand up for an opinion, and this situation hadn't gotten there yet.

4

RESPONSIBILITY

ELDSDAY, 4TH OF HEARFEST, 1162.111

Carter thought he had died, but then the pain hit him, and he knew he was alive. Every single muscle in his body ached, and stiffness filled his joints; the simple act of moving his arm to see what he lay on brought tears to his eyes.

The surface was smooth and cold, most likely something made of metal. Stretching out his arms, he crawled forward, feeling his way as he went. The darkness was so absolute that he thought he may have gone blind.

He determined that he was trapped in a confined space. The walls had no doors or windows, and without being able to see, he didn't know if there was a way out.

Being careful to keep his lines short to use as little power as possible, he traced kölprufta. When he had finished, the agyl, no larger than a tooth, sprung to life. The light was dim, but enough for him to make out the room. The walls rose two-and-a-half parses high, which was too high for him to jump or climb, but he could lift himself using higher magic. That would be risky because there was nothing stealthy about casting a true spell. There was also the wooziness. Whatever he had done to the dragon was still taking its toll on him. He was lucky that it hadn't burned him out.

Crunching, like rocks under boots, sounded from above.

Carter unraveled the agyl with a simple tug, and the place went dark. A heartbeat later, a halo of light appeared above him. Standing on the edge of the pit was the man who had been a dragon. A big nose filled most of his face, and his chubby cheeks completely hid his jaw bone. Rough stubble, what would take Carter at least half a week to grow, covered the man's face.

"About time you woke up."

"Are you going to eat me?"

"Why in the name of Eadimor would I want to eat you?"

"'Cause you said you were going to?"

"You don't know a thing about dragons." The man bobbed his head. Not once but repeatedly, and it was such an odd action that it drew Carter's attention to the way he stood. The man's whole body was rigid and tense as if ready to strike.

"So this isn't like a pit where you keep boars or whatever it is you plan to eat?"

"When was the last time you bathed?" The man asked.

"What does that have to do with anything?"

"Answer the question."

"Uhhh," Carter scratched his chin. "Maybe three days ago? Or four?"

"That's why I put you in there. You reeked. Still reek."

"I reek?"

"Reek. As in smell bad." The man stepped out of sight. Seconds later he reappeared with a rope. He tossed one end to Carter. "You smell like ashes mixed with sweat mixed with some god-awful herbs mixed with I don't know what."

Carter sniffed his shirt and armpit. He didn't smell any kind of funk and instead got the hint of a fruity sweet scent he didn't recognize. "Why do I smell like a perfume shop?"

"Tine berry juice. I doused you with it before flooding the bath."

"Is that what this is?" Carter tried to picture the round pit from above. The depth and shape would make it perfect for a dragon bath tub. He didn't see any agyls, which meant there must be some other water source or drainage system. "Wait, you gave me a bath?"

"Would you rather I had killed you?"

"Good point. Thank–" He didn't know what to call the former dragon. "What's your name?"

"Doug."

"Doug the dragon?"

"Doug."

"It's not very dragon sounding."

"It's not the name I was given at birth."

"Is it because your real name is so intricate it can't be pronounced by human lips, so it's easier if I call you Doug?"

"I was right. You are daft in the head." In an almost human-like manner, Doug rubbed his forehead with the back of a hand. "Now boy–"

"Carter. My name is Carter."

"Alright," Doug said with a bit of gruffness in his voice, "Carter, I was kind enough to let you live. I think the least you can do for me is turn me back into a dragon."

Now Carter understood. Doug had been buttering him up. He wanted something. "About that, I wasn't trying to turn you into a human. I tried to disintegrate your body."

"Intentions aside, undo it, and I will let you go."

"I can't. I don't know how."

"You did this." Doug drummed his fist against his bare chest. "You have to be able to undo it."

"I don't know what went wrong. I can't even think of where to begin with designing a counter to the spell." Which was true. Magic was funny like that. The quirks of intention with the words and raw power. Undoing a spell wasn't like washing a pair of dirty clothes or erasing ink from parchment. Magic altered reality. Undoing it, when possible, required more effort than doing it in the first place.

"You wrent-sucking child!" Doug leaned over the edge of the bath's rim. He was still buck naked. "For three days, I put up with your insufferable snoring and stench. You will undo this, or I will pick you up by the scruff of the neck and throw you off the highest cliff I can find."

Three days? Carter had never been knocked out that long by overusing higher magic. It also meant the spell would be much harder to undo. "I believe you. I do, but I don't know how to fix you."

Doug kicked a makeshift rope ladder over the side of the tub. "Then prepare to fly."

"But... I might know someone who can help."

When Carter and Doug entered the cottage, they found Owen reclined in a chair reading a book. The old man didn't bat an eye. Instead, he flipped a page and ignored them. Carter faked a cough, and when it still didn't gain Owen's attention, Carter stomped his foot on the floor. "Hello!"

"Oh you," Owen said, refusing to look up. "Decided to return home?"

"I know it's been a few days," Carter said. "But I can explain."

"It's not as if I were worried sick about you." Owen stared at his book. "Why would I be concerned when you rushed into a dragon attack?"

"There was really a dragon attack?" Doug asked. "I thought the kid made it up."

Owen slammed the book closed. Puffy bags hung under his eyes. He wore a dark navy jacket with a placketed front. Its puffy sleeves had no cuffs, and the trousers matched it perfectly, down to the silver buttons. Owen's usual attire for reading in the evening was a long night shirt with billowy pants. The way he was dressed now was what he preferred to wear when working or heading into town, which meant, sometime during the past few days, he had been out searching for Carter.

Owen stared at Doug, taking in the naked man. His pupils dilated. "What are you?"

"This is Doug," Carter said. "Doug the dragon."

"By the light, what have you done boy?" Owen threw his book. It landed on the hardwood desk in the corner of the room. "Out with it!"

"I tracked the dragon to a cave near the base of the mountains," Carter said. "I went in to face it, but instead there was a big blob–"

"Hey!" Doug scowled at Carter.

"Sorry, but it's true." Carter shrugged. "I saw a big blob and realized it wasn't the same dragon we saw flying and spewing fire. But I was kind of backed in a corner. Doug was going to attack–"

"You invaded my home. You threatened me!"

"Ok, well yeah, I didn't say you didn't have your reasons. But the long straw of it is that I cast a spell and then, poof, Doug the dragon is Doug the human."

"You are not one of the dragons that has been plaguing the southern towns?" Owen asked.

"There have been other attacks?" Carter shut his mouth as Owen glared at him.

"I've not seen another dragon in years," Doug said. "I was unaware my kind had resurfaced. If what you say is true, it is unusual."

Owen ruffled through a mix of papers on his desk. He chose one whose back was clear of writing. Lifting a quill, he tapped off the excess ink and then nodded to Carter. "Write down the exact spell you used."

Carter did as he was told, though he wasn't confident about the precise spellings of the second half of it.

Owen took the paper. He read it. He read it a second time and then looked at Carter with his brows raised. "Where did you learn this?"

Carter dropped his gaze to the floor. He took three steps backward and placed his left hand over a knot on the side of the desk. He pushed his palm down. The desk slid sideways, revealing a spiral staircase.

"How long have you known about my library?"

"Since last winter."

"Show me the book you used." Owen, as if seeing Doug again for the first time held up a hand. "Wait a moment, let's get you something to wear first."

"I don't want to wear any of your human clothing."

"That may be the case," Owen said, "but the clothing will not only keep you warm, but also protect your skin from snagging, scratching, and normal wear and tear."

They argued back and forth, but Owen got his way, and Carter was forced to head to the back shed. They kept a stockpile of shirts, pants, and robes stored in an air-sealed room. With the kind of injuries Owen treated, having clean clothing for patients was a must. After rummaging through the shelves, Carter found a single pair of trousers and a fluffy cotton robe. The robe was tight on Doug's broad shoulders, and he couldn't button it shut, but was able to use the sash to tie it mostly closed.

Satisfied, Owen led them down two flights of stairs and into the library. Upon entering, several agyls activated, washing the room in a warm light. The space was larger than the cottage above it. Carter estimated it went halfway across the lake. Rows of bookshelves ran down the center of the room while a wood counter lined the entire outer wall. Papers, parchments, books, and half-scribbled notes covered every bit of the counter.

"This place smells," Doug said.

Carter sniffed. The air was dry and yet it did have a slight musty odor.

"I've never seen so many books in one place." Doug's eyes widened.

"It's deceiving," Owen said. "At least half are my own journals and notes."

"Any written in Bakat?" Doug said.

"What's Bakat?" Carter asked.

"The language of the Norrbakai," Doug said.

Carter opened his mouth, but Doug spoke again before he could say anything. "The Norrbakai is what the dragons call themselves."

"Dragons have their own language?" Carter scratched his chin. He wondered how different Norrbakai was from Etriä or some of the other lost languages.

"You thought we all speak human?" Doug said.

"No, well..." Carter said. "I didn't know dragons could speak until–"

"Carter," Owen said with his usual no-nonsense tone. "The book you used. Now."

Several months had past since Carter had last snuck into the library. With every shelf built from the same dark stained wood and cluttered with no sense of order, finding the book might be a fool's errand. A leather book about identifying herbs could sit next to a wood-bound book about anatomy.

At every aisle, Carter placed two fingers on the spine of the first book on the top shelf. Feeling nothing, he moved to the next aisle. Upon touching the book in the eleventh aisle, a probing wet sting ran along his bones, numbing his entire arm. It hurt, but other books had left him burned or sent him flying backwards. This one by comparison was mild.

"Here it is!" Carter picked up the book next to the one that had zapped him. It had no cover, and a metal thread was the only thing that kept it bound together. Lifting it with two hands, he held it out, but Owen shrank away.

"You imbecile." Owen pointed to the wood counter, and Carter set it down. "Do you know what that book is?"

"A spell book." Carter was confident about that much.

Using the back end of a quill, Owen flipped open the book and examined the yellow pages and intricate text. "Your guess is as good as mine because I can't read this. There is no telling what the spells, if they are spells, do."

"Only half the spell was from that book," Carter said.

"And where did the other half come from?" Owen said in a flat tone.

"Remember the whole Cartina incident?" Carter bit his bottom lip. He hated bringing up the Cartina incident.

"I will never forget it," Owen said.

"What incident?" Doug asked.

"A few years ago,"–a smile slid across Owen's face–"my ignorant protégé was turned into a girl."

"Not true," Carter said. "I was still a boy. It was an illusion spell. I merely looked like a girl to everyone else."

"And how did you get turned into a girl?" Doug asked.

"There was a witch lady and these wolves..." Carter trailed off thinking maybe it wasn't the best kind of story to be telling Doug. "The details don't matter. The point is that the spell I used on you was based on the spell that was used on me. I merged the witch spell with the spell from the book, and together, they should've destroyed your physical form and disintegrated you."

"And that didn't happen, so can we get to undoing it?" Doug said. "I don't want to stay in this soft body any longer than I have to."

"That's a problem." Using the quill, Owen closed the book. "I dare not attempt to undo such an amalgamation of spells. Too much could go wrong. You could end up a Greker, a house cat, or a pile of mush."

"If you can't, then who can undo it?" Doug asked.

"No one living." Owen leaned close and wiggled his nose as if he were sniffing the book. "The text is from before the Scourge."

"I don't know what that means," Doug said.

"The Scourge," Carter said.

The blank expression didn't leave Doug's face.

"It happened like eleven hundred some years ago," Carter said. "When the Alder, Urkish, Ketchka, Cylphana, and Erediä vanished from Majerä and all of Elderealm."

"I didn't know you humans used a term for it," Doug said. "So you are saying this spell is from one of the vanished races?"

"Precisely," Owen said. "If I tried to undo it, I could kill you or turn you into something else."

"I don't care." Doug clenched his fist into claws. "I'd rather die than be stuck like this."

"I can walk you through the merging of the spells." Carter opened the book and flipped to the page he had used. "It's simple stuff."

"You don't have the slightest idea about what you've messed with." Owen pinched the bridge of his nose. "How did you think to combine the two spells?"

"You know how sometimes with magic you can feel things?" Carter traced the text with a fingertip. "I can't read the words, but I can sort of feel them, and they had the same feeling as the spell the witch woman used on me. I could tell they would fit together."

"There may be hope." Owen opened his eyes and looked at Doug. "You can travel to Compitum and see the Oracle. She might be able to help you."

"You can tell me how to get to Compitum?" Doug asked.

"I can arrange travel." Owen turned, walking back toward the stairs. "I'll do so in the morning."

"Looks like we will be parting ways." Doug slapped Carter on the back. The blow was so hard that Carter had to brace himself on the wood counter to keep from falling over. "Not a moment too soon. Another day of you, and I likely would rip off your head out of frustration."

Owen stopped and looked over his shoulder, meeting Doug's gaze. "Carter will be going with you."

"I'm a dragon, not a wet nurse."

"And you could get there and be told the only way for the spell to be undone is for the original caster to undo it," Owen said. "He must go with you."

"You can't make me go." Carter crossed his arms. "Not alone with a dragon. You have to come with us."

"I dare not leave Hal," Owen said.

"Lies!" Carter was sick of all the big talk nonsense. For as long as he could remember, Owen had mentioned the big picture. He referenced nonsensical things, and in eighteen years, Carter had never seen a single sign that any of it was true. He found it easier to believe The Silver Lady was real. "You always do this. You always take the coward's path instead of doing what is right."

"I'm sorry you feel that way." Owen climbed the staircase. He didn't look back, and when he passed through the secret door, the magical lights of the library autodimmed, leaving Carter and Doug in darkness.

5

BEING HUMAN

ISLEDAY, 5TH OF HEARFEST, 1162.111

Doug awoke to a sharp pain in his stomach. At first he thought he might be sick, but as his belly gurgled, he realized he was hungry. As a dragon, he could go a week without eating and be fine, but as a human, he needed constant sustenance.

He searched the cottage, looking for the magician and Carter, but neither was around. Deciding he couldn't bear the pain any longer, he headed to the kitchen, hoping to find something to eat.

Along the back wall of the room was an oven, but he saw no hearth or place to ignite it. The side wall had a wooden prep table with three mortars and pestles on it. Above the table hung dozens of vials filled with dried herbs. Or at least he thought they might be herbs. They could easily have been something magic related.

There was a basin with a drain and stopper he thought might be for holding water, an alcove that formed a pantry, and in the corner stood a vault-like stone box with agyls drawn on it.

Wherever the food might be, it was out of sight.

His belly rumbled.

The sensation of hunger, this need to end the pain, was a horrible trait. He didn't understand how humans dealt with it. They were so weak and fragile. No. Now he was weak and fragile. He needed to accept it. Accept that for the time being he was human.

He sniffed and caught a mixture of odors that were hard to separate. Clove. Berry juices. Smoked hickory. Cheese. Lots of cheeses. Lots of nice-smelling cheeses, the aromas of which emanated from the stone box. It was as tall as he was and had a forward-facing door. When he peered inside, he was surprised to find that the contents were cold. That must be what the agyls were doing. They kept the items inside from getting warm and spoiling.

The shelves of the box were packed with eggs, meat, vegetables, and five different kinds of cheese. Doug selected a yellow cheese with a bloomy rind. It was soft to the touch and stunk, but it had a good kind of stink, in the way cheeses do.

He loved cheese, and it had been years since he had gotten the chance to eat any. He was tempted to search for bread or maybe a sweet fruit to complement the cheese, but he didn't have the patience. He bit into the wheel.

The cheese melted on his tongue like butter, and although creamy, it had a tangy citrus flavor with a hint of sweetness. It was glorious, and he devoured the whole thing.

Doug re-opened the stone box and looked for more food. He settled on a bundle of carrots. They had an earthier than normal flavor, and he wondered if, as a human, his taste buds had changed. His sense of taste didn't seem as dulled as his sight and smell.

Closing his eyes, he listened, trying to decide if his hearing was also diminished. The cottage creaked in the wind. He heard tapping on one of the windows, maybe a bird or rodent. Past the walls of the cottage, he could make out a repetitive thumping sound followed by a groan he recognized as belonging to Carter.

Following the sound, Doug exited the cottage and found Carter outside the shed where they had gotten the clothes the night before.

The boy was using some sort of paddle to mash the contents of a wooden barrel.

"That is foul." Doug winced, covering his nose. "It smells like rotting fruit."

"Huh?" Carter ran his hands through his short hair, flicking away beads of sweat. He looked down at the barrel and then nodded. "Well yeah. It's decomposing fruit that has been fermenting."

"Poison for a magical potion?"

"No, I'm making mash for alcohol." Carter went back to slamming the paddle into the barrel. "We are almost out, and Master Owen might need some for treating patients while we're gone."

"Where is Owen now?" Doug asked. "I woke up, and the house was empty."

"I don't know. We weren't exactly on speaking terms this morning. I saw him. He got dressed, packed his stuff up, and left. I guess he went into town, but I don't know for sure."

"So this..." Doug pointed to the barrel. "Isn't some sort of punishment?"

"We are going to be on the road for at least two stints. It needed to be done. That's all." The handle of the paddle thudded against the barrel as Carter let it go. He curled his arms upwards, stretching out his shoulder. "You are welcome to take a spin. It's fun."

"I'm too smart to fall for that."

"Was worth a try." Carter ran the paddle around the side of the barrel. "If you change your mind, let me know."

Doug grunted. He did not feel like helping out. He did not want to help out. He wanted to be home. He wanted to sleep in his own den. He wanted to live his normal life. He wanted to deal with his garden and the mite situation. If it went on for too long, he wasn't going to have food this winter and would be left foraging. He did not want to be here.

"You can't do that," Carter said.

"Do what?"

"Grunt like that." Carter let out a long sigh. "It's not normal. It stands out."

"Humans grunt."

"Yes, but your grunt is like a dog or animal grunt. I don't know how you make that sound."

Doug grunted again. "Like that."

"Well stop it."

"Why does it matter if I stand out?" Doug asked.

"Humans don't..." Carter's face scrunched.

Doug wasn't sure what the expression meant. It looked like Carter was in physical pain.

"Humans are not fans of what they think is different," Carter said. "If you act different, then they won't like you."

"I don't need to be liked."

"If they don't like you, they may pay more attention to you and might figure out you aren't human."

"So let them know. There is no shame in being a dragon."

Carter's face twisted up again. It then calmed, and he spoke in a soft tone. "The world out there isn't too great, and if what Master Owen said is true about dragon's attacking the Southern lands, then it might not be too safe if people learn you are a dragon."

Doug had faced dragon assassins, knights trained and armed specifically for killing dragons. He knew the stigma that came with being a dragon. His kind had been in hiding for so long that humans thought of them as monsters and beasts, forgetting they were sentient and intelligent. The attacks meant the sense of fear and hatred would be on the rise. Doug did not want to face a trained dragon killer while stuck in his current soft form.

"Alright." Doug tilted his head, conceding. "If I didn't want to stand out, what other things might I have to be aware of?"

"This will be great!" Carter chuckled and clapped his hands together.

~

Doug spent the rest of the afternoon listening to Carter drone on about fitting in. Most of it was extraneous, ranging from superfluous topics like Kelsam table manners or which greetings were appropriate to use with someone from Gara but not someone from Arwyn. It all boiled down to one thing: Keep quiet and try not to talk to anyone.

Owen returned an hour before sunset. He had several sets of clothes for Doug he promised would fit, and he informed them that, in two days, they would be taking a caravan to Compitum. Their passage had been paid for, and they would have a private hut.

During the conversation, Carter didn't say a word. It was the longest Doug had seen the boy keep his mouth shut. When they were done, Doug showered and insisted Carter do the same because, even with a wall between them, he could still smell the teenager.

Time dragged, and Doug spent the next two days learning more basic human etiquette. Some of it he knew, and some of it, like basic facial expressions, was helpful since to him most human faces looked alike.

On the eve of their leaving, Carter went to his room early. He and Owen still were not on speaking terms, and Doug was getting tired of it. Both clearly wanted to talk to each other, and yet neither spoke up.

Doug decided the situation needed to be addressed before they left. If not, Carter might be distracted on their journey. So he waited till after dinner and approached Owen while the old man worked at his desk.

"You should talk to him," Doug said.

Owen set down his quill and met Doug's eyes. "Should I?"

"Every day you don't speak, he gets a bit more angry. Considering what he did to me, it might not be a good thing to have his emotions all out of whack."

"Did he apologize to you yet?"

"For changing me into a human?"

"Yes."

"No, he didn't apologize. Did you tell him to?"

"I didn't think I needed to. I raised him to be better than that." Owen lowered his gaze. "For what it is worth, I am sorry. If I had done a better job, you wouldn't find yourself in this situation."

"I learned a long time ago that only the individual is responsible for their actions."

"True. Yet there are things in the world that shape who we are." Owen put his palms together. When he pulled them apart, an image made of light sprung to life, an amber flower reaching for the sky.

It was like looking through a window or seeing a reflection on a still lake. If Doug hadn't known better, he would have thought the perfectly straight flower was real.

The image zoomed out and revealed a pine tree that cast the flower in shade. The flower wiggled, and instead of growing straight toward the sky, it grew slanted, trying to escape the tree's shadow.

"Carter is his own person. He always has been," Owen said. "But it would be inaccurate to say my parenting hasn't influenced him. I truly am sorry for what you are about to face."

The image between Owen's hands twinkled and then faded away.

Doug had seen magic as a fledgling, but dragon magic was different from human magic. Or at least he thought it was. He had left the clans before he was old enough to learn such things. He had never seen any of the elders command light like Owen could. Of course, he had also never seen a stone box where fresh food was kept cold.

"You and Carter are about to head down a long, painful road," Owen said. "At times you will feel overwhelmed, like all decisions have been removed from your hands. When those times come, remember free will. No matter what has shaped you, you have the right to make choices, even if they lead to mistakes."

Doug didn't know what he was supposed to say, so he nodded

his head and looked away. Carter had emphasized in their lessons the importance of eye contact. Making eye contact meant something, and the lack of it meant something else, often that a person held a secret or didn't wish to converse.

"Enough of this." Owen stood. "I do believe you might be right. Carter and I should at least attempt to make amends before he leaves."

Owen walked down the hallway and stopped at Carter's door. The door swung open, and the old man stepped out of sight. "I know you are awake," Owen said.

Doug wasn't trying to eavesdrop. He didn't want to be involved in the particular details, but with his sharp hearing, there was no way for him to block them out.

He detected the sound of a fake snore.

Owen spoke a single word Doug didn't recognize. There came the rush of air and blankets rustling.

"Put me down!" Carter yelled.

Something, most likely Carter, thudded against a creaking bed.

"That was–" Carter stopped mid-sentence, and his tone changed from outrage to concern. "What's wrong?"

"In the morning," Owen said, "you will be gone."

"I know."

"You leave and don't come back."

"Am I going to die?"

"I only know your time here is finished. This part of your life is over."

"I'll try harder."

Owen laughed. "I'm not getting rid of you. You are leaving home. You might come back to visit, and should you, you'll always be welcome. As far as anyone is concerned, I consider you my son, and no matter where your journey takes you, you'll always be in my thoughts."

"What if I don't want to leave home?"

"You and I both know that's a lie. You've wanted to visit Compitum for years."

It must have been Carter's turn to laugh 'cause Doug heard a light chuckling.

And just like that, days of awkwardness between them seemed forgotten. Part of Doug was envious. It had been a long time since he had been close enough to someone to have a fight. Being in a fight meant caring, and Doug didn't care about anyone.

6

PIEROGIES

ULESDAY, 7TH OF HEARFEST, 1162.111

The odor hit Doug before he and Carter entered the Square Boulder. For the first time since leaving his cave, the scent of human stench didn't drown his nose, instead the smells flowing throughout the restaurant were of roasting meats, fried foods, and steamed vegetables.

"Want something?" Carter said. "The caravan we are taking doesn't load for a half hour so we've got time to kill. Plus it's basically against the law to go on a quest without first eating a bowl of pierogies."

"We aren't going on a quest," Doug said. "What's a pierogies?"

"Pierogi, singular. And the only true way of knowing what it is, is by experiencing it yourself." Carter sucked in his nonexistent gut and squeezed between the backs of two chairs, shuffling to an empty round table in the middle of the dining room. He set down his bags and then looked back to Doug. "Watch the table. I'll grab us the grub."

Doug didn't see a route to the table that would allow him to get there without bumping or slamming into one of the other patrons. Drops of water formed on his temples, and his palms felt equally moist. It was unnerving how much he sweated as a human. Sometimes it had nothing to do with how hot he was and had everything to do with how he felt. He missed many things about being a dragon, and of the utmost was the lack of sweat glands.

Taking in a deep breath, he pushed past a half-full table. His stomach, rubbed against it, scooting it into a tired-looking man. Turning to apologize, his butt bumped into a waitress who carried two mugs of hot cider.

The woman lost her balance.

Doug grabbed her by the waist to keep her from falling over, and a bit of cider splashed onto the already damp floor.

With every step, more sweat ran down Doug's cheek, and his heart didn't slow until he took a seat at the table Carter had chosen. He felt like all eyes were on him, and he never wanted to get up again. There was a mother with two teenage sons, and he was sure both kids were ogling him. A woman with curly, grey hair sipped from a wooden bowl and narrowed her eyes at him, and a round-faced girl sitting with a big brute of a man was definitely staring.

The brute was older. Not ancient like Owen, but not as young as Doug's human form appeared to be. Streaks of grey peppered the large man's dreadlocks, and the way he held himself reminded Doug of the dragon assassins he had come across. The tan, laced vest he wore did nothing to hide his gargantuan biceps, and strapped across his back was a long sword.

The girl looked as rough as the man, and her eyes were puffy, as if she hadn't slept or had been crying. Her rich, golden skin was smooth with no wrinkles around her eyes or the corners of her mouth, making her age easier to pinpoint. She was in her late teens or early twenties, somewhere near Carter's age. Strawberry highlights coursed through her braided hair that hung over her right shoulder. Narrowing the scents in the room, he locked on to hers, and strangely enough, it had a musty smell like Owen's house, but also a sweetness like honey.

"It's rude to stare." Carter returned and placed two wooden trays on the table, both packed with saucers. He followed Doug's gaze and saw the girl. "She's cute."

"Her?"

"No, the beefy guy with her." Carter rolled his eyes. "Yes the girl."

"She looks squishy to me."

"You don't know what you're talking about."

"It's true. I don't really understand human attraction and what is desirable or not."

"It mostly comes down to curves. Guys like when a woman has curves, and women don't like when a guy has curves. Those aren't set in stone, but those are the basics."

Doug ran his hands along his chunky belly. "Then it's a good thing I'm more into dragon women than human women."

"There is more to it. Sometimes a guy will like a guy and a woman will like a woman. Plus personality counts for a lot too. Like the girl may look pretty, but if she's not a nice person, it would make her ugly. It's a balance thing."

"And what do the human women think of you?" Carter had a lankiness about him. That must be what humans saw as a first impression. But what else might they notice? Carter's nose was short. He had thin, light-colored eyebrows that matched his short hair and steel-blue eyes. His face was a tad long and ended with a not-so-square jaw.

"Like I told you, in your cave, I'm a great magician. Women are into that kind of thing."

"Hubris. It's a word you should learn if you do not already know it."

"I know what hubris means. There is a difference between pride in your skills and excessive pride. I simply have the former." Carter took a handful of something mushy off his tray and shoved it into his mouth. "So good. I could eat these all day. I normally never get the garlic sauce 'cause Dale and Allison say it makes my breath smell, but they aren't here."

The tray in front of Doug had five plates on it, and each had multiple bulging dough things on them, which he assumed were pierogies.

Doug poked a pierogi. The outside was tender and crusty as if it had been sautéed. Leaning down, he sniffed it, catching a hint of sage and a smoky savory essence. He smelled each of the five plates and distinctly caught whiffs of boar, lamb, and crenzel. Grimacing, he pushed the tray away. "I won't eat that."

"What's your problem?"

"I don't eat meat."

Carter leaned forward, glanced over his shoulder to make sure no one else was listening, and then gave Doug a blank stare. "You are a dragon."

"So? You are an obnoxious little boy. It doesn't change the fact that I don't eat things with faces."

"You threatened to eat me!"

"We've been over this. I was trying to scare you off."

"What about last night when Owen roasted the–"

"I only ate the vegetables."

"But..."

"I don't eat meat. End of story." Doug slammed a fist on the table, cracking the wood. Startling himself, Doug jumped backward and rammed his chair into the chair of a bleach blonde woman sitting behind him. The woman flopped forward, smacking her head on the table and knocking over a bowl of pierogies.

"God dammit Kenzie, you are a worthless piece of crap!" The man seated across from the woman yelled. He was tall, dressed in furs, and an unkempt beard clung to his face. A wooden club hung from his belt. "Bad enough you waste my money on food, but then you spill the food all over the floor."

"It's not her fault," Doug said. "We will reimburse you."

The man stood, looking dead into Doug's eyes. "And who do you think you are? Do you see me? Do I look like someone who needs the charity of a fat slob? Get out of my sight before–"

"Jack don't." Kenzie put herself between Doug and Jack. She was almost as tall as Doug, and her blonde hair was cut shorter than Carter's. "I'll pay you back, Jack, I swear."

"No you won't," Jack said. "But you will eat every morsel of food you dropped."

A pierogi flew over Doug's shoulder and smacked Jack in the forehead. The gooey onion sauce oozed down Jack's cheeks, dripping into his fur clothing.

"Back off the lady," Carter said. He stood on the cracked table with a handful of pierogies.

"Get down," Doug said between clenched teeth.

"There are two ways this can go." Carter ignored Doug. "Let us pay you back and treat you to a nice meal or end up walking out of here with your tail between your legs."

Jack unhooked his club from his belt.

"Have it your way." Carter moved his hands in a strange pattern. A trail of light followed his fingertips, and when he was done, a ball of fire hovered in the air above the boy. He quickly drew another pattern, and a gust of wind hurled the fire at Jack. The ball struck Jack in the chest, and his fluffy shirt caught on fire.

"You should've minded your own business." Jack drew his own symbol in the air. The trial of light flashed, and water fell upon him, dousing his clothing. "If you had, you could have left this alive, but now I'm going to kill you, and I'm going to enjoy it."

"Prösenta." Carter pointed an open palm at Jack.

A loud crashing sound ripped through the restaurant. Mugs and dishes flew off the tables.

A solid wall of air collied with Jack. It lifted him off the ground and threw him into one of the booths along the back of the restaurant.

People screamed, fleeing in all directions. The big man with dreadlocks drew his sword. He and the round-faced girl were the only ones not running.

"See." Carter nodded to Doug and tapped his chest. "Great magician."

Doug slapped a hand to his forehead and groaned.

A wooden chair exploded against Carter's chest, knocking him from the table. He spun, landing face first. Jack kicked a table out of his way, and brought down a foot on the small of Carter's back, pinning him to the floor. "The problem with magicians is they are all fluff and peacocking. There isn't much you can do in a situation like this."

"Let him go, Jack." Kenzie kept her head tilted so her hair hid her face. "If you do, I'll not give you anymore trouble. I swear."

"I think it's time we further your education." Jack gripped his club with two hands. "That way in the future, you can think back to this moment and understand what exactly will happen to you."

Doug didn't see any option. He had to step in. Carter being taught a lesson or two was fine, but Carter's brains being reduced to sludge was a deal breaker. He potentially needed the boy alive.

"Jack..." Doug tried to sound threatening, adding a low rumble-like growl to his voice. "I get it. I've wanted to kill him several times in the past few days."

"Not helping!" Carter said.

"But we are at odds because, as much as you want to kill Carter," Doug said, "I need him alive."

Jack's eyes narrowed as if measuring up Doug, and then he laughed. "Unless you are a 'great magician' too, I see very little you can do to stop me."

Dragons don't punch. Dragons claw and bite, which left Doug unsure about the mechanics of making a fist. He knew he didn't have time to figure it out, so he slapped Jack in the jaw with an open palm.

Jack crashed into a wooden table. He rebounded by swinging his club at Doug's head. Doug caught the club with his right hand. It snapped in two.

"How...?" Jack looked from the splinters embedded in his palms to Doug's bloodless hands.

"It's a vegetarian thing." Doug slapped Jack again. A muffled wheezing slipped from Jack's lips. He collapsed and didn't get up.

"Bloody apples!" Carter snatched Doug's hands, flipping them over and inspecting them. "Did you see how fast you moved, and there's not a single scratch."

"My hand stings." Doug flexed his fingers. His whole hand ached as if he had shoved it into a pile of snow and left it there for a long time.

"No gorph." Carter let go of Doug's fat fingers. "Every bone in your hand should be–"

Sobbing from somewhere in the room interrupted Carter.

Kenzie sat on Jack's chest. With tears pouring down her face, she repeatedly punched him over and over again. His lip was swollen, and blood covered Kenzie's knuckles.

"Ma'am, you don't need to cry." Carter caught her wrist and helped her to her feet. "We won't ever let him hurt you again."

Carter paid the Square Boulder's owner several wheels. Doug had no idea how much it was, but based on Carter's reaction, Doug estimated it was a fair amount of money to cover the broken furniture and loss of business. Carter insisted they still had more than enough to cover traveling to Compitum and back, but they would have to be careful about how much they spent on food. That didn't stop him from buying a whole new bowl of pierogies for all three of them.

To prevent the risk of another incident, the three of them were led to a private room that had no windows. An agyl lamp hung in the corner, and when a serving man brought their food, they ate it in silence.

Doug didn't admit it to Carter, but he enjoyed the radish filled pierogies. The texture was nothing like the food he could prepare as a dragon, and the creamy red filling must have been made from at least two kinds of cheeses.

Kenzie killed her bowl, and Carter bought her a second round. She had stopped crying, but her eyes remained bloodshot, and she had a funky smell to her. It was outdoorsy but not grimy the way Carter smelled. It was more like a hare or other forest creature mixed with damp leaves and something he couldn't recognize.

He wasn't sure what they were supposed to do with the girl. In many ways, she was like a kitten in need of protection, and Carter seemed too confused by her fair skin and sky-colored eyes.

"It happened so fast," Kenzie said to Carter. "My father warned me about him, but Jack had a soft side no one else but me could see. We ran away together, but as soon as we got out of Compitum, things changed. He became a different person."

"It's not your fault," Carter said. "You didn't know."

"I should've," she said.

"It doesn't matter now." Carter pointed at Doug and then back to himself. "We are going to Compitum, and it's not a problem for you to come with us."

"She can't come with us." Doug realized he must have missed that part of the conversation earlier. Otherwise, he would have put an end to the idea sooner.

"Why not?" Carter said. "We can afford one more fare."

"And my father will be sure to pay you back when we get to the city!" Kenzie finished off her second bowl of pierogies by slurping down the buttery juices left behind.

"I don't like it," Doug said. "You can barely watch out for yourself."

"It doesn't matter if you like it or not. It's what's happening." Carter held Doug's gaze as if daring him to say something different.

"I don't want to be trouble, and I don't want to cause any discourse between the two of you." Kenzie stood moving away from the table. "I'm grateful for the food, but I'll go and won't be a bother."

"Don't listen to Doug. He's a jerk."

"Yes, I'm a jerk," Doug said. "That does not change the fact that she can't come."

"You are not in charge of me," Carter said.

"Wanna walk back to the cottage and see what Owen says about it?" Doug let a smirk crawl across his face.

"Don't bring Master Owen into this," Carter said. "You need me. You want me to go to Compitum, and I'm not going unless Kenzie comes with us."

Doug glared at Carter. He was tempted to smack the boy. Not hard enough to do permanent damage, but enough to knock him out. He could throw Carter over his shoulder and carry him to Compitum if he had to.

"I have no idea what is happening right now," Kenzie said. "But again, thank you for all your help. I never thought I'd get away from Jack, and you made it happen. I can find my way to Compitum on my own."

Kenzie stood as if to leave, and Doug noticed a shift in her scent. There was a sourness, like her sweat glands kicking in. Was she nervous or scared? Something caused her body to react to the idea of leaving them. "Wait. How old are you?"

"Twenty-one," she said.

"Do you have any siblings?" Doug asked.

"Two younger sisters," Kenzie said."Both from my father's second marriage. They are eight and six."

Her scent shifted again. Her nervousness fading.

"How about we strike a deal?" Doug gestured to Carter. "You help me keep him out of trouble. As long as you do that, I'll count it as your payment for traveling with us. Sound fair?"

"Really?" Kenzie said in a whisper.

Doug nodded.

Kenzie's rigid stance went loose, and she visibly let out a long sigh. Before Doug could stop her, she wrapped her arms around his neck and hugged him. Her body, pressed against his, felt warm. Her lips brushed his cheek, and goosebumps sprung awake on his arms and legs.

Like hitting a lever, the beads of sweat returned to Doug's temples.

"Thank you." Kenzie let go and sat next to Carter. "You going to finish your pierogies?"

Carter passed Kenzie his half-finished bowl and gave Doug a cocky smile.

7

COMPANIONS

ULESDAY, 7TH OF HEARFEST, 1162.111

Carrying their travel bags, Carter, Doug, and Kenzie climbed a three-story staircase. At its peak was a walkway that extended to the back of an ollip. The beast was four times bigger than a dragon, and that was not counting its long neck that stretched past the tree tops. It had a tan, furry underside and a hard, blocky shell on its back. Attached to the shell was a platform with railings and an octagonal hut in its center.

A rope bridge ran along the left side of the platform, spanning the ollips both in front of and behind this one so the caravan formed a string of more than a dozen of the behemoths. It didn't seem safe to Doug, but with no ground to argue, he followed Carter and Kenzie into their private hut.

The room inside wasn't too big, but it had enough space for them to lay down without having to rub elbows. Benches lined the walls, and leather straps protruded from the floorboards. Kenzie explained the caravan could get bumpy and by strapping in an arm or leg you could make sure you didn't slosh around and get hurt.

It took over an hour for the caravan to load all the passengers, but finally, they were on their way. Doug sat by one of the three windows. The rolling hills and mountains were pretty with the vibrant reds and yellows of fall, but they didn't compare to what the same sight looked like while flying.

"She's out cold." Carter sat down next to Doug and pointed to Kenzie who lay curled on the floor with a leg tucked into one of the leather safety straps. "We should talk about what happened."

"I think it's a mistake to let her come, but if–"

"No, I mean about what you did in the fight with Jack. A human couldn't have done it."

"I'm not human."

Carter stared at him without blinking.

"Ok, technically I'm human," Doug said. "But you get what I mean."

"You must have some of your dragon strength or something. It's the only way you could have stopped the club."

"I have but a fraction of the strength I used to have." Doug flexed his arm and mimed lifting something heavy then dropped his hands to his sides. "If I do have some sort of altered strength, then I can't imagine how weak and fragile you must be."

"I took you down, and I totally would have had Jack if you hadn't stepped in!"

"You need to understand, when you do things like that, you not only put yourself at risk, but me too. What if something had happened to you and then I got to the Oracle and learned only you can turn me back into a dragon? You need to not be selfish."

"I wasn't being selfish. I was looking out for Kenzie."

"It's the pretty thing you mentioned before, isn't it? You helped her because she is pretty?"

"No," Carter said. "I think she does have a nice smile and a cute laugh, but I helped her because she needed help. You've only been around me and Master Owen. We live a good life. Out here in the rest of the world, it's a harsh place for people."

"You don't need to tell me how harsh it can be."

"Last week you were a dragon. Powerful and top of the food chain. What do you know about life being harsh?"

Life was loss. The only reliable thing was that eventually everyone leaves, if not by choice, then by death. It didn't matter what the species–human, Greker, or dragon. Death was the universal common. Doug had seen it time and time again. He doubted Carter had the faintest clue.

"It's done." Doug pushed away his anger. Arguing with Carter would get him nowhere.

Doug crossed the hut, resting his elbows on the windowsill. On the horizon, he could make out the Anber Mountains. They were a faded blue, almost too far away to see. Beyond them lay the Scourge, and beyond that, farther to the northeast, was Dras. Once more, he was leaving what he considered home, and he hoped by Eadimor's desire that this time it wouldn't be as painful.

Kenzie slept for hours, and when she finally awoke, she and Carter spent time playing something called Ryth. They tried to explain the rules to Doug, but he didn't understand and had trouble reading the frilly writing on the stone tiles.

At suppertime, a girl with a cart powered by agyls brought food. Carter bought them all a round of leek soup served in bread bowls. It was a bit salty, but otherwise good. Doug particularly liked the earthy undertones that balanced out the creaminess.

A half hour later, another knock thunked on the door to their hut. It opened, and in walked the round-faced girl and the dread-locked man Doug had seen in the Square Boulder.

"Sorry for the intrusion," the girl said. "I'm Alex, and this is Gideon. We overheard something and thought you should know."

"What?" Doug put Carter and Kenzie safely behind him.

"The man from the restaurant," Alex said. "The one the two of you fought, he's on the caravan in one of the back compartments. He's offering a whole sun to anyone willing to help kill you."

"We can handle Jack," Carter said.

"Maybe you can, but can you handle him and three other guys?" Gideon said. "A little bit of gold can feed a family for a long time."

Gideon didn't smell right. Not as in bad but different, and unlike Alex, he didn't show signs of nervousness or stress. This, whatever it was, was no big deal to him.

"I'll be sure to watch our backs," Doug said.

"Can you?" Alex patted a pouch on her belt, jingling coins. "If not we could help, for a price."

Doug wasn't even slightly surprised. He had seen the way they reacted in the chaos of Jack and Carter's confrontation. They had both been ready for a fight. "Mercenaries?"

"We are travelers heading south," Alex said. "And who couldn't do with an extra coin or two?"

"I don't feel good about this." Kenzie's knuckles were white as she clutched Carter's shoulders. Her fair face looked paler than before.

"I agree," Carter said. "Jack thinks he is cool because he can whip out an agyl. That's amateur's work. I can do the real–"

Carter winced and bit his lower lip. Both he and Kenzie were acting particularly strange.

"We are grateful for the offer and the warning, but this is a personal matter," Doug said. "We have–"

Now Doug felt it. Fire ripped through his gut. There was a swirling sensation, like being caught in free fall without being able to get his wings open. His eyes watered, and before he could stop himself, his stomach heaved, forcing the partially digested leek soup out of his mouth. It ran down his chin, leaving stringy tendrils that seeped into his shirt leaving wet, grainy stains.

Bile overrode all other scents, and Doug fell to his knees, puking brown sludge.

"Gorph!" Alex sidestepped a spray of vomit as Carter dropped into a fetal position.

Kenzie made a groaning whimper that bled into a staggered gagging. A moment later, Doug felt a wave of wetness run down his leg, filling his right boot. He dared a glance and saw the rim of his boot filled to the ankle with cream-colored vomit.

The sight of the gunk sloshing and the wetness on his toes caused his own abdomen to flinch. Before he could do anything else, he broke into another round of puking.

Spasms rippled across Doug's body. He blinked, focusing long enough to see Gideon draw a long sword. The big man held the sword's handle with one hand while he tugged on a strap with his other hand. The cord released the sheath so it fell to the floor, allowing the blade to come out in a smooth clean motion. The tip of the oversized weapon scratched the ceiling of the cabin.

This was it then. Alex and Gideon had feigned being there to help, but had been hired by Jack to kill him and Carter. They had poisoned the soup and were going to take them out without any effort. Doug couldn't let that happen.

Gasping between hurls, Doug lunged at Alex. Vomit splashed as his shoulder struck her behind the knee. She screamed and fell over.

"Don't touch me!" She kicked him in the temple with the heel of her boot.

Doug rolled onto his back and puked again. This time, it came out like a thin mist raining down on both himself and Alex.

"No, no, no!" Alex panted as if trying to hold her breath. Her face stretched, and her jaw dropped. Barf poured from her mouth. It was tanner and grittier than his own vomit, possibly oats or a grainy porridge.

"You alright?" Gideon didn't look at Alex. He kept his eyes locked on the door to the cabin.

"Yes," she said between gasps. "Just sympathetic–"

She puked again.

"Stay down," Gideon said this with an air of bossiness that reminded Doug of Owen. "I'll handle this."

Doug didn't want to be handled. He didn't want to die as a human. He had to fight back. Why weren't Carter or Kenzie fighting?

He twisted his hips and spotted them hanging out of separate windows, vomiting. Both appeared unaware that anything else was happening.

"I won't let you kill us." Doug's own barfing had evolved into dry heaves. Distracted and annoyed, at least he could stand and make a fist.

"Kill you?" Gideon raised a brow. "We didn't poison you. It must have been Jack or one of his men. Since you are still alive, I'm guessing they didn't use nightblade. Maybe heartlocke? If so, it's not deadly, which means someone will be coming to finish the job."

The door to the hut flew open, the force snapping it off its hinges. Jack stood in the doorway. His right arm was wrapped in bandages, and he held his left hand out, as if preparing to trace an agyl. "What's a revenge killing if you don't get to gloat before making the kill?"

Two men dressed in rags stood with Jack. They both had beady eyes and rat noses. Doug suspected they might be related. The rounder one held a rusty dagger, and the other a dull dinner knife.

"It's unfortunate you and the girl interrupted this," Jack said. "But lucky for you, I am a fair man. I have no quarrel, and if you sheath your sword, I'll allow you to leave. Or you help us, I'll give you a sun to split."

Without warning, Gideon lowered a shoulder and swung his sword. Gideon was the opposite of Carter. No whippy quips or smart responses. No talk at all. Just action.

The flat edge of Gideon's blade smacked the man with the dagger in the face. The weight of it knocked out two molars, and the guy crumpled crying.

"For the honor of The Silver Lady!" The butter knife bearer charged Gideon.

Gideon backhanded the man and stomped on the side of his shin. The man's leg bent wrong. A gut-wrenching snap echoed off the walls, and Doug had to hold his mouth shut to keep from dry heaving again.

"I gave you the chance to leave. Your mistake." Jack traced two aglys in the air. A fireball the size of a melon sprung to life and smashed into Gideon's chest.

Gideon dropped his sword. The blast sent him crashing into the wall of the hut. The smell of burning leather overrode the acerbic stench of bile.

Jack was drawing a second set of agyls when Doug saw Alex. The girl, though covered in vomit, had recovered. She had drawn her short sword, and with Jack unaware, she swung at his calves.

Like a puppet with its cords cut, Jack fell. Blood oozed from the back of his leg, and he screamed in pain.

Alex pointed her sword at Jack's neck. "I've already cut the tendon in your leg. You move a mark, and I'll kill you."

Doug couldn't tell if Jack had heard her. The man was hunched over and yelling slurs while pushing his palms against his bloody calf.

"Gideon?" Alex asked. "How are you doing there?"

"I'll need new gear, but otherwise I'll survive." Gideon's vest was charred, and blisters blotted the deep russet skin of his exposed upper chest. "I can't say that about Jack here. Clean slice. Deep. It will scar, but the question is, will we let you live long enough for it to heal."

"I will kill you," Jack yelled. "I will find your taintson of mother and father and kill them too. If they are already dead I'll slit the throat of your gorphing dog–"

Alex kicked Jack in the face.

He blinked, looking stunned.

She kicked him again.

His eyes rolled backward, and he blacked out.

"Sorry, I couldn't take it." Alex slipped on the sticky floor and jammed her sword into the boards to keep from falling. "What do you want to do with him? Well, all of them?"

The two men who had entered with Jack cowered in the corner of the hut. Their already-filthy clothes were drenched in puke.

"Your call," Gideon said.

"Let them go." It took all Doug's effort, but he sat up. He was weak, but the dry heaving had ended. "Let them all go."

"Alex?" Gideon asked.

Alex looked at Doug. Her once tightly braided hair was loose with frizzy bits floating above her ears. Her clothes were damp, and her eyes were watery, most likely from puking. She was an outright mess, and yet something about her, her stance or confidence, made Doug realize she wasn't someone to mess with.

"He's right," Alex said. "Let them go. They won't bother us again."

Doug couldn't have made it through the night without Gideon's and Alex's help. They arranged a change of rooms and convinced the caravan's coordinator to stop long enough for all of them to bathe in the river. None of it was cheap, but Carter had enough coins to cover it.

By morning, Doug felt fully recovered from the vomiting incident, though he never wanted to eat leek soup again. Carter and Kenzie weren't as lucky. They spent the entire next day sleeping. Alex kept herself busy, but Gideon stuck close to Doug, as if not trusting him.

When Doug sat by the window, Gideon sat by the window. When Doug placed himself at the entrance to their new hut, Gideon sat on the opposite side.

"What is this?" Doug finally asked. "You've been shadowing me all day."

"I merely want to keep Alex safe," Gideon said.

"And you think I'll hurt her?"

"You and the boy are like fish walking through the forest. Something is not right with you two, and you shouldn't have been able to recover from the heartlocke so quickly."

"And you and the girl aren't suspicious?"

"Fair enough." Gideon nodded to Alex. "Came across her like you did Kenzie. She was in the woods cornered by two gentlemen who wanted to do more than introduce themselves. After I helped her, she asked if I could escort her to Elene."

"Where?"

"Elene. Southeast of Compitum. Surely you've heard of it?" Gideon raised his brow.

"Oh Elene." Doug vaguely remembered Carter mentioning a place named that, but Carter constantly named too many blasted places. Doug couldn't keep track of them all. "I didn't hear what you had said."

"What about you and the boy?"

"He's the apprentice to a magician." Doug knew there was no reason to try and hide that fact. Carter had made it obvious who he was during the fight at the Square Boulder. "I was hired to travel with him to Compitum and back. In return, the magician plans to heal a sick relative of mine."

"You must love your relative," Gideon said. "Protecting that boy is a full time job."

"You have no idea."

"I know that's not the whole story."

"Neither is yours," Doug said.

Gideon nodded but didn't offer further explanation.

After what happened with Jack, Doug hadn't questioned Gideon and Alex's motives, but not once did the two ask for money or any kind of reparation for their assistance. From what Doug knew of humans, it was an odd behavior.

8

THE INFILTRATOR

ALLSDAY, 8TH OF HEARFEST, 1162.111

The shapeshifter was frustrated. The goal had been to wait till everyone fell asleep and then slip out, but Doug refused to close his eyes or move away from the damn door to the hut.

In the morning, the shapeshifter used the excuse of needing the privy compartment to slip away. Thank god for bathroom problems.

The privy hung over the edge of an ollip's shell. It had a bench with a hole. When peering through the cavity, the shapeshifter could see the worn ground below. Taking the form of a spider, the shifter crawled through the hole and down to the ollip's belly, hiding in its fur. It bent a leg in an awkward angle, and the indigo crystal appeared at its tip.

"Medrayt?" the spider asked.

"I'm here."

"The boy and dragon have left Hal and are headed to Compitum on a caravan."

"To speak with the Sisters?"

"Why else would they be going there?"

"We can't let it happen."

"I know."

"I still do not wish to provoke Owen into taking action. However, I see no other choice. You cannot let them talk to the Sisters."

"There is something else. Good news." The spider's mouth shifted, forming an eerily human smile "The princess is here."

"That is quite a surprise. What is she doing there?"

"Your guess is as good as mine, but having her could be useful."

"I agree. I'll contact the Red Hounds and have them ambush the caravan. In the commotion, kill the dragon and the boy. Then if you have a chance, capture the princess."

"It will be my pleasure."

9

THE RED HOUNDS

ISLEDAY, 10TH OF HEARFEST, 1162.111

As far as Carter was concerned, things were going great. In less than a stint, he would get to see Compitum. He was on a quest to restore Doug's dragonity or whatever the equivalent of humanity was for dragons. Plus, he now had two new friends.

It's not that Dale and Allison weren't cool, but Kenzie told neat stories about high life in the city, and Alex had faced more creatures and scary things than he realized were real. It was nice to meet people with different backgrounds. It gave him a better idea of what the world was like outside of Hal.

Both were pretty, which also helped. He was a bit more partial to Kenzie only 'cause Alex acted on edge. Alex's sea green eyes had a fierceness, and she was always ready to unsheathe her sword.

Not that Carter had time for such things. The last thing he wanted was to accidentally have a kid. Magic had to come first. He had to learn. He had to pay his dues. The rest would come. Someday. Not now. He didn't want to be like Dale, who was counting down the days till his twentieth birthday so he could propose to Allison. Dale thought their love was so grand that they would one day be as famous as Brundal and Evalore. Fat chance for that.

"It's your turn," Kenzie said.

Carter looked up, and it took him a moment to process. He had zoned out. Kenzie had been talking about the significance of using the proper forks for the proper courses. Alex had butted in to correct her, and Carter had stopped paying attention at that point. "My turn?"

"You have to have some good stories about magic and being a hero." Kenzie's eyes were as dark as coffee, and the longer Carter looked into them, the more distracted he got. "Please?"

"Alright." Carter stood and cracked his knuckles. "I think the two of you are ready to hear about the horrible dragon I chased down and fought."

Doug and Gideon, who sat on either side of the hut door, both looked up at this. Carter felt his cheeks flush. Maybe this wasn't the best story to tell right now, at least not without a few alterations.

"Don't joke about dragons," Alex said.

"What does it matter?" Kenzie said. "Dragons aren't real."

"Of course they are," Alex said. "They are dangerous and deadly. If you ever see a dragon, the best thing you can do is run."

"I don't believe you." Kenzie looked from Alex to Carter. "Is she telling the truth?"

"Dragons are real." Carter's eyes flickered to Doug, and he hoped no one noticed. "One attacked the fields outside of Hal only a few days ago."

"I saw the burned crops on our way into town," Alex said. "I should have recognized the signs of a dragon attack. I'm surprised the town survived."

"I trailed it from Master Owen's cottage," Carter said. "Before it got to town, it diverted north to the mountains."

"Owen the Magician?" Alex asked.

"Yeah, he's my guardian. I didn't think anyone outside of Hal knew who he was."

"I've heard a thing or two," Alex said. "I'm sure most of it was exaggerated pub talk."

Their ollip halted.

The whole hut bucked forward and then snapped back.

Cater rolled and banged his face against the wall of the hut. His lip fattened, and he tasted blood. The others, who had been hooked to the floor straps, were unharmed.

Kenzie and Alex beat Carter to the window, and he had to push his way between them to see what was going on.

Nothing seemed to be happening.

Periwinkle streaks ripped across the sky. The sun, already behind a ridge, didn't offer enough light for them to see beyond the mountain road. Thanks to agyl lamps strung along the rope bridges, Doug could see that the caravan curved around a bend in the road.

"I hear yelling," Doug said.

The ollip in front of theirs let out a gurgling whistle. Its fluffy stomach swelled and ballooned out of its shell. The ollip's legs gave out, and as it fell to the ground, its intestines ruptured, spraying green goo and stringy bits. The fleshy shrapnel made wet plopping sounds as it struck the road and the side of their hut.

"I'm going to be sick. Please, by The Silver Lady's hand, don't let me vomit again." Kenzie ducked below the windowsill and covered her mouth as she gagged. "The smell is worse than the taste."

The hut and platform that had fallen with the ollip were now crushed under a pile of twisted shell and broken bones. If anyone had been inside, they were now dead.

"That's not natural." Carter didn't see any traces of agyls being used and didn't know of any combinations that could have caused such an effect. He supposed it could be high magic, but outside of Master Owen and the witch woman from the Cartena incident, he had never met anyone who could work real magic.

"Carter!" Red flooded Doug's cheeks, and he frantically waved his arms. "Pay attention. We are going."

Gideon, Alex, and Kenzie were already out the door with their gear in tow while Doug held both his own and Carter's travel sacks.

"Hustle!" Doug's voice transitioned into a threatening growl.

Carter followed Doug onto the platform surrounding the cabin. With the ollip in front of theirs down, the rope bridge that would have led to it hung trailing in the dirt. Alex, Kenzie, and Gideon descended it like a ladder.

"Look out!" Kenzie called to Carter.

A shiny blur whizzed past Carter's neck. He heard a thunk and turned to see an apple-sized ball sticking to the door. It had metallic needles like a bur, and the cracks along its surface pulsed with a maroon light. It was magic. He could see the strands, but he didn't know what kind of magic.

"We don't have time to stare." Doug wrapped his arm around Carter, and before he could object, Doug jumped off the platform.

The bur exploded, or at least that's what Carter figured it must have looked like to everyone else. With his second sight, he saw the truth. Dozens of prözrupta agyls were bonded together, and on impact, the bond broke, releasing a blast of wind, but also a huge wave of pressure.

Had they been standing on the platform, it would have ripped them in half, but thanks to Doug, the wave hit them midair, catapulting them.

They spun out of control, soaring over the trees, and crashed into a particularly large sycamore. Sticks and branches scratched Carter's arms and legs as they fell, but Doug held the boy tight and shielded him from the worst of it.

Carter stood, and already he could feel an aching sensation down his back. By tomorrow, he would be covered in bruises. "Are you alright?"

"No," Doug said. "Our bags are going to smell like damp leaves for days."

Carter took that as a sign that the former dragon wasn't hurt. "We need to find the others." The forest was old with no shrubbery and wide spaces between the trees. Even being able to see twenty or so parses in all directions, he had no idea which way the road was.

Doug nodded over his shoulder. "That way, but they are coming to us."

"How do you know?"

"I can hear them."

By the time Doug got to his feet and brushed away the twigs from his thick hair, Gideon, Alex, and Kenzie had arrived.

Kenzie wrapped her arms around Carter and kissed him on the cheek. "You're alive!"

"Barely," Carter said. "What the heck happened back there?"

"It's the Red Hounds," Gideon said. "A nasty bunch from out west that take particular delight in hunting dragons and doing other dastardly things."

"Why would they be here or in the Freelands at all?" Carter asked. The second the words passed his lips, he knew why. They had to be after Doug. It was the only thing that made sense. Yet, how could anyone know that he had turned Doug into a human?

"We go to where we are paid to go." A mannish thing sat straddling a branch above their heads. It was short, would not reach Carter's shoulders, but it had long hairy arms that stretched past its knees. It wore a ruby-colored metal chest plate, and in its hand was metal bo staff. The creature rolled backward, falling off the branch. It somersaulted and landed on its feet. "It's been a long day. I hate traveling. All I want is a cold ale by a fire. So let's be mature about this."

At the same time, Alex and Gideon drew their swords.

"No need to get all close and pointy," Carter said. "I'll blast him with a spell. Easy peasy and we'll be out of here."

The monkey-man swung its staff. He moved so quickly it was a blur.

A strike landed in the back of Carter's knees. He hit the dirt, falling on his back. Then the man-thing shoved the tip of the staff against Carter's throat.

"What are you?" Carter asked.

"I am Mogul."

"But what are you?" Carter stressed the word what 'cause whatever Mogul was, it wasn't human.

"Leave the boy be." Gideon sidestepped, putting Alex behind him.

Mogul winked at Carter and broke into a back handspring, flipping over Gideon. The speed was unnatural and reminded Carter of how Doug possessed enhanced senses and strength.

Gideon brought his sword over his head, deflecting an attack from Mogul. He then threw his entire body at the monkey-man.

Doug pulled Carter to his feet, and the two of them, along with Alex and Kenzie, stepped back, ceding the space between two large pines to Mogul and Gideon.

Metal clashed against metal. The blade ground the staff, sending sparks into the air.

Gideon had the advantage of height and strength, but Mogul was faster, which made the fight more even.

Gideon's moves were defensive in nature, not leaving himself open to attack, while Mogul ferociously beat at Gideon as if to wear him down.

"You can't win this fight." Gideon kicked Mogul in the chest.

Mogul rolled, flipping back to his feet. He grinned and blood drizzled off a gash in his lip. "This fight was never about winning. It was about stalling."

Gideon's eyes went wide, and he spun in the opposite direction.

Carter followed Gideon's gaze and was shocked to see three approaching figures.

"Hello, sorry about being late. That hill was a bit steep for me," a woman said. She wore no armor and had layers of clothing wrapped around her as if staying warm was a constant struggle for her. Her hair was white and curly, peeking out through a hooded shawl. She easily had as many wrinkles as Owen did. In the crook of her arm, she held a woven basket filled with the explosive burs.

"Not a problem, Cooke," the monkey-man said. "We were merely making introductions while we waited."

"Oh excellent, manners are important in these dark times," Cooke said. The old lady then tilted her head to the brute of a man who stood beside her. "This is Bash. Say 'hello,' Bash."

"Hello." Bash stood taller than Doug and Gideon by two parses. His legs were thick, like tree trunks, and unkempt auburn hair hid his face. His clothing was patched together from multiple fabrics and too skimpy for anyone to feel comfortable. With both hands, he held the shaft of a war axe that rested against his shoulder. "Pleasure to meet you."

"That's enough Bash," Cooke said. "We do intend to kill them. There is no need to give the wrong impression."

"Sorry, Headmaster." Bash puckered a lip.

"I know I said I would kill you, but you can make this easier." Cooke reached into her basket and withdrew one of the metal burs. "Give us the dragon, and the rest of you can walk away from this."

"You all are crazy." Kenzie turned heel and bolted deeper into the forest.

"No, don't," Gideon yelled. "We have to stick together."

Kenzie didn't stop.

"Death to all of you then." Cooke twirled the bur she held and pressed the end with her thumb. She winked and then tossed it underhand toward Doug.

The bur hit the ground, rolling to a stop in the damp leaves.

"I think not!" Doug stomped on the bur, burying it into the dirt.

The bur ruptured, and the ground shook with rippling waves.

"You stupid taintson!" Cooke sneered at Doug "This whole region is limestone and chock-full of limestone caves."

"Headmaster!" Bash wore a horrified expression and covered his mouth with one of his giant hands. "You said..."

The ground broke into cracks, sliding under Carter's feet.

Unable to keep his balance, Carter rolled backward.

Dirt gave way beneath him, opening a sinkhole.

A cracking roar ripped through the forest as the nearest trees went root-up.

"Carter!" Doug dove for Carter, but was too slow.

A tree crashed between them, and the earth swallowed Carter.

He curled into a ball, trying to protect his face. The world swished by so that he couldn't tell which way was up and which was down.

Dirt and rock filled his nostrils.

Something hard bashed his temple and then hit him in the small of the back.

He landed sideways on something hard and felt something heavy collapse on top of him.

Laying there, Carter heard a low ringing in his ears. He knew he wasn't moving, but it felt like he was. Waiting for the spinning to fade, he practiced breathing slowly and calming his nerves. Once sure he knew which direction was up, he tried to rise to his knees, but discovered his left leg was caught on something.

Tracing the air above his chest, he drew kölprufta. The agyl snapped to life and shone with a strong, white light. Carter lay in a shallow cave. The ceiling collapsed inward with rocks and a broken tree blocking the way out.

The fork of a branch pinned his left ankle, trapping it. He delivered three hard stomps with his right boot, and it snapped.

He rolled over, intending to stand, but the sense of vertigo was too strong. He feared his eardrums might have ruptured. If so, there was little he could do about it.

Minutes passed, but it felt like hours. The pain eased, and so did the spinning sensation, which allowed Carter to climb to his feet. Like a toddler crossing between pieces of furniture, he staggered, using the wall of the cave to steady himself.

The limestone cave was natural. It twisted in a downward slope with the walls practically joining in several places. The ceiling was barely taller than Carter himself, and the walls were wet with water trickling down into lower caverns.

It was possible that there would be no way out of it.

Carter tapped his magic. He pulled it forth, not as an overpowering force, but as a slight sip. "Prosentä!"

The air around him bent to his will, but instead of forcing it to submit, he allowed it be and instead felt it. It stirred, suggesting a draft.

He cut the magic off and proceeded deeper into the cave. A draft suggested a way out. That was good. Now he needed to find it.

After about ten minutes, Carter reached a intersection of four tunnels. He was on an upper branch. Ten parses below was a still lagoon, and seated beside it was Cooke. The old woman sat cross-legged. Next to her was the deadly basket of burs.

"You." Her lips curled up. She tilted her head and opened her eyes, staring at Carter. "I thought I was the only one who ended up in this abyss."

"Nope," Carter said. "I'm here too."

Carter tapped into his magic again. This woman had tried to kill them at least twice. No reason to give her another chance.

"We've met before," Cooke said.

"What?" Carter's focus slipped, and feeling confused, he looked down at her.

"I saw you when you were a child. Soon after Owen took you in."

"That's creepy."

"My point is that I've been studying magic since before you learned to stop pissing yourself. This isn't a fight you can win." Cooke stood, wincing. She stretched and then picked up her basket of burs. "Help me find the dragon, and I'll let you live to see Owen again."

Someone had to have made the explosive burs, and whoever did knew magic. It was possible Cooke wasn't lying. Of course, true magic was a mental thing. If Cooke was a magician, then the best way to shake her up was to mess with her focus. "If you knew Owen, why has he never mentioned you?"

"Because Owen refused to teach me. He used you as a reference, saying your own strength as a toddler was more than I would ever have."

"You shouldn't feel so bad about being weak. It's not your fault. I am a great magician." He patted his chest this time, trying to make his bragging as large and flashy as possible. "You saw Doug, right? I did that. I turned him from a dragon to a human."

Cooke moved her free hand and traced a pattern in the air. Sölbrumta. Instead of finishing the agyl, she let it hang in the air. Before it could fade away, she whispered to it. Carter could feel the higher magic. It was weak, but it held enough power to alter the agyl.

Carter had no idea what it would do, but knew it would be bad. He couldn't let her finish. Using his own agyl would take too long, so he did what he thought she might not expect. He slid down to the lagoon and rushed her while shrieking at the top of his lungs.

A twitch rattled Cooke's left eye. She looked from the warped agyl to Carter and appeared to lose focus. The agyl flashed and faded away.

"You are an insolent brat," she said between gritted teeth.

Carter continued to yell incoherent words. A moment of reprieve could be enough to allow her to regain her focus.

Cooke swept her arms in a large arc, tracing kölprufta. Carter had but a moment to try and shield his eyes. Light flared, changing the cave to resemble the brightest part of day. It dissipated quickly, but Carter's eyes took another five minutes to adjust to the darkness. When they finally did, Cooke was gone, and he was alone once more.

Cooke must have fled, but he couldn't figure out which direction she had taken, nor did he see any signs of magic being used. His only hope now was to find the others before coming across anymore of the Red Hounds.

10

BETRAYAL

ORNSDAY, 11TH OF HEARFEST, 1162.111

The longer Carter stumbled through the cave system, the more his body ached. His eyes felt dry. His legs kept cramping in the cool air. His back and arms were so bruised that every step was filled with pain.

Twice he thought he heard fighting or shouting and changed the direction he was walking, but neither time did he locate any of the others. It was maddening to know that friends and enemies were near, but for all the magic he knew, nothing he was aware of would help him find them.

Carter pinpointed the draft he had felt earlier and meticulously tracked it to its source, an opening just large enough for him to crawl through. The tunnel opened onto a thin ledge that was two parses wide. A quarter of a league down, an unbroken forest stretched. Golden light from the freshly risen sun reflected off the trees' canopy, bathing the rocky precipice in a warm hue.

Having the sun to orient himself, Carter figured he was looking west at the Garan side of the mountains, which meant if he wanted to find the road, he needed to head in the opposite direction.

Carter heard a woman scream. It had to be either Kenzie or Alex.

The narrow ledge wrapped around a bend, and as fast as was safely possible, Carter shuffled up. It rose and connected to a wide, U-shaped bluff. Carter stood on one side while Doug, Kenzie, and Bash, the giant man, stood on the other. Between them was a chasm with a deadly drop. It would take minutes for Carter to run around and reach Doug.

Bash, twirled his axe, shepherding Doug and Kenzie to the cliff's edge.

"Do something," Kenzie said.

"Like what?" Doug asked.

"Like something Carter would do."

From across the chasm, Carter heard Doug's low, rumbling groan.

"Alright you taintson, you want to fight, let's fight." Doug stood his ground, and when the axe came toward him, he caught the top of its shaft. Grunting, he pushed back toward Bash, and the metal pole bowed.

"That's not nice." Bash let go of the bent axe pole and grabbed Doug in a bear hug. "Manners matter."

Doug kicked his feet, but had no leverage to break free.

"Apologize," Bash said.

"You are trying to kill me!" Doug said. "I'm not apologizing for defending myself."

"Not for fighting. Fighting is life," Bash said. "You said a bad word. That's wrong."

"Attacking people is wrong too, but that hasn't stopped you or your friends!" Kenzie lifted the head of Bash's oversized axe to belly button height. She rocked it back and forth and flung it at Bash.

The curved axe blade sliced through the front half of Bash's right foot.

Bash dropped Doug and fell onto his butt, pulling his injured foot toward his chest. Tears ran down the man's cheek. "I will pop both of your heads."

Kenzie heaved the war axe at Bash again, though he saw it coming this time and rolled out of the way. As if he had completely forgotten his surroundings, the man-giant rolled right off the cliff. A blood-curdling scream filled the air, and as abruptly as it had started, it stopped.

From where he stood, Carter could see a smear of blood against the light-colored stone at the base of the cliff. No one could live through a fall like that.

Kenzie pressed herself against Doug's chest. "I didn't mean to kill him."

"You saved me, and I don't know if what you did counts as you killing him," Doug said. "There was something off about that guy."

Carter made his way to the pair, and Doug gave a sigh of relief. "I saw what happened," Carter said. "It's not your fault Kenzie."

"I'm a monster." Kenzie's sulking bloomed into full snotty tears.

"You alright?" Doug asked. "I wasn't sure if you had survived that bur going off."

"Hurting, but I'm still here," Carter said. "Any sign of Alex or Gideon?"

"No," Doug said. "And I don't think we will see them. I'm pretty sure they were working with the Red Hounds. I heard Gideon talking to the monkey-man. There is some history there. I'm glad you are alright. I thought..."

Kenzie's crying drowned out Doug's voice. She pushed her face deeper into Doug's chest, and he stumbled as though caught off balance by her weight.

"Easy there." Doug awkwardly patted her back while soundlessly pleaded to Carter for help. He was out of his league.

The crying became wailing, and Kenzie slammed her palms against Doug's chest. She repeated the action, only this time she hit Doug hard enough to propel him into the air and off the cliff.

Carter saw everything in slow motion.

Kenzie's lips twisted into a crooked smile while Doug's eyes widened as he clearly realized that he was about to face the same fate as Bash.

Carter cleared his mind and called forth his magic. "Prösenta!"

The wind roared, catching Doug. For a moment he hung there, floating over the cliff. Then the air shifted and flung him over their heads and back onto solid ground.

"By Eadimor's breath, what the abyss was that?" Doug scrambled to his feet, putting more distance between himself and Kenzie.

"This." Kenzie rubbed her hands together. "This is always my favorite part."

The bleach-blonde hair flowing from Kenzie's head expanded out of her skull and grew to reach her shoulders. The tint darkened until it became a solid black. Her body pulsed and shifted, so instead of looking petite and trim, she looked fit and muscular. The features on her face stayed the same, but her cheekbones rose and made her look slightly older.

Carter's second sight didn't kick in, which meant that the transformation wasn't magic. It was natural. Whatever Kenzie was, she was powerful and something special.

"Don't get me wrong, sometimes putting on the act is fun,"– The being that had once been Kenzie stretched her arms out with fingers interlaced, cracking her knuckles–"but Kenzie was pathetic. I'm not sorry to see her go."

"I don't understand," Doug said. "What is going on?"

"Shapeshifter assassin." Not-Kenzie pointed at her chest and then at Doug. "Dragon I was sent to kill. I would've done it over a week ago but the brat had to turn you into a human."

Kenzie wasn't real. She never had been real. She was a persona Carter hadn't seen through. He liked Kenzie, and learning she had never truly existed hurt as much as if she had died. It also meant that the shapeshifter was dangerous. She intentionally killed Bash and for days had befriended them all. Someone who could do that so easily was sick in the head.

Carter mouthed the words "be careful" to Doug. He had intended to say it with snark, but he couldn't find the energy to speak. The world blurred, and the fatigue of commanding magic made it hard for him to remain standing.

"I won't be easy to kill," Doug said.

"I saw what happened with Jack." Not-Kenzie flexed, and her hands shimmered as they transformed into swords that glistened in the morning light. "But I'm much more deadly. If you don't believe me, ask Bash. Though, in my defense, he had it coming. For months, I've been looking for a way to kill him without having to take the blame."

"What about Jack and us saving you from him?" Doug asked.

"A ruse," she said. "He had a part to play and did it well. He will be compensated."

"Look Kenzie–"

"Kane," she said. "My name is Kane. Kenzie isn't real."

"Ok Kane." Doug's lips smacked as if saying the name left a bad taste in his mouth. "We can work something out here. I don't know who would want me dead, but there is no reason for this."

"There most definitely is a reason, but I don't have the time to bother explaining it. I have work to do." Her hips swayed. She moved her blade arms in a rhythmic, circular motion and Doug had to scramble to keep out of their path through the air.

"You are crazy." Doug dove under her blades, jamming his shoulder into her ankles. She flopped sideways and fell over him. He rolled onto her and repeatedly drove the butt of his fist into the back of her head. He continued to pound her so hard her face sunk into the dirt.

A ripple rolled across Kane's body. Her hair parted, and the bony back of her skull morphed and became her face. Her arms and legs also reversed direction. "Oh sweetie. You didn't understand, did you?" Her eyebrows pulled together, and she spoke out of the corner of her mouth in a motherly tone. "Remember, I said I'm a shapeshifter."

Doug didn't slow his assault. Her nose bent from the impact of his knuckles, but by the time he lifted his fist to prepare another punch, her face had returned to normal.

"You are boring me." Four extra arms with gangly fingers grew out of Kane's sides. She gripped Doug's limbs and lifted him off her chest. He attempted to wiggle free, but she held him. She ran a blade arm across Doug's cheek in a loving manner and then brought the appendage to his throat. "Let's see how tough your dragon skin is."

"Stop this," Doug said.

"Shhh, we are experimenting." She applied pressure to the tip of her blade arm, creating a dimple without breaking Doug's skin. "Hmm, let's try a bit more force."

A dribble of his blood ran down his neck. "That hurts."

"I'm sure it does." She pivoted her arm so that a scarlet line wrapped around the bulge of his larynx. "It's a good sign though. For a moment, I had feared your skin was impenetrable. That would have made killing you a bit more complicated."

Carter wanted to do something, but he was still too weak to risk magic. At best, the spell would fail, and at worst, he could burn himself out. Maybe he could muster an agyl or two? With two fingers, he tried to make a line in the air. He was so unsteady that he lost his balance.

A pair of hands caught him and he was surprised to discover it was Alex. "I got you," she said. Gideon was beside her. His long sword was leveled at Kane. Blood dripped off its cross guard, and Gideon's replacement for the vest that had burned was now stained red.

"Let him go, Kane," Gideon said. "This is between us."

"You silly goose,"–Kane twisted her neck a full one hundred and eighty degrees–"I'm here for the dragon."

A gurgling squeal sounded from the forest. All heads turned to see Mogul staggering toward them. In his right fist, he held his metal bo staff, and in the other, he held nothing, for his left arm was gone, severed at the shoulder. It wasn't a clean cut. Tendons and thin strips of skin flapped in the breeze. The ape-man's pupils were swollen to the point that the whites of his eyes were no longer visible. A teal froth flowed from his nostrils, streaming around his mouth like a beard. He moved in a maddened state, increasing his speed upon seeing Gideon.

Gideon sprung to intercept Mogul.

Their weapons clashed. Gideon was stronger, but Mogul moved with inhuman speed.

"That will keep them busy." Kane leaned in close to Doug as if to kiss him. "Which should give us time to end this thing we have going on between us. I'm thinking decapitation."

Doug head butted Kane. Their foreheads made a cracking sound, and her grip loosened. He kicked off her chest and broke free.

"Give him to me." Doug snatched Carter from Alex.

"What are you doing?" The words came out slurred, but Carter didn't care. He was happy to be able to vocalize his thoughts.

"We are leaving." Doug tucked a hand under Carter's armpit and dragged him backward, away from the others.

"We can't leave them," Carter said.

"Which them?" Doug asked.

"Alex and Gideon." Carter had clearly heard what Kane had said. She called Alex a princess and someone named Med-something wanted her.

"Nope," Doug said. "I don't trust them."

"Trust me," Carter said. "We can't leave them."

Doug ignored Carter and continued to drag him away from the action. Already they were a good thirty parses away from Kane.

Kane pivoted to follow them, but Alex, with her silver sword, intercepted the shapeshifter.

"I'll deal with you later." Kane swung an arm blade at Alex's gut, but she sidestepped the blow and drove her short sword into Kane's chest.

"You will deal with me now." Alex twisted the blade.

Kane shut her eyes. She took in a deep breath and let out a long grumble. "So be it."

The goo of Kane's body oozed and hooked around the blade of Alex's sword. It rippled and pushed the sword out of her chest.

"What are you?" Alex gasped, backing away.

"That's right." Kane snapped and tapped her temple. "You missed the whole reveal."

Kane's raven hair went blond as it was sucked back into her skull. Her lips grew a bit fuller, and her cheekbones dropped so that she looked like Kenzie again.

Alex's eyes widened.

"Ta da!" Kane smiled, showing off Kenzie's perfectly white teeth.

Alex kicked Kane in the crotch. It was a futile attack, but while Kane shuttered, recovering her balance, Alex rolled, retrieving her sword.

Kane feinted right and then slapped Alex in the face. She repeated the action, and Alex blocked the strike with her sword.

A lizard's tail grew out of Kane's butt. She spun. The tail caught Alex in the shins, and she landed on her back. In less than a heartbeat, Kane smashed a foot into Alex's abdomen, pinning the girl to the ground.

"Don't hurt her," Cooke commanded. Her voice sounded so loud that Carter's ears rang once more. The old woman emerged from the forest.

"I don't take orders from you," Kane said.

"We need her alive." Again Cooke had a booming cadence. She must have been using magic to alter the distance her voice could reach with such volume.

"Alive doesn't mean unharmed." Kane lashed out with her tail, stomping Alex's chest, causing the girl to break into a coughing fit.

Gideon glanced over his shoulder to where Alex lay moaning.

Mogul took advantage of the opening and slammed his bo staff against Gideon's face. In rapid succession, the ape-man struck at the pressure points along Gideon's neck and back, forcing him to the ground.

"Cooke," Kane said. "Do be a dear and toss one of your air bombs this way? I think shoving it down Doug's throat might be an interesting way to end this."

Carter looked from Kane to Cooke. The older woman still held her basket of burs. He could see the agyls and the energy they held. He didn't know exactly how they worked, but the braids were clear. It should have been fairly simple to break them.

"Set me down." Carter tapped Doug's forearm.

"No," Doug said. Already they were so far away from the others it was hard to hear what was being said.

"Give me a few seconds," Carter said. "I have an idea, but you dragging me away is too jolting."

Doug released Carter, who sunk to his knees. That was fine. He didn't need to stand or to appear threatening. This might work better if the Red Hounds didn't see it coming.

Reaching out with his magic, Carter felt for the power held in the basket of burs. There were dozens of the air burs. All he needed to do was find the weakest thread and pull.

Cooke must have sensed what was happening because she threw the basket into the air and turned tail, running into the forest.

"Prösenta!" Carter didn't call the winds. He dominated them.

The air surged and threw Kane and Mogul backward. It swept across the cliff, lifting Alex and Gideon. The two floated to where Carter and Doug sat, and then the wind coiled around their entire group like a cyclone, forming a barrier.

The dozens of agyls inside each of the burs ignited. The basket and metal balls ceased to exist, while a wave of pressure ripped into the cliffside and shot out in all directions. Trees that were hundreds of years old ruptured into dust, and the ground fractured.

Kane's arms and legs became roots, digging into the dirt. She yelled something, but Carter couldn't hear it over the roar of the wind. If his eardrums hadn't been damaged before, they surely were now, but he couldn't worry about it. He had to block out the pain and the sense of his vision shrinking. He needed to direct all his attention at the sphere of air protecting them from the pressure wave.

The front of the wave hit Kane, and her body morphed into pudding, flattening against the broken ground. Soil shot into the air, and the rocks that made up the cliff crumbled. A fresh canyon formed that reached all the way to the valley. Its walls were unstable, and the entire stretch of the mountainside collapsed in on itself.

The others screamed as the dirt beneath their feet disappeared, but Carter wasn't worried about it. He had known he wasn't strong enough to resist the pressure wave, so he didn't fight it. He rode it.

The wave struck their protective bubble of air, and Carter allowed it to shoot them into the sky.

The mountains shrunk, becoming no bigger than wrinkles in a bed sheet. It was mesmerizing and terrifying at the same time because, as the seconds creeped by, Carter felt a weariness come upon him. It started in his arms and traveled in a web across his body. The worst of it was his eyelids. They felt heavy, the weight unbearable. His body begged him to give in, but he didn't. He refused to blink for fear he wouldn't be able to open his eyes again.

An eternity seemed to pass, but finally the sphere of air reached an apex and arced, falling back to the ground. That was when the numbness came. Carter could no longer feel his fingers, and a horrible sense of coldness overwhelmed him. It was as if his pool of energy had run so empty that it was now drawing every speck of heat from his body. His teeth chattered, and his arms shook. Still, he didn't release the magic, for doing so would be instant death.

11

THE PRINCESS

ORNSDAY, 11TH OF HEARFEST, 1162.111

The world flipped, spinning around Alex. She saw flashes of the sun, a blur of trees, and a swirling mix of blue. They all congealed together, becoming an endless cascade of motion.

Alex knew Carter had created the bubble of air around them and that he had caused the explosion on the cliff, but her knowledge of magic was so minuscule that she didn't know how long he could keep it up.

She got her answer when the bubble collapsed, and they crashed into a pool within a winding stream.

The winds died, and if not for Gideon's quick thinking, Carter and Doug would have drowned. It wasn't until Alex stepped onto the mucky bank that she saw Gideon with one arm wrapped around an unconscious Carter. With the other, Gideon offered support to Doug, who could barely keep his head above the water's surface.

Alex rushed back into the pool and escorted Doug to land. The big man fell on his back and coughed up water.

Gideon set Carter down on the ground. The boy's cheeks were sunken, and his skin had lightened, as if all the blood had drained from his body. Gideon held the back of his hand against Carter's nostrils. "He's breathing. Are you...?"

"Fine," Alex said. "I'm fine. What was that?"

"He's Owen's ward," Gideon said. "What did you expect? You've heard your father's stories."

"Hearing is different from seeing," Alex said. Arywn wasn't a backwater kingdom. They had amenities that rivaled the finest in Compitum. Yet those were all agyl based. What happened on the cliff was new to her.

Doug rolled onto his side and spit out a splooge of water. Shaking, he crawled to Carter and shooed Gideon away. "Leave him alone."

"As I see it," Alex said. "We are in this together. No need to be rude."

Doug sniffed Carter. "He smells dead, and his heart is slow."

"Side effect of using that much magic," Gideon said. "I've seen it a few times before. He will either recover or not. There is nothing we can do but wait it out. Our concern, though, should be the Red Hounds. I think we landed too far away for them to follow, but to be sure, we might want to put a few more leagues between us and them before nightfall."

The forest around the companions looked different now. Gone were the trees with needles and those with leaves had a more greenish tint, as if autumn had yet to arrive. The forest floor was damp, with plush ferns, but no grass. Moss-covered logs filled the gaps between the trees.

"We must be in Gara," Alex said. "We should head south. Eventually, we will hit the Alsend River or the canal that bridges the northern and southern parts."

"Let's say we do." Gideon waded back into the water. "Compitum could be dangerous. We might want to avoid it completely and head directly to Elene."

"Do what you two want," Doug said. "Carter and I are going to Compitum."

"You will go wherever we go," Alex said.

"We are going to Compitum." Doug stood. His hair was in tangles, and his clothes were torn. He looked rough, like an alley cat refusing to back down.

Alex waited for Gideon to back her up, but she realized that he was underwater. Most likely he was searching for his sword and her dirk. She hoped he would find the dirk. She thought she had been holding it when the wind knocked Kane down, but it had all happened so fast she wasn't sure.

Gideon surfaced and had not only their weapons, but both Carter's and Doug's travel sacks. That was good. At least they weren't without supplies. She had her pouch and a few personal valuables tied to her belt, but she would miss her Ryth deck and a few other accoutrements.

"Did you decide what you wanted to do?" Gideon laid the bags on the ground and went back to the edge of the pool. Kneeling, he used reeds and scrubbed Mogul's blood off his arms and vest.

"Doug insists he is going to Compitum," she said.

"I am going to Compitum with or without you," Doug said. "I'll carry Carter the whole way if I have to."

"I heard what they said about you," Alex said. "You are a dragon."

"And I heard what they said about you. You are a princess." Doug said the last bit in a slow drawl and winced as if speaking the word produced a bad taste in his mouth.

"Don't you dare." She poked Doug's squishy chest. "I know what your kind can do. I wouldn't for a second trust you with Carter's life."

"I don't trust you either." Doug returned the poke, jamming a finger into Alex's shoulder.

Stepping backwards, Alex slipped and landed butt first in the mud.

"Hold it! Do not touch her again!" Gideon picked up his long sword and stood, staring at Doug. "Be careful about what you say or do next."

"I have this under control." Alex gathered a ball of mud and chucked it into Doug's face. She knew enough from the past few days that it was one of the worst things she could do to him.

The man-dragon roared.

Alex took a defensive stance in case she had judged incorrectly.

Doug charged, not her, but the pool. He dropped to his knees and feverishly threw water into his face, trying to clear away the mud.

Gideon rolled his eyes. He set his sword back down then popped open the travel sacks.

"That was disgusting." Doug pinched his right nostril shut and blew out the left, shooting a wad of mud into the pool. "All I can smell now is dirt. Grimy dirt with things moving and growing in it."

Doug was not like other dragons she had come across. He might be able to offer some insight into what they were dealing with.

"I was in Bryton when the city fell," Alex said.

"You didn't tell me that," Gideon said.

"I didn't want you to know," she said. "But I want Doug to know. I witnessed a dragon attack firsthand. I saw a schoolhouse collapse with children inside. I saw people in flames running down the street. Their skin blackened and cracked as their bodies broke down becoming ashes."

Of the all the tragedies Alex had witnessed in or out of court and in life, what had happened in Bryton nearly broken her. Remembering the horrors caused her heart to quicken and her breath to grow short. She could smell burning flesh and feel grimy soot on her arms, knowing that it used to be people. People she had failed to save.

Alex's eyes watered, but she didn't cry. Doug must have noticed because he slouched and looked away from her as if he were the one embarrassed.

"I didn't do that. I didn't hurt anyone," Doug said. "I've not seen another dragon in years."

Alex sat and slipped off her boots. As much as Gideon might want to get moving, they weren't going anywhere till they had dry shoes. "Maybe you can help us. Arwyn and the Freelands have been overrun with dragons. Not dragons capable of speech or thought, like you, but demonspawn, intent on killing."

Doug looked northeast then back at Alex. "I don't know why it's happening."

"What about Kane?" Alex said. "Why did she want to kill you?"

"I don't know that either," Doug said.

"Kane wanting to kill you and the dragons attacking. They have to be connected. It's too strange not to be." Alex pointed to Doug's boots. "Off with them. You need to let them dry before we can get going."

Doug sat on a log that was particularly moss-free and took off his shoes.

"We have at least two days' worth of food if we are careful." Gideon shut the travel sacks and folded them shut. "We have maybe a day of water."

"What about an agyl?" Doug asked. "Jack made one to create water."

"That is not where my skills lie," Gideon said. "Alex can't do them either. We will have to follow the stream south. If Carter wakes up, he can always supply us with some."

Carter had saved their lives, and now the boy looked dead. They needed to dry him off and do what they could to care for him.

Alex unlaced Carter's boots. His skin was cold to the touch, like an agyl-powered ice box. She lifted the lids of his eyes, and his steel-blue pupils held their size, failing to contract in the sunlight. She didn't know much about the medical arts, but she knew that wasn't good.

"Doug, why are the two of you going to Compitum?" Alex asked.

"I don't think you need to know that." Doug fidgeted on the log. "But it's nothing bad. We aren't trying to harm anyone."

"Gideon?" She knew Gideon well enough to know he must have figured it out by now.

"They are going to see the Oracle," Gideon said. "And if I had to guess, I would say Doug wants to find out how to become a dragon again.

The Oracle. She had heard her father mention the Oracle, often in passing or in hushed tones. The Oracle was said to possess insight about a person and the events of their lives. If that were true, if the Oracle could foresee what was to come, then maybe they knew how to stop the dragon attacks. "Doug, I like your plan. Gideon and I will escort you to Compitum."

"Alex." Gideon said her name as if giving a warning. "I'm under strict orders to bring you back to Elene."

"And only a few minutes ago," Alex said, "you didn't have a preference if we went through or around Compitum."

"The Oracle is different," Gideon said. "Your father–"

"My father is not here," she said. "My father is at home in his palace sitting behind his walls while his kingdom burns."

"The Oracle is dangerous," Gideon said. "Your father and I have dealt with her in the past. I fear what path she may put you on should you speak to her."

Gideon was not one prone to lying. Alex couldn't think of a single time when he had lied to her. Not told her the full truth sure, but never a flat-out lie. That meant the Oracle truly was dangerous, and yet, what choice did she have?

Owen, the greatest magician in the land hadn't been able help her stop the dragons. Maybe this Oracle could and if it was dangerous then so be it.

~

It took a quarter of the day for Alex's clothes to dry and even longer for Gideon's boots. Once all the companions gear had dried, they left the pool, heading south. Gideon created a makeshift sling from the travel bedding in Doug's bags. They used it to strap Carter to Doug's back. The former dragon had some sort of enhanced strength, and he could carry the injured boy without much trouble, though they had to make frequent stops to allow Doug to catch his breath.

Hours before sunset, Gideon suggested they make camp. He pointed out that as long as they didn't make a fire they were too deep into the forest for anyone to track them.

They set up camp on a rocky knoll surrounded by blackberry bushes. Gideon cleared a space for everyone deep inside the thorny tangles and explained that the brambles would deter any of the mountain creatures.

The companions had two bedrolls among them. One was dedicated for Carter. Gideon said he would sleep on the ground, and although Alex wanted the other bedroll, she didn't want Doug to think she was acting unpoxed, so she let him have it.

For dinner, they ate blackberries and shared grain bars that Owen had packed in Carter's sack. They were dry and tasted like dirt, but at least they had filled their stomachs.

Sleep didn't come easily for Alex. The forest was a cornucopia of sound. The constant trickle of the stream. The hoots of owls. The crunching of branches and twigs. With every noise, Alex reached for her sword, sure that someone or something was coming to kill them.

When she was unable to take it anymore, Alex pulled a small agyl orb from her belt pouch. The device was no bigger than a peach, and its surface was a milky amber. She shook it, and the object emitted a soft, yellow light.

"Get some sleep," Gideon whispered. "I'll stay up. You know you are safe with me here."

"I'm tired," she said.

"Then sleep."

"Not that kind of tired. I'm tired of being on the run. Tired of searching for answers and not finding any."

Gideon laughed.

Actually laughed. Mr. Cool-as-Stone chuckled at her expense! "That's a bit rude."

"I'm not laughing at you," he said. "I was thinking about your father when he was your age, well a bit younger. He and I had a very similar conversation."

"Dad was worried about the kingdom?"

"No, I was." Gideon crept closer and hiked up his left sleeve. A curved scar ran across the bottom of his bicep. "We were hunting a blood cult, and I was bitten by... I still don't know exactly what it was. Whatever it was bit my arm, and my arm turned chalk white. I was feverish, and if I died, I knew your father wouldn't make it either. He had a broken leg from a bad fall."

"Dad has never told me this story."

"I'm sure he didn't. You see, we were debating if we should amputate my arm, and then he stood up, hopping on his good leg, and skittered deeper into the cave system. No explanation. No words of confidence. He just left me alone in the dark."

"That doesn't sound like Dad."

"Well, wait for it... an hour passes. Then another. I hear several sets of footsteps, and your dad shows up with the blood magician and three other cultists. Your father demands proof of their dark magic. He says if they show that The Silver Lady is a falsehood, that she wasn't real, then he will turn Elene over to them!"

"He did not!"

"He did."

"No wonder Dad never told me."

"It gets better. 'Cause I was pretty out of it by that point. I couldn't pick up on what your dad was trying to do, so I fought for my life. I thrashed out at the cultists, and it took all of them to restrain me. They tied me down. Did some sort of magic, and then the next thing I knew, my arm no longer burned and it was back to its normal color."

"What did Dad do?"

"He said he was belittled by their power and was so moved that he was going to make me the first blood sacrifice to their twisted cause. The cultists bowed, chanting, and your father raised his sword to behead me."

"I see where this is going now."

"Well yeah, instead of killing me, he pretended to trip, playing it off as his broken leg. He swung the sword and decapitated the cult leader. It was a mess. The thing about blood magicians is that their bodies can hold an obscene amount of blood. It gushed from his neck like a fountain. The cave walls dripped blood, and all the other cultists were dumbstruck. I think maybe none of the underlings knew any actual magic."

"So what happened then?"

"We put an end to the cult, but I still felt uneasy. Maybe it was the magic or the thing that bit me, but I always felt as if we had never truly done what we were supposed to do. On the journey home, I couldn't sleep, and finally one night, your father looks at me and says 'If you can't gorphing sleep, then at least start cooking breakfast so I can wake up to a hot meal.'"

Gideon broke into another round of laughter.

Alex laughed too. Not at the joke. It was a bad joke, even by her father's standards, but that was Gideon's humor. It was nice to see that, after all he had survived, he still had a sense of humor.

"So your point," Alex said, "is that I either need to shut up and sleep or that I should start cooking?"

Gideon cackled and made a snorting sound.

Doug stirred and lifting his head off the bedroll. He leaned over, checking Carter's breathing and then sat up to stare at Alex and Gideon. He let out a yawn and then smacked his lips. "I'm hungry. Did we have any extra berries, or is it almost breakfast?"

Alex and Gideon laughed louder.

~

By breakfast, Carter showed no signs of improving. His temperature rose, and instead of feeling cold to the touch like it had before, his skin burned like an infected wound. His shirt and pants clung to his skin, drenched in sweat, and no matter how they tried to give it to him, he wouldn't keep down any water or food.

With Carter's condition worsening, moving camp didn't make sense, so they stayed in the bramble patch, which allowed them food and easy access to water.

Noon came, and with it Carter's body convulsed. Gideon recommended shoving a stick in the boy's mouth to keep him from biting off his tongue. The only thing that calmed Carter was the coolness of the mountain stream.

Doug's loyalty to Carter confounded Alex.

The former dragon meticulously cared for the boy. Twice Carter crapped himself, and to Alex's surprise, it was Doug who dealt with it. He didn't say a word or complain. He merely hefted Carter into his arms and carried him to the stream.

From camp, Alex watched as Doug once more waded into the water with Carter.

"Do you think Carter will live?" Alex asked Gideon, hoping Doug was far enough away to not over hear the answer.

Gideon ran a greasy rag up and down his long sword. He had made sure to oil Alex's first.

"I told you yesterday," he said, "it's magic. He will die or not die. Little we can do."

"How do you know?"

"I've seen Owen like this. Maybe not quite this bad. Well, maybe once."

"Why is it happening in the first place?" she asked.

"Magic has a cost. You think someone can do what Carter did on that cliff and not have consequences?"

"What about agyls? I've seen workers draw them all day without being effected." She pulled out her glow orb and shook it. "This has lasted years without breaking."

"Agyls are a different kind of magic."

"Dad has told me countless stories of you, him, and Owen going on adventures. Then there are accounts of what happened on the Crimson Plains. I knew Owen's magic was different, but I guess I always thought the extent of that difference was exaggerated."

"Magic is easy for us non-magicians to understand." Gideon held up his sword, catching it in a ray of light that fell through the tall trees. He spun it, and she knew he was checking to make sure every speck of its surface had been properly treated. "Agyls are tools that the educated person can use to manipulate the world around them. Agyls have limitations, and to create things like your lamp, it takes multiple aglys drawn and–"

"I know what agyls can do."

"Hear me out," Gideon said. "Think of higher magic, the stuff that Carter and Owen can do, as the same thing as agyls, only instead of using tools, they manipulate the world directly. Theoretically, if Carter had planned and had enough time, he could have drawn thousands of agyls to summon the wind like he did. Instead he did it directly without tools. He forced the air to his will. That kind of power takes a toll."

"How do we lessen the toll?"

"You can't. All we can do is wait."

"I don't like waiting," Alex said. "I don't like sitting here and feeling powerless. We have to do something."

"Haven't you done enough?" Gideon propped his sword up against the base of a bramble root and turned to face Alex.

"What is that supposed to mean?"

"This. All of this. Our being here is because you decided that you had to be the one to do something. You couldn't trust that your father had things under control."

"He didn't." Alex stood. She had no desire to hear a lecture she had heard a dozen times already.

"Don't walk away," Gideon said.

"I'm going to see if Doug needs any help." She ducked, and shuffled through the cut brambles and made her way to the bottom of the hill. On the bank of the stream, a slight breeze nipped at her cheeks, and she pulled her travel cloak tighter around her body.

Doug must have heard her approach because, before she was more than fifteen parses from the water, he looked up at her. "Everything alright?"

"Yes," she said. "How is he doing?"

Doug stood waist deep in the water with one hand cupped in the small of Carter's back. With the other hand, he splashed armfuls of water against Carter's legs and thighs, cleaning up the latest mess.

"I don't know enough about human bodies," Doug said. "I can smell that something is off. I can hear his innards moving slow. I do not know if he is getting better or worse. I hope it is better."

"I hope so too," she said.

12

GREKERS

ORNSDAY, 14TH OF HEARFEST, 1162.111

After two more days of being trapped at the same camp, Carter finally awoke. He was borderline delirious and only kept consciousness for an hour or so, but Gideon said it was a sign that the boy would make a full recovery and that it was safe to move him again.

By the fifth day, Carter could walk on his own and even though he had been at death's door, he seemed energetic and excited about their journey. Too excited. It grated on Alex's nerves so much so that she found herself walking side by side with Doug to avoid having to answer childish questions.

That night they made camp in a cave. Gideon and Doug said it was clear of nasties, and for the first time since they had been traveling together, they made a fire. Curled up against a rock, Alex held out her hands, letting the flames warm her fingers. She thought travel before had been rough, but making do with no supplies was a new low, and something so simple as being warm was a luxury she didn't mind indulging.

"What's it like being a princess?" Carter lay on his stomach, using a stick to sketch runes or some strange language she didn't recognize.

"I don't know." She wondered if his questions would ever stop. "What is it like to be a magician?"

Carter missed the sarcasm in her voice because he sat up and looked at her with glee. "I've never been anything else. I always knew I would grow up and do magic. It's who I am."

"Then you know what it's like to be a princess. I've been a princess my whole life, and because of that, I don't know what it means to not be a princess."

"But you get to live in a cool castle and go on crazy adventures, right?"

"She tries," Gideon slouched against the cave wall with his eyes closed. His turn for watch was but a few hours away. "Don't stay up late tonight. If we push hard tomorrow, we might get out of this forest and reach the plains."

Gideon shifted his weight and turned his back to them. Alex couldn't tell if he was going to sleep or merely trying to give them privacy.

"What does he mean, Alex?" Carter asked. "How can you try to go on adventures? Don't you either have one or you don't?"

"I'm lucky if I get an hour to myself," she said. "I train daily with Gideon. Then there are meetings, social calls with visiting dukes or emissaries from the other kingdoms, not to mention my classes at the university and other household responsibilities."

"Your parents make you do all of that?"

"My father is busier than I am. I don't know how he has time to sleep."

"What about your mom?"

"She died giving birth to me," Alex said. "I never met her."

"Master Owen makes me do the laundry and take the trash out

to the compost pile." He paused. "I have my magic lessons with him and have to assist when he treats sick people, but I still have time to visit my friends or to read for fun. I read a lot."

"Sounds nice."

"Maybe your dad keeps you busy on purpose because he is over-protective and too worried that if you weren't busy, something bad would happen to you."

"Where do you come up with these things?"

"I told you, I read a lot." Carter shrugged.

"What about your parents? Why do you live with Owen?" She had asked Doug the same thing when Carter had been recovering from the magic, but Doug had said he didn't know.

"Master Owen won't tell me." Carter set down his stick and used his palm to erase the drawing in front of him. "I know my parents were ordinary people, nothing special, but he won't tell me how they died."

"You are sure they are dead?"

"That's what Owen told me."

"Maybe he's lying."

"Not Owen. He either tells you the truth or doesn't tell you anything at all. He said one day when I'm older he'll explain to me how my parents died, but until then..." Carter sat up and drew his knees to his chest. "It doesn't bother me too much because I think of Owen as my father. He's raised me since I was a baby, and I know he loves me."

"He won't tell you the truth?" She raised her voice making a dramatic gasping sound. "Maybe it's because you are secretly the son of a great wizard, Owen's mortal enemy, and you are destined to grow up and kill him!"

Carter glared at her. "You are making fun of me aren't you."

She grinned back at him. "Pretty good impression, huh?"

"Please, my theories make way more sense than that, and I don't sound as goofy."

"You keep thinking that."

"Like half the books I read are real!"

"Real fiction."

"No, I mean histories of the lost races and the time before."

"Why waste your time?" Alex said. "It's gone. It's now that matters. I guess I could understand the histories of the kingdoms. I hate having to read about my great-great-great-grandfather and how he fought a war over whatever, but it's practical. What you are talking about isn't useful."

"Sure it is."

"Like what?"

"The Coming of Erediä," Carter said. "It's one of the oldest tales I've read and it's important."

"Never heard of it." She of course knew of the Erediä, but she didn't know that books or tales from that time existed anymore.

"Back then, humans lived in a world where they were the masters. The bravest of these was a man named Ailwin. He was fearless and traveled the lands searching for adventure. It was in one of the darkest lands that he found the Erediä."

"This Ailwin is like a role model for you, isn't he?"

"You are ruining the story!" Carter cleared his throat and continued. "The Erediä came on the clouds, like angels, and all noted their beauty. Their skin was colorful, like flowers, free of blemishes and wrinkles. They showed no signs of aging. Both the men and women wore their hair long, and they moved with a grace that no human could match.

"The Erediä said they came from a beautiful world, more beautiful than anything the humans had seen, and since the ugliest of them was a wonder to look upon, the humans believed them and asked if they could see the place the Erediä call home. Not everyone wanted to leave, for humans were masters of their world, and so the majority of those who left were downtrodden and looking for a better life.

"Ailwin didn't hesitate and was the first to enter the clouds. Thus, he was the first to be put into chains, for the Erediä were not there to help humans but to help themselves. They brought hundreds of humans to Elderealm and used them as pets and servants. Seeing them as no different than we see livestock."

"Everyone knows that humans were slaves before the Scourge," Alex said. "But the rest of that sounds made up. Clouds. Other worlds. It's fairy tales."

"No, it's not," Carter said. "It's useful."

"It's not useful." Alex rubbed her temple. Trying to convince Carter of anything was like trying to get a banker from Kelsam to admit that money didn't matter.

"It's got a lesson."

"Which is?"

"Gifts from the clouds are often false." Carter crossed his arms and smirked.

"There are a dozen kids tales that do the same thing."

"I think it's useful." He leaned forward "How about–"

"How about we get some sleep?" She faked a yawn, but it transformed into a real one. "Tomorrow you can think of a better story and fail again to convince me why it matters."

The scraping sound of loose gravel snapped Alex out of her sleep. Across the fire, she saw ten small creatures carrying Doug out of the cave. He was limp, and even with ten of them, they struggled to lift him.

She suspected the creatures were Grekers, though she had never seen any in person. They had chubby cheeks, exposing a pale green skin and full heads of hair that wrapped down around their necks like a mane. The most striking thing about them was their oversized eyes, which made them resemble children. Their cherubic faces combined with their delicately woven clothes made them look cute.

Since they seemed to have no interest in her, she kept still, and once they had managed to lug Doug out of the cave, she shook

Carter awake. "Grekers took Doug, and since Gideon didn't stop them, I think they have Gideon too."

Carter walked two fingers along the back of his arm and then flopped them upside down.

Alex raised an eyebrow.

He repeated the motion, but flopped his hand harder.

"What?" she whispered.

He grunted and brought his mouth to her ear. "We should follow them but be quiet. Grekers have hypersensitive hearing."

Curling her lip, she repeated the hand motion he had made. "How is this a signal for 'let's follow but be quiet'?"

He ignored her and walked out of the cave on his tiptoes. His boots crunched with every step, so much so that she knew anything with heightened hearing would not be able to miss it. She waited, keeping her distance, and followed in complete silence.

Alex couldn't see any stars between the leaves and branches, and she had trouble tracking the Grekers. Carter must have had the same idea because, a moment later, she saw a glowing agyl being traced in the air. "Put that out," she said.

"I need it. I can't see a thing out here. I'm likely to fall and break my neck."

"The Grekers will see it."

"I don't know," he said. "I think they may be gone."

"They can't have slipped away so swiftly."

Carter drew a second agyl in the air. This one was much larger, and its light pierced the darkness, illuminating the forest in all directions. "See. Not a trace of them. You sure you weren't dreaming?"

"I wasn't dreaming. If I was, how do you explain Doug and Gideon going missing?"

"Good point." He spun, looked around the forest, and then turned back to her. "Your guess is as good as mine."

The Grekers could have used some sort of magic, but she hadn't seen any sign of that. They hadn't cast a spell or used an agyl to move Doug. They had picked him up. The dragon's weight, evenly dispersed across that many feet would still be boulders. If Alex and Carter backtracked to the cave's entrance, she might be able to track them.

"There." Carter tapped her on the shoulder and pointed to the trunk of an ash tree. "I think that's a pile of clothing?"

She recognized the vest. "It's Gideon's."

"Why would he take off his clothes?"

"I don't know."

"Maybe the Grekers removed his clothes. Was Doug naked when they took him?"

"Eww, no." The image of Doug's hairy, pudgy body burned into her mind.

"Then Gideon must have done it himself."

The vest had a new hole in it and was damp with a green liquid. She pulled the garment close, sniffing it. It was sour but had a mintiness to it.

"What is it?" Carter reached out to touch the goo.

"Idiot." She jerked the vest away. "It's parpah root. Assassins use it. A few drops can knock a person out in seconds. A bit more kills a person, causing the heart to slow and throat to swell."

"I know what parpah root is," Carter said. "A solution made with water and parpah root can dull the pain from wounds."

Alex folded the vest, being careful to keep the parpah root away from her skin. "Let's go."

"Go where?"

"Back to the cave," she said. "We should douse last night's fire and get our gear. We won't be coming back."

Alex had expected Carter to give her a hard time about being able to track the Grekers, but he didn't react other than nodding and listening. They made the short trek to the cave, packed, and headed out again. On the way out, Carter drew an agyl on a smooth pebble. It radiated with a dull light, and he offered it to her.

"I don't want that," she said.

"I thought you could use it to find the tracks easier."

"We want to do this as stealthy as possible."

Carter flicked a finger. The agyl unraveled, and he threw the pebble into the underbrush.

"Now my eyes aren't adjusted to the dark." Alex threw her hands up in frustration.

"I only wanted to help," Carter said.

"I don't need help. I got this."

"I'm not going to stand here and do nothing."

"This isn't some 'adventure' as you like to call it. This is real. Those things took someone I care about, and for all I know, he's already dead. Gideon is like an uncle to me, and I don't want you doing anything stupid to mess this up. I'd leave you here if I could, but there is no telling how far I will have to track them, or what what trouble you might get into on your own."

Carter mumbled something under his breath.

"What was that?" she asked.

"I said, 'You aren't half as smart as you think you are.'"

Enough. She turned her back to him, not caring if he followed and headed deeper into the forest. The cluster of imprints in the dirt and broken shrubbery made it beyond simple to follow the Grekers.

Carter did follow, not saying a word, and Alex felt an awkward tension. She was part mad and part annoyed, but at the same time, all she wanted was to focus on solving the problem at hand. Things had been simpler when traveling with Gideon.

By the time the sun rose, they had reached the flat plains that Gara was known for. She had traveled along the main roads only in Gara, and it was interesting to see the rolling hills as they transitioned into level land used for farming and livestock. It also made following the Grekers effortless. The band had left flattened paths through the tall grass.

Because following them was so easy, Alex feared that she and Carter were stumbling into a trap, but that didn't make sense. If the Grekers had wanted them, why hadn't they taken them at the cave?

For that matter, why had they taken Doug and Gideon? They weren't known for being aggressive, only for avoiding interactions with humans. The whole situation was strange and got stranger when they stumbled upon the Greker's camp.

From a low knoll, dense with shrubs, Alex and Carter assessed the site. There were twenty-two Grekers in total, and their camp was nestled in a willow grove along the shore of a creek. There was no watch, which made sense because their hearing was so acute they would wake before anyone could enter the camp. In the middle of the sleeping rolls and snoring Grekers, she saw Doug and Gideon tied to ornate wooden thrones. Neither moved or fidgeted, so Alex had to assume that they were still under the influence of the parpah root.

"What should we do?" Carter said.

"You do your magic thing and put them to sleep or blast them across the stream so that we can run down there." She didn't want to rely on Carter's magic and risk him exerting himself, but she saw no other choice. There were too many Grekers for her to fight.

"I don't know a spell like that."

"What do you know?"

"I know the spell to manipulate air and the spell I used on Doug." Carter looked down as if embarrassed. "We only started covering high magic on my last birthday."

"What about agyls?"

"I..." his brows sank together and a smile spread across his lips. "I think we should revisit our argument from earlier."

"There are so many that I don't know which one you mean."

"The one where you claimed my story about the Erediä isn't useful."

"It's not."

"It is when you consider that the Grekers worship the Erediä like gods."

13

THE EREDIÄ

ULESDAY, 17TH OF HEARFEST, 1162.111

Drool leaked from the corner of Doug's mouth, pooling in a rose blossom that had been carved into the arm of the throne. As he came around, the first thing he noticed was his own smell. From what he could guess, he must have been unconscious for a day, if not longer. That's hours and hours of not washing, which allowed the funk of sweat, musk, and urine to penetrate his clothes.

More disturbing was that he smelled the unmistakable wet dog smell of Grekers. He hated Grekers, and a whole squad had managed to capture him and Gideon. Once the critters realized he was awake, they would drug him again.

"About time you woke up," Gideon said.

Gideon was strapped to a similar throne with bindings around his armpits, elbows, neck, waist, and knees. That would explain the chafing Doug had felt around his gut. "Quiet. We don't want to wake them."

"Too late for that." Gideon nudged his head to the right, and sure enough, three Grekers were sitting on mats looking back at them. "Can you get free?"

"I doubt it."

"You're stronger than me. Try."

Doug did, but the ropes around his arms were triple wound, and he had no leverage. Same with this legs. "No go."

"That's a shame."

"Where are Carter and Alex?"

"I was hoping you knew. I've not seen a sign of them. The buggers stuck me, and I was out cold before I saw them."

"Grekers," Doug grunted. "I hate Grekers."

An hour before daybreak, the Grekers packed up their camp. Doug expected to be drugged again, but once the creatures seemed to conclude neither he nor Gideon could break free, they ignored them.

A low fog drifted off the creek. From within it came a buzzing sound. The Grekers chittered away in their strange language and then dropped their sacks to take up spears.

"They are saying a dark spirit is in the mist," Gideon said.

"How do you know?"

"I can speak every language spoken on Majerä."

"Even Ba–"

"Even Bakat."

That made Gideon only the third human Doug had met who could speak his native tongue. "There's no such thing as dark spirits, so what do you think is making that noise?"

"There are dark things," Gideon said, "but that's not one."

The wall of fog swallowed the willow trees, and Doug shifted his weight to see what was happening. A feminine figure floated on the fog. Bright light shone from behind her, making it hard to see anything but her silhouette. "*Mont ja höltaæz gy stobälalo.*"

The voice had a sweet cadence to it along with a scratchiness. It sounded familiar to Doug, but he couldn't quite place it.

A ripple of gasps flooded through the Grekers as the woman approached. They dropped to their knees and bent their heads as if kissing the ground.

"What are they doing?" Doug asked.

"Praying."

"What language is that thing speaking?"

"Etriä, which is odd. It's the Eredïän language."

"*Fulta ty nartizälo. Fulta ja mont kot stobötilo kæt ral keftälalo.*"

The tone of the Grekers chants shifted, and they repeatedly said the word, "Arg'Natz." Doug didn't like that.

A pattering of feet filled the air, and the Grekers fled into the surrounding field, leaving their supplies and all all of their bedrolls.

The fog shrank and the shadowed figure sank to the ground. As she did, the backlighting faded, and Doug saw that it was Alex.

"Camp is clear." Alex untied a cloth that covered her mouth and wrapped over and around the back of her head. Three agyls were burned into the cloth, and as she removed it, her voice began to sound like normal. "You two ok?"

"We are unharmed," Gideon said. Alex used her dirk to cut away his bindings and then she freed Doug.

"Where is Carter?" Doug asked.

"Here." Carter approached them from the stream. He was breathing hard, and Doug could hear the boy's heart drumming in his chest. "I'm getting tired of this. Literally tired. You need to stop relying on my magic to get you out of trouble. It's draining. As soon as I get caught up on sleep, I end up exhausted again."

"That was all your magic?" Doug asked. The boy clearly had raw power. He had seen that several times, but the finesse of making Alex float and creating fog had a more sophisticated touch to it.

"Like I told you–"

"I'm a great mage," Alex said in a mocking tone.

"Hey!" Carter said. "I was going to say that."

"What did you say to the Grekers to get rid of them?" Doug asked.

"I said that I had returned on the clouds and that they should spread the word of my return," Alex said. "Or something like that. I basically repeated what Carter told me to say."

That made sense. The Grekers were obsessed with the Erediä. If the beasties thought the old ones had returned that could be more of a problem than a good thing. "There might be consequences for what you told them."

"I'm not worried about it." Carter covered a yawn with both hands and then held his stomach. "They left all their supplies. I bet we can find something other than vegetables or fruit to eat."

"We don't have time to search," Gideon said. "Grab whatever bundles or sacks you think might be useful, but be quick. If those things return, we don't want to be around."

Doug sniffed, focusing on an oily smell mixed with pine. He picked up a satchel and opened it to find a half used bar of soap. He slung the bag across his back. The moment they got far enough from the Grekers, he was going to wash himself, and it would feel wonderful.

14

WORM FOOD

ELDSDAY, 19TH OF HEARFEST, 1162.111

Kane knew she was a sore loser, but being aware of it didn't dampen her emotions, and thanks to the bratty magician boy, she had hours upon hours to reflect on what had happened.

When the mountain collapsed around her, she shifted into a worm, shrinking down to the smallest possible form her mass would take. In the process, she had jettisoned Medrayt's indigo communication crystal. It had been too big and was now shattered and broken somewhere in the rocks. That meant she was on her own, and there was no one to keep her company but herself.

Never before had she so royally screwed up a job. Part of it was on Medrayt. The man should have let her kill the dragon days ago. That was a mistake she wouldn't make again. She was officially off book and didn't care what the would-be-despot wanted. Of course, the first thing she needed to do was escape.

The act of digging was quite degrading. A worm's mouth connects directly to their digestive track, which is why worms prefer to eat soft dirt or decaying plant matter. Eating hard dirt caused her insides to reel and felt worse coming out her back end. Once she cleared a hollow space, she tried to shift into something larger with claws. She had thought being a mole would work, but the ground was so unstable that, when she took a different form, the earth shifted, threatening to squash her.

Reverting to a worm, she took the safe route, slowly twisting and turning toward the surface. After more than week of digging, she broke free to see a bright, sunny sky. She instantly shifted back to human form, without bothering to create clothes for herself, and lay in the sun, enjoying the warmth on her skin. She wasn't one to get claustrophobic, but it was nice to be able to stretch her legs out and relax with her arms tucked behind her head.

Medrayt would want her to touch base or regroup with the Red Hounds that had survived. That wasn't what she wanted. She wanted to go after Doug, and she knew exactly where they were going. Compitum.

She could go as a dragon, but dragons felt played out. Maybe a griffin or great eagle? Flying was the fastest way to get there.

Kane settled for functionality over style. She warped her arms into a hollowed-out exoskeleton, keeping the shell flat and thin, like the egg cases used by stingrays. She narrowed her body, letting it take on a snake shape.

She waited for a wind gust, and when it hit, she jumped into the air. The second her feet were off the ground, she blended her legs together and formed a mermaid-like tail, but instead of its being made of a fatty flesh, she made it hollow like she had her arms.

Kane flapped her tail, creating a powerful thrust that sent her soaring into the clouds. The horizon curved in the distance, and she leveled off her incline. Flying too high could be risky.

It took only a day to clear the mountains, putting her about halfway to Compitum. She didn't enjoy holding a shape for too long. It felt off. She could get cramps and feel jittery. Already her back end ached, like knuckles needing to be cracked.

By this point, she decided that she had to be ahead of the brat and dragon. A few hours with dirt under her toes wouldn't delay her too long. Plus, once she got tired of running, she could take to the sky again.

Kane landed on a grassy plain that stretched as far as she could see. The ground, too rocky for trees, was perfect for wild flowers and small rodents that made dens in the shrubbery.

Hunting for field mice could be fun. She had time to spare, but it would be irresponsible. So instead of taking on the shape of a fox or dire wolf, she settled on a kirin. The big reptilian creature, like a mini-dragon without wings, was common enough in the region, and its sleek form was perfect for running. Naturally, they could only sprint for a limited distance, but that wouldn't stop her. Her endurance levels were unmatched.

The pads on her claws made a drumming sound on the hard earth. The serenity of the rhythm soothed and relaxed her.

An hour into her sojourn, a fluffy strand of black clouds crept along plains, delivering a downpour. Rain beat on Kane's golden-green scales. The coolness felt refreshing though she had to shift her innards from being cold-blooded to warm.

The downpour transformed the hard earth into a sloshy mess. Instead of running for speed, Kane had to adjust her stance, digging into the ground with her claws with each stride. Mud flew in all directions. It coated her hindquarters and clumped on her back.

It became a game to see how long Kane could slide in the mud before needing to use her claws to keep from falling. This was living. Being free and feeling the beating heartbeat of the world.

A burning sensation tore through her right hind end.

Kane stumbled.

Her face smacked a puddle, and she rolled.

Lifting her stiff neck, Kane saw an arrow's shaft sticking out of her thigh, its head, buried too deep to see.

Kane told her legs to shift, intending to shove the arrow out of her body. The wound itself was superficial. Nothing more than a hindrance, yet her legs didn't warp. In fact, she couldn't feel anything past her midriff.

"I got it!" a man yelled.

Kane curled her front half around and caught a whiff of something spicy. The arrow had been doused with drug or toxin. That's why she couldn't shape shift.

"Hold up," someone else said. "Let the juice sink in first. You don't want to approach it until it does."

The numbness spread, covering Kane's entire body. There was nothing she could do to stop it, but that was alright. It would wear off, and when it did, she would kill whomever was responsible for it.

Two men, one in his twenties and another older than crap, scooped Kane up and dumped her in a cart. From where she lay, Kane could only see the dark clouds and hear the pattering of rain.

The men took her to a log cabin nestled on a hill that overlooked the plains. They dumped her in a wooden cage and left. She heard mugs clanking from inside the cabin and assumed they were celebrating their catch.

When the numbing agent wore off, Kane discovered that her cage was but one of a collection of ten. All the rest were stocked with kirin, though none had scales as shiny and beautiful as hers. The others looked as if they had been injured from arrow wounds, including two cubs that could have been only a few stints old.

The storm intensified, and lightning danced across the plains. Thunder cracked, and the other kirins cowered in the corners of their enclosures.

Kane appreciated that the cages were wooden and not metal. She had been struck by lighting before, and had no desire for it to happen again. The last time it had almost killed her.

The hunters could not be collecting kirin for food or clothing.

Kane could forgive such a thing. Nothing wrong with making your place in the world. To have this many kirins alive could be for only one thing. The men intended to sell the animals to a fighting ring.

Compitum, being at the edge of Gara, Kelsam, and the Free-lands, had a particularly high-class rich sector. Despicable unpoxed aristocrats who hadn't worked a day in their lives and were so bored that they did asinine things like bet on kirins fighting in an arena.

This would not do.

Kane shifted into her human form, but shrunk small enough to fit through the bars of her cage. On the other side, she returned to normal height.

Seeing her, the kirins bristled and hissed. She couldn't blame them. They were hurt, trapped, and scared. None of which was right.

Now that she could see it clearly, she realized that the wooden cabin was hardly bigger than a shack. It must be a hunting lodge that had been passed down within a family for generations.

She could set the cabin ablaze and burn the men alive, but that felt a bit impersonal. She could charge in and with a few swings of an arm blade kill them, but that felt a bit too personal. She needed something in the middle.

Kane grinned. Justice sometimes had a perfect sense of irony.

Shifting, she grew to giant size so that the kirin cages reached her knees.

Careful not to make any noise, she picked up each of the cages and rearranged them so that they formed an arc around the entrance to the cabin.

Kane tore off the doors to each of the cages.

The kirins' hissing grew to howls.

The door to the cabin burst open, and both men rushed out. The bewildered expressions on their faces made it clear that they were unprepared to face the loose animals. The kirins, on the other hand, were itching for a fight.

Thunder boomed, drowning out the screams.

Kane didn't stay to watch the whole ordeal. She wasn't a monster. She watched just long enough to make sure that the kirins had everything under control. The last thing she wanted was for them to be further hurt.

Satisfied with her work, she stretched, taking in her surroundings. Earlier in the day, the rain had felt fun and carefree, but now it felt bothersome. Evening was coming, and the stars would be out. She felt a particular urge to be closer to them. Maybe she would shift into a falcon or a roc? Something with feathers. It had been a few weeks since she'd had feathers.

15

THE ORACLE

ULESDAY, 27TH OF HEARFEST, 1162.111

Carter raced up the hill to join Alex. The view was unimpressive. Protruding from the mostly flat horizon were jagged buildings. They didn't seem tall enough to be the fabled four towers of Compitum. "You sure that's it?"

"What else could be that big?"

"Doesn't look big to me."

She laughed and continued down the other side of the hill. Two hours later, when they still hadn't reached the city, Carter found out why. They must have been more than four leagues from Compitum, and as they got closer, the towers grew and grew and grew. He had never witnessed structures so tall, nor imagined that they could stand without toppling over.

Compitum sat smack dab in the middle of the Alsend with three bridges leading to it; one from Gara, one from Kelsam, and one from the Freelands. On their side of the river, the lake ended in a dam with a series of locks that ran for a dozen leagues connecting to the North Alsend. Carter had always envisioned the manmade canal to be no more than a stream, but it was a full river packed with barges, fishing boats, and ferries.

"Get a move on it." Doug prodded him. "We are almost there."

Carter hadn't realized he had stopped walking and followed the others across the Garan Bridge. They passed merchants with carts and the carriages of those unwilling to make the walk. The outer walls and inner buildings were the same cream color as the towers, and Carter was confident that they must have been originally built with magic because he didn't see any seams breaking their smoothness. Smoky clay slates covered the roofs, but the residents made up for the monochromatic drabness by imbuing everything else with over-the-top vibrant colors. Door trims ranged from a bright pink to baby blue. Rainbow awnings covered shop entrances, and second-story balconies were filled with ivy and blooming flowers.

There were too many things and too many people to look at, and if Carter felt overwhelmed, he wondered how Doug was managing it. When he asked the former dragon about it, Doug wrinkled his nose and grimaced. "They try to cover up with fragrances, but it's not working. Thank the light, I'll soon be a dragon again."

Gideon led them to the park surrounding Compitum's central tower. Closer now, he could see that it was teardrop shape and it wasn't white like the other buildings, but a crystal that reflected the cream colors of the surrounding buildings.

"Is that where we are going?" Carter asked.

"No, the Oracle is in there." Gideon pointed to a black obelisk sitting in the shadow of the crystal tower. It had no windows and only a single rectangular door at its base. The interior had a sunken floor, lower than the ground outside, and in the center of the room was an azure pool of water.

A woman in a loose white dress draped across one shoulder watched them as they entered. Her pale skin was perfect, without a blemish, and her bleached white hair ran to the center of her back.

"Hello chickens," the woman said.

"You!" Carter, Doug, and Alex yelled in unison. The three shared a confused expression and then glowered at the woman.

"It's not cheating. I never committed to messing with only one of your futures at a time." She licked the tip of her finger and held it up in the air. "Oh look at the time, I must be going."

"We came to see the Oracle," Doug said. "Are you her?"

"Ohhh sorry," the woman said. "The oracle no longer oracle-izes."

"What does that mean?" Doug's fingers curled into a fist.

"Maybe if you come back on the third Tuesday of the month in the second leap year of a new millennium." The woman shrugged.

A pink poof of light flooded the room, and when it faded, the woman was gone.

"What in the name of the abyss was that?" Alex stomped a foot and punched at the air. "She helped me slip out of Elene without my father finding out. You two recognized her too?"

"She was there the day I left the Dragon clans," Doug said. "And she looked exactly the same as she did now. As if she hadn't aged."

"She was the one who turned me into a girl," Carter said.

"You got turned into a girl?" Alex's mouth dropped

Carter felt his cheeks redden. "Kind of, but it was an illusion. I wasn't actually a girl."

"Calm down, all three of you." Gideon pushed passed them and stepped into the pool of water. Instead of making a splash, his boots passed right through the surface, as if the water were not there. "She was goading you. Having a little fun."

"An illusion?" Carter strained his eyes staring at the pool. He did not see the smallest trace of magic.

Gideon answered by walking deeper into the pool. Step by step, he sank until he was completely out of sight.

Carter followed and felt a strange sensation. His eyes told him he stood in a pool of water, while his body told him he was dry.

Unable to see where he was stepping, he dropped his head below the surface. The moment he did, the water faded away, and he saw he was at the top of a large staircase. The walls were made of blue crystal and shined with light. "There are stairs under here," he yelled to Alex and Doug. "Take small steps, and you'll be fine."

The four followed the stairs to a long hallway. Several rooms branched off, and at its end, it opened onto a large chamber. Floating in the air were three women. The one they had just seen and two others who looked identical except for their hair color. One had brown hair, and the other was a yellow blonde.

"We are disappointed in you, Gideon." The one with brown hair said.

"We like when the chickens discover us themselves." The white-haired woman gave Gideon a deadly scowl.

Gideon shrugged, not seeming to care.

"I told you," The blonde pointed at the white-haired one. "I should have been the Oracle today. You always mess it up."

"It didn't matter which of us it was," the white-haired one said. "They would have found us no matter what."

"Can I do the voice?" the brown-haired one asked. "I never get to do the voice."

"It's 'cause you aren't good at the voice."

"True, but I still like doing it."

"Stop it!" Doug yelled. "Stop this nonsense and explain what is going on."

"Don't you dare raise your voice with us." All three women spoke as one.

"In all fairness, you were being rude," Gideon said. "The brunette is Atropos. Clothu has the yellow hair, and Lachesis is who you met upstairs."

"Spoilers," Clothu said.

"Together they are the Oracle," Gideon continued.

"We are more than a mere oracle," Lachesis said. "And you, my ducklings, have been caught in a dangerous web."

"Gee," Doug said in a snide tone. "I wonder who made the web?"

"He's a smart one," Clothu said.

"He always was." Atropos narrowed her eyes.

"Maybe we chose correctly?" Lachesis asked.

"Forget it." Doug threw his hands in the air. "I don't want a lecture or to know what game you are playing. I came here to find out how Carter can turn me back into a dragon. Tell me so we can be done."

"Carter cannot help you." Clothu waved her hand. The light dripping from the crystal ceiling expanded, taking the shape of a floating image. It shifted and morphed to become a purple flower, one that Carter had never seen in nature or in any of the books he had read. "This is the Dragon Lotus."

"It is what you seek." Atropos clapped her hands.

"Well..." Lachesis added. "It is what you will seek now that you know it is what you seek."

"A flower?" Doug leaned closer as if he hadn't heard right.

The Dragon Lotus's shape reminded Carter of the water lilies that grew in the lake by Owen's cottage, but its shades of mauve and mulberry were entirely new.

"Not a mere flower." Clothu held up her hand, correcting him. "It is a Dragon Lotus."

"You can repeat its name all you like, but it doesn't explain anything." Doug puffed out his cheeks, and Carter wondered if the woman were playing with him again, simply for the fun of it. "How can a flower turn me back into a dragon?"

"The Dragon Lotus is tied to the origin of dragons, hence the name," Atropos said. "If you eat a flower, it will restore you to your true form. Not so much undoing Carter's spell, as going around the root of the problem."

"Where can I find the flower?" Doug asked.

"We will get to it. There is a rhythm in how these things must be done." Lachesis snapped her fingers, and the image of the Dragon

Lotus zoomed out to reveal a bed of flowers circling a black pit. "You see the Dragon Lotus are also what Alex desires."

"I desire a way to end the dragon attacks," Alex said.

"And we will tell you how to stop them," Clothu said. "But first, we must show you how they started."

"No. Tell me now where–"Doug barged forward waving his hands through the light projection.

Atropos snapped her fingers, and Doug went from stomping around like a child to hanging upside down from the ceiling. Silver cords of light coiled around his body and covered his mouth. He squirmed and Atropos giggled. "I love making omelets from the eggs."

Once again, Carter saw no sign of magic being used. He heard no words of power and didn't sense any threads. These women and what they were doing, or at least what they were capable of doing, was something old.

Lachesis cleared her throat, drawing attention back to the light projection. In it was the silhouette of a man. From the way he moved, Carter could tell he was older, but without more light or seeing the man's face, he couldn't peg the man's age. "The flowers are located deep inside the Island of Kale. This is Medrayt, the one responsible for the dragon attacks. Kane works for him."

"Does she?" Clothu asked. "I never understood that relationship, and Kane doesn't let anyone tell her what to do. Even us."

"I agree," Atropos said. "They are more like allies."

"Fine," Lachesis said, "they are allies."

Medrayt kneeled and cupped his hands around one of the Dragon Lotuses. He plucked it, pulling it protectively toward his chest. The image swirled then showed Medrayt standing on a bluff overlooking a valley.

Doug made a muffled noise while wiggling in his bindings.

"What is he saying?" Carter asked.

"He wants to say he recognizes the place. It is Dras. Homeland of the dragon clans." Atropos flicked her wrist, and their view within the light projection moved down the snow-covered sides of the mountain, over a forest, and then paused as a dozen or so dragons soared into and then out of view. "Medrayt used the Dragon Lotus to take control of the dragons."

"How?" Carter asked. "How can the same thing make Doug a dragon again and allow someone to enslave other dragons? That's too much of a coincidence, and magic doesn't work that way."

"Of course it isn't a coincidence," Clothu said. "We had to work very hard to lead things onto this branch."

"A coincidence!" Atropos scowled at him. "One more insult like that, and Doug won't be the only one hanging from the ceiling."

"I'm not..." Carter took a deep breath. "I wasn't trying to be rude. I was trying to understand."

"You are a kitten speaking to a lion." Lachesis seemed to sense his lack of comprehension and nodded. "If your understanding of magic and the nature of this world was a single drop of water, our knowledge would be an ocean."

"That still doesn't explain," Carter said.

"In time, you will understand," Atropos said with a hint of sadness in her voice. "For now, know that the Dragon Lotus has the ability to alter and restore a dragon's form. In Doug's case, it will turn him back into a dragon. In the case of the others, it will restore their minds."

"Why is this Medrayt doing this?" Alex said. "The lives he is destroying and the sense of terror surrounding the people is awful. Let alone controlling a sentient race like the dragons and forcing them to his will is wrong."

"People are dicks." Clothu rolled her shoulders backward. "What can you do?"

"What my sister means..." Atropos gave Clothu a disapproving look. "Medrayt wants your father to surrender Arwyn. Elene is the gateway to the west, and if it falls, so will the other kingdoms. By this time next summer, Medrayt could control all of Majerä."

"We can stop him... with the Dragon Lotus?" Alex asked.

"It is our hope," Lachesis said. "A magician armed with a single petal could free the dragons. That would end Medrayt's plans."

Carter now understood why he was here. He saw the path that brought him to Compitum. He was meant to be the magician who would free the dragons and save the world. "You planned this. I was supposed to turn Doug into a human so we would come here and so you could tell us about Medrayt. You want me to go with Alex. You want me to undo the spell!"

"We want lots of things," Clothu said.

"We see lots of things," Atropos added.

"We plan and line things up," Lachesis said. "What we want does not matter. In the end, it comes down to choice. You brought yourself here."

Doug made a smothered noise, and his body swung back and forth like a swaying chandelier.

"We can't hear you, but we know what you are thinking," Atropos said. "You did bring yourself here. Your choices. Your actions. Did we exert influence? Yes, but in the end, it was you. No matter what you leave here today thinking, know that."

Doug mumbled something else. Then something else. Then something that made the three mystical women wince. Lachesis nodded and waved her hand. "Then go."

The bands of light loosened, and Doug thumped onto the crystal floor. He climbed to his feet and turned his back to the group, as if he meant to leave.

"Where are you going?" Carter asked.

"I'm going to go eat a flower," Doug said. "I know now that I don't need you, and as far as I'm concerned, I'm done with the lot of you."

"You can't leave," Carter said.

"I can," Doug said. "I don't like knowing my whole life has been changed by meddling. I want nothing to do with any of this madness."

"What about your own kind?" Alex asked. "Don't you care that Medrayt has enslaved the dragons?"

"The problems of the dragons stopped being mine a long time ago." Doug exited the chamber without looking back.

"That could cause things to unravel," Clothu said.

"We knew he had authority issues." Atropos snapped her fingers, and the light projection faded away.

"For good reasons," Lachesis said.

16

WAKING DRAGONS

ALLSDAY, 23RD OF HEARFEST, 1162.111

Cooke held an open envelope flush against the tree and ran a razor blade across its bark. The idea was not to cut it. She needed to lightly scrape it to create a powder. If she cut the bark, it decreased the number of berries the tree would produce. Besides, shavings didn't always dissolve and mix properly.

She thudded the rim of the envelope against the tree. The dry brown residue inside fluffed up. She estimated that she had harvested maybe two ports, which should be more than enough. With a bit of water and sugar for flavor, dragon flight might be marginally bearable.

"Headmaster!" Devina's high-strung voice rang throughout the arboretum. "Headmaster?"

Cooke sighed. She had been back to Stobnyk Kol for less than a day, and she hadn't gotten a moment of peace since arriving. "I'm on the other side of the nightblade bushes."

Grey clouds hung above the glass roof of the courtyard, making the arboretum a bit darker than usual, but still, if the girl had opened her eyes, she should have been able to spot Cooke.

"He is awake." Devina's bare feet hustled across the terra-cotta tiled path. Everything was so urgent and rushed with the girl. "Mogul is awake."

"Calm down," Cooke said. "His bindings will hold."

"Yes, but his yelling it's..."

"The man lost an arm less than a stint ago and nearly bled out. He is allowed to yell as much as he'd like."

"Yes... but Headmaster, the first years are taking their quarterly exam."

Cooke set down her razor blade and folded the envelope's flap to close it. Clearly she wouldn't be able to get anymore work done today. "If the first years are distracted by a bit of yelling, then we can always keep them as first years."

Devina's tiny mouth opened, and a wrinkle ran across her forehead.

"It's fine," Cooke said. "I'll deal with Mogul. Take the first years down to the longhouse and–"

"We have the forth years down there sparring today."

"My father managed to get every lord from each of the great houses of Caerkaldor into those halls. If you can't manage to fit sixty–"

"Eighty-nine."

"Excuse me?"

"With word of the dragon attacks in Arwyn, we have had an influx of students the past few months."

"Deal with it. If you still can't fit them, make them run the hill down to Demral. Most need the exercise anyway. A trek in the snow will do them good."

"Yes, Headmaster." Devina dashed out of the courtyard as if she were rushing to put out a fire.

Cooke stood. Her knees ached. Being old did not make life easy. Even more, the family estate she had loved so much as a child was now a hindrance. She never dreamed she would hate the blasted hills and stairs as much as she did now.

Taking her time, Cooke passed through the arboretum. The students were doing an adequate job watering the trees and plants, but they had a way to go in learning to handle the weeding. She would need to speak with Devina about that.

In the arboretum's atrium, she stopped to retrieve a heavy shawl from a wooden rack. She coiled it around her abdomen, up over her chest, around her neck and back down her back. The fabric felt cozy to the touch, and simply wearing it made her think back to the days when she and Devina's father would head into the city for hot cider.

The wind outside the arboretum was crisp and smelled like snow. She knew that by nightfall new flakes would be falling. Not that they didn't already have enough snow on the ground, but that was life in Brekka. Snow came early in Hearfest and stayed till at least Sowe.

Cooke buried her hands in her shawl and crossed Stobnyk Kol. The villa was abuzz, and it was nice to see the old home full of life. Instructors waved as she passed while students whispered and pointed with gaping eyes.

One girl who was maybe sixteen, hopped on one foot while trying to throw on leather sparring armor and bracers. She slipped on a stone step and rolled down half a flight of stairs. At the bottom, she got back to her feet and ran toward the longhouse. That kind of commitment or fear of being late couldn't be taught. Cooke would have to find out the girl's name. For the most part, all the children looked like babies to her, and with the number of students who were expelled or died, she generally didn't bother with names until they were at least fourth years.

Black smoke billowed from the furnace at the metalsmith's shop. A cluster of boys and girls stood around watching the basics of how to stoke the fire and work it using a mixture of agyls and coal. They had to be third years, fifteen and sixteen year olds. She knew that due to the curriculum. A decade ago, they started teaching metal workings to the first years, but too many ended up with burns or serious wounds that hindered their fighting abilities. Cooke was all for weeding out the weak, but unnecessary injuries or death didn't make sense when the whole goal was to grow the Red Hounds.

Past the forge, flush against the wall to the villa, was the infirmary. It had once been a temple to The Silver Lady and was the only wooden structure in Stobnyk Kol. Although three-stories tall from the outside, it had only one main floor with high arching pillars cut in intricate designs.

A few students slept on cots. Two with burns, one with a puncture wound, and another with stitches. She had set up Mogul in a private room along the back of the infirmary, and before Cooke was halfway to it, she could hear his cursing.

The door creaked open, and Mogul's big ape eyes narrowed at her. Leather straps secured him to a stone table. He was topless, and white bandages covered his left shoulder where his arm used to be.

"'Bout time you showed," Mogul said in a slurred voice. "You bound me up like a wounded goat. Ain't right."

"You left me no choice." Cooke approached the stone bed. She loosened the leather straps bolted around Mogul's ankles. "You thrashed about when they carried you in. If you didn't hurt someone else, you were going to hurt yourself."

Cook unhooked the strap around Mogul's chest, and he sat up. With only one abnormally long monkey arm, he looked almost human again. Almost.

"What do you plan to do?" he asked.

"About what?"

"My missing arm."

"I can't do the impossible."

"You are the queen of concoctions."

That was true. To her knowledge, not even Owen possessed her mastery of mutating agents or the ways she could twist agyls. Still, she knew of nothing that could grow a creature's arm back, though that might be something she could look into. She thought of the number of soldiers wounded that, instead of having to lay down their swords and leave the Red Hounds, could keep fighting.

"There is nothing," Cooke said. "And we have been together long enough for you to understand that, when I say there is nothing I can do, I mean it."

"You have done it before. You fixed my lungs and saved me from that gultrak bite."

"And look at how that turned out." She brushed a hand across his long arm and stopped at the wrist to check his pulse. "Anything else I may try would not work or would make you even less human."

"I don't care." Mogul jerked his arm back. "I'm faster this way. The best fighting shape I've ever been in, but that means nothing without a second arm. I can't properly use my bo. I can't fire a bow and arrow or hold a long sword. You have to fix my arm."

"You will have to make do. We can always pull you out of service, and you can stay here teaching."

"I'd rather die than not be able to fight." Mogul spit on the floor and swung his legs off the stone table. He stood, lording over Cooke and walked out of the room. "Fix it or don't expect to see me ever again."

Cooke sighed. This was but one more thing added to the list of things that she needed to handle.

~

A black and silver female dragon came three days later for Cooke. It landed on the snowy hills outside of the walls of Stobnyk Kol. It was the fifth time a dragon had arrived to drop her off or pick her up, and still the students reacted. They rushed for their armor and weapons.

It was like watching children play dress-up. To think that these soldiers-to-be might become Red Hounds one day. It was sad to think that the future rested on their shoulders.

Devina barked a series of orders, and the fourth years took over. They were trained enough to at least do as told without acting foolishly on their own. They loaded the dragon with supplies, and when they were done, Cooke climbed aboard, all the while dreading the long journey north.

Dragon flight made Cooke sick. A solution of diluted zewik bark helped, but it didn't completely rid her of the vertigo or pressure around her eyes. It took an entire day, but Cooke was ecstatic when the dragon landed on the solid stone streets of Gwen.

Cooke walked through the abandoned city.

Her steps echoed off the peculiar curved buildings but did nothing to hide the heavy breathing of the sleeping dragons. She couldn't see them, and that always gave her chills 'cause she knew they were there. They were on the roofs, inside the structures, or the next street over, all waiting to awaken upon Medrayt's command.

She found Medrayt in the temple. She didn't know if it was an actual temple. The first time she had arrived in Dras was after the dragons had been brought under control, so she knew nothing of their culture, but to her, the high ceilings, engraved columns, and dais felt reverent.

"I've lost complete contact with Kane." Medrayt didn't open his eyes or look her way. He most likely was somewhere else seeing through the eyes of a dragon or dragons.

"Right to business?" She bent her aged frame forward, stretching out her spine. She was sure the small of her back was bruised, and in a day, she would be so sore she would have trouble walking.

"The situation is escalating quickly."

"The situation is what it has been."

"You met the boy and dragon. They are new players–"

"And they can wait," She approached Medrayt. He didn't look unhealthy, but he didn't look as fit as the last time she had seen him. Gone were his hard muscles, and his shoulders no longer filled out his tunic. Where his usually clean-shaven face should have been was a nest of whiskers that knotted into an unkempt beard. "First I want to know how you are doing. I see you've been eating this time."

He took a long, drawn-out breath and then opened his eyes. "The nonperishable wafers have made it easier for me to make the time."

"You are the key. Without you, we have nothing. You need to take care of yourself."

"I am..." He twirled a finger in his beard and gave it a tug as if noticing it for the first time. "I am doing my best."

"Do you think Kane is dead?"

"I do not know if Kane can be killed."

"Then let's assume that she is still on mission." Cooke sat next to Medrayt and stretched out her legs. "Do we send anyone else after Carter and Doug?"

"Is that the dragon's name?"

"It's what he called himself."

"I could send a few dragons after them, but I don't know if I can spare the effort. The next few weeks will be taxing."

"It's why I am here." It was a good thing too. This was the critical hour, and it was embarrassing to think that their savior smelled of piss and fermented eggs.

"Can we send Mogul after them?"

"He will need time to recover in Stobnyk Kol. He will be ready when we make our final move, and to be honest, he would be a bit outmatched."

"Owen's ward is that powerful?"

"More than you and me combined." Not that Cooke had much power in her, but Medrayt was probably second only to Owen himself. "With Doug no longer being a dragon, can his blood still be used to free the rest of his kin?"

"I don't think so, but there is no precedent for this type of thing."

"Kane is out of contact. Carter and Doug are for the moment beyond our reach." She put a hand on his shoulder and felt something that was both crunchy and sticky. Getting him bathed, fed, and rested would have be the first priority. "What can we do?"

"We do as planned," Medrayt said. "I start waking the dragons."

"How many can you control at once?"

"The most I've tried is twelve."

"And how many are there?" Cooke asked.

"Not counting the children, there is just shy of four hundred dragons."

"Then we have a lot of work to do if we are going to save this world."

17

THE FORMER SERVANT

ULESDAY, 27TH OF HEARFEST, 1162.111

Gideon waited for Alex and Carter to ask a barrage of questions. Some were important, some weren't, and maybe a quarter were answered so that the the children understood. The Sisters gave Carter a flat stone with a spell carved onto its surface. The spell was long, a full sentence and the language looked like Urkish, but Gideon didn't get a good look at it so it might have been something else.

When readying to leave the chamber, Gideon felt it was time to tell Alex his decision. "I can't go with you to Kale."

"I know." She didn't sound upset or surprised. "You are going to Elene."

"You understand?"

"Someone needs to tell father. I could go, but what do I know about preparing for war or how to defend against an army of dragons. He needs you."

"Edgar will be furious at me for letting you go on your own."

"I'll be there," Carter said.

Gideon looked at Carter. Opened his mouth. Decided it was best to not say what he was thinking and turned back to Alex. "Any message you wish me to pass on?"

"Tell him I'm coming and will do what I can to save our people." Alex wrapped her arms around Gideon's waist and squeezed. "Tell him I love him and he shouldn't do anything stupid."

"He knows, and I'll look out for him." Gideon leaned down and kissed the top of her head. "Be safe, please."

Carter grumbled something under his breath.

Gideon insisted Alex keep all the travel supplies. He needed only his sword and the clothing he wore. They shared goodbyes a second and a third time. Then finally, Alex and Carter headed out of the chamber, leaving Gideon alone with the Sisters.

"To what do we owe the pleasure of your company?" Clothu said in a grandmotherly voice.

"Cut the bull," Gideon said. "What game are you three playing?"

"You lost the privilege to know such things," Atropos said.

"You know the reasons why I left your service. I had no choice," Gideon said. "Edgar demanded it, but that's no reason to keep me in the dark."

"Like you have kept Alexandra in the dark about Medrayt and the kind of threat he poses?"

"There are some secrets that aren't mine to reveal. A chunk of them are yours," Gideon said. "For starters, I recognized the dragon and the boy."

Clothu flexed, as if showing off massive muscles. "Ohhh big man."

"Big words." Atrops tapped her temple.

Lachesis crossed her arms. "You dare threaten us?"

"I'm keeping many secrets," Gideon said. "My point is it's probably best for all involved if I keep my mouth shut, but if there is something you can tell me, please do."

"Can't we give him a little something?" Clothu stuck out her lower lip. "He did serve us longer than anyone else ever has."

"He has earned a tad of information," Lachesis said. "I suppose."

"Go ahead, Gideon." Atropos clasped her hands, in a grand-motherly fashion, that didn't seem quite natural to her. "Ask us what you wish to know."

"The end of the world is coming, isn't it?" Gideon said. "That's what it has to mean if Doug and Carter are here."

"This is not the end," Clothu said. "Only the beginning of the end."

Atropos shook her head. "Our plans may yet blossom."

"True," Lachesis said. "But which plan? Right now the threads are in conflict."

"What can I do to help?" Gideon asked.

"So sweet." Atropos laughed. "But your time has passed. There is another we have tapped as our champion."

"He's a good one too," Clothu smiled.

"He wears glasses." Lachesis curled her fingers, forming tunnels, and peered through them, as if using a double spy glass.

"And where is this new champion?" Gideon waved across the room. "Guiding Alex and Carter should be his main priority."

"Oh my poor poor gosling," Atropos sighed. "You forget there are many worlds and some in far worse shape than this one. We have many seeds that we have planted. For now, we have to hope they take root."

"There is nothing you can do to stop Medrayt's dragon army?" Gideon asked.

"There is a thing or two more we can attempt," Clothu said. "But for the most part, we can do nothing now but wait. We have done our best to not alter the course of lives, but to highlight choices that may have been overlooked. Let's see if our ducklings make the right choices."

"Free will?" Gideon laughed and rolled his eyes.

"Quite right," Cloth said.

"The decisions have always been theirs." Atropos nodded.

"They forge their own paths," Lachesis said.

"Don't forget our history," Gideon said. "I know how you manipulate the threads. Take this as a warning from an old servant, be careful how much you push Doug. You wouldn't want what happened to Medrayt and Kane to happen to him."

The women were quiet and looked at each other. They then floated to the floor and nodded to Gideon.

"Your advice is noted," Atropos said.

"Also, my loyalties now lay with Edgar and Alex. I'm not sure where your games are leading, but if they mess with my obligations, I'll have no choice but to oppose you."

"My pet, do you not understand?" Clothu giggled.

"Your working for King Edgar has always been part of our game." Lachesis smiled.

Goosebumps formed on Gideon's arms.

No more words needed to be shared. Not even a goodbye. He bowed his head in respect and left.

Upon hitting the streets, Gideon toyed with the idea of getting supplies and extra boots, but, within the city, there was a flourish of activity, more than normal, and he realized it was Sahene Eve. Best to be gone while the bridges were still open.

He reached the Freelands bridge in time. Already it was packed with locals preparing for the night's festivities, but he was able to slip out of the city without any complications.

By night, he was more than ten leagues outside of Compitum. He rested in a dusthole of a town, where he resupplied with water, and hit the road again.

There were limits to how hard he could push himself. On a good day, he might be able to cover sixty leagues. At that pace, he might be able to reach Elene before the end of the month. He hoped it would leave enough time for Edgar to prepare for the dragon army.

18

THE QUEEN-IN-WAITING

ULESDAY, 27TH OF HEARFEST, 1162.111

Alex knew that the Arwyn embassy was located in the southwest section of Compitum, near the Freelands bridge, but she had rarely been in the city on her own, and so maneuvering through the tangled streets slowed their travel. She stopped and asked directions to Council Way, one of the main roads through the city, twice. When they found it, she had no problem leading Carter to the embassy.

She picked up her pace when she spotted the grey stone of the embassy's towers. It would feel nice to bathe and sleep in her own bed. Plus, it was the day before Sahene. That meant there would be all kinds of pastries and cakes made in preparation.

"It's big." Carter said. "Like big-big."

The embassy took up four city blocks and had walls higher than all the buildings around it, but both Kelsam's and Gara's embassies were equal in size, and all three were designed to be fortresses. In comparison, she knew that Saul Western was more than ten blocks wide, and the other university on the north side of the city was bigger. "The palace in Elene dwarfs the embassy, but my room here is way bigger."

"I'm excited for someone to wipe my bum for me. 'Cause that's what they do in embassies and–"

She punched him. In the shoulder. Hard.

It shut him up.

The only entrance to the embassy was through a fifty-foot metal portcullis that remained closed and manned with Arwynian soldiers. When her father or Gideon weren't present, the embassy was run by Jintzy Bardock, a former high ranking baron. Bardock was a decent guy. His family had died in a flood when Alex had been a kid. He gave up his lands and was going to kill himself, but somehow, her father had convinced him to serve as ambassador instead. Her father had a way with people.

Alex approached one of the two soldiers at the embassy's gate. "I need to speak with Jintzy. It's a matter of emergency."

"Go away," the man barked. "No refugees allowed here. Go find the Registrar."

Alex knew she and Carter looked travel worn, but to be accused of being a refugee was a bit too much. Her cloak was dirty, but it had no rips and was clearly made from Ralkan fleece. Straightening her back for maximum height, she placed a hand on her hip and pointed to the portcullis. "I am Alexandra Eos, the queen-in-waiting. You will open the gate."

The second soldier, a lean woman with a crooked nose, laughed. "If you are the princess, then I'm King Edgar himself!"

"Get lost." The first soldier shooed them away. "We see at least three Princess Alexandras a day, and every one is more convincing than you."

"There is a ding on the right side of your breastplate." Alex circled the man, inspecting him. "Your surcoat is frayed at the bottom, clearly not tailored to your height, and I believe those are food stains on the bottom corner."

"Mind your own business and get going, or I will call the City Watch!" The man reached out to grab Alex, and she ducked under his arms, using the opportunity to draw the long sword from his waist.

"This is interesting." Alex held the sword level and close to her face. "It's not been properly oiled, and it looks dull."

The female soldier drew her own sword. "Drop it now."

Alex was a bit unused to the weight of the longsword. She didn't have the height or arm length needed to use it properly, but she made do and swung it with both hands. Alex struck the female soldier's blade right above the hilt to cause maximum vibration. The female soldier dropped her sword, and Alex swooped in to catch it.

"Let's review, shall we?" Alex laid both swords on the ground to make it clear she was not being an aggressor. "A woman shows up at the gates. She says she is your queen-in-waiting. She easily points out your dress code violations and the lack of care for your weapons, and she disarms you both with little effort. I know neither of you are university students, but this should suggest that the woman might be who she claims to be."

The male soldier kicked Alex in the chest. She landed on her butt and skidded backward. Both soldiers picked up their weapons, and Carter defensively stood in front of Alex with his arm raised as if to cast a spell.

"Carter, no." Alex stood, dusting herself off. "I have this."

"Let me blast them," Carter said. "Then you can call the Jitsy man and get this straightened out."

"His name is Jintzy and no." She made sure to use the same stern tone her father used when telling his barons something they didn't want to hear. "I can handle this. I don't need your help."

Carter narrowed his eyes and grunted. He didn't like it, but he stepped aside, deferring to Alex.

The moment he did, the female soldier grabbed him from behind and held her sword to his neck. "Stand down girl," the soldier ordered. "Or he will be the one paying the price."

"You are lying," Alex said.

"Am not."

"I spent my whole life memorizing every rule, law, and policy of Arwyn. Right now, the proper thing for you to do is to call for backup."

The woman glanced over her shoulder to the closed portcullis and then back at Alex. "Who are you?"

"I told you. I'm your queen-in-waiting, and I'm growing annoyed. This is your last chance to appease me before I embarrass you in front of every soldier stationed here." Alex spoke with a calm voice, being sure not to appear a threat. "Decide."

The female soldier kicked Carter in the back of the knee, knocking him over. She then raised her sword.

Alex drew her dirk in time to parry the soldier's longsword. She took a firm stance while watching the soldier's legwork. They traded blows, but Alex kept her attacks light and testing. The soldier was stronger but slower and relied too much on her strength so that, with every swing, she left herself open.

"Hurry up and end this," the male soldier said.

"I'm trying, Donny. She's too bouncy."

Alex parried another slash and for fun smacked the female soldier on the thigh with the flat of her dirk. "You are putting too much into your swings. Which means that, when I dodge an attack, you leave yourself overextended."

"I'll handle this." The male solider raised his longsword into an attack position, but before he took another step, Carter summoned a gust of wind, lifting the soldier off his feet and bashing him against the portcullis. A sharp ringing of metal on metal echoed off the walls of the nearby buildings.

"You killed him!" The woman soldier turned her attention away from Alex and to Carter.

"He's fine," Carter said. "Maybe a bit concussed, but he'll be fine, I swear."

The female soldier swung her sword wildly at Carter's head. He dropped to his belly to avoid the attack and then rolled away as she slashed at him.

"Alex!"

"Idiot." Alex sheathed her dirk. She sprinted at the female soldier and bashed her shoulder into the woman's hips. The woman toppled over, and Alex grabbed the soldier's arm and pinned it behind her back. Alex jammed her thumb into the armor's joint at the woman's elbow pit, being sure to hit the pressure point. "I'm sorry. This escalated further than I wanted."

The woman grunted and spit out a glob of blood.

"Thanks," Carter said.

"Thanks?" Alex gritted her teeth. "I told you I had it. I told you I didn't need your help."

"I disagree. I could have taken them out without risking either one of us being cut to pieces."

"I wasn't trying to fight them."

"Then you suck at trying not to fight people."

"I maybe misjudged how much I was provoking them, but that doesn't change the fact that until you got involved, I had things under control."

"Doesn't matter now." He bent down and touched the unconscious male soldier's neck. "He won't be out for long, I don't think. How do we get to the people who might recognize you?"

"Left side of the gate," Alex said. "There should be a chain. Give it a hard pull. It will ring a bell in the guardhouse."

Carter rang the bell.

A moment later, a soldier appeared on the other side of the gate. He looked at his downed comrades and then bolted out of sight. Alex heard some shouting followed by the sound of metal boots on stone. The portcullis shook and rose, allowing ten fully armored soldiers to pass beneath it.

"I am Alexandra Eos." Alex let go of the female soldier's arm and stood.

"Your highness." An older soldier with dusty sideburns bowed his head. "We were not told you would be arriving."

"This is Arwyn land, is it not?"

"Yes, ma'am."

"Do I need to announce when I will walk upon my own soil?

"No, ma'am."

"Summon Jintzy." Alex waved a dismissive hand to the two downed soldiers. "And send these two back to basic training. Their swordsmanship is pathetic."

19

HUNGER

ULESDAY, 27TH OF HEARFEST, 1162.111

Doug had no idea where to go. Sure, he knew Kale was his ultimate destination, but in terms of which direction or how to get there, he didn't have a clue. He couldn't even find his way out of Compitum. The blasted buildings all looked alike with its white walls and people scuffling about. The streets weren't laid out in any pattern that made sense. One would be walking toward the outer quarters of the city, and then the street would loop back for no reason. It was like trying to maneuver through a labyrinth.

The whole situation stressed him out, which meant he was sweaty, which meant the more he went in circles, the more he got into a funk. His usual method for dealing with stress was flying. He could fly for twelve hours or more without touching the ground, and when he soared above the clouds, any problems he had faded away.

Since he couldn't fly, he did the one thing he could do. He walked. He walked for hours, and by nightfall, he found his way to one of the many harbors on the outskirts of the island city. A cool breeze blew across the lake, causing the humans to pull their hoods up and tighten their cloaks. But Doug embraced it, allowing it to wash away the flush of his cheeks and dry the dampness under his armpits and in the small of his back.

From what he could tell, he was somewhere on the south side of Compitum. He didn't see any of the three bridges that led into the city. Swimming wasn't an option. White choppy caps raced across the lake, and even if they had not, his not knowing how to swim would have stopped him. He could try stealing a barge or boat, but he didn't know how to use them.

His stomach rumbled. That might be something he could fix. A problem that had a solution... except he didn't know how to get food. If he were in the forest, he could easily sniff out edible vegetation. But in the city, he would probably need human money, and Carter had all their money. It had been stupid of him to storm out as he had without taking any money or supplies.

The scent of roasting pecans flooded his nostrils. Without thinking, he locked on to the smell and followed it back into the city. The deeper he went, the taller the buildings got, blocking out the stars. Hanging from balconies and shop awnings were metal lamps. They glowed with the same quality of light as Carter's agyls. However these ranged in various colors so that, even at night, the city felt bright and vibrant.

Doug followed the smell of pecans and soon picked up on a potato and squash soup with a touch of dill, grilled vegetables cooked right to have a smoky essence, and all kinds of breads. He broke into a run. Three blocks later, he found himself on the edge of a grassy park that was surround by a canal. Ornate lattice bridges crossed the waterway, and on the other side were dozens of bright booths. It reminded him of the spring festival back in Gwen. There was food for sale, but also art dealers and craftsman. Doug perceived a general sense of jovialness, something he hadn't felt since arriving in Compitum.

Every vendor Doug passed yelled to him. Some with a sultry voice, some with direct brashness, and others asking questions.

"Sweet treats from Kelsam that will make any woman or man fall in love!"

"Agyl-imbued mask to celebrate Sahene in style!"

"Embrace your inner demons with spiced whistlebugs! One stone for two points. Best deal you'll find in the Ivory Rainbow."

By the time Doug passed the second row of booths, he had figured out that eye contact only made the merchants yell louder, and the best thing to do was to stare at his feet.

Doug had hoped that, with such a crowd, he could slip in and steal a morsel or two of food, but the booths were set up so anything edible was on the inside, out of the reach of any passersby.

"Dragon?" Doug stopped dead in his tracks and turned to see a girl about Carter's age. She smelled of beans, though her curly autumn hair had a hint of sweetmelon. "Would you like a dragon sculpture?"

On the cart before her were nine sculptures of dragons made from shells. The dragons had various poses with wings unfurled and maws open as if ready to breathe fire, but what caught Doug's eyes were the types of shells. They had fat openings with spirals wrapping around them and ranged from no bigger than an ant to the size of apples. "What are these?"

The girl narrowed her eyes. "You aren't going to buy one, are you?"

"I don't have any money."

"Then move along."

"Please," Doug said, "I saw one of these a long time ago, but never knew what the creature living inside was called."

"They are garden crab shells." The girl scooted the largest of the sculptures, back and out of Doug's reach. "My pa gets them imported from the East Reach Sea."

"It's lovely." He meant it. There was a sense of motion in all the sculptures, as if each of the dragons were seconds from leaping off her cart. "I've not seen work of this nature before."

The girl shrugged. "Something I'm playing around with. I thought with all the dragon talk maybe they would sell, but so far they ain't doing it. You sure you don't want to buy one? I'll sell it to you for five rounds!"

"I would,"–Doug patted his belt where a pouch should hang–"but I really don't have any money."

"You came in with the group from Holton?" She nodded answering her own question. "I bet you've not visited the Registrar yet, either?"

"I don't know what that is."

"Same thing happened to me and pa when we got to Compitum." The girl rolled her eyes. "These things probably ain't gonna sell. Let me take you to the Registrar."

Doug's state of hunger had reached the point where his belly constantly ached. He felt a strange bubble of pain, like he had to hiccup, but instead of air needing to escape his insides, it was a sense of emptiness. He needed to find food. "I appreciate the offer but..."

"You are tired and hungry?" She finished for him. "That's why I'm saying I'll take you to the Registrar. It's where all the refugees are supposed to head for food and a place to sleep. It gets cold in the city at night."

Food. She had said the magic word.

It took her but a few moments to pack up her cart. The entire thing folded down to a trunk with wheels, which she loaded and was able to pull with a single hand.

"We got here a year ago." She led him over one of the lattice bridges and out of the park. "I'm Francine, by the way, but you can call me Frankie. We weren't the first survivors to arrive in Compitum, 'cause they did have the Registrar all set up, but we were one of the earliest groups to survive a dragon attack.

"You lived through an attack?"

"Pa and I watched the fabric shop and our apartment above it burn."

"Your mother?"

"Gone." She paused at an intersection, looking right and then left. "We should avoid the Painter's Brush area tonight. The Guild House Players are performing in the East Center. It's gotta be crowded like heck, which could be why Clover Market was so dead. Though on Sahene Eve, you'd think more people would show, you know?"

Doug didn't know what to say, so he kept quiet hoping whichever route she choose would soon take him to food.

"Back home, Pa was a third generation seamster, and after the dragon attacks we had no stock or supplies, so we came here to start over. There are guilds and politics, so even if we had the funds, he couldn't open a new shop, but he scored a nice teaching gig at Saul Western. It don't pay much, but I get to take classes for free, and we eat at night, so it ain't bad. What did you do for work?"

Doug gave a nonanswer. It became a series of nonanswers as she led him through the maze of the city. With every step, his belly grumbled, desiring that anything be placed inside it. Block after block, Frankie talked, and only a fraction of what she talked about made sense to him.

After twenty minutes, he could tell they had reached a different section of the city because he kept sniffing hints of straw and barnyards. There was a funk in the air, and his biggest concern was no longer eating, but trying to avoid breathing through is nose.

"This is it." Frankie stopped in front of an arched doorway. "There should be a clerk on duty who can help you. By The Silver Lady's graces, I hope you get back on your feet."

"Thank you for this."

"It's a big city. Lots of bad things can happen. I'm doing what I wish someone had done for me a time or two."

She wheeled her cart away, but her words lingered in Doug's head. Outside of Owen, who also seemed to lack a filter, she was the most sincere human he had come across since this whole ordeal began.

Doug walked through the doorway and the stench of livestock grew.

The building was long with a high ceiling, like a warehouse. It was stuffed with rows and rows of bunk beds, each filled with humans. Dirty humans who had not bathed in days, or maybe weeks. Feces. Fish. Ashes. Sensory overload. He grimaced and took a step backward.

"New arrival?" a mustached middle-aged man asked. He sat behind a desk that had been placed sideways in front of the entrance to a side room. Behind him were shelves of blankets, clothing, and food.

"Yes," Doug said. "I arrived to the city today."

"Let's get started," The man waved him over. "I need your name and city of origin."

"Doug. I'm from Holton." He had been lucky Frankie mentioned the city earlier.

"Ahhh yes, I heard the City Watch missed a whole group of you today. Sorry about that, chap." The man made a mark on a piece of parchment and scribbled notes next to it. "Any skills?"

Doug nodded, trying to come off confident.

"You a farmer? You look like a farmer."

"Uh no."

"Then what? I need to know where to place you."

"Midwife," Doug blurted. He felt foolish for saying it, but for some reason, his mind had narrowed in on a story Carter had told him about Owen overseeing births in Hal.

"I don't have anything open in the medical field right now, but you look strong. I'm going to put you down as a dockhand."

"A what? I'm sorry. I'm a bit confused."

The man ran a thumb down one side of his mustache. "Right, right, right. That's on me. Compitum does its best to take care of its citizens. The more that are fed and have a roof, the less crime we have. Begging is illegal here, and so we will provide a place for you to sleep and food for you to eat. In return, you will work for the city to pay off your cost of living. In time, if you are frugal, you should be able to make it on your own without any assistance. Make sense?"

"Yes." It didn't. Not in the slightest.

"Since you are a big'n, you'll excel at being a dockhand, loading and unloading the ships. As long as you aren't lazy, I have a feeling you might prosper at it." The man went into the little room behind him, and when he came back, he had a blanket roll he passed to Doug. "This is yours. An olive loaf, freshly baked this morning, is inside. Think of it as a welcome gift, but don't expect treats every day. Meals are served at dawn and dusk. Make sure you are back in time, or you'll be eating nothing."

Doug sniffed, trying to smell the loaf of bread, but the stench of the room hid it. "Where do I go?"

"Grab any spot you can find." The man waved an arm to the row of bunks. "When the morning bell rings, make sure you get up and head over to the docks. You know where that is, right?"

Doug nodded. He had no intention of going to the docks. All he needed was food and a place to sleep. In the morning, he would figure out where Kale was and how to get there.

"Move along then," the man said.

Doug clutched his blanket roll and walked into the tangle of beds. The paths between the rows were so tight in places that, when turning sideways, his gut or butt still shook the bunks. The first few times it happened, Doug apologized, but soon he realized it didn't matter because the bed occupants were used to it.

The bunks along the center of the room and back were filled, but he did find a series of empty ones on the side of the room near the privy. He drew the line there. The pungent odor was too much, and he'd rather sleep outside.

"Try the mess hall," a man told him. "When the bunks fill up, there are usually spots under or on the tables. You'll have to get up early, but it means it will be impossible for you to miss the next meal."

Doug followed the man's instructions, shuffling to the back right corner of the warehouse. From there, he took a catwalk, crossed over a street, and entered the building on the other side. To his relief, the smell was much better. There was still a stink, but also trace smells of onions and broth. At least here he would be able to sleep.

Picking a spot as far away as possible from other people, Doug rolled out his blanket so it was halfway under a table. He picked up the olive loaf and breathed it in. Rosemary and a sweet oil coated the loaf, keeping the entire thing soft.

"What's that?" a child asked.

Doug looked up to see the face of a boy peering over the edge of the table. The face was thin, but more notable were the scars. A blotchy patch of wrinkles ran down his neck. "I'm about to eat the bread they gave me."

The child stared at him with wide eyes. Doug knew what the boy wanted. The boy wanted the bread, but Doug didn't care. It was his bread.

"Welcome bread is good stuff." The boy smiled, but it was lopsided thanks to his scarred cheek, which didn't move. "All we get is the stale stuff. It's so tough that when you soak it in stew it never softens."

Doug's stomach grumbled. It wanted the food. Yet his heart ached 'cause it wanted to share. Maybe he could give the boy a quarter? That would still leave plenty for him. "Would you like some?"

"You eat. I'll watch and smell." The boy rolled off the table, landing on his butt. "I like the smell, but I think I'm getting sick, so I may not be able to smell it."

"You sure? I don't mind sharing."

"I would of course, what idiot turns down bread?" The boy looked over his shoulder and then leaned in and whispered. "It's my baby sisters and mama. I wouldn't feel right sneaking food and not giving them any. I'm the man of the family now. It's my job to provide for them."

The gurgling hunger in Doug's stomach screamed. It knew what he was thinking, and it rebelled against the idea. "Take the whole loaf."

"You mean it, mister?" The boy's mouth hung open.

"Yes."

"Thank you." The boy snatched the loaf and ran across the mess hall. Doug lost sight of him, so he resorted to listening instead. He was able to pick out the boy's voice easily.

"Worked like a charm," the boy said. "Always does."

"Did you mention dragon fire this time?" a man asked.

"Naw, I did what you said. I let him make his own assumptions."

"Good," the man said. "The more attention you draw to it, the greater the chance someone will realize it's not a burn from fire."

Doug had been played. Again. First by the Sisters and now by a boy who had tricked him out of his food. He was tired, hungry, and done with letting people take advantage of him.

Standing on his table for a better view, Doug found the ragged boy. The kid sat against the far wall with a bearded man eating the olive loaf. Doug's olive loaf.

In three leaps, he crossed the mess hall and landed in front of the boy and man. Both continued eating the bread. "That's mine," he told them.

The man's eyes were clouded over, and instead of looking at Doug, he pointed his ears toward him. "The guy found us, didn't he?"

"Yep," the boy said.

"Of course, it's yours." The man fumbled for the boy's hands and took the bread. Then the blind man held the two remaining chunks out to Doug. "We want no trouble. Take it."

Doug did so and protectively held them against his chest. The moment he did, the boy fell to the floor screaming. He shouted, cried, and yelled, flailing his arms about.

"What's wrong with him?" Doug asked.

"What do you expect?" the man yelled. Every head in the mess hall looked up and over to see what the commotion was. "You steal food from a child and then want to know why he cries!"

"You stole the bread from me!"

"I'm blind, and he's but a child. How could we steal anything from a monster like you?"

The doors to the mess hall swung open, and three soldiers wearing platemail entered. They held drawn crossbows.

"You better run." The blind man smiled at Doug. "The City Watch has a strict policy regarding theft."

Doug didn't think of himself as violent, and yet he wanted to pick up the blind man and throw him across the room. This whole situation was wrong. Flat out wrong. It was his bread. They had conned it from him, and now they were going to get him in trouble with whatever the City Watch was.

"What's the problem?" the soldier in the lead said.

"We were minding our own business when this brute stole from us." The blind man turned his head in the opposite direction as if speaking to someone who wasn't there. The move was so choreographed and over the top that Doug didn't know how the soldier didn't pick up on its fakeness.

"Sir, is this true?" the soldier asked Doug.

"No. It's my bread. I arrived today from Holton, and they stole it from me."

"Give me the bread." The soldier lowered his crossbow and held out his palm. "Now."

Doug handed it over. The soldier dropped it onto the ground and stomped on it. "I don't know whose bread it was, but now it's no ones."

The boy with scars stopped crying. He wiped away the fake tears and crawled to the flattened bread. He peeled the shrapnel off the stone floor, making sure not to miss a crumb.

The tips of the crossbows drooped. The soldiers seemed as surprised by the boy's actions as Doug was. The boy, with a satisfied grin, leaned against the wall, chewing the bread extra loud, as if on purpose.

"That settles that." The soldier pointed his bow back at Doug. "Unless you still have a problem?"

Doug clenched his jaw, showing the soldiers his teeth. He could bash their heads in before they knew what happened. He could throw them off the catwalk and onto the streets below. He could–

A rumble surged from Doug's stomach.

He was hungry and wanted nothing to do with humans. Blowing past the soldiers, he stepped onto the catwalk and leapt to the street below. A gust of wind nipped at him, and he thought Frankie had been right. The city was cold at night.

20

FEAST

ULESDAY, 27TH OF HEARFEST, 1162.111

Jintzy was not around. He was attending a play in the Painter's Brush and would not return till dinner time. It gave Alex and Carter a much-needed break because once word spread that the queen-in-waiting was present, the embassy's staff scurried about drawing baths, cooking food, and trying to cram a week's worth of preparation into a few hours.

Luckily, Arwyn had little in the way of internal politics. There was still some tension with the eastern barons, but for the most part, Alex could be herself without having to put on a show. Had she been attending a dinner with representatives of Gara or Kelsam, it would have been all drama and the meaning of unspoken things.

The warm salt bath was relaxing, but what Alex treasured was getting back into some of her own clothing. Since she and Gideon lost their travel gear back on the caravan, she had been stuck wearing the same clothes. She didn't have Doug's super smelling skills, but even she knew they stunk.

She picked a loose ivory undershirt with a chartreuse leather tunic and black leather pants. She of course wore her dirk at her side and had her personal pouch attached to her belt. The outfit gave her an air of seriousness, not that Jintzy wouldn't believe her, but she felt it was important for the rest of the staff to see she was here on business.

A woman from the kitchen told Alex the food was ready. She headed to the royal family's dining room, which was two floors above her personal quarters. She used it only when dinning with her father or Gideon.

Glass covered an entire wall of the dining room, providing a splendid view. As night loomed, the city glimmered with twinkling agyl lamps. The mornings were always her time with her father, and they had spent more mornings than she could count eating in front of the window.

Carter sat at the dining table. His ratty, torn clothes were gone, and instead, he wore a puffy teal shirt and black velvet vest. The vest was covered in an alabaster floral pattern and was a bit too big for him.

"What are you wearing?" Alex asked.

"What they gave me." Carter fiddled with the vest's silver buttons. "Does it look bad?"

"It works," Alex said. "If you were trying to look like an actor pretending to be a pirate."

"Hey! I like the vest." He straightened it. "I feel fancy."

She took a seat across from him. "Did they tell you yet what the kitchen staff whipped up?"

"I've got no clue. I assume some frilly fancy slop like sautéed goose liver."

"No way. Dad hates that crap. Maybe it's smoked mutton or roasted crenzel. Either way, I hope there are potatoes with lots of butter."

A thin man dressed in Arwynian blue entered carrying two plates. He placed one in front of each of them. The food wasn't attractive. It was a pile of meat with a cream sauce and a biscuit on the side.

"What is it?" Carter leaned down and sniffed his plate.

"Boar. Pulled and separated and then covered with gravy." Alex picked up the biscuit, dipped it in the gravy, and then took a huge bite. "The biscuit is sweet potato and so good."

Carter mimicked her and nodded his approval.

They ate mostly in silence, both enjoying the hot meal, the best either had eaten in weeks. When they were done, the blue garbed kitchen worker took their plates and brought out strawberry tarts stuffed with custard. They were so delicious Alex asked for a second helping.

"I'm not complaining," Carter said. "It's nice to not be walking, but how long are we going to be here?"

"Depends," she said. "A ship is going to be the fastest way to Kale. I don't know what is docked here. We might have to wait a day or two for something seafaring to arrive. Jintzy will know when we talk to him."

"I've never been on a ship."

"It's smoother than riding a caravan and way faster. What has me worried is the journey back from Kale. We will probably have to dock in Brand and make the rest of the trip on foot. I don't know if we have that kind of time."

"I still can't believe this is all happening."

"It's like the kind of stories my dad tells about when he was our age. Going on big adventures to do some great thing, but he never mentioned the weight or the queasiness that forms in your stomach."

"I think it's the boar." Carter palmed his belly and stuck out his tongue.

"That was some fine boar. You ate too much." Alex rolled her eyes. "Are you trying to tell me that you aren't nervous? You have to be the one to do the magic to free the dragons."

"No. It's magic. I started studying agyls over ten years ago. We finally moved on to high magic this past year. It's kind of what I've been raised to do."

"I wish I had your confidence. All I can think about is if we screw up, it's my city, my people, my father who are going to die."

"I keep thinking about the guy Kane threw off the cliff."

"The giant, Bash?"

"Yes," Carter said. "I've seen people sick. I've seen people die. It happens when you are learning medicine, but I've never seen someone murdered. I keep picturing his blood glistening on the rocks."

"I get it. The things I saw traveling to Hal have stuck with me. I wish I could shake them, but I can't."

"Do you have nightmares?"

"Nightmares? No, but what I saw still haunts me when I close my eyes to go to sleep."

"Do you think it gets any easier?"

"I don't know, but I expect what we've seen so far is only the beginning."

A silence settled over the room. It hung there as they both sat lost in their thoughts and starring out at the sparkling city.

The Freelands Bridge was ablaze. The Saheners were already out burning this year's constructions. She wished she had gotten to see them earlier in the day. One of her favorite memories as a kid was the sunset parade when the locals wheeled out painted wooden doors, each decorated with a theme. Some might honor the tales of Coteth, The Silver Lady, or Owen, while others were intricate works of art made to look like peacocks, thylazines, or dragons. Once the sun had set, they were burned. Hundreds of hours of work turned to ash. It was always a spectacle to witness.

Ten minutes passed, and the silence broke with the door opening and Jintzy entering the dining room. It had been several months since Alex had seen him. He looked older. Heavy shadows hung under his eyes, and his clothes were loose, as if he had lost weight.

The embassy kept a full staff. There was no reason one of the tailors couldn't mend Jintzy's overcoat and baggy shirt. She would have to speak to him about it. If he was attending public gatherings as a representative of Arwyn, he needed to at least look the part of an authoritative figure.

"Your highness." Jintzy bowed his head slightly. "I returned the moment I got word of your arrival."

"I'm here on pressing business." She stood and took a deep breath. "The dragon attacks plaguing the Freelands and Arywn are not random. A man named Medrayt is behind it. Gideon has already left for Elene to warn father, but I have need of a ship."

"Are you sure the name you heard was Medrayt?" Jintzy asked in a worrisome tone.

"Yes," Alex said. "He's a magician who has taken control of the dragons. Have you heard of him before?"

"I have, but not in over twenty years."

"Who is he?"

A redness rose on Jintzy's cheeks, and sweat beaded on his forehead. "It's not my place."

"Just say it," Carter said. "She's going to hound you until you do anyway."

Alex grumbled. She wouldn't "hound" Jintzy. She would order him to share what he knew. It may not seem like a big difference to Carter, but to her it was. "Elene is in immediate danger, and all of Arywn is too. Anything you can share with us would be a boon. Now is not the time for secrets."

"There are things not spoken of." Jintzy walked to the window, peering out at Compitum. "Though I am surprised you've never heard the name before."

"Why should I have heard of him?"

"He is your father's brother. Well, half brother, but still they grew up together."

"My father was an only child."

"It's true your grandmother had only one child, but your grandfather had another from a previous marriage," Jintzy said. "I assure you Medrayt and Edgar were brothers. I trained both boys myself."

"Then why haven't I ever heard of him?"

"For a time in their late twenties, your father and Medrayt disappeared." Jintzy lowered his head. "It was a rough time for Arwyn. We thought them dead. Two years later, your father and uncle returned with you. Someone was not happy about their return, and your uncle was killed, though I guess that is not the case anymore. He somehow survived."

"I've read every account of Arwyn's history. I've had more tutors than I can name. No one has ever mentioned father having a bastard brother."

"Half brother," Jintzy said. "Medrayt was the rightful heir not a bastard."

This was ridiculous. How could her dad have never brought up having a brother? It made no sense. Sure, there were some things off topic, like Alex's mother. Her dad never talked about her mother or the span of years from when they had met till she had died giving birth. But never mentioning a brother was the same as lying. Her dad never lied to her, or so she thought. "If this Medrayt is my uncle, why would he be attacking the kingdom or threatening my father?"

"I can't answer that," Jintzy said. "From what I remember, your uncle was a patriot. He loved your father, and he loved Arwyn. To know Medrayt has been the one causing the dragon attacks and creating the overwhelming number of refugees, it's a tragedy."

"Have there been many refugees?" Carter asked. "I'm from Hal and only learned about dragon attacks in the past few weeks."

"Have there been many?" Jintzy snorted. "Compitum is overwhelmed with thousands of refugees. That's not taking into consideration those who have fled to Brand or Elene."

Alex had walked through the ashes of what was once a town. She had seen the horrors done to the people. Whoever Medrayt was, he was a terrible person. "We shouldn't waste any more time.

Carter and I need to reach the East Sea. How long before you can get us a ship?"

"We have none here that could handle rougher waters, but I could send you down river to Brand."

"When can we leave?"

"By first light," Jintzy said. "I'll send word now to the harbor master. They will start stocking supplies and preparing to sail."

"Thank you, Jintzy."

Jintzy bowed his head. "Although times are turbulent here, I could clear my schedule and travel with you to Brand."

"You don't have to do that," Alex said.

"I think I do," Jintzy said. "No disrespect to your own skills, but I wouldn't be doing my duty if I didn't do everything I could to help."

"I'll be there," Carter said.

"What skills do you offer?" Jintzy asked. "Are you a hunter or tracker?"

"I'm a great magician."

"Are you?" Jintzy nodded with approval. "Certainly, it would make you qualified. I guess then the two of you do not need me?"

"Don't be silly Jintzy," Alex said. "We'd love to have you come, but I know how important your duties are here. Gideon would never have left us if he didn't think the two of us could handle it."

"Well, gorph." Jintzy stood and stretched. His grey hair shifted to a rich brown, and his features slimmed, taking on the familiar form of Kane. "I had hoped the two of you could lead me to your dragon friend, but it seems he is no longer around, is he?"

"Where is the real Jintzy?" Alex threw her chair aside, keeping the table between her and Kane. "You better not have hurt him!"

"I assume your ambassador is still at the play," Kane said. "I only caught a quick glance of him from a distance when he left earlier. I'm surprised that you didn't figure out who I was. I know I didn't get his facial details or build perfect."

"You need to stop being so mean and tricking people," Carter raised his hands, readying a spell. "And for the record, I liked Kenzie better. She was nice. And prettier."

"Fool me once, shame on you. Fool me twice, shame on me." Kane flexed her arm, and it stretched like taffy. It lashed around Carter's wrists, binding them together. She repeated the motion with her second arm, coiling it around Alex.

"Not fair." Carter shook his wrist, trying to break free.

"You want to talk fair?" Kane said. "I've been in this blasted place for more than a week posing as a maid. People are nasty. Then after all this, you didn't bring Doug? Tell me where the dragon is, and I'll make your deaths quick."

"We aren't going to tell you anything." Alex bent her knees, trying to reach her dirk, but Kane tightened her grip.

"I expect simplicity from haystack over here." Kane retracted her arm drawing Carter in close. "But surely, you must see more is going on."

"I don't believe a single word you've ever said to us," Alex said. "You are a liar who can't be trusted."

"Ahhh I see. This is about dear old daddy." Kane nodded. "You think I made up the whole story about Medrayt being your uncle. I didn't."

"Lies." Alex squatted and pushed with her legs, trying to pull free of Kane's stretchy arm. Kane pulled back, flipping Alex upside down so she was stuck dangling in the air by her feet.

"Believe what you want." Kane retracted her arm.

Alex ended up face to face with Carter. He winked at her, which wasn't a good sign.

"For an assassin, you suck at assassinating," Carter said. "Remember the time you didn't kill Doug and I blew you to shreds?"

"I was unprepared," Kane said. "Things have changed."

"You talk a good game," Alex said, "but have nothing to back it up."

"Let's fix that," Kane said.

The hair along Alex's neck stood on end. She maybe shouldn't have provoked the crazy shape-shifting lady.

Kane flung Alex toward the glass window that overlooked Compitum. Alex hit it, butt first, and it shattered outward.

"Prösenta!" Carter yelled.

For a split second, Alex felt relieved. Carter was going to use his magic and throw her back into the room, and everything would be ok. That didn't happen. A wall of wind erupted in the dining room that launched Carter and Kane out the busted window.

"What did you do?" Kane yelled.

"Shame on you!" Carter said. "I don't need my hands to cast spells. I only use them for aiming."

"I hate you." Kane's back bubbled, and feathered wings grew from her shoulder blades. She spread the wings, and they unfurled, stopping both her own and Carter's descent.

Alex, on the other hand, continued to fall. In less than eight stories, she would be nothing but a stain on Compitum's pristine white stone streets.

21

AMBUSHED

ULESDAY, 27TH OF HEARFEST, 1162.111

Doug decided the only solution was to leave Compitum. Once he was out in the farmlands and forests, he could forage for food and feed his aching belly. He no longer cared about giving himself away or drawing attention. He walked up to the first people he saw, a drunk couple stumbling from a pub, and asked them for directions.

The man laughed, said something Doug assumed was crude, and then vomited. The sour-bile smell was not as bad as the fish stew, which was so poorly chewed Doug could still see slices of carrots and peas.

Doug grabbed the drunkard by the scruff of his neck and demanded directions to the Freelands Bridge. The man vomited two more times and then passed out. Luckily, a woman accompanying the man was not intoxicated and she pointed Doug in the general vicinity of where he wanted to go.

Doug repeated his abrupt direction asking five more times, each went much more smoothly than the first. Finally, he came in view of the Freelands Bridge. It was impossible to miss because it was on fire.

Flames shot higher than full-grown trees, and the light reflected off the water, bathing the city in a speckled orange glow.

As he got closer, he saw that the stone of the bridge was not burning. Bulky skeletal frames, the size of buildings, blazed. The fiery-box shapes blocked the bridge, and people cheered, drinking and celebrating on the streets.

A sober-smelling man stood in front of an easel, painting the jubilee, or at least that's what Doug assumed he was doing, though the coloring on the canvas looked more like spilled paint than intentional strokes.

"What's going on?" Doug asked.

"Sahene Eve." The painter dipped his brush into a brownish glob and smeared it into a peach smooge.

"I'm from out of town."

"They are exiling the demons and burning the entryway to our world."

The humans who were dancing and shouting all wore masks.

"When will they be done?"

"By morning I expect." The painter looked up from his work for the first time and stared at Doug. "You have exquisite eyes. May I paint you?"

"I don't want paint on me. It smells like wet stone and will take forever to fade."

"Not on you, but make a painting of you?"

"I don't have time. I need to get out of the city. Can you tell me the fastest way to either of the other bridges?"

"The other two bridges are closed," The man said. "You aren't going anywhere for hours."

Doug's shoulders sagged forward. He was so hungry, and all he wanted to do was leave this human infestation, but it was as if everything was conspiring against him.

"I can pay you." The painter rummaged through a sack at the foot of his easel. "Two copper rounds or five Kelsam halfpents?"

"Don't need any money..." Doug sniffed the air. "You have food in there?"

The painter held up a jar and something wrapped in parchment. "Half a bin of sweet lemon jam and bit of crusted rolls."

Doug snatched the food from the painter and sat cross-legged, spreading the paper across his lap. Inside were... Well, he wasn't sure what they were. They were like round slices of bread, but instead of being soft, they were hard, and yet not stale tasting. There was a bit of crunch to them, and when dipped into the jam, they became the most amazing thing he had ever eaten. Of course, if he tried them again on a full stomach, they might not taste as good. But as of right now, the sweet creaminess mixed with the sharp acid and the salty crunch of the bread was fantastic.

Doug licked the jar clean. He was still hungry, but at least the pain of the hunger had subsided. Making it through the night while waiting for the bridge to become passable again would be manageable.

"Where are you going?" The painter asked as Doug stood up.

"I finished the food."

"I'm not done painting you."

"Not my problem," Doug said. "Unless you have more food..."

The painter bit his lower lip and frantically glanced up and down the street. "Ok, don't move. I'll be back."

It took three sessions of food running before Doug finally felt full. In that time, he got to try spiced grits topped with tine berries, grilled yucca, which was like a savory sweet potato, and a seaweed wrap filled with spring greens and rice. It was the best meal he had eaten since leaving home. He was so content when the man offered to buy him a fourth round of food, Doug said he was ok and allowed the painter to continue working.

With a full stomach, waiting for the Sahene celebration to end became less of a burden. Already, the fires were down to a fourth of the height they once were. It would be an hour at most, and then he could finally get back to the mainland. That was when he heard shattering glass.

A block away, seven or eight stories up, he saw a girl falling. There was a gust of wind, and then a woman and boy were also thrown from the same window.

It took half a heartbeat for him to recognize all three.

Kane grew wings from her back and flew in a circular pattern, holding on to Carter, but Alex continued to fall. Doug didn't debate it or contemplate it. He sprung into action. He couldn't allow the girl to die, not when he could do something about it.

Doug sprinted, going solely for speed. He angled his body, and with each step, he pushed off the pavement, propelling himself forward. With each jump, he gained more height, and timed it so he connected with Alex while at the zenith of a leap.

"Got you." Doug put a palm against the center of her back and tucked his other arm behind her knees. "Go limp when we hit the ground."

She did as he commanded, and when his feet hit stone, he bent his legs, trying to soften the impact as much as he could. It was too much, though, and instead of a smooth landing, his heels kicked forward, and she landed on his pudgy belly, knocking the air from his chest.

"Thanks." Alex rolled off him and was back on her feet before Doug had a chance to catch his breath. "We need to get Carter though."

"Do we have to?" He asked between coughs.

"Not funny."

"Kind of funny."

"Do something!"

Kane half glided and half flew while wrestling with Carter, who squirmed in her arms like a hatchling not wanting a bath.

"Hey Kane, stop flirting with the kid and come face someone who stands a chance against you."

Kane and Carter's struggle stopped as they both looked down. A moment later, Kane released her grip on Carter, dropping the boy.

"Prösenta!" Carter pointed his palms to the ground, and a rush of wind rose, catching him. He landed in a huff and gave Doug a cold stare. "What are you doing here? We don't need your help."

"I was minding my own business when I stumbled upon you getting yourself into trouble," Doug said. "And don't worry, I plan on leaving as soon as I deal with Kane."

"I had things under control." Carter staggered and dropped to a knee.

"Sure looks like it."

"It's the magic." Carter propped his fingers on the ground to keep from falling over. "I'll be fine in a minute."

"We don't have a minute." Alex pointed to the sky. Kane was mid-shapeshift. Gone were her wings and human body. Her neck grew long, and she bulked up, taking the form of an ollip. "She's going to crush us!"

Alex helped Carter to his feet, guiding him farther down the street, but Doug didn't budge. Maybe the hunger had gotten to him or his overall patience had hit maximum capacity because he no longer wanted to run. He wanted to see exactly how strong he was.

Doug jumped and collided with the ollip.

The ollip plowed into Doug, driving him into the street.

Intense pressure coursed through his body. Not so much pain, but the sensation he would pop, as if his blood and innards were going to squirt out through his eye sockets or ears.

The feeling eased, and as it did, he realized Kane was shape shifting again. Her mass slid off him, and other than an achiness, he felt-light headed to the point that sitting up was a no-go.

Stone shrapnel and dust blew through the air, and when it faded, Kane stood straddled over him. "I was worried you wouldn't show up to play,"

"I had to get something to eat first," he said. "Ever tried grilled yucca? You should."

"You can't distract me." She flexed her wrists, and her hands became forked blades.

"You can walk away from this. I want nothing to do with Medrayt or the other dragons. All I want is my old body back."

"And I can't let that happen."

A Greker dart struck Kane in the neck. Her eyes rolled up and she collapsed, landing on Doug. He was too sore to move her, but by shifting his head, he could see a squad of Grekers shuffling out from a sewage grate.

Doug knew what was coming. They would stick him next, and this time there would be no escape. He hoped Alex and Carter were safe.

22

THE ARG'NATZ

ALLSDAY, 28TH OF HEARFEST, 1162.111

Alex watched the Grekers emerge from the sewers. There were at least as many as there had been at their camp, if not more. Their strangely cute bodies stood out, for in all the time she had spent in Compitum she had never seen a nonhuman walk the streets.

Kane went down, and a moment later, they shot Doug. Alex knew she and Carter would need to act fast if they were going to intervene. "Carter, blast them!"

Carter's eyes rolled back and he fainted.

Alex felt a prick on her thigh and looked down to see a dart oozing with parpah root. Well that was different. She didn't expect to be hit too. The last time, the Grekers had left both her and Carter alone. Guess she pissed them off with the whole Erediä thing.

The world blurred, but the extract wasn't as fast acting on Alex as it was with the others. She had time to draw her sword and square up her stance.

The Grekers picked up Kane and Doug, dragging the pair toward an open sewer grate.

"Don't touch them," Alex tried to yell, but the words came out jumbled.

The grip on her sword waned. A moment later she heard it rattle on the ground, not realizing she had dropped it.

She crumbled, and only barely managed to bring her arms in front of her face to keep from breaking her nose on the stone road.

The effect of the parpah root wasn't like being asleep. It was more like being sick. She kept seeing and hearing flashes of things. She stirred when the Grekers picked her up. She saw the night sky disappear as she was carried into the sewer, and she vividly remembered being laid in a cart full of hay.

Less than an hour later, the root had worn off completely. She caught glimpses of an underground tunnel and the others bound in the hay beside her. As soon as the Grekers realized she was awake, they shot her with another dose. It wore off even faster.

The fourth time the Grekers attempted to drug Alex, the parpah root it had no affect, and they gave up trying to sedate her. Instead, she was left seated in the cart with hands bound while the others slept in the hay.

The tunnel ended in a cavern with a subterranean river, and the Grekers followed a worn road along its bank. Unable to use the most basic of aglys, the Grekers relied upon flickering torches to light the cavernous spaces. Alex didn't know what the torches were made of, but they lasted a long time and released a sangria-colored smoke that smelled like rotten eggs.

Escape wasn't an option. Sure, she could get away, but it would mean abandoning Carter and Doug. She couldn't do that. Not only did it feel wrong, but she needed Carter to cast the spells to free the dragons.

The first time Alex climbed out of the cart, the Grekers stopped and pointed their spears at her. Alex tried to explain why she had climbed out, but they either didn't care or didn't understand.

Instead of worrying about communication problems, she undid her belt, squatted, and took a pee. She shook dry, and from then on, they didn't give her any lip when she decided to stretch her legs.

With no way to tell the passing time and no view of the sky, the days blurred for Alex. Alex figured they were heading somewhere in the Redrock Mountains, but without the stars or daylight, it was impossible to pinpoint where exactly they were or how far they had traveled. If she was right, it meant they were heading east and closer to Kale. But she could be wrong, and for all she knew they were traveling north.

"Where are we going?" She had tried to speak to them several times, but they never responded or acted like they understood. "We going east? North to the Scourge? Where?"

The Grekers pulling the cart stopped. They spoke and then a particularly cherubic Greker with grey whiskers on his cheeks climbed into the hay cart. "You are the one who posed as Erediä?" He stressed every word, dragging out the question in an awkward but understandable manner.

"Yes," Alex said. "You had my friends."

"What do you know of the Scourge?"

Alex must have touched a nerve. But what? Why did the Grekers care if she knew about the Scourge. Everyone knew about it. "It is the wasteland to the north. It once belonged to the lost races."

The Greker said something to his companions, and the cart lurched forward.

"What does the Scourge have to do with anything? Why speak to me now after ignoring me for so long? Why capture me and my friends?"

"Too many questions." The Greker sat down in the hay, leaning his back against the frame of the cart. "I shall explain, but in my way. I will tell you the story of Bakero."

~

Bakero shuffled the coals fueling the stone oven. The heat singed the whiskers on her cheeks. A good sign, soon it would be hot enough for the dough. She couldn't allow a single thing to go wrong at the meeting with House Fengar.

She reached for the bellows, only intending to give it a slight push, but her hand passed through it. She lost her balance and toppled to the floor. Instead of landing on the hard cherrywood, she fell through it, as if it were made of mist.

The entire mansion became translucent as did the fountain in the front of the estate and the town houses farther down the street. There was a dull flash of light, and everything vanished. The ground remained, but all the vegetation was gone, and a sickly, flaxen crust, like burned dried oats, had replaced the dirt.

Her first thought was that she had died and that this dead world was Yorndrak, but none of the tales she had heard ever described the spirit world like this.

In that moment of ponderment, when Bakero could not decide if she was alive or dead, she saw The Silver Lady.

Bakero knew who she was for all know The Silver Lady in the same way our instinct tells us what is up or down. The lady's skin was like a mirror's surface, and she was as angelic as the legends said.

"Little one." Her voice was music, so sweet Bakero forgot to respond. The Silver Lady snapped her fingers, breaking Bakero from her trance. "Pay attention."

"Yes m'lady." To keep from being distracted again, she bowed her head and locked her eyes on the gritty soil.

"You must leave this place. If you do not, your entire race is doomed."

"Is this one of Yorndrak's rings?"

"You have not left Elderealm. The northern lands are what have left. If you wish to survive, you must flee south. Seek Agnar. It shall be your salvation."

Bakero made the mistake of looking up at The Silver Lady to ask a question, and in doing so, she became lost in the lady's eyes. They had an infinite depth and twinkled with starlight. The lady smiled at her in the way a mother smiles at an infant mesmerized by a shiny button.

From within her flowery robes, The Silver Lady withdrew a curved dagger. The hilt was bent to match the arc of the blade, so the entire thing formed a perfect crescent. Its inner edge had jagged teeth, while the outer bit was smooth and glistened in the light emanating from The Silver Lady's skin.

"Hold out your hand." The Silver Lady pressed the teeth of the danger against Bakero's wrist. A bracelet of blood soaked into her thin coat of fur.

The Silver Lady spun the dagger around and placed the pommel into Baker's quivering palm. The lady pressed the dagger along her own wrist, drawing blood.

Bakero's arm hurt, but only for a moment, and the pain was followed by a rush of energy. Her wrist tingled, and when she examined her own wounds, she saw they had closed, leaving no scar.

"You have been given the Argnot kot Natzul kæt. Use the gift wisely and lead your people."

Like the city of Zora, The Silver Lady vanished. The only proof of her visit was the odd dagger left at Bakero's feet.

"Bakero became the first Arg'Natz." The Grekers spoke in such a hushed tone that Alex had to lean closer to hear. "She led my people out of the Scourge."

"Interesting," Alex said. "I've never heard a story of what the Scourge was like, but it doesn't explain why you've taken us or drugged my friends."

"We shall reach Agnar. Until we do, hold your tongue. Speaking of things that are considered sacred could provoke negative repercussions. You are lucky you have not been killed for impersonating the Erediä."

Alex had been to enough state dinners to understand. The wrong thing done at the right time could lead to death or worse. She had once seen peace talks to end trade sanctions between Kelsam and Ralk fall apart because a fork was thrown in the trash during a dinner course. Dozens were killed. It was tragic.

As much as Alex wanted to demand more answers from the Greker, she respected the wisdom of keeping quiet. It was a good thing she was the one awake and not Carter. "I get your meaning."

The Greker nodded and leaned back in the hay, taking a nap. Alex envied his ability to fall asleep so quickly and wondered if it was a racial thing, an elderly thing, or simply the way he was.

Less than two hours later, an emerald light flooded the tunnel. At first, Alex thought something was wrong with her eyes. Maybe she had been underground for so long that daylight seemed off, but as the tunnel opened into a huge, underground cavern, she realized that what she saw was not the sun–or at least not the normal sun. Hundreds of stories up and floating dead center in the cavern was a ball of light. It was too bright to stare at, but in quick glances, she saw that the artificial sun had patches of brighter and darker spots, which flowed across its surface like oil failing to mix with water.

Having no more need for the torches, the Grekers doused them in the river and stacked them in the back of the cart. The noise woke the elder Greker. He sat up, looked around and crawled over Doug to stand next to Alex.

The cavern under the green sun stretched, so far that she couldn't see the other side. Red vines thicker than tree trunks lined the walls, and from beneath their bushy, turquoise colored leaves, sprouted pale flowers as big as Alex's head. Grekers scrambled up and down the vines plucking scaly looking fruits.

"Parpah fruit," the old greker said. "Good for medicine and for eating."

Past the vines, were fields of wheat or maybe barley–she always got the two mixed. There were several hut-like cottages made from smooth stones, and in the distance, near a kink in the river were the outskirts of a city. This must be Agnar.

The buildings were slanted, coming to points at odd angles. Though she had expected them to be stubby and designed for Grekers, they were instead open and large. At the heart of the city was a steep pyramid, higher than any other structure. A disc rested upon its top, drowning a section of the city in permanent shade.

It was into one of these darker areas that the Grekers led the wooden cart, and the farther they traveled, the larger the crowd grew that had formed around it. Children, elders, and every age in between chittered. Most spoke in their odd language, but every now and then Alex recognized a word like Compitum or Arg'Natz.

They stopped the cart in front of a bland building, and the onlookers kept their distance. One by one, the Grekers picked up Kane, Doug, and Carter and carried them inside. When it was Alex's turn, the older Greker offered her a hand, helping her out of the cart, then led her inside the building.

The interior walls were cream-colored and lacked any design, but the floor sparkled, and golden stripes ran through it, in a grid pattern. Alex's companions lay separated, sprawled unconscious on the floor. The air between them had a shimmery quality, like heat rising off stone on a hot summer day.

"Please walk forward," the Greker said.

"Why? What is this?" Alex asked.

The Greker prodded her forward. "Nothing will harm you."

She still had the option of fighting. Overcoming the old Greker would take maybe two well-placed strikes, but Carter and Doug were still out cold, and she couldn't defend the building from the dozens of Grekers outside. Feeling like she had no option, she walked onto the strange floor. It sunk under her feet, and she had second thoughts.

Alex stepped backward, trying to retreat, but her rear slammed against a wall. She didn't see anything but a soft shimmer of the air. She kicked and felt for a way around the invisible barrier.

"What is happening?" She banged on the wall, and with each thump, she could feel it hum with a surge of energy.

"The Domo will explain all." The old Greker turned to leave and glanced over his shoulder one final time. "May The Silver Lady watch over you."

Alex kicked the wall. She punched it. She rammed her shoulder into it. It had to be some sort of magic. She hated magic. Letting out a long sigh, she slouched against the wall and let her feet slide forward until she landed on her butt. There was nothing she could do but wait.

23

FAMILY MATTERS

ELDSDAY, 39TH OF HEARFEST, 1162.111

The waiting took a day, and to Alex's dismay, Kane was the first to awaken. The shapeshifter banged on her magic walls while shouting and screaming, but the barriers that imprisoned them somehow allowed sounds to enter and blocked them from getting out. That meant Alex could put her back to Kane and not think twice about the assassin.

Doug was the next to wake up, and his reaction was a bit odd. He looked around, wrinkled his nose, and then lay down. He didn't try to speak or test the barriers.

Carter did not take their imprisonment so gracefully. Upon awakening and finding himself trapped, he cast a spell. She assumed it was the same one that allowed him to summon the wind because one moment Carter stood in the center of his cell, and in the next, he flew upward and was plastered against the ceiling. He must have smacked his head because he fell back to the floor and didn't move for over an hour.

The second time Carter awoke, he ran through a series of agyls. There were puffs of smoke, streaks of lightning, and what looked like rain, but nothing the boy did was able to break through the invisible walls holding them.

In what felt like evening–she wasn't sure because the constant glow of the green sun meant it always looked like day–a crew of Grekers brought refreshments. Jugs filled with wine and metal trays were passed through the one-way walls. They trays were circular and had divots filled with earth-tone-colored mush. A spongy flat bread was stacked in the center.

Not sure what to do with the food or if it was safe to eat, Alex looked to the others. Carter acted as confused as she felt. Kane was using the bread as a brush and painting the walls of her cell with what looked like a series of stakes with Greker heads on them.

Doug propped a piece of the flat bread onto three of his fingers, and then pinched a pile of mush, picking it up. He folded the bread over once more and ate the bound wrap in one bite.

Alex mimicked his action, but with her smaller hands, it was harder to deal with the flat bread. The bread had a sour taste that balanced the spiciness of the mush. It was odd, but tasted nice. She quickly finished off her whole tray.

The wine was similar to a Tull Gold with a light feel and a hint of citrus in the aftertaste. Not sure when the Grekers would bring more to drink, she took only a few sips, intending to ration it.

Alex ran her tongue over chapped lips. She was dehydrated already, and anything to help hydrate her was a good thing, so she took another swig of the wine, a big swig. Not enough to make her cheeks flush, but enough to help quench her thirst. Of course, it made her fully aware that she hadn't used the privy in hours.

Alex waved, getting Doug's attention. He acted as if he knew this place, and if that was the case, maybe he knew how to call the guards. When he looked her way, she mimed taking a pee. He pointed at the golden strips in the floor and stepped on them in a specific looking pattern. The instant he finished, the walls for his cell turned opaque. A moment, later they reappeared.

She watched him do it two more times and then was able to do it herself. When her walls lost transparency, a bench with a hole in it rose from the floor. She relieved her bladder and then stood there, enjoying the sense of privacy. Not wanting the others to think she was doing something other than peeing, soon she repeated the step pattern, and her walls once more became see-through.

Carter's cell spazzed. It flicked from clear to solid, and between the flashes, it looked as if he were dancing. Finally, he smiled and traced an agyl.

"Can you hear me?" he asked.

"Oh my goodness, yes!" Alex hopped up and down with excitement.

Carter pointed to his ears. "I can't hear you. This is only one way. Give me a moment, and I should be able to fix yours too."

It took a half hour, but when done, Carter had disabled the sound blocking on all the cells. Alex had hoped he could pull down the barriers completely, but he said the walls trapping them were too complex and that only through a loophole in the system, was he able to take down the sound barriers.

Carter had lots of questions for Alex. Doug seemed to not care, and Kane kept her mouth shut. Alex answered what she could, and when finished, she decided it was time to get some answers from Doug. "How did you know how to open the privy?"

Doug cracked an eyelid and squinted at her. "I've been here before."

"How? When?" Carter asked.

"Long time ago," Doug said. "And if this is anything like my last visit, you all should get comfortable. There is no way to escape from here."

"That won't cut it," Kane said. "If we are to get away from here, we need all the information you can provide."

"Since when are you part of our 'we'?" Doug asked. "Last time I checked, you were trying to kill us?"

"I'm not a fan of confinement," Kane said. "Thus a truce would be in all of our best interests."

"Why not shape shift and break out?" Alex asked.

Kane held up a hand. Nothing happened. "As you can see, I've lost my abilities. The green light is not natural. I'm stuck in human form."

"Fun, isn't it?" Doug said sarcastically.

Kane raised the corner of her lip, showing her teeth like a dog growling.

"Why would the green light make a difference?" Carter asked. "I had figured your shape-shifting was an inborn magic."

"Sunlight fuels me." Kane pointed toward the green light oozing in through the door to the prison. "That makes my stomach churn."

"It's not sunlight," Doug said. "Agnar was, well I don't know what it was, but it's old, maybe even older than the Erediä."

"This is all your fault." Kane punched the wall of her cell.

"My fault?" Doug laughed. "None of this is on me. Carter turned me into a human, and you've been trying to kill me. All I want is to be left alone."

"Is that why you ditched us in Compitum?" Alex asked. "If you had been with us when Kane first attacked, we never would have been on the ground for the Grekers to nab us!"

"The point is," Kane said. "You should be dead like all the other rogue dragons. If you were, I wouldn't be trapped like a pet pig. Instead, I should be sitting pretty in Dras, relaxing in a hot spring while Medrayt finishes preparing his army."

"What is wrong with you?" Alex kicked her metal tray, and it slide across the floor, letting loose a ringing sound. "My people have done nothing to you or Medrayt. What you are doing is wrong."

"It's not about your people," Kane said. "You lot are dense. By now you should've figured it out."

"Figured what out?" Alex asked.

"The Fates are behind all of this," Kane said. "They are the bad guys not me or Medrayt."

"The Fates?" Alex raised a brow.

Kane rested her head in the palm of her hands. "The Weird Sisters. The Oracles. The Sisters Three. Call them whatever you want. They are the pissholes that are behind all this. They are the ones you should be mad at. If not for them, not a single one of us would be locked in these cells. Their strings are tied to each of you like puppets."

"We know this already," Doug said. "It's why I ditched the kids. I don't want to be a part of anyone's game."

"That's why you left?" Carter asked.

"Yes." Doug rubbed his temples. "I'm not going to ask why you thought I left."

Alex told the story of the sister she had met. It was the day she had left Elene. The woman had pretended to be a maid in the palace, and she had shown Alex a secret exit, a way to slip out of the city without anyone knowing. Alex had taken it, and if she hadn't, there was no way she would have ended up in Hal or met Carter and Doug.

"See!" Kane rapped her knuckles against the wall, pointing at Alex. "Medrayt and I are trying to save the world. Well, your uncle is. I want to piss off the Sisters."

"My uncle?" Alex's face contorted, and her mouth dropped. When Kane had revealed her disguise in Compitum, Alex figured the story about Medrayt had been a ruse, but if so, why keep it up.

"Did you think I lied about that?" Kane laughed. Not a chuckle. Not a snicker, but a gut-busting laugh that caused her to gasp as she desperately tried to catch her breath. "Oh that is great. Yes, Medrayt is your father's brother."

It was a lie. It had to be. Or did it? Alex didn't know who or what to believe anymore.

"Back it up," Doug said. "You said Medrayt wants to save the world. How is possessing dragons saving the world?"

"I thought you didn't care?" Kane winked at him. "That all you wanted was to be alone."

"I don't care." Doug lay back down and stared at the ceiling.

"Even if you are right. Even if we have been manipulated, so what?" Alex said. "There is still right and wrong, and what you and Medrayt are doing is wrong."

"It's for the greater good," Kane said. "Something bad is coming, and only the human kingdoms united under Medrayt can stop it."

"How could you know such a thing?" Alex still didn't believe Kane. The shapeshifter was an actor at its core, skilled in deceiving and putting on masks, but a small piece of the story nagged at her. What if it were true?

A stubby Greker entered the jail. She had tufts of white hair protruding from her ears and wrinkles around her eyes. She was tugging at her whiskers with her head cocked sideways. "You bypassed the cell's sound proofing. That's a new one."

"Who the hell are you?" Kane said. "Never mind. It doesn't matter. Let me out now, and I won't kill you."

The Greker pressed her face against Kane's cell, smooshing her nose into a pig-like shape. "You intrigue me."

"Cut the crap, Bova," Doug said. "What do you want with us?"

The Greker pulled a pair of bifocals from a breast pocket and perched them on her nose. "How do you know my name?"

"What, don't recognize me?" Doug stood and twirled, showing off his body. "I guess I look a bit different than last time I was here."

Bova's mouth dropped open. "Doug?"

"In the human flesh."

"How delightful." Bova smiled revealing rows of sharpened teeth that looked out of place with her grandma-like demeanor. "When the scouts said they returned with the Arg'Natz, I was disheartened to learn it was not a dragon."

"I want you to let us out of here," Doug said.

"I can't do that," Bova said. "You have to understand."

"As Arg'Natz,"–Doug paused as if it let the weight of his words sink in–"I order you to let us out."

Bova grimaced. She looked over her shoulder to the jail's entrance and then back to Doug. "Things have changed since you were last here."

"You are the Domo," Doug said. "The Pontis will obey your orders."

Bova shook her head. "The factions war. The power of the Pontis is not what it once was."

"You're the Arg'Natz?" Alex asked.

"Not now," Doug said.

"Yes, now." She didn't yell and made sure her voice was controlled, but at the same time she put her own authority into it. "Enough with your secrets."

"I'm the Greker king or emperor." Doug rolled his eyes. "The word doesn't have an exact translation."

"Being the Arg'Natz is so much more!" Bova spoke faster, growing excited. "The Arg'Natz is our spiritual leader. He or she is destined to bring back the Erediä. Can you imagine if it were to happen in our lifetime? The return of the Erediä!"

"Stop." Alex held up her palm. "Doug, the human, who used to be a dragon, is the spiritual leader of the Grekers?"

"Greker society is complicated." Doug said "I kind of inherited the gig after I left the dragons."

"Twelve years ago, when the last Arg'Natz died,"–Bova kissed the palms of both her hands and covered her eyes–"May The Silver Lady lead him in Yorndrak, Doug witnessed the passing of our last Arg'Natz."

"It wasn't so sweet sounding as that," Doug said. "I stumbled upon a squad of Grekers that had been torn to shreds by a roc, a nasty dragon-sized bird. The only Greker still alive was a young one. He couldn't speak, his throat was slit, and bleeding out, but he placed his hand on my snout, and I felt a bit of heat. From then on, I've been able to heal extra fast."

"Why do you make it sound like a bad thing?" Carter asked "It sounds cool to me."

"Because, Carter, I am a dragon, remember?" Doug glared at him. "I live to fly. To feel the sun's rays on my wings and the wind whip around my body. I can't live underground in a creepy cave, but that's what the Grekers did. They tried to keep me here against my will. It was only through dumb luck that I escaped last time."

"If you are their ruler, couldn't you order them to let you go?" Alex asked.

"Greker society does not work that way," Bova said. "In fact, things have only gotten worse. As I said before, the various factions are at war. The people demand a new Arg'Natz or proof that Doug deserves to be its bearer."

"They are opening the arena?" Doug asked.

"Yes, in a few days' time." Bova motioned toward the door to their prison. "Right now, there are over a hundred soldiers guarding this building. All the factions are here and all plan to challenge you in the arena."

"What happens in the arena?" Alex asked.

"Any who thinks they deserve to be the Arg'Natz may challenge the current Arg'Natz in a trial by combat. If they manage to kill the Arg'Natz, then they can claim the sacred spirit for themselves."

24

THE RETURN HOME

ISLESDAY, 40TH OF HEARFEST, 1162.111

The hills of the Freelands flattened, and in the distance, Gideon could see the Redrock Mountains. Their rust-colored peaks faded into craggy snowcaps that rose above the clouds.

Three days later, the familiar sight of Elene's azure towers greeted him. The city sat nestled in a pass connecting the Freelands to Arwyn. Shear, unscalable cliffs protected it from the north and south. To Gideon's horror, the road leading to the city was clogged with a shanty town made by hundreds of refugees. They had no permanent structures or any kind of defense, and when the dragons attacked, they would be the first to die.

Elene's outer ward wasn't much better, having been transformed in the months since he had gone on the road to track Alex. Rows of wooden hovels butted the walls, and the foot traffic was ten times what it should be. The market district and inner ward were equally packed.

Making his way to the palace took far too long, and once inside, it took him twenty minutes to track down Edgar. He found the king in his study, asleep at his desk. The ruler looked older than when Gideon had last seen him, and his face was puffy with big bags under his eyes. His grey hair was long, but neatly kept, tied back in a ponytail.

"Majesty." Gideon shook him. "We need to talk."

Edgar yawned, and a disoriented look crossed his face. He then blinked and looked past Gideon. "Where is Alexandra?"

"That's what we need to talk about."

"Is she safe?"

"She was the last time I saw her."

"And you return without her?" Edgar's cheeks flushed with anger, in the way that Alex's did.

"I did what I thought was best," Gideon said.

"I'm sure you had your reasons." Edgar crossed the room and poured a glass of water then handed it to Gideon. "Sit and drink. Have you eaten? No, of course not. Look at you. Let me have food brought up, and then you can tell me everything."

Gideon was hungry, though waiting another hour to eat wouldn't kill him. Still, he didn't protest. He knew there was no arguing with Edgar when it came to this kind of matter. At the same time, there was one thing worth mentioning.

"You should know," Gideon said. "Medrayt is alive."

Servants brought lunch, and when the sun had set, they brought dinner. Gideon held nothing back, sharing everything from the moment he left to track Alex, finding her, their journey to see Owen, meeting Carter and Doug, and of course the meeting with the Sisters.

"And so, my daughter and Owen's boy are finally dragged into this?" Edgar pushed back his chair and stared at the ceiling. "This was never what I wanted."

"Since when has that mattered? Besides Alex is her father's daughter."

"And her mother's." A rare smile danced across Edgar's face. "We are going to have faith because if not, we are doomed anyway."

"You could turn Arwyn over to Medrayt."

"Maybe, once," Edgar said. "But it's been twenty years, and clearly he's not in his right mind."

"I could be biased," a rich voice said, "but I'm confident that I'm the only one who is thinking clearly."

Medrayt stood in the door to the study. He wore no armor nor a sword at his belt. Beige robes hung off his worn frame, and in his hand, he held a glass orb.

Gideon didn't waste a second. He drew his longsword and lunged at Medrayt.

As if Medrayt were a true ghost, the blade passed through him and embedded itself into an oak book shelf.

"That is quite precocious," Medrayt said. "You thought I was actually here? No, I am too busy. This is merely a projection."

Grunting, Gideon sheathed his sword.

"How can you do this?" Edgar asked.

"It's not too hard." Medrayt twirled the orb. "My skills in magic have increased quite a bit since we last spoke–"

"Not this." Edgar waved a hand through Medrayt's misty face. "How can you do this?"

Edgar threw open the curtains. Below were the streets of Elene, and beyond them and the city walls was the camp of refugees.

"I do what I must, brother."

"These are our people." Pain showed in Edgar's eyes. "It is our duty to protect them, and instead, you destroy their homes and kill their loved ones. My brother, the brother I loved and who died all those years ago, he would never do something so cruel."

"I've learned a thing or two about cruelty," Medrayt said. "I can thank both you and Lady Zera for that."

"That's what this is about?" Edgar asked.

"No," Medrayt said. "But it was the first sign. The second being when the assassin tried to kill me."

"Too bad he failed," Gideon muttered.

"What's that?" Medrayt spun to face him. Now that he was closer, Gideon could see the same marks of age that showed on Edgar's face, and eerily, the same sense of tiredness.

"Are you here for a reason or just to mock us?" Gideon asked.

"Never were one for small talk, were you Gideon?" Medrayt narrowed his eyes. "How is the favorite puppet of the Sisters? I was quite surprised to learn you were escorting my niece through the lands. I didn't think they would let you off your leash for such a personal matter."

"My allegiance no longer lies with the Sisters," Gideon said.

"Has Yorndrak stopped spinning? Is the sky now below and the ground now above?" Medrayt leaned in so close that his ghost-like pointy nose protruded into Gideon's forehead. "You are telling the truth, aren't you? My, my... things have changed."

"You too have changed." Edgar stepped closer. "Growing up, you always put others first. You were full of honor and cared more for protecting Arwyn than anything else. What has happened to you? How could you subvert the dragons and kill the same people you used to protect?"

"Why?" Anger erupted in Medrayt's voice. "From the time I was your daughter's age The Weird Sisters groomed me. They trained me to be the greatest leader the world has ever seen. I put honor and virtue above all else. And what happened? Assassins were sent to kill me, and nearly did."

"This is revenge then?" Edgar said. "I had nothing to do with your assassination and have grieved for you ever since."

"This is not revenge," Medrayt said. "Merely what I must do. In another life, I would have done it in a gentler manner, but that was before I took a dagger through my heart."

"I can't let you do this," Edgar said. "I can't let you kill innocents."

"And so, we come to why I am here." Medrayt paced the room. "Cede your crown to me, and I'll spare Elene. With my dragon army and your forces, we will be unstoppable. The other kingdoms will fall in line without fighting. Thousands of lives will be spared."

Edgar lowered his head. "You know I can't do that."

"You can," Medrayt said.

"If all you wanted was Arywn, I'd give it to you in a second." Edgar met his brother's eyes. "But if I back down, nothing will prevent you from conquering the other lands. It wouldn't be right."

Medrayt turned away from Edgar and gave Gideon a quizzical look. "Does he not know?"

Gideon kept his mouth shut.

"This is grand. You don't know." Gideon spun back to face his brother. "I must rule all the kingdoms because, if I don't, the world will be destroyed."

"Is that true?" Edgar asked.

Gideon felt his throat tighten. He had to say something, but wasn't sure how much was safe to divulge.

"Of course, it's true!" Medrayt blurted. "The Sisters showed me long ago the horrors we are to face, and unless we are united, the human race will be wiped clean."

"And when did you last speak with the Sisters?" Gideon asked. "It is true they once choose you to be the protector of this world, but fate is fluid, and now others have been picked to replace you."

"You are a pet, a mouthpiece with no brain attached. I do not expect you to understand." Medrayt closed his eyes and gave Edgar a pleading look. "Surely brother you see that this is the only way. Instead of wasting precious resources fighting me and my dragons, join me."

"I'm sorry," Edgar said. "I'm sorry to learn that you have been alive this whole time and I didn't know. I'm sorry that now, having come back, instead of once more being my most trusted friend, that we are to meet on the battlefield."

"Fighting me is death," Medrayt said. "Don't make me kill you."

"You do what you think you must do," Edgar said. "I will do the same."

"Then I, too, am sorry." Medrayt's misty visage faded to nothing.

~

Gideon and Edgar spent the night talking. It wasn't until after three in the morning that Gideon returned to his chambers.

He had an entire suite to himself, even though he insisted over and over again that he didn't need so much space. In the years that the room had been his, he acquired few items to fill it. Personal property did not matter to him.

No art or tapestries adorned the walls. No ancient vases sat on end tables.

A plain, double-sized bed, custom built for his height, sat in the middle of the room. An oak chest that held his clothing, rested at the foot of the bed. A small table with two chairs abutted against a window. He took meals there, so it served a purpose.

A wooden rack holding three lutes was the only bit of frivolousness in the room. The instruments, hand crafted decades ago borderlined ostentatious. Built by masters, in a time when music meant more, they had jewels embedded in them, and intricate staining that looked beautiful, no matter what the lighting.

Gideon picked up the center lute, its body shaped like an avocado cut in half. He ran a finger along its smooth finish and plucked a string. It twanged out of tune. When was the last time he had picked it up? A year ago? Longer?

He kept meaning to make time to learn to play. Sure, he could strum a few chords, but that was all. He wanted to learn how to make real music. To invoke emotion in a way that only music can.

If he could to that, if he could learn to play, then he could make the music he heard in his head when fighting, a real thing that existed in the world. The rhythm and beat of weapons clashing, hearts beating, the pulse of life that fueled him.

The music of a battle had kept him alive more times than he could count. He had done his best to teach it to Alex. He thought she might get it. She might hear it like he does, but he didn't know for sure, and so the song stayed trapped inside of him. If he could get it out and share it with the world, a weight would be lifted from his shoulders.

Gideon twisted a peg on the lute's head and strummed the bottom string. Still off. He gave the peg another turn. It sounded much better, and he worked his way up both sides of the head, tuning all fifteen of the lute's strings.

Closing his eyes, he played "The Devourer's Winter."

He didn't try to sing. He didn't then, nor would he ever, have a voice capable of singing. Instead, he focused his thoughts on the chords, drinking them in, letting them drown out the months of exhaustion and stress.

Gideon played the chorus for "A Bride's Blackberry Pie." He didn't know the full song. He finished up with "The Drunken Ballad of James Frey." The reprise, in particular, brought back memories of his childhood and flickering flames on cold summer nights.

If they survived–

No.

When they survived the dragon attack Gideon would let Edgar know that he wanted a tutor. The best musician they could find. He would make it a priority then to learn how to play.

Gideon set down the lute.

Tomorrow they would begin to evacuate the city, and he would need all his strength for that. Best to stop fantasizing and start worrying about what he needed to do to make sure the city survived.

25

BOUND

ORNSDAY, 41ST OF HEARFEST, 1162.111

Carter had an escape plan in place. He choose not to tell the others in case the Grekers had a way of listening to their conversations. On the second day of their imprisonment, he saw an opportunity to put his plan in action.

Bova and two other guards brought manacles for the group and had everyone lock their wrists behind their backs. Carter waited patiently, clearing his mind and doing as he was told. Bova pulled down the barriers on their cells and led them single file out of the building.

Carter was halfway through drawing an agyl when he stopped and let it fade away. Thousands of Grekers waited for them in the streets. They hung out windows, sat on roofs, and stood shoulder to shoulder in the streets.

"By the light," Kane said, "you people are like an infestation. There are so many of you."

"The Arg'Natz has returned," Bova said.

"How did you find us?" Carter asked. "Your scouts found us in the woods and again in Compitum. How?"

"We have a way to track the Arg'Natz," Bova said. "For years, the ways have been dormant, but a month ago, they came alive again. We assumed that Doug must have been killed and that the essence had passed on to a new host."

"Nope." Doug patted his chest and his manacles clanged. "Still here."

"How does your tracking work?" Carter asked.

"I do not know," Bova said. "Magic is not my specialty. You'd need to speak with someone from the Solt faction."

Everything Carter knew about the Grekers was turning out to be a lie. He had thought, like most people did, that they were primitive creatures that lived in small tribes in the mountains or rural forests. Instead, they had escape proof cells and some sort of magic technology that wasn't agyls nor higher magic. It was something in between, and Carter wanted to know more.

Bova led them through the horde of Grekers and out of the permanent shadows of the inner streets. The sun that floated at the top of the cavern was more impressive than Alex had described. She had seen it with regular eyes, but Carter could see it on a whole a different level. It looked like a ball of yarn wound around itself but instead of fibers, it was strung together from strings of pure energy. He saw all of the threads of magic and connections to all the schools of magic. He doubted any one person could manipulate and wield such forces. It would have taken a team of magicians, working together, to create such a thing. Whoever or whatever had done it knew magic far more powerful than what Master Owen knew.

The group slowed and turned a corner, having to wait while their escorts cleared onlookers from the street. "Where are we going?" Carter leaned in close to ask Alex.

"The museum," she said.

"I thought we were going to the arena so Doug could fight people."

Bova had told them the day before that the arena was the big disc that cast their prison in shadow. Now it was easily half a dozen blocks away.

"Were you not paying attention?" Alex glared at him.

"There is a green sun woven with magic unlike anything I've ever seen," Carter said. "You can't use that tone with me. It's not my fault I was distracted."

"We have to get Bakero's Blade," she said. "It can be used to draw the essence of the Arg'Natz out of Doug which could kill him or it might not."

"Ok but why bring us..." Carter spun his finger in a loop at all of them. "Why not bring the knife thing to the arena?"

"Excellent question." Bova slowed her pace, falling in step between Alex and Carter. "We are here as a group because only the Arg'Natz may retrieve Bakero's Blade."

Carter did a double take looking from the Bova to Doug. "Wait, you want Doug to get a magic blade so that Grekers can then try to kill him with it? That seems stupid."

"Those that challenge Doug will not be trying to kill him," Bova said. "They merely need to stab him and hold the knife in place long enough for the essence to flow out of Doug and into them. Historically it has only killed the current Arg'Natz twice."

"Out of how many times?" Carter asked.

"It's been used twice," Bova said.

"That is idiotic." Carter nodded to Doug. "You should tell them 'no.'"

"Doug can't say 'no.'" Bova rolled her eyes. "That wouldn't make any sense."

"No." Doug said.

"What?" Bova's eyes went wide.

"No," Doug repeated. "I'm not going to get some stupid knife so that you can kill me with it. Why would I?"

"Because you are the Arg'Natz." Bova said it as if she were explaining something factual like up being up and down being down. "Only you can get it and if you don't the factions will surely go to war. You can't want that. You wouldn't do that. Plus we don't know that it will kill you."

"Let's go." Doug shuffled past Kane and back toward the direction they had come. "If we hurry maybe we can make it back to our cells in time for midday meal."

"Stop messing with him." Kane grabbed Doug's shoulder, halting him. Her dangling manacles clanked against his side. "You know you are going to do it, so let's get it over with."

"I'm not," Doug said.

"You will." Kane rolled her eyes.

"Is that a threat?" Doug squinted, narrowing his eyes at her.

"You aren't thinking ahead," Kane said. "You are bitter and angry at the Grekers, but you aren't yet looking at the whole picture. For example, what is it you most want in the whole wide world?"

"I want to be a dragon again."

"Great!" Kane smiled "Now, can you do that while you are here and trapped as a prisoner?"

"No," Doug said. "But we will escape somehow."

“That might be true," Kane said. "No one has been able to keep me locked up, but how long do you think that might take? A week? Two weeks? A month? And in that time, what do you think Medrayt is going to do to Arwyn and the other kingdoms?"

"She's right," Alex said. "We don't have time to waste. You have to do this."

"I don't have to do anything." Doug crossed his arms and leaned away from both Kane and Alex. "None of this is worth dying for."

Carter understood where Doug was coming from. Doug wanted to survive, and this whole situation wasn't one where it looked like they would. He didn't blame Doug for not wanting to get the knife. That being said, he had to side with Alex. They didn't have time to waste, and as much as he liked Doug and felt guilty for what had happened to the dragon, they had a mission to complete.

"So what is worth dying for?" Carter asked.

"Excuse me?" Doug said.

"You heard me," Carter said. "What would you put your life on the line for?"

"I intervened in Compitum when I saw you two numbskulls brawling with Kane," Doug said. "I had thought Gideon would keep you safe and when I saw just the two of you, I had to do something, even though I knew it was a risk."

"So what do you think happens to us if some Greker takes the Arg'Natz from you?" Carter asked. "You think they will let us go?"

"I don't..." Doug turned to Bova. "What does happen to Alex and Carter if I die in the arena."

"There is a provision in the accords. Give me a moment." Bova closed her eyes and twirled her cheek fur with her smallest finger. "If the host of the Arg'Natz has been sundered and separated from it, then no matter if he lives or dies, his kin are exiled from Agnar."

"That's great but..." Carter threw up his arms. "We aren't his kin!"

"No, you aren't are you?" Bova said. "In that case I'd expect the new Arg'Natz to order your deaths. No reason to keep you around."

"There's nothing we can do?" Alex asked.

"Maybe." Bova paced back and forth in front of Doug. "What are your feelings on adoption?"

"What do you mean?" Doug asked.

"We could file the paperwork," Bova said. "It would make Alex and Carter your adopted children. They would be spared should you die or lose the Arg'Natz."

"Hey, Dad. Dadddd." Alex winced and shook her head. "Nope. That sounds weird."

"That would really work?" Doug asked. "I sign some parchment and they are protected."

"I'd have to witness you signing the paper and approve," Bova said. "But that is the short of it."

"What about me?" Kane jerked her hands apart forcing the chain between them to crack like a whip. "I can't shapeshift, which means I can't pose as one of Doug's children. And if I don't get a free pass out of here, I'm not about to let any of you get one. I assume I'm too old to be adopted?"

"Quite right," Bova said. "The legal age for an adult here is twenty-five, but you could marry him."

Kane's face paled. She looked sick as if she were going to vomit. Doug's own expression mirrored hers. They saw each other's disgust and both their faces shifted to furrowed brows and taut lips. "You got a problem being fake married to me?" Kane asked.

Doug growled. "Only that you've tried to kill me more times than anyone else in my life."

"If I had gotten a real chance to kill you," Kane said, "you would be dead."

"Then why should I marry you?" Doug asked.

"This truce between us is a light one. I can't shape shift." Kane held up her manacled hands. "But with these I could choke Carter or Alex before a single guard could stop me."

"And if I don't care?" Doug said.

"Shall we put it to a test?" Kane's eyes drifted from Alex to Carter. "Which shall it be?"

Carter cleared his mind, preparing a spell. If Doug didn't give in, Carter wasn't about to let Kane hurt Alex or himself.

"Tick. Tock. Tick. Tock," Kane said.

"No." Doug said it in a flat cold tone.

"So be it." Kane grabbed Carter.

By the time Carter, realized what she was doing, she sat on his chest with the manacles wrapped around his throat. The metal chains coiled so tightly that he couldn't speak.

"There is no need for violence!" Bova paced behind Doug, as if scared to get closer to Kane.

"He can still breathe," Kane said. "But a bit more force, and it's bye-bye Carter."

Carter thrust his pelvis up and kicked, but Kane weighed at least twice as much as she appeared. The bulk of her on his chest, restricted his breathing far more than the pressure around his throat.

"Threatening him or Alex will not get me to fake marry you," Doug said. "And keep in mind that your shifting may be disabled, but I still have my strength. You aren't a match for me."

"Huh." Kane loosened her hold on Carter's neck and leaned back driving more weight into his chest. "That's a valid point."

Kane rose into a crouch and slapped Carter. "Stop goofing around and get up."

Carter kneed Kane in the crotch. She rolled her eyes and left him on the ground as if he weren't anything to worry about.

"How about I give you something you want," Kane said. "You fake marry me and ensure I escape this hellhole, and I'll make sure you have the best wedding night of your life."

"You have nothing I want." Doug sneered at Kane.

Alex's chains clanked as she covered her mouth and laughed.

Carter found it equally amusing, but he knew Doug had missed the double entendre and had meant the statement in a factual manner.

"That's how it's going to be?" Kane's upper lip curled into a snarl, and her cheeks reddened.

"Unless you can turn me back into a dragon or tell me how to do it without the blasted lotus," Doug said. "Then yes, that is how it's going to be. I will not marry you."

Understanding crept over Kane's face, and she relaxed her stance. "What if I told you when Medrayt plans to attack or why specifically he needed all the rogue dragons killed? Don't you want to know why you are a threat to him?"

"No," Doug said. "All I care about is being a dragon again."

Carter chewed his lip. Every bit of him wanted to tell Doug to accept the deal, that it would be useful to know why. But Carter couldn't justify supporting a fake marriage to a monster like Kane.

"How do we know you would tell the truth?" Alex asked.

"You don't," Kane said.

Alex tugged on Doug's manacles, pulling him down to her eye level. "You should do this."

"Why?" he asked.

"It's a win-win all around," she said. "It keeps the truce. It keeps us safe, for a time at least. It potentially gets us good intel, and besides it's a Greker marriage. It's not real."

"It matters that much to you," Doug said, "that I do this?"

"I think you should," Alex said.

Doug swung around and looked Carter in the eyes. "And you?"

"It would be good to know," Carter said. "And its no different than playing house as a kid. It's meaningless."

"Alright." Doug pointed a fist at Kane. "You step out of line, you act up in anyway, and the wedding is off. Consider it our insurance that you behave. The second it happens you tell Alex what it is that she wants to know. Agreed?"

Kane winked and blew him a kiss.

Acting as if nothing had happened, Doug headed up the street away from the prison. "Where is the museum? I'm getting tired of all the walking."

Bova took the lead, and there was extra pep in her step, as if she were happy to have everyone on board.

They passed two more blocks of wrongly shaped, geometrical buildings and stopped in front of a dome. The dome's curve was smooth, and if they could see below street level, Carter suspected it would have made a perfect sphere. There were no seams on the walls, and Carter thought what the Grekers called a museum at one point might have been some sort of magical vault.

Bova led the way into the dome, and Carter took up the end of the line. The throngs of Greker followers stopped at the entryway, and Carter couldn't tell if they were too scared to enter or merely showing respect for the place.

Carter figured a museum would be like Master Owen's study. There would be rows and rows of book shelves and tables with ancient things on them. That's not what this place was. Lamps, not fueled by agyls or oil, hung from high ceilings and washed the room in a warm light.

"Classy stuff here, Jeeves." Kane reached out to pick up coins from a metal table, but her fingers struck the same type of invisible wall that their prison cells possessed. "I'm growing to hate this place."

"Preservation is our highest priority." Bova ducked between Carter and Alex then crossed the room. "This museum houses our collection of Erediä artifacts. Some respect, please, while you are here."

As they made their way through the maze-like corridors, Carter was surprised at the number of everyday items. He was sure he saw at least two hairbrushes, a washing tray, and six or seven mortars with pestles.

Bova led the group past a courtyard filled with statues and stopped in front of a stone slab as wide as two doors and as tall as two people. The charcoal-colored slab was a finger's width thick. Its center was sunken in, and an agyl-like rune was carved into it. A circle of glowing gems lined that section, and they flickered from light emerald green to a bleached yellow.

Carter heard a buzzing sound like the hum right before a lightning strike. Whatever the stone slab was, it was old and oozed with power. "What is it?" The stone felt unnaturally cold under Carter's fingers.

"You'd have to ask one of the Creen." Bova tugged on Carter's wrist pulling him away from the slab. "I do not know how it works or what it is called, but I know that it will allow Doug to retrieve Bakero's Blade."

"I don't like it." Doug scrunched his nose. "It smells like something, something I can't place, but something I know from home."

"It will take but a moment," Bova said. "Place your palm in the circle."

"It's on the tip of my tongue. It's..." Doug took another long sniff and then jumped backward. "Are you mad? It reeks of Yorndrak."

"It is perfectly safe," Bova said.

"Yorkdrak is real?" Carter pushed past Bova and placed his hand on the stone a second time, though this time he tried to see and feel it with his second eyes. Although the slab appeared to be stone, it wasn't. It was compressed threads of magic packed so tightly–

Carter blinked trying to clear away the haze. He lay on the floor looking up at the others. They were talking, but their voices were muffled. "What happened?"

"You fainted," Doug said, though the words were hard to make out. "Proof that, whatever that thing is, it shouldn't be touched."

"I told you, he is not the Arg'Natz." Bova snapped two fingers at Doug. "You are."

"What did it feel like?" Alex whispered into Carter's ear.

"It was like sensory overload," he said. "Like I thought I was drinking a glass of water, but it was a barrel."

"Don't be unpoxed." Kane grabbed Doug's wrist and slammed his hand against the slab. Doug pulled back, but Kane didn't release her grip.

An ivory halo of light leapt to life, tracing the circle and pooling around Doug's hand. The light spilt over, connecting in straight lines to each of the glowing gems.

"Let go, or I swear–" Doug's and Kane's hands slipped into the pool of light, as if they were reaching into a vertical puddle.

Their arms sunk in less than a head, and Kane jerked her hand out while Doug fumbled around for a moment as if he was trying to pick something up. When he finally pulled his arm out, he held a curved dagger.

The light faded, and the portal shut down.

Doug held Bakero's Blade awkwardly out to Bova. "What do I do with this?"

"Hold onto it." Bova counted on her fingers and then spun to leave. "We should get going. We do have a slight amount of downtime before we must get to the arena. If we hurry, we can squeeze in a wedding and an adoption."

~

The adoption happened first because Bova struggled to convince a member of the Baloc faction to officiate for the wedding. Doug, Carter, and Alex signed several parchments. Bova stamped them with a wax seal, and in less than an hour, Doug became their rightful guardian in Greker society. It meant nothing to Carter, and he was sure Alex and Doug felt the same way, which was good because he didn't like the idea that he and Alex were foster siblings.

With the adoption out of the way, they were locked back in their individual prison cells. Eventually, Cholton, a member of the Baloc faction, arrived. He was the only other Greker in attendance besides Bova. The burly, robed man was younger than Bova, and other than a few moans and grunts, he didn't speak a single word. Carter wondered if that was because he disapproved of what was happening, because he couldn't speak, or because of some odd vow of silence.

Once more, Bova was all business and failed to understand that to all of them the wedding was a farce. Leading up to the ceremony, she kept Doug and Kane separate with their cell walls opaque and spoke in a low, solemn voice as if they were in a temple or holy place as opposed to a prison.

After what seemed like way too long, Bova brought down the walls to the cells. Doug was dressed as he always was except for the addition of Bakero's Blade, which was wrapped carefully in a thick hide and hung from his belt.

Kane, on the other hand, looked like a demonic angel bent on both saving and destroying the world at the same time. Her hair was pulled back, showing off her angular face, and somehow the

Grekers had found a strapless dress for her to wear. It had a rusty-metallic sheen and contrasted sharply with her pale skin. It was both ominous and beautiful in the way it fit her curves, making her look as feminine as she had when she had taken on the guise of Kenzie.

Alex elbowed Carter in the gut, and she looked at him with exaggerated wide eyes.

"What?" Carter whispered.

"You were staring," Alex said.

"So?" Carter shook his head, annoyed.

"It's rude." Alex pursed her lips.

"I was trying to figure out where–"

Bova coughed loudly giving Carter a glaring look.

Carter rolled his eyes, but didn't open his mouth again.

"Face each other and take hands," Bova told Kane and Doug.

The pair interlocked fingers in an awkward manner.

Kane grunted, let go, and motioned for Doug to cup his hands upward. He did and she gripped the tips of his fingers.

Bova wrapped a silver braided cord around Doug's wrists and then took the other end and did the same thing to Kane's.

"It's warm." Doug jangled the cord so it slid to the butt of his palm.

"It's Galvoryan bark," Bova said.

Carter had no idea what that meant, and judging by the expressions on the others' faces, they didn't either. No one acted concerned by it, but Carter had an uneasy feeling. Something was off, but he didn't know what.

Cholton, in a booming baritone voice, chanted in Etriä. The Greker strung the words together in a lyrical manner, making it hard for Carter to translate. He was able to pick up only a few words here and there, and most were the cliché things you'd expect to hear at a wedding. The union of two people and that sort of fluff.

"I stand witness between equals who pledge their bodies and minds to each other." Bova and Cholton both stepped away from

Doug and Kane. "Separate they are weak, but as one, they are strong. Let them pledge their commitment to each other."

Alex picked up a large parchment and unrolled it, on the table. In unison, Doug and Kane read it out loud.

"Your needs, are my needs. My heart, is your heart. My strength, is your strength. Before time and after time. In this world and all others. You are my home. We are one."

Cholton brushed his fingertips across the braided Galvoryan bark.

The butterflies in Carter's stomach grew, and he knew why. There was magic in the cord. "Stop the wedding!"

Everyone but Cholton looked at Carter. The grumpy Greker either did not understand or didn't care and, instead, spoke in a booming voice. "*Tikætto zyn ty aktälalo. Zo zyn kot kæt hanitohæz kæt setälalo. Zo koltætto zyn ty aktötilo*."

The bark surged with energy. It happened so fast that Carter couldn't pick out all the threads, but he recognized twists of heat, light, and strokes from both the school of destruction and alteration. The magic took on the detailed curves of the bark, intertwining, so the single strands melded into bold light. The light flowed into Doug's right arm and out the left then flowed into Kane. It repeated the motion, moving faster and faster in a blinding surge that only Carter could see. It grew so bright that Carter had to look away.

Doug yelped.

Kane reeled, slinging the Galvoryan bark off her wrist. "What the bloody hell was that?"

"It burned me!" A pink welt swelled on Doug's arm.

Kane grabbed Bova by the neck, lifting the Greker so that her feet dangled helplessly in the air. "What did you do?"

Bova made a choking sound.

"She can't answer if you kill her." Alex moved a hand to her waist, preparing to draw her short sword.

Kane's face contorted. Her eyes went squinty. Then wide. Her jaw dropped, and she let go of Bova. Spinning on her heels, she glared at Doug. "I feel you. In my head, I can feel you. You're... hungry."

"And you're furious." Doug cupped his forehead. "But I guess that's how you always are."

"What did you do to us?" Kane demanded of Bova.

"I married you." Bova nodded to the other Greker. "Well, Cholton did the real work."

"If I closed my eyes and spun in a circle," Doug said, "I could point and tell you where Kane stood."

"That's marriage," Bova said.

"Undo it now!" Kane curled her fingers into a fist.

"I can't!" Bova pressed her back against the wall, moving as far away from Kane as she could."

"For once I agree with Kane," Doug said. "Undo this!"

Carter picked up the braided piece of metal. It was cold, but he could see power running through it. It was old, ancient magic from the Erediä. "I don't think they can. Not with this anyway. It serves one purpose, to bind two souls or spirits or essences. I'm not sure about the exact translation of the spell that was spoken, but I know for sure it can't separate two souls into one. You'd need another device or spell for that."

"This is what you agreed to," Bova said. "You signed documents. I do not understand why you are so angry about this."

"You never once mentioned that magic was involved," Doug said.

"That is what marriage is." Bova spoke in a condescending tone that was sure to only make things worse. "The binding of two."

"That is not what marriage is, and if you don't undo it this second, I will, one by one, rip the head off every one of you rat faced retched creatures until your race is extinct." The skin on Kane's arm rippled as if she were trying to shape shift, but lacked the full power to do so.

"A marriage cannot be undone. It is permanent," Bova said.

"The bond can only be broken by death, and even then, the survivor can never remarry."

Kane snarled and leapt at Bova.

Cholton's hands sunk into the shadows of his robes. There was a blur of motion and then Carter saw two darts sticking out of Kane's back. From how quickly she dropped, it was obvious that both had been dipped in parpah root.

"That's strange." Doug held out his arms to steady himself. "I felt her go down, and now it's quiet."

"I am sorry that neither of you understood the commitment you were making, but what's done is done." Bova took a deep breath and then stepped over Kane's unconscious body. "If we can all move forward from this, it is about time to start heading to the arena."

"I am not pleased with this situation." Doug towered over Bova. "This ends today. If I don't die in the arena. If there isn't a new Arg'Natz, and you don't let me free. I will help Kane tear this place apart."

26

THE ARENA

ORNSDAY, 41ST OF HEARFEST, 1162.111

The fourteenth Greker rushed Doug. Like all the other attackers, it held Bakero's Blade. Where it would have been a small dagger at best if held by Doug or another human, the Greker had to use it as if it were a two handed sword. The cumbersomeness of which cost the creature precious time.

Doug mocked a yawn.

The Greker swung the blade overhand. Doug sidestepped it, and delivered a bone-breaking punch to the Greker's nose.

Three medics rushed into the arena to pull the fallen Greker off the field.

"Is that it?" Doug picked up the dagger, holding it so the crowd could see it clearly. "That's one from every fraction. You all sending in another, or can we call it a day?"

Stomping feet, the equivalent of boos, drummed out the sound of Doug's voice. He didn't care. Of course, the creatures were unhappy with him. He contemplated throwing a fight and letting one of the challengers prick him with the knife, but ultimately, the risk of losing his own life was too great. He wanted to live. He wanted to be done with the arena and this place.

The arena was more of a pulpit. The fight took place on a raised platform, and circular stone pews surrounded it. Bova, Carter, Alex, and Kane sat in the front row, with armed members of the Pontis surrounding them on all sides. Members of the various factions filled out the rest of the arena seating, each designated by their signature uniforms.

Of the hundreds of eyes on Doug, it was Kane's gaze that was the strongest. He could feel Kane. Not in a physical sense. He couldn't feel the iron wrapped around her wrists, but he could tell she was bored. This whole ordeal was growing old to her. She was ready to leave, and yet at the edge of her thoughts, there was excitement that was slowly bubbling to the surface.

"Will there be anymore that wish to face the Arg'Natz?" Bova looked to the two nearest factions. The stomping stopped. Bova faced the rest of the arena, but none of the faction members made a sound. "Then if there are no more challengers–"

"Wait," Kane said. Her excitement crescendoed. "I wish to challenge Doug."

"You can't do that!" Carter said.

"Of course, I can." Kane looked to Bova. "Isn't that right?"

"I'm not sure." Bova leaned down, whispering to Cholton and another Greker. A scowl crept across his face. "The laws do not state that a challenger has to be a Greker."

"Would someone please remove these?" Kane batted her eyes and gave a dainty grin as she held up her cuffed hands. "It will be hard to kill my husband if I'm still tied up."

"No!" Doug could feel Kane's excitement bubble over. She was fully enjoying this. She thrived off not only being the center of attention, but also the showmanship of it all. "I don't agree to this."

"You have no say in the matter," Bova said. "The rules are clear."

"Besides Dougy, you should have seen this coming." Kane's manacles were removed by Cholton, and she stepped onto the sandy floor of the arena. "If I defeat you, I get to become the new Arg'-Natz, which means I get the power. It also means I get to stop you and my stepchildren from continuing with your quest. It's a win-win situation. I can't pass that up."

"Taintson wench!" Alex stomped on Kane's calf, knocking her over. "I hope Doug kills you."

Members of the Pontis swarmed Alex, pulling her back down to the stone bench.

"Please." Kane stood, brushing sand off her dress. "Did you expect anything else? If so, shame on you."

"Any questions?" Bova asked.

"I'm good." Kane clapped, drawing Doug's attention. "I need the knife."

Doug cocked his arm and threw the knife full force. It twirled in the air, sailing directly at her pointy nose.

She ducked.

The crowd scattered, and the knife clanged into one of the stone benches.

"This will be interesting." Kane tapped her temple as she retrieved the dagger. "I could sense what you were doing before it happened. Never fought anyone before that could read my mind. Well... there was that one guy in Yemto, but that was more of a future sight thing."

"I'll admit," Doug said, "it was nice, at least for a few days, to not have to worry about you trying to kill me."

"You do understand that it's not personal, right?" Kane hoisted herself onto the raised pulpit. "This is business."

"You are lying. I can feel it."

"Well sure, I'm going to enjoy killing you. I can't help that. You and Owen's whelp have been at the top of my dunglist since I met you, but this is more about the big picture than you."

"How so?" Doug circled the rim of the pulpit, keeping as much distance between himself and her as he could. "'Cause no matter how you try to spin it, killing someone is pretty damn personal."

"Contrary to what you think, I don't enjoy the act of killing." She wasn't lying. Or if she was, she was lying to herself and didn't realize it. "I enjoy having the last word and pissing people off, but that moment when you feel a life slip away and you watch a creature's eyes dim. I'm not into that."

A rush of regret poured through the bond and with it came a surge of anger. "That's how you justify what you are?"

"I do what I do because it is what the Sisters made me to be!" Anger hadn't been the right word to describe the emotions radiating from Kane. It was pure loathing. Hate. The central core of who she was, and it was borderline overwhelming. "We are all their pawns, and the only way to get back our lives is to fight the Sisters."

"And killing me does that?"

"It does."

Kane came at him. Not in a sloppy way like the Grekers had. Not in brute force like she had on the cliff. This time she moved with grace. She slank from side to side in an unpredictable manner like a sheet caught in the wind. If it weren't for the bond, Doug would have had no hope in evading the attack.

As it were, he knew that she expected him to punch her, which wasn't surprising. That had been his go-to move when fighting the Grekers. If he tried it with her, she would flip him and slit his throat before he could do a thing.

Since she was expecting a punch, he decided a hard kick to the chest would be the best counter. Though the second he decided it, he felt a shift in her. She now knew he was going to kick her, and thus was adjusting her own movements. Now she was going to roll left, dodging the kick, and slam the knife between his lower two ribs.

Doug decided to go back to punching her.

Kane stopped in her tracks and tilted her head. "This is getting us nowhere. At this point, we aren't fighting a physical battle, we are playing out scenarios in our minds."

"Seems like it."

"Then give in. Let me stab you with Bakero's Blade, and I'll make it quick. No strung-out torture."

"Don't believe that for a second." Though, through their bond, he could sense truth in her words.

"I'm trained in more fighting styles than you could possibly know. Eventually, I'll think of a maneuver that you won't be able to counter, even if you know it's coming."

"Maybe," Doug said. "Maybe not. But you can't forget my strength and imperviousness."

Through the bond he felt a rising sense of annoyance.

"I didn't want to play this card, but I guess it's time." Kane's dress melted into her skin, and her entire body took on its rust color. Quills sprouted from her back, and the rest of her curved over, taking on the shape of a mountain cat.

Kane moved at speeds so fast that by the time Doug sensed them, it was too late for him to react.

She darted left, broke into a zigzag, and pounced on him.

With her weight pinning him to the ground, she shifted again. Her feline haunches fractured with each part becoming a squirming tentacle that wrapped about his limbs, while her upper chest and face reverted to human. "You should've figured out that I was lying about not being able to shapeshift."

He could feel the truth in her words. That only made him feel more frustrated, and through their bond, he could tell that his frustration delighted her, which frustrated him even more.

"Now to be fair, I didn't completely lie." Kane tilted her chin to the green sun. "That thing is disgusting and doesn't nourish me like real sunlight, but it wasn't weakening me. Not feeding on light is no different from you not eating for a few days. Sure, it will make you tired, and your reaction time might be slower than normal, but you'll still be able to lift your arm as easily as I can still shape shift."

Kane's chest opened, revealing a cavity. A third arm holding

Bakero's Blade grew from it. She held the knife to Doug's throat, preparing to slit it, and leaned in as if to whisper in his ear.

Doug head butted her.

She plunged the knife into his shoulder.

It went in slowly, as if his skin were trying to resist it. The orb on the pommel flickered with a sharp, mossy sheen. The wound hurt, as it should, but the pain felt off balance, like a mix between the heat of an infected wound and flesh burned by frostbite.

The cold ran down his arm and across his chest. His lungs burned, unable to suck in air, and his body convulsed.

Doug screamed.

A mixture of pain, fear and anger, poured from his throat.

Kane wobbled, lost her grip on him, and fell to the sand.

Doug's pain didn't diminish, and it took all his focus to reach up and grab the dagger's handle. The grip was so cold that he thought his fingers might freeze to it.

Pulling, he jerked the knife out. Blood gushed from the wound, and with it came a warm release of heat.

"That didn't go as I thought it would." Kane, now fully in human form, lay next to him with her jaws chattering. "I expect round two to go smoother."

Doug placed a hand over his wound and applied pressure. The pain of which caused his eyes to water and forced a grunt from Kane's lips.

"You felt that didn't you?" Clenching his teeth, Doug shoved a finger into the cut. Shooting pain rippled down his arm and into his neck.

"It's not pain." Kane rolled into a fetal position moaning. "I can barely feel that. It's the hatred and anger. So much of it is nauseating."

He focused on his anger. His anger at Carter for turning him into a human. Anger at Kane for trying to kill him constantly.

Using the anger as a distraction, he crawled to the edge of the pulpit and rolled himself off it.

"Don't forget, it works both ways." Her words slurred.

A wave of hatred struck him, and he slumped over, unable to move.

"How does that feel?" She laughed, and the hatred shifted to amusement.

"I wish I had never married you." He meant it. The marriage was supposed to be something on paper. Not real. He never thought he'd really be married. Dragons choose their mates and mate for life, but there is no ceremony or paperwork, and he had given up the idea of finding a mate back when he was a fledgling.

"That's different." Kane stood on the edge of the pulpit, looking down at him. "That's a hell lot of anger, but it's not directed at me."

Had Kane read his thoughts? Did she know about Bellalyn? Could she see the limp body and the other images that haunted his mind.

"Stop! It's too much." Kane swayed and she had to kneel, to keep from falling over. "Stop thinking about her!"

Doug did the opposite.

"Her name was Bellalyn." He used the lip of the pulpit to pull himself to his feet. "She was my best friend."

"I can tell what you are planning. It won't work. Nothing can stop me from killing you and taking the power."

"We were fledglings together, and there wasn't a second that went by when we weren't hanging out." Instead of pushing the memories away, he embraced them, giving in to his emotions. He heard Bellalyn's snorting laugh, her brave voice, and smelled the scent of her scales.

"Stop."

"She was in danger, and when I went to the dragon council, they wouldn't help. I tried to save her, I truly did, but I failed." Doug thought of not only the pain he felt about her death, but also thought of his anger toward the dragons for doing nothing. He thought of the overwhelming sense of loneliness. He held back nothing.

"No more." Kane buried her face in her hands.

"I didn't turn from my own kind. They turned on me. They are soulless monsters and when I heard what Medrayt had done, I didn't feel bad for them. I was happy, but in the end, it doesn't matter. You know why? 'Cause Bellalyn is dead and never coming back."

Doug drove Bakero's Blade into Kane's chest.

"You get a star for effort." Her body went soft, like gelatin, and absorbed the dagger. "It was smart to distract me like that, but foolish to try and harm me with a knife."

"To the abyss with you." He spit in her face.

"An eye for an eye, right?" She smiled. "How about I show you real pain."

Their bond sprung to life, and he understood why his memories had overwhelmed her. Lost in the feelings, there was no separation. Her experiences and emotions became his.

Being alive caused pain, and he felt the lack of desire to exist. With it came hatred, not directed at the world, but directed at himself. He felt disgusted with who he was and knew there was no hope of ever ridding himself of the feeling. There would be no salvation, only a constant downward spiral, and the only thing that could end it was death. He wanted to die. He wanted the world and everything to go away so that he could rid himself of these feelings and, for the first time ever, experience peace.

Outside of the bond and the feelings, Doug was only vaguely aware of himself and his surroundings. Most of his vision was taken up by the green sun, which suggested he had fallen over. Peripherally, he could see Kane's face and that she held something in her hand. He tried to focus his vision, but couldn't. A crippling sense of regret and jealousy surged through the bond.

Bakero's Blade slid into Doug's gut.

The burning cold overrode his emotions, and he blinked to see that Kane held the dagger in place. Its pommel once more glowed.

Blood spilled from his stomach, and with it came a sense of

tiredness. He wanted to throw Kane to the ground. He wanted to fight back but he was too weak. His eyes were heavy and everything grew cloudy.

The last thing Doug saw was a quivering aura at the sides of his vision. It surged, growing and swallowing Kane, wrapping around her body as if caressing her.

"It's mine."

The ribbon of light twisted and then pushed its way into Kane's mouth, and only then did Doug realize that he was the Arg'Natz no more.

27

STABBED

ORNSDAY, 41ST OF HEARFEST, 1162.111

Alex wanted to avert her eyes. She liked Doug, and she had no desire to see him die, but she couldn't look away.

Kane pulled out the dagger. The light pouring into her faded, and she flopped across Doug's chest. Like two lovers post-sex they lay there unmoving surrounded by a pool of blood.

Carter pushed past Alex, practically knocking her over as he ran to the base of the pulpit. He dragged Kane's limp body off Doug and kneeled, inspecting Doug's shoulder wound and then the gash. "For gorph's sake, I can't see how deep it is. There is too much blood."

Carter drew an agyl in the air. From the bottom stroke poured a steady stream of water. It crashed against Doug, mixing with the blood and soaking Carter. "Get off your ass and help me!"

"I don't know what to do to help!" Alex said.

Carter pulled off his shirt and shoved it into Doug's chest. His pale skin looked sickly in the green light. "From what I can tell, nothing serious inside was pierced, but if we don't stop this bleeding, he will die. We can't let that happen. I need something metal that I can make hot."

"Well?" Alex turned to Bova. "You heard him. I need metal."

"I don't, I mean, well..." Bova took a deep breath. "We have nothing here. This entire building is stone, and no weapons other than Bakero's Blade are allowed in the arena."

"Carter, the dagger!" Alex pointed at Kane's fist, which still clenched the knife. "Will that work?"

"Get it. We can try."

Alex pried the dagger from Kane's fingers. The metal radiated with an unnatural warmth that caused goosebumps along the back of Alex's neck. "Here."

"Wait." The usual overconfidence that Carter displayed was gone. His tone was serious and to the point. "The second I let go, I need you to hold my shirt against his stomach and press the palm of your hand into the shoulder wound. Understand?"

Alex kneeled, her shoulder blocking the water agyl.

"It's fine," Carter said. "I'll unravel it once my hands are free."

Alex laid the dagger down and put her hands in place. The bloody shirt wasn't so bad, but touching Doug's shoulder made her feel queasy. She could feel both sides of the wound, and when she slacked on the pressure, a gurgling warmth enveloped her hand soaking under her nails and staining the faint blonde hair along her wrists.

The amount of blood pouring from Doug didn't disgust her. It scared her. From the destroyed towns to soldiers hurt in battle she had never seen someone lose so much blood and live.

Carter tugged at the water agyl, and it faded. He took up the dagger and stopped, staring at it.

"What?" she asked.

"This isn't normal iron or silver. I don't know what it is."

"So?"

"So I don't know how it will respond to heat."

"We don't have anything else."

"So be it." He traced a series of agyls in the air and muttered under his breath, summoning the wind. Where as before he always brought forth a powerful gust, this time it the air was controlled and focused, lifting Bakero's Blade from his hand.

"What are you doing with that?" Bova asked in a concerned tone.

"I'm saving my friend," Carter said. The air lifted the dagger and held it, hovering, so that its blade crossed through the tiny agyls.

The blade turned crimson.

"No!" Bova hustled past the stone benches to snatch the dagger.

"It is too hot to be touched," Carter said. "Those are four heat-forming agyls. It will melt your skin."

"But the blade!"

"The blade isn't my concern."

The Grekers in the crowd stood shouting and yelling.

"It should be fine." Carter curled his hands and opened them, as if releasing something. The agyls dimmed, and the fiery dagger floated toward Doug. "We are going to have to do this together. The second I tell you to let go, you need to not only get your hand away, but remove my shirt from the wound and try to wipe away enough blood so that I can clearly see where it is."

"What about his shoulder?" she asked.

"That can be stitched. You ready?"

Alex took a deep breath. So far she had done her best to forget Doug's blood as it soaked into her clothing. Having to look down at his gushing wound made her feel sick. "I'm ready when you are."

The blade hovered over the top of Alex's hand. The molten glow of the metal faded, but the air around it still quivered with heat.

"Go when you are ready," Carter said. "But be fast."

Alex didn't lift the soaked shirt. Instead she pushed, grinding it toward his legs and using her forearm to wipe away the blood.

Carter didn't waste a moment. The dagger pressed against

Doug's skin. It sizzled, and the smell of burning flesh was all too familiar.

Bile rose in Alex's throat, but she caught herself, swallowing it back down.

Doug's body jerk involuntarily, but neither he nor Kane awoke.

With immense precision, Carter cauterized the wound, being careful to not burn any skin that he didn't have to. When done, the wound, which had been leaking so much blood, was now covered with a black burn in the shape of a triangle.

"It's done." Carter dropped Bakero's Blade into a puddle of pink water. It boiled in a flash of steam. "The cut was deep, but missed his intestines. He might live."

"You did good," she said.

"I only gave him a chance. He may have lost too much blood."

"What about the shoulder? Can I move my hands away?"

"No, but we can deal with that now." Carter turned to Bova and said something in Etriä. Bova shook her head. Carter repeated his words. Bova nodded and frantically ran into the crowd.

A moment later, Bova returned carrying a small bag that the Greker medics had used when treating the fallen challengers.

Carter took a needle and thread from the bag and shooed away Alex's hand. "This is the hardest part. The waiting. There were so many nights when Owen would treat someone, do everything he could, and then we'd have to wait to find out if the person would pull through."

"I don't think we have time to wait," she said.

"What do you mean?"

"Kane." She tilted her head to the unconscious shapeshifter.

"What do you want to bet she wakes up before Doug?"

"Honestly," Carter said. "I don't understand why she fainted in the first place. If she..."

"What?" Alex asked.

"The marriage spell. We know that the two of them are linked. I'm guessing the binding reacted to Doug being wounded and losing the essence of the Arg'Natz. If Doug were to stabilize or die, I wouldn't be surprised if she woke up immediately."

"She won't let us leave here alive," Alex said. "Even if Greker law says we should be spared."

"What can we do about it?" Carter asked.

Alex only saw one option. "We kill Kane."

"I don't think we can," Carter said.

Alex could. She had killed in self-defense before, and the only difference now would be that she was saving not only herself, but others and possibly her kingdom. Would Carter think less of her for suggesting it? He had a strict line of what was right and wrong. "I can. If I have to."

"That's not what I was saying," Carter said. "I don't think we have the means to kill her. She's something different. Then you factor in the Arg'Natz, and I literally don't know how to kill her."

"Oh. Then what do we do?"

"I don't know."

The Grekers brought two carts, one for Doug and one for Kane. The two were loaded, and a crew came in to clean the arena of the blood and water. None of them wanted to touch Bakero's Blade, so Alex took it. She expected the blade to be melted with rounded edges, but it appeared to be as sharp as ever.

On the way back to the shade drenched side of the city, Bova told them that they would all be placed in their cells and held until it was confirmed that Kane was in fact the new Arg'Natz.

"That's not good enough," Alex said. "We need to leave now."

"My hands are tied," Bova repeated for the third time. It was as if that was her answer for everything.

"I read your codex when you were busy signing paperwork with Doug," Alex said. "The challenge has been completed. Carter and I must be allowed to leave."

"You can leave, but Doug cannot."

"He is no longer the Arg'Natz! You saw what happened."

"I did, but these things are complicated, and we must be sure."

"Kane will kill Doug."

"We can keep her under control."

"Even if she is the new Arg'Natz? The factions will follow and listen to her, won't they?"

"Well no." Bova frowned. "It has been a long time since we had a new Arg'Natz. My people will most likely embrace Kane, but there are legal documents and precedents. If you let me use them and do what I do, I can help you."

"No." Alex didn't need Bova's help. Alex needed to get to Kale, and she was tired of waiting and jumping through hoops. Besides, Bova made a mistake showing Alex a weakness. The Grekers thought Doug could still be the Arg'Natz.

Alex pulled herself onto the cart that carried Doug.

"What are you doing?" Carter asked.

"Getting us out of here," she said. "Cover my back?"

"Got it." Carter followed her and held his hand outward, ready to summon the wind.

Doug's breath crackled, as if his lungs held water. She did her best to ignore it, focusing on what she could control, and placed Bakero's Blade against his neck. "This is pretty simple. Let us go, or I kill Doug."

"You wouldn't." Bova snapped her fingers and pointed at two of the other Pontis members, telling them to go around to the rear of the cart. The second they did, Carter unleashed a blast that threw them backward.

"Leaving Doug here for Kane is the same as killing him," Alex said. "At least this way, I know his death will be quick and painless. Besides if the Arg'Natz didn't pass to Kane, and I kill him, then I'll be the new Arg'Natz, and trust me, you wouldn't want that."

More Grekers surrounded the cart, and Bova held up a hand. "What is it you want?"

"I want you to let us go," Alex said. "Doug, Carter and myself. You keep Kane. Keep in mind you can try to use your little darts, except they don't work on me. And if someone so much as thinks of pointing a spear or sword in my direction, I'll drive this dagger through Doug's throat."

Cholton whispered something to Bova. The two chatted back and forth.

"Alright," Bova said. "We can take you to the tunnel that will lead you to Compitum."

"We don't want to go back to Compitum," Alex said. "Is there another way out of Agnar?"

"There is only one way in," Bova said. "The tunnel that follows the underground river."

"The river!" Alex snapped her fingers and pointed at Bova. "I saw barges on our way into the city. We want one of them stocked with supplies to go down river."

"That's not wise."

"Does the river lead back to the surface?"

"Eventually yes, but those tunnels have not been cleared since–"

"And where does it resurface?"

"On the eastern side of the mountains."

Depending on how far north or south they were, that would put them halfway to Kale. "Make it happen."

Bova chittered to Cholton. The guards and robed Grekers split off and followed Cholton, who directed Kane's cart down the hill and back toward the prison.

The Grekers that remained steered Doug's cart in the other direction to the where the river cut through the center of the city. It took them more than a half hour to reach the port. There Alex saw twenty or so barges, each thirty parses long. Most were stocked with fruit, though some had piles of what looked like salt.

"This one," Bova motioned to a near-empty barge. It had three oars on each side and a round wheelhouse. Half a dozen woven baskets were stacked aft. "It's prepped for a squad of eight for a week-long journey. It should met your needs."

Carter climbed aboard, holding his arms out to keep balance. "Can you steer this?"

"We are taking it down river." Alex didn't fully know how to steer a ship. She had been on plenty that sailed both the East Reach and West Reach Seas, so she had a vague idea of how it worked, but in this case they wouldn't be dealing with tides, sails, or any of the complicated stuff. "So we can let the river do most of the work."

Carter summoned the wind, lifting Doug out of the cart and placing him on the deck of the barge. Alex made sure to stay near him in case the Grekers changed their minds about letting them leave. She certainly wouldn't kill Doug, but they didn't know that.

"How do we know they won't attack once we get underway?" Carter stared at the bridges and buildings that spanned the river. "A few spears and we'd be dead."

"Not before we could kill Doug," she said.

"Before we allow you to go," Bova said, "we need Bakero's blade."

From a distance, the dagger looked fine, but up close, it wouldn't pass inspection. Alex wasn't sure how the Grekers would react to their holy relic being damaged, but she guessed there would be no diplomatic solution for it. "Carter, can you put some distance between us and the shore?"

"I can," he said, "but I don't got much left. I'm already feeling groggy, and this thing must weigh half a boulder or more."

"Be ready." Alex nodded toward the barge's moorings. "Bova, take care of those, and the knife is yours."

"You heard her," Bova said.

The Grekers untied the ropes and threw them onto the deck. The barge lurched. The second it did, Alex threw Bakero's Blade into the fast-moving water.

"No!" Bova shouted and dove in. She was followed by all of the other Grekers.

"Now!" Alex yelled.

Carter flicked his wrist, and a tempest slammed into the boat pushing it to the middle of the river. Within minutes, they drifted past the bridges and buildings and passed through a huge gate, entering the dark cavern on the other side of Agnar.

Alex fumbled for the pouch on her waist to retrieve her tiny agyl lamp, but before she had it open, Carter drew glowing lines in the air that illuminated the roof and walls of the tunnel. The agyl hung in place, and a few seconds later, the river pulled them out of its reach. He drew another.

"I can keep this up for a while," Carter said, "but it will grow old fast."

With the aid of the agyl, Alex retrieved a sparker from her pouch. She went to the corners of the barge and lit the oil lamps that hung there. They weren't as bright as Carter's magic, but they could see well enough to steer without crashing.

"That's nice," Carter said.

"What?"

"Yellow light. I was sick of seeing green, and I wasn't sure we'd get out of that damn place alive."

"I knew we would. We had to."

"I guess I don't have your faith." Carter sat down beside Doug and checked the man's bandages. "Do you think we have a chance anymore to turn him back into a dragon or to stop the army of dragons?"

"I don't know." This journey started because she wanted to make a difference. She wanted to do something because she felt her father wasn't, and now that she had a goal, a thing she could do to help her people, it felt impossible. For all she knew, the dragons had already attacked Elene. Her father and Gideon could both be dead. "What do you think?"

"I want to be confident and tell you that everything will be alright," Carter said. "But I'm tired. I've never been so tired in my life. The constant drain of using so much magic... it's worn me down. It's hard to think."

"If you've lost your faith how am I supposed to stay strong?"

"I didn't say I was giving up," Carter said. "I may be tired, but I don't think we are beaten. We are going to give it our all, and no matter what we face next, you can know that you won't do it alone. We are a team."

"Thank you," she smiled. For the first time since Gideon had left, she didn't feel alone.

Carter slouched down leaned his back against the wheelhouse. His head dropped, and he let out a large yawn.

"The magic?" she asked.

"Yeah, I gotta be careful." He blinked at her, and his eyes watered from fatigue. "I've been overexerting myself. Walking that line where, if I go too far, I could potentially burn myself out."

"That's a thing?"

"Oh yeah, Master Owen had me start small. One of the reasons there are so few magic users is that most burn themselves out before knowing they could use magic."

"How can they do magic when they don't know they can do magic?"

"I heard a story once," Carter said. "We were at the Square Boulder and these merchants were saying how they saw a woman and a boy attacked by a pack of boars. The largest was about to spear the kid right through the gut, but all of a sudden the boars caught on fire. They stopped in their tracks and panicked then ran into the forest. The mom fainted, and when asked, she described feeling angry, scared, and tired all at the same time. Now these weren't educated people, and of course they thanked The Silver Lady, but I bet you that the woman used magic. Real magic and burned herself out doing so."

"I've seen you do impossible things. Things that compare to stories my father has told me about Owen." There were many, and it was hard to pick her favorite, though she was partial to the one where Owen, Gideon, and Edgar ended up trapped in a tree because anything that touched the ground instantly crapped their pants. "What's stopping you from burning out?"

"Since I was a kid, I've been learning agyls." As an after thought, he traced one of the glowing markings in the air. It sparkled and washed his face in a soft light. "Agyls are substandard to real magic, but they require a certain focus, kind of like..."

Carter stood and unhooked the travel satchel from his belt. He pulled a stack of Ryth tiles.

"You play Ryth?" she asked.

"Good. This will be easier to explain." He fanned the tiles out. "You know how when you get a good match going and you are trying to decide not only what your opponent will do next but what they will do like three turns later?"

"That's the whole point of Ryth."

"Exactly, it's that thinkyness." He handed her tiles, and she flipped through them. The artwork was worn, and it was clearly an older set, nothing like her personal deck that she had lost back on the caravan. "That thinkyness helps you grow that part of the brain that is used to control magic. Owen made me spend years practicing and training so that I wouldn't risk burning myself out."

"Up for a round?" She shuffled the tiles and split the stack.

"Can we do it later?" He yawned again. "I don't think I'd play very well right now."

"Sure," she handed the tiles back to him.

28

YORNDRAK

ORNSDAY, 41ST OF HEARFEST, 1162.111

Kane stood in her childhood home. Her first thought was that she was dead. Something had finally killed her, and she was now in hell paying for all the sins she had committed. Then she saw Doug and knew that wherever they were, it wasn't the afterlife.

Doug stood by the window. His eyes were wide. "By the light, this place..."

"Did you do this?" she asked. "Did you bring us here?"

He growled and turned to look at her.

"You stabbed me." Doug touched his chest, but his clothes were intact with no visible wounds. "I remember. You stabbed me, didn't you?"

She thought about the incident. She definitely had the memory of stabbing him, but she didn't know how long ago it was or if it had been real. Maybe she hadn't stabbed him? "Something is not right."

It was impossible for them to be in this house. This house must be what was wrong. Yet the living room was as Kane remembered...

No. It wasn't.

The antique cherrywood side table by the window had been Kane's great grandmother's, and her mother had sold it when she was ten or eleven. This was not her childhood living room. It was more like an idealized version of it. "I don't think this is real."

"You did this," Doug said. "When you stabbed me with Bakero's Blade, this happened."

"Shut up." Kane knew Doug was right. They were somehow locked together, and they were either in her head, or some other metaphysical realm. She hated mystic hoo-ha and did her best to avoid it.

"Come on, we are leaving." Kane walked to the front door then flicked the bolt lock. The world outside transitioned. At first, it was a brown, unkempt yard, and then it shifted.

Egg-shaped beads of light, no larger than a grape, formed the ground. They twinkled with pastel colors and hummed like the sound of lightning the moment before it strikes.

The colors rippled through the horizon and sky, and the world around them faded. The sky became deep shades of olive, sage, and emerald, mixing together, while a black nothingness formed a void around the house.

"I've seen this before." Doug squatted, looking at the swirling ribbons of light dancing around his boots. He pressed a finger into the ground. The spot he touched turned white, pushing the colors away. When he lifted his hand, the colors rushed back in, filling the spot.

"When, where?" Kane asked.

Doug ignored her and closed his eyes. "I don't smell anything. We aren't here. At least not in a physical sense."

"I know that already, but where is here?"

"This is Yorndrak."

Kane's suspicions had been right. They were in some mystic

hoo-ha place. The kind of place where Bartleby would be a huge help. It was a shame that he was not around. "Do you know how to get out of here?"

"No, but it's good we aren't really here. Yorndrak is death for the living. I guess it's a matter of getting our minds to wake up, probably has something to do with you stabbing me."

"Can we drop it for now? You keep bringing it up."

"Kind of hard to forget."

"Then let's talk this out. I stabbed you. Why would that put us here? Is this what happened when you absorbed the Arg'Natz?"

"No," Doug said. "There was a bit of light and an odd sensation, and that was it."

"So what's different now?"

"We are married."

Kane had many regrets in her life, only a few rivaled getting married. "Ok, so we are bound with whatever Erediän magic linked us, and at the same time the Arg'Natz switched between us. Why would that bring us here?"

Doug shrugged. "You got me."

Kane knew there were other worlds. Though in reality only two mattered. This Yorndrak was one of the many spaces between them and it was not her first time here. Somehow their bond had brought them here, and it meant that maybe their bond would get them out?

The field of lights flickered. One by one, they winked out and were replaced by fog. A rolling pink mist blocked out the sky and through it three shapes approached. Kane knew instantly it was the Sisters. They had a habit of meddling when she least wanted them to, but for once, maybe it was a good thing.

"Our sweet chickadees, why do you do these things to yourself?" Atropos spoke.

"Maybe they like a challenge?" Clothu said. "Instead of choosing the paths we suggest, they wish to pick the hardest to prove their strength? It could be an honor thing?"

"I'm confident that they merely lack intelligence," Lachesis said.

"Can you picture the others we have touched constantly getting themselves into so much trouble?"

"Tegan," Atropos said.

Clothu nodded as if agreeing. "But she is still a child."

"We get it," Kane said. "You are all knowing, all mystic, and you are here to help us if we swallow our pride and listen."

"It's not that simple." Lachesis floated behind Kane. "You know that."

"Then what?" Doug said. "Stop the games. Stop the showmanship. Tell us how to get out of here."

"Games?" Clothu said in a sharp voice.

"We are not our nephew." Atropos pointed to her siblings. "We do not do the things we do for our amusement. We do it for the sake of reality. For the sake of all the worlds."

"Then tell us what we need to know and begone," Kane said.

"So snooty." Clothu chuckled. "Let's have some fun!"

"And teach them a lesson?" Lachesis asked.

"There is no need," Atropos said. "They will learn for themselves."

"Learn what?" Doug said.

"That what you face is bigger than either of you," Atropos said. "This is more than mommy and daddy issues. More than bitterness to your kin."

"You will either step up or you won't," Lachesis said. "And the time to make that choice has not come yet, but when it does–"

"Go to hell." Kane was done. She had tried to hold her tongue. She had tried to be mature, but the Sisters got under her skin like no one else could. Arrogant, uppity bitches. They could take their warnings and vague hints and shove them up their corporeal asses. "I thought you were here to get us out of this, but you know what? I don't want your help. I'd rather be stuck here and die than let the three of you lift so much as a finger to get me out of this warped reality."

Kane turned her back to the others and walked into the mist.

"You can't go." Atropos teleported and materialized in front of Kane.

Kane ignored the woman, walking through Atropos' non corporeal body.

"I'm not dumb," Kane said. "The three of you aren't here. You can't do jack to stop me from walking away."

"Not true," Clothu said.

Lachesis spread her arms, and the pink mist washed away. In the distance was a cyclone of energy. It breached the pale sky, sucking in strips of light. The sizzling beams whipped around it, funneling into a black hole.

Beside it stood a giant.

Though giant felt like too small of a word. The being was hundreds of stories tall and its skin sparkled as if imbued with glimmering sheets of mica.

"Think carefully," Atropos said.

The giant spun its hulking body, to look in their direction.

Clothu snapped her fingers, and the pink mists returned, hiding them from the giant's view. "You walk a thin line."

Kane knew she should care about the godlike being beyond the mist, but pissing off the Sisters seemed more worth it. She barreled forward.

"Wait." Doug ran to her side. "I don't like you. You don't like me, but we are in this together, at least for now. Listening to them might be the only way to undo whatever has happened to us."

Kane stopped.

Although she wanted to stick it to the Sisters, the idea of getting Doug out of her head and severing their link would be worth it. "Alright, no more ollip fodder. You got thirty seconds to be clear, or I'm walking straight out there, which I have a feeling will bork your plans."

"This is Yorndrak," Clothu said. "Particularly, you are on the fringes of Felloe and Cyrin."

Kane sighed. This was the problem with mumbo jumbo. It

didn't make sense. Felloe and Cyrin were pointless words. From the context, she knew they had to be places, subdivisions of the spirit realm, and yet they were meaningless names.

"There is nothing you can do to escape this place," Atropos said. "Only time will free you."

"Time for what?" Kane asked.

"Time enough for the Arg'Natz to heal Doug." Lachesis floated toward Doug and leaned in close, as if to inspect his chest. "With your link, you failed to fully absorb the Arg'Natz. Instead the two of you now share it and are forever bound. The trauma of stabbing him and splitting the power forced your minds' eyes here."

"Undo it," Doug said. "Surely, you can cut the bond between us."

"In all the branches we see," Clothu said, "the only way to sever your link is with your death or Kane's."

"That can be arranged," Kane said.

"For now, what do we do?" Doug asked.

Kane bit the inside of her cheek. Doug seemed to be taking the news much better than she was, and that ticked her off.

"Being here in spirit…" Atropos said. "You both are vulnerable."

"Like insects crawling in the treads of boots." Clothu clapped her hands together as if squashing a bug.

"Return to Felloe and wait," Lachesis said. "Any other actions will lead to your destruction."

"Return how?" Kane said. "This is a place of illusions."

Clothu parted her arms. The mist swirled and formed a corridor of light. On the other side, Kane's childhood home stood.

"I'm not going back there," Kane said.

"That house is a construct," Lachesis said, "a part of the substance used in dreaming. If you do not wish to go there, then when you arrive make it become something else."

Kane glowered. She had no choice. She had to go with Doug

and return to the dream place, but it didn't mean she had to act happy about it. "Whatever."

On the plus side, once they were awake in the real world, she could kill Doug once and for all. That would end the weird bond. Then she could get back to other things, like helping Medrayt unleash a dragon army on the kingdoms. She desperately wanted to be there when Elene fell, and she hoped that the Sisters would be there too and that they could see their plans fail. That would be justice. It wouldn't fix the things they had done, but it might make them pay in a way that nothing else could.

"We know your thoughts," Clothu said. "You cannot hide them from us."

"I've never tried to hide my feelings toward you," Kane said. "In fact, I've been nothing but open about my aspirations to thwart your plans."

"This path will lead you to pain and suffering," Atropos said. "A torture unlike anything you have ever felt."

"But it's not too late." Lachesis lowered her head as if pleading. "Turn from the road you walk."

"No." Kane's lip formed a slim smile. "I'm good."

"We have warned her," Clothu said. "That is all we can do."

Lachesis shrugged. "We knew she wouldn't listen."

"Not true," Atropos said. "There was a chance. There is always free will."

"What about me?" Doug said. "All this talk of fate and paths and destiny. What of me?"

The Sisters broke into a fit of giggles.

Before Kane or Doug could ask anything else, they vanished.

"That's it?" Doug looked to Kane. "No hints or insights? They spent the majority of that conversation talking to you and talking around me."

"What can I say?" Kane shrugged. "I'm more important."

~

Upon returning to her home, the first thing Kane did was erase it. In a way, it felt good. One moment it was there, and the next, she bent it so that it melted like a snowman on a hot day.

After an excessive amount of effort, Kane had been able to create a stone structure like the bastard amalgamation of a church and castle without any sense of refinement. It had cyclopean masonry, high arches, and a glass ceiling that allowed the rainbow lights of Yorndrak to flood it with vibrant colors. Most importantly, down the center of the structure was a solid wall that had no doors or windows. Kane claimed a side for herself and banished Doug to the other half.

Keeping the construct intact took more effort than Kane would have thought. Whenever her mind wandered, the cobblestone walls waned and shifted back into those of her childhood home.

Whenever the construct broke, Doug tried to dematerialize the unwanted bits, but he had no conscious ability to destroy or build anything. Sporadically, glasses of water, fruits, or other exotic foods Kane didn't recognize popped into existence, so Doug had some skill, but no way to intentionally direct it.

Days passed, and they knew it was days because Yorndrak had a cycle where it shifted from lighter to darker tones. At night the void in the sky became blacker than the abyss while during daylight hours it took on a navy blue.

They did not need to eat, drink, or sleep. Kane felt it was manageable, but as a week passed, she grew itchy for they had no sign of when their stay in Yorndrak would end.

"Kane?" Doug's voice was followed by a thudding on the wall between them.

"Go away."

"Where do you want me to go?"

Kane grimaced. It would be best to deal with him and nip this in the bud so she could go back to sitting in silence.

One by one, Kane dematerialized enough stone blocks and the

mortar between them so that there was a window to Doug's side of their home. "What?"

"Can you shape shift?"

"You know I can shape shift. I'm a shapeshifter. By definition, that means I can shape shift."

He shook his head. "I mean here, while in Yorndrak."

Kane hadn't tried. Her body wasn't real. She felt no physical sensation when touching things, like the floor or wall. She felt resistance, but not texture.

Looking down, Kane saw that her body lacked exaggerated muscles and unnecessary curves. She ran a hand along her cheek, nose, and through her hair. Sure enough, her facial features were equally plain. She was in her natural form, and she didn't like the idea of Doug seeing her in this way.

Picturing her cheekbones, Kane tried to raise and thin them out, but nothing happened. She imagined herself taller and with longer hair, and again, nothing happened.

"Well," Doug asked, "can you shape shift?"

"No," she said.

"Drats." He looked through the glass ceiling to the magical sky. "I've been trying to turn myself back into a dragon. I thought maybe, for at least a little while, I could fly, but I'm not having any luck."

"You miss flying?"

"Feeling the wind rush around me. Seeing the sun creep up on the horizon. There is nothing like it."

"The sense of peace is my favorite, especially at night when you can fly above the clouds and its only you and the stars above."

Doug cocked his head sideways and smiled. "I hadn't thought of that. That you would know what it was like to fly or that you might understand what it would feel like to be grounded."

"I'm special like that." Kane waved a hand, and the rest of the stone blocks in the wall melted, leaving an opening large enough for Doug to walk through.

"When was the first time you flew?" Doug lay down on the floor beside her, with his hands resting on his chest.

"The first time was more falling than flying."

Doug laughed. "Fledgelings have a saying that goes 'You are doing it wrong if you don't fall.'"

"Then I must have been doing something right. It took me hundreds of tries to learn how to fly. Shaping my wings, making sure I was aerodynamic and had enough thrust. It's not easy."

"I guess I had it easy, being born with wings."

"You have no idea."

She expected him to say something sappy. To keep pestering her. To do something Doug-like. He didn't. He merely lay there looking at the stars.

Although it curled her toes and made her stomach churn to admit it to herself, Kane thought, at least for a little while, it was nice not to be alone.

It wouldn't last and she couldn't let herself get attached. The moment they were free of Yorndrak she would have to kill him. Not because she wanted to, but because their link was a weakness she couldn't afford.

29

IN THE DARK

ULESDAY, 42ND OF HEARFEST, 1162.111

Alex had no trouble steering the barge. They encountered a few spots of white water, but those were only due to a sharp bend in the tunnel. She did grow bored. Doug slept. Carter slept. She stood and then sat in the wheelhouse, not knowing how far they were going or how many hours had passed.

When Carter awoke, he tried to estimate the distance based on how often Alex had needed to refill the oil in the lamps, but he couldn't settle on an accurate number. So travel became a matter of shifts, napping, eating, and waiting. It was the most peaceful time Alex had had since leaving Elene.

They talked about lots of things because there was nothing else to do. It was interesting to hear Carter's thoughts on the world, considering he didn't know much about it. On the flip side, with all her schooling and training, Alex didn't know the first thing about stitching a wound or how to judge if crops should be harvested early.

When talking grew old, she gave Carter basic fighting lessons in which she covered stances and making sure to protect the vital parts of one's body. When he was too tired or sore, they went back to talking or sleeping.

Checking in on Doug became part of the routine. They moved the former dragon to the wheelhouse, and whoever was on duty also had the responsibility of regularly dripping water into his mouth.

They explored every bit of the barge and found a stash of clothing. Most of it was far too small, but both Alex and Carter found travel cloaks that fit them. The fabric was different, none she had ever seen and it was perfect for rolling up in when she was tired.

The days passed, merging into each other, but Alex was confident their time on the barge lasted under a week. The first sign that it was coming to an end was the noise.

A distant, low hum echoed off the cavern walls, causing Alex and Carter to stop sparring and pay more attention to the river. For an hour they listened, its intensity growing.

"That's different," Carter said.

"With our luck it's bad different."

The sound grew to a gurgling, and when they passed another S-curve in the river, the barge slammed to a stop.

Alex kept her balance, using the wheel to brace herself, but Carter tripped then slid into the barge's low wall.

"I think we hit something." He righted himself and looked downstream.

Alex had done her best to keep the barge in the center of the river where the current flowed faster, and now she wondered if that had been a mistake. "What is it?" She hoped it wasn't some under water creature. She was not in the mood for dealing with some twisted monstrosity.

"I don't know," Carter said. "I don't see anything breaking the surface."

"Can you do anything? I'm turning the wheel, but nothing is happening."

"Like what?" Carter shrugged. "There's..."

The bow of the barge stayed where it was while the rest of the ship pivoted. A scraping vibration shook the entire deck.

"Anything?" she asked.

Carter drew an agyl as tall as himself. Its bright white light blinded her.

"Watch it!" she yelled.

"Sorry, but we need to see what's going on."

Dotted along the river were rotted pylons and rusted pieces of metal. Farther ahead, stone blocks formed a dam. The blocks, easily the size of a cart, had channels drilled into them, that allowed the water to pass through, but otherwise obstructed the tunnel.

"That has to be the way out," Carter said.

Taking her eyes off the water, Alex looked up to see that the ceiling rose into a cone shape. A spiral roadway crawled hundreds of parses along the side of the cavern, funneling into a gorge in the ceiling. From it spewed a reddish-yellow glow. If they were lucky, it was sunlight and their way out.

Storefronts and other crumbling buildings lined the spiral road. There were windows and doors, though from a distance, Alex couldn't tell if the windows had glass or any kind of covering.

The base of the road formed at a beach on the river's bank. This place was another city, one as old as Agnar and the pylons and stones blocking the river must have been the remnants of a harbor. Someone back in the day had used the river to send goods, people, or whatever between the sister cities.

"How do we go from here up to there?" Alex pointed to the top of the spiral road. "Can you lift us with a bit of magic?"

"Unless you want to carry me along with Doug," Carter said. "That's way too far for me to lift us."

"Then we will have to make it on foot." Alex climbed onto the deck railing and hopped to one of the grey stone blocks that formed the dam. She landed on a slimy surface. Her boots slid and flew up past her head, and she landed on her butt, sliding. Clawing with her fingernails, she snagged a crevice and stopped herself before she slipped off the other side of the stone block.

"You ok?" Carter asked.

"Yes, but don't come this way." The rushing roar they had heard was the river falling to unseen depths on the other side of the dam. "There is a pit on this side."

"Can you make it to the bank?"

The stone blocks had a few gaps and cracks, but if she was careful, she could cross them. "I think so. Can you magic-up Doug and the supplies?"

"I'm good for more than magic." Carter gathered together three of the woven baskets and married their contents.

"I know. I saw how you treated Doug's wound."

"Well, I'm good for more than magic and medical stuff."

"Like rushing head first into something you shouldn't be involved with?"

"Says the girl whose rashness got us out of Agnar."

"Rash?" Keeping one foot firmly planted, she made her way along the blocks. "I thought what I did was pretty darn cunning."

"Bova wanted to help us."

"She might have wanted to help, but that didn't mean she could."

"I think we should have taken her help." Carter stacked an overstuffed basket onto three bedrolls and then cracked his knuckles. He pointed, and Doug rose into the air, bumping his head against the doorframe to the wheelhouse. "Oops."

"We want him to get better, remember?"

"He's fine, I think..." He set Doug down by the bedrolls, took a moment to inspect him, and then nodded in approval. "We are golden. He's good."

Alex reached the widest gap in the stone blocks. It was maybe two strides wide. She would have to jump it or let Carter lift her, though any extra exertion on his part wasn't good. He needed to stay as rested as possible to carry Doug at least until they could put together a makeshift sleigh or something.

She jumped.

Her toes touched down on the other side of the gap and the stone block crumbled.

Letting momentum take her, she flopped forward, making her body as flat as possible. Her chest and hands crashed into the crumbling stone block while her feet dangled over the white water. Laying there, she could feel the stone cracking beneath her. She army crawled across the rotting stone, not daring to stand. She imagined this must be what it felt like to cross melting ice.

Reaching the next stone block, she pounded it with a fist, testing it. It held strong and she slid her weight onto it. Standing, the rest of the walk was without incident, though she grumbled at Carter beating her to the rock beach.

With a single word and flick of the wrist, Carter lifted himself, Doug, and their supplies the fifty or so parses. "We should camp here, or at least give me some time to recover."

The start of the spiral road lay but five steps away, and the glow from the gap in the ceiling teased her. They were so close to seeing daylight again, but if Carter needed to rest, she couldn't argue. "That's fine. I was thinking we could make a hammock out of one of the bedrolls for Doug. Maybe together we can drag him instead of you having to magic him?"

"That sounds good." Carter drew an agyl, lighting up the beach. The rocky walls lining the cavern twinkled. "What is that?"

From the corner of her eye she saw a bit of movement.

"Did you see that?" he asked.

"No, what was it?"

"Something small and quick."

Carter put his back to her, and when he did, she saw a smooth lump on his neck. It matched the color of his skin, but as she stared at it longer, six limbs squished against a pod-like body became clear.

"Ahhh." Carter swatted at his neck, and before his hand struck the lump, the creature had crawled out of reach. "Something cold."

"Don't move."

"What, why?"

"Because there is something on you." Alex drew her short sword. Stabbing the thing would be too risky, considering how quickly it moved, but if she could get the blade underneath it, she might be able to pry it free.

"Then get it off!"

"What do you think I'm doing? Hold still." Feigning as if she would move in from the right, she instead went left and jammed the flat of the blade against Carter's neck. Too slow. The thing hopped out of the way.

"What is it? It's so cold it burns."

"It's the size of a frog, but smooth. It jumped off your neck and..."

Doug lay sprawled on the beach. Six of the things clung to his arms and face.

"Prösenta!"

A blast of wind slammed into Doug. The egg-like centers of the creatures' bodies popped into the air, and two were thrown off. The rest held on with suction-tipped legs.

Alex wrapped her forearm in her cloak to keep the things from sticking to her. Together with Carter's magic, they wiped the things off Doug.

"What were they doing to him?" She asked.

"From what I felt on my neck, I think they were eating or drinking his body heat. Sucking it up like pasta."

"We can't let that happen again. You take watch that way, and I'll watch..."

The rock walls along the beach shifted from a midnight black to a bright blue. Hundreds of the creatures skittered back and forth while more descended from the glowing cavern above.

30

EVACUATION

ORNSDAY, 4TH OF WINEWEN, 1162.111

Gideon had no control over the crowd. He knew that, but he wasn't ready to give up. He could still end this in an orderly manner. The palace had been easy to evacuate. All nonmilitary personnel were ordered to leave, and they left. Trying to clear out the rest of Elene had been a disaster.

Shop owners and residents whose families had resided in Elene for generations didn't want to leave, and the refugees felt a false sense of safety in the city. The mandate from Edgar had been clear and warned the people of the coming army. Still they refused to go. The people did not want to believe that an army of dragons was on its way, and so what should have been an orderly evacuation was on the verge of turning into a riot.

Gideon stood in one of the smaller city squares watching two soldiers, with swords drawn, break into a potter's store. Behind him, the crowd hissed, and several threw chunks of hardened food.

"Enough!" Gideon shouted so everyone in the square could hear. "You know me. I would not be here if this was not dangerous!"

"Gorph licker!" An elderly woman with thin eyebrows threw a glass bottle at Gideon. It struck him in the chest, bouncing off his leather armor, and shattered on the cobblestone. "I don't pay taxes so you can force me from my home!"

"If you stay you will die," Gideon said. "The dragons will see to that!"

"Lies! There is no dragon army." The woman yelled, making a guttural sound, and those around her did the same, showing a force of solidarity. "A plague upon the king and his spoiled daughter!"

A soldier wearing armor a size too big, tapped Gideon on the shoulder. Speaking low, he leaned in close. "There is a problem in the potter's shop."

"What?" Gideon asked.

"Two teens attacked Goderik."

"How bad did he hurt them?" Dead teenagers would be a fuel to send the crowd into a full riot.

"He didn't," the soldier said. "The teens ran a spear through his shoulder. They said the next one to enter the shop will get it through the heart."

"I'll deal with it. You deal with this." Gideon nodded to the crowd. "Keep them calm and in no circumstances use any kind of violence."

The soldier thudded his chest.

Gideon entered the potter's shop. It was dark. The windows were boarded, and a single agyl lamp lit the room.

Two teens sat behind a pathetic attempt of a barricade made from tables that had been turned over, baskets, and wooden crates. "Leave or we'll kill you." It was a girl who said it. She had fair skin and couldn't have been a day over twelve.

"I've done it before." A boy, maybe fifteen or sixteen, held a Kelsam spear. It was an ornamental piece. Its metal cap and tip were polished and sharp, but it would break against any real weapon.

"There is no need for anyone else to get hurt," Gideon said.

"We agree," the girl said. "Leave and we won't hurt you."

"The king has ordered–"

"He ain't our king," the boy said. He had a western accent that Gideon hadn't picked up on at first. These two weren't Elene locals.

The dragon attacks hadn't spread past the Freelands. Depending on where exactly the children were from, they may not know about the dragon attacks. From their clothing and the meat on their bones, they surely weren't refugees.

"Where are your parents?" Gideon asked.

"In Yorndrak." The girl spit on the floor. "May The Silver Lady bless them."

"Quiet," the boy said. "We don't have to answer to him."

Although the children had dismantled the shop to make their barricade, they hadn't wrecked anything. No broken ceramics or pottery lay on the floor. What they had done, they had done with care.

"Last warning. Get out." The boy tightened his grip on the spear. Clay had caked beneath his fingernails.

"Who else is here?" Gideon looked toward the back of the shop where a set of stairs led to the second story.

"Aunt–"

"Cynthia, I told you to hush!"

Cynthia scowled at the boy. "You can't tell me what to do."

"I don't have time for this." Gideon pushed through the barricade. Wooden crates toppled and the boy had to dive out the way to keep from being hit.

"You asked for it!" The boy drove the spear at Gideon.

Gideon caught it, jerked it away from the boy, and broke it on his knee. He threw the spear tip at the ceiling so hard that it stuck in the wood and hung out of the reach of both children.

Cynthia rushed to the stairs, and Gideon followed. She spun then slapped him across the face with an open fist.

When he kept coming, she screamed.

Gideon lifted her out of the way and continued up the stairs.

A horrible funk, like pig vomit and fermented meat, filled his nostrils. "What is that?"

"Don't hurt her." Cynthia was crying now, her false bravado completely torn away. "Auntie is all we have."

The apartment was modest with a small kitchenette and living space. On the floor next to the bed was a lump of rags and blankets that moved up and down.

The closer Gideon got, the more he wanted to shield his nose.

In the pile of wet clothes was a woman, or at least what was left of a woman. She barely breathed, and fever raged across her body. On her face and the backs of her arms were blue scaly strips where the flesh had rotted and died.

No doubt it was the blue pox. It wasn't a highly contagious sickness. Often annoying to kids, it was deadly to adults. There was no cure and nothing Gideon could do to help the woman. She would beat it on her own, or she would die. Judging by how she looked, he guessed it would be death.

"Can you help her?" the boy asked. "Please?"

"I can ease her pain," Gideon said, "but that is about it."

"It's our fault. Pa's ship sank, and Auntie came to get us. I got sick along the way, though after a week I was fine. But Auntie got sick too, and she kept getting worse and worse."

Gideon ran his arms behind Auntie's neck and another under her butt. She was wet. He didn't know if it was urine, vomit, sweat, or a mix of all three. It didn't matter. He couldn't get sick, and it was nothing that wouldn't wash off.

"We have to go." Gideon lifted her from the bed. Wetness ran down his arm. "I'm going to take you and your sister to the palace, alright?"

"Alright."

"What's your name?"

"Conner."

"Well, Conner, I want you to be strong. You need to be strong for Cynthia. Can you do that?"

Conner nodded.

"Then let's go see if we can get your Auntie some help."

The woman was no trouble to carry, and Gideon made it down the stairs and back to the front of the potter's shop easily. When he and Conner got there, they found Cynthia staring out the open doorway with her mouth open.

The sound of battle flowed in from the street. Metal on metal and yelling.

The locals had broken into a full riot.

Gideon saw a few of his soldiers, but most were out of sight, trampled, or fleeing while the residents threw anything light enough to lift and were in the process of lighting carts and kiosks on fire.

"What do we do?" Conner asked.

"We do nothing. I will end this." Gideon exited the building and turned to gingerly lay the sick woman against the doorframe. In the daylight, she looked worse than he had realized. Her eyes cloudy and bald clusters of rotted skin formed patches in her crusty hair. "Wait here."

"Enough!" Gideon yelled. It wasn't loud enough. The mob's chanting drowned it out.

Gideon drew his long sword. He angled the blade and ran it against the stone street, causing a high-pitched ringing.

The chanting lulled, and all eyes turned toward Gideon.

"We aren't leaving!" It was the older woman again. "You can't send us from our homes claiming a fake army is coming."

"Then you will die," Gideon said. "The dra–"

A chorus of yells sounded, and the mob turned on him.

Gideon realized his mistake. They thought he was directly

threatening them as opposed to warning them about the imminent dragon attacks.

The rioting people pelted Gideon with rocks, bags, and whatever else was in reach. The largest items he deflected with his sword, but he couldn't do that for much longer. Soon, those in the lead would reach him, and when they did, he dared not have his sword. Killing these people to save their lives was not a solution he could live with.

Gideon sheathed his sword as a big man with soot stains on his tunic, swung a fist at him. Gideon ducked. The man had a familiar face. He might have been the metalsmith's apprentice, but wasn't sure.

A weight slammed into Gideon's back, and two arms wrapped around his neck. It was the elderly woman. Gideon suspected she meant to choke him, but she had underestimated his height, and now she dangled on his back, refusing to let go.

"What are you doing?" Gideon pried the woman's fingers off his leather armor, but she was like a frantic rodent, quickly grabbing to keep hold on as if falling from his back would kill her.

The metalsmith's apprentice dealt Gideon another punch. It connected with his jaw, and he saw a flash of white and heard a drumming in his ears.

Gideon twirled and grabbed the old woman's legs. He jerked her off his back, and still she fought, resorting to scratching.

A fist jammed into Gideon's temple and then another in his gut. Two more people joined the metalsmith's apprentice, beating Gideon to the ground.

Gideon didn't see a favorable outcome to the situation. He could truly fight back, but that would anger the mob further. He could stop resisting and take their hits. That would most likely end with his being knocked out or killed. What he needed was something big. Something grand and shocking that would snap the locals back to their senses.

The sky went dark. Not like it would at night when there is no sun and one could see the stars. It was dark like a room with no windows or doors.

The men restraining Gideon let go, and the people screamed.

A bolt of magenta lighting arced above their heads, but instead of fading, it hung in places allowing a floating figure to be seen descending from the sky.

"Imbeciles," the shadowman said. His voice echoed off the streets so loud that everyone in the square could hear him. "This place will be besieged by dragons. You think I am scary? Then you have no idea what is in store."

The lighting came alive once more, striking the stone street. It erupted in a wave of light, and everything the light touched shimmered.

The buildings were gone, burned to ashes. Brick foundations were broken, and the streets were filled with deep holes. The walls of Elene, which had stood for thousands of years were toppled. Through the smoke and falling flakes of soot, a dragon appeared. It was big, twice the size of any dragon Gideon had ever seen. He knew it could not be real, or if it was real, it was something much darker and wicked then a dragon.

The people screamed, and when they tried to run, they found they couldn't. A magenta light held their feet to the streets. Most still strained, trying to lift feet held in place by magic, while a small portion crouched down, tucking their heads between their knees as if attempting to hide.

When the last one averted his gaze, the dragon and the darkness vanished, and in their place stood Owen, leaning on a worn cane. The damage to the walls and buildings faded away, no more real then the dragon had been.

"Go now," the magician said. "Save your lives and leave this place."

A few shouted his name in recognition, but that didn't hinder them. The city folk fled.

"Kal ah!" Gideon said.

"Kel eh." Owen took off an imaginary hat and then bowed. "Seeing you twice in a single season? If I didn't know better, I'd say the world is ending."

"It is."

"Oh, right." Owen smiled and shifted his gaze to the highest towers of the palace, visible over the walls of the outer ward. "Then I guess we should do something about it, shouldn't we?"

"We can try, but this isn't our fight."

"No it isn't, is it?" Owen let out a long, slow breath. "How was he when you last saw him? I miss him."

"Carter is like you when you were that age."

"I was never that young."

"You were, once. I remember clearly." Gideon let out a laugh and placed an arm around Owen. "He's got your sense of dramatic flair."

"What dramatic..." Owen met Gideon's eyes. "Oh posh, fine."

"When the world is ending, you have to savor the moments you can," Gideon said. "Even when they are at the expense of a borderline senile man."

"I've not been senile since that time in Ralk, and that wasn't my fault."

Gideon laughed. "No, it wasn't was it?"

"Let's go see Edgar. I'm sure he would be disappointed to miss out on the ribbing."

"In a moment, there is something else first," Gideon said.

The pair crossed the deserted square toward the potter's shop. Cynthia and Conner sat on its stoop. Both were in tears.

"It's ok," Gideon said. "The dragon wasn't real."

They acted as if they hadn't heard.

"Oh my." Owen bowed his head.

Auntie was still seated where Gideon had left her, but the shallow rise and fall of her chest had stopped, and blue strings of snot dripped from her eyes and nostrils.

Owen muttered something beneath his breath. A breeze washed the woman's face clean and closed her eyes.

"I'm sorry," Gideon said.

Conner's sobs were so strong that his chest heaved as he made a gasping sound. Cynthia draped her arms around her brother. "It's ok. You still have me."

31

WRENTS

ULESDAY, 7TH OF WINEWEN, 1162.111

Doug woke to shouting. He sat up, and his whole body ached. It was an abrupt transition from Yorndrak, where he had no physical needs, to the real world where everything hurt.

"What in blazes do you want me to do?" Carter screamed.

"Wind bubble or anything to keep them back," Alex said.

Doug cracked open an eye lid and saw Alex spinning in a circle, swatting at what looked like fat gnats. She was good. Kept most off her, but one or two managed to land on her back and shoulder in the unprotected spots. The longer the gnats stayed on her body, the more it looked like frost formed around them. Odd, if he didn't know better, he'd say they were wrents.

The wounds where Doug had been stabbed with Bakero's Blade throbbed, but without warning the pain eased, becoming a pleasant cooling sensation. He glanced down to see three twinkle pods gripping his chest.

He blinked.

They were wrents!

Instinct took over, and he backhanded them so hard they flew against the stone wall of the cavern, splattering. Their purple innards leaked down the wall, and other wrents jumped to the spot to absorb the residual warmth before it fully leaked away.

"Wrents!" Doug brushed off Alex's back and spun to clean three from Carter's side. "For gorph's sake where are we?"

The three of them stood on the banks of an underground river. To the right, at the base of the cavern wall was a wide spiral road that appeared to be carved directly in the rock. The road coiled up to a gorge in the cavern's ceiling. Along it were crumpling storefronts and shops.

"Thanks." Alex kicked away a trio of wrents that had landed on Doug's calf. "We are... I don't know where we are. These things showed up and they won't leave us alone."

"What do you have for creating heat or fire, anything?" Doug asked.

"I got my agyl sparker," Alex patted her belt pouch.

"I can make a heat agyl," Carter said.

"Heat, do it!" Doug moved so the three of them now stood shoulder to shoulder in a circle, facing out, kicking and hitting away the wrents. "As much heat as you can!"

Carter traced a man-sized pattern. When finished, it flared and heat radiated out of it.

"We need to move away from that, now!" Doug ran up the curved road. Carter and Alex matched his pace. "Those things are wrents. They are attracted to heat. The only way to get rid of them is to get near a source that is warmer than us."

"I can keep drawing agyls," Carter said.

"They won't work for long," Doug said. "There are too many of the purple suckers. We need something warmer."

"Think we can make it into the city?" Alex took out another two wrents. "Maybe a house or store has some flint or wood to burn"

"You see this place?" Carter said. "It's ancient. Anything burnable will be rotten and decayed to a pile of nothing."

Doug punched another wrent as it sailed at him, and gave it all he had, more testing his own strength than trying to destroy the wrent. It exploded on impact, which was nasty since the vile things smelled like dung. But he noticed no pain or restriction in his movement. However bad his stab wound had been the power of the Arg'Natz had healed it.

Without wasting time to warn them, he grabbed each teenager with an arm, bent into a crouch, and jumped. He cleared twelve parses. His boots left purple stains on the cavern floor. He leapt forward another three times, pinging in different directions so that his movement was too erratic to predict. Still the wrents came, but a final jump upward took them onto the lowest ring of the spiral road.

Carter drew a new light agyl, giving them a better look at the cliff city. The doors to shops were extra wide and extra tall, not made for Grekers. The road curled, always moving upward. There were no railings, and a fall would drop them into the watery pit below.

The wrents continued to come from both below and above the companions. They had bought a bit of time, but soon they would be sandwiched between two massive fronts of the critters.

"We have to run!" Alex scrambled out of Doug's grip and sprinted ahead.

"Nowhere to run to." Carter drew a series of heat agyls and linked them together. "We need to fight."

"There is no fighting when it comes to wrents." Doug leaned over the edge of the road. One hop at a time, the critters were following, though some had broken off the main group and were hoping directly up the walls.

"I've never heard of them before," Carter said.

"You aren't a dragon. Buggers are a pain in the arse. They cling to your underbelly or back, and they always know the exact places you can't reach. Their grip is something fierce. If you've got a friend to watch, and there are only a few, you can clean them off. Otherwise, heat is the only thing that can save you."

"Hustle. Those things are catching up fast." Alex kept the lead, sprinting and then stopping at every new building and glancing inside. "Nothing useful in here either."

Doug was already sweating from the heat of Carter's agyls, and the running caused damp patches to form around his pits and down his back. It smelled horrible and the first chance he got, assuming they lived through this, he was going to bathe.

The angle of the road was steep, and by the time they did a full turn to reach the second level of the road, Doug's lungs felt as if they were going to explode out of his chest. His breathing was heavy, and no matter how much air he sucked in, he felt he wasn't getting enough. His heart thudded, and he felt a bit light headed.

The distance between Doug and the teens grew father apart while the distance between Doug and the wrents shrunk. Doug gave up walking and resorted to taking the massive leaps, but it wore him out faster. "I can't keep this up."

"In here." Alex darted into a building.

Doug tried to object, but the words came out slurred.

By the time Doug scrambled inside, Carter had drawn new light agyls, illuminating the room. It looked like a workshop with an abundance of tables, benches, and stone tools.

"Hurry up." Carter put a hand on Doug's back, ushering him up a stone staircase to the right of the door. Everything in the blasted city was made of stone.

With every step up the stairs, a cramping pain surged in Doug's side. To his horror, when he reached the top, he found himself in larger stairwell that headed both up and down.

Doug couldn't think. His chest hurt, his side hurt, his lungs hurt. In fact, he hurt way less when he was being stabbed than in that moment.

"Move it!" Alex grabbed Doug's arm and pulled him up another flight of stairs. Looking up, he saw that the stairs continued as far as the agyl's light shined.

"I need to rest." Doug sat. Not having to move. Not having to support his own weight. It was glorious.

"We don't have time." Carter tugged, as if attempting to lift Doug, but it didn't work.

"Do something!" Alex was two flights above them.

"Prosentä!" Carter summoned the wind.

Air swirled around them.

They were lifted into the center of the stairwell and rose, zooming upward so fast that, in only a few seconds, they were in near darkness. The only light was a warm glow higher up the tunnel.

The cushion of wind shot from the stairwell, reaching the upper echelon of the city. The cavern they found themselves in was easily three times the size of Agnar. Spires rose out of the ground, each a twisted building with windows twinkling with light.

In the ceiling of the cave hung not one but five red suns of various sizes. Around each, Doug saw scaffolding and stairs.

Carter set them on a catwalk that was fifty parses above the ground and spanned two spiral pyramids. Alex had to hold Doug up to keep him from falling. He sank to his butt, still winded from all the climbing.

"That wasn't smart," Alex said.

"We had to get out of there." Carter planted his own ass next to Doug. "At least we are away from the wrents."

"We aren't." Doug said.

The blinking lights that were spread throughout the underground metropolis shifted and moved. Each was a wrent, and judging by the size of the cavern there weren't thousands, but hundreds of thousands.

"I can float us maybe one more time," Carter said. "But then I'm done. If I do, where could we go to get away from those things?"

"The suns!" Alex said.

"Carrying us to the suns wouldn't do us any good," Carter said.

"The wrents like heat right?" Alex held her hands together like a sphere and expanded them outward. "Can you magic the suns, beef them up or something, to draw the wrents away from us?"

The suns formed a ring in the center of the cavern. Their shape and color suggested they existed in various stages of completion. The smallest had a burgundy cast and was dense, while the largest looked like a swirling sphere of fire.

"I'll kill us." Carter stared at the suns. "The threading and the magic is old and coming apart. If I mess with them at all, they could destabilize."

"We are dead anyway," Alex said.

"Yeah but–"

"Carter, I don't know much about magic," Doug said. "But right now we have two options. We get frozen to death by wrents, or you magic the suns and make them burn hotter."

"It doesn't work like that." Carter whisked his wrist in a mock gesture. "I can't wiggle my fingers and tell them to burn hotter. The braids of that magic are beyond anything I've ever seen. This isn't magic. Not like the magic of now. This is old magic, pure energy."

"Do it." Doug said in flat, commanding tone.

Carter sighed and then closed his eyes.

Doug groaned. "What are you–"

"Quiet, I need to focus." Carter used a snappish tone Doug was used to hearing only from Alex. "You and Alex need to buy me the time I need."

Doug still hadn't caught his breath, but the stitch in his sides had eased. "I'll take the front," he told Alex. "You take the back."

She drew her short sword.

Doug took a defensive stance, rooting his heels.

They waited.

The twinkling wrents continued to creep closer to the companions, like a deadly fog sneaking across a river. There were so many that the twisted and pointed buildings writhed.

Never had Doug seen a nest of wrents so huge, but without any predators to kill them and a forever-burning heat source, it made sense that they would take over the fallen city.

The first wave came not from below, but from above.

Dozens of the heat suckers, fell upon Doug. He knocked a few away, but spun, allowing the rest to clamp onto his posterior. The burning cold ran down his spine and when it became unbearable, he jumped and landed on his back, squashing them. Their wet innards, for once, feeling warm.

Alex handled them in a more efficient manner. She spun as if in a dance. She deftly sliced them in half or batted them away with her blade.

Doug knocked a wrent off Carter's shoulder, and it stuck to his hand. He shook it fiercely, but the creature held tight. With all else failing, he clapped his hands, summoning his brute strength. It popped like a cherry tomato.

The onslaught grew, and Doug realized they had no chance of keeping all the wrents away. Instead, he put himself as close to Carter as possible. He had more body mass than either of the teens, and he could shield them.

"I can't keep this up," Alex said. Two wrents perched on her neck. "It hurts."

"Help her," Carter said. "I'm about ready, and you two need to be as close to me as possible."

Doug plucked and squished the wrents on Alex, and she returned the favor by clearing away those that had stuck to his shin.

"There!" Carter clapped.

Nothing seemed to happen.

"What did you do?" Alex split three more wrents with her sword.

"I didn't want to mess with the magic of the suns. It was too much," Carter said. "But I found a weak spot in the bindings that were holding the suns in place."

Doug squinted, and sure enough all five suns were moving, sliding downward at a snail's pace. "What good does that do?"

"You wanted it hotter," Carter said. "I couldn't make the suns hotter, but they are blasted hot as it is. So instead, I'm bringing them down to the city."

The farther the suns fell, the faster they moved.

Doug felt the warmth on his skin rising. The wrents must have felt it too because after a final push, they retreated, hopping down the buildings.

"You slurping idiot." Alex sheathed her sword, the metal ground against the scabbard.

"What?" Carter threw his hands in the air. "You asked for the impossible. I did the next best thing."

Doug realized Alex's concern. The five suns were hot. Hotter than any furnace or fire he'd ever seen. So hot they would melt rock and metal alike.

The first and largest sun hit the ground.

Doug braced himself, expecting to feel it, but there was no shake or vibration. The largest sun oozed onto the rock floor of the city, devouring all buildings and structures in its way. Smoothly they sunk, and a band of molten rock arced out from it, like ripples in a pond.

"Oh, that's what you meant," Carter narrowed his eyes, looking at the smaller suns and then back to the big one. "Oh gorph. Gorph gorphity gorph."

"What?" Doug asked.

"There were primitive agyls mixed with threads of magic to bind the suns in place," Carter said. "That's why it was so easy to release them, but they weren't merely holding the suns in place. They were holding each one together. All five of them are unstable."

The largest remaining sun expanded. Its fiery rim, swallowed the smaller ones. Tendrils of energy exploded out of it, licking the cavern ceiling. Stalactites melted, and freshly molten lava, rained down on the city.

The wrents, still seeking heat, flooded toward the inferno, their twinkling fading out as lava swallowed them.

As the ring of viscous rock spread farther from the suns, the bottom of the cave bowed and sank. The catwalk where they stood was far enough away to prevent its collapsing, but still the whole thing shuddered.

"Get us out of here, now!" Doug scooted as close to Carter as he could. Alex did the same.

"Prösenta!" Carter pointed his hands to the ground, and they rocketed into the air. "Where are we supposed to go. This whole cavern is going to be destroyed."

The ash and embers, clouded Doug's view. As far as he could tell, the now-melting walls of the cavern blocked the city. "We need to get out of here."

"There!" Alex yelled.

To their back was a cylindrical tower, like a lighthouse. It rose higher than all the buildings around it, and at its zenith was a bridge leading to a closed iron gate.

Between them and the tower was the field of raining lava.

"We won't make it," Doug said.

"I don't see any other way, do you?" Alex said.

"It's fine." Carter spoke slow between deep breaths. "I have this."

Carter brought his hands together, and the wind moved, becoming a bubble around them, as it had on the cliff. The overwhelming currents not only kept the heat at bay, but they slung away any drops of melting rock that touched it.

The companions floated over the center of the city. Below them, geysers of liquid fire erupted from the mega sun. In seconds, buildings that were thousands of years old became glowing pools of nothing. Their history and any clue to the past was burned away by uncontrolled magic.

"Brace yourselves!" Carter yelled.

A column of fire slammed into the base of the bubble and plowed them into the ceiling. The air cushioned the blow, but the heat was all encompassing. Sweat matted Doug's hair to his forehead, and every bit of his body dripped with it.

"I'd like to have a few of those wrents now," Alex muttered.

Doug agreed.

"I'm doing my best," Carter said. His tone was intense, his face caught in a permanent frown. The veins on his temple pulsed. Either it was a trick of the light, or his blood was glowing.

A chunk of lava landed on top of the bubble, and Carter grunted as if the blow physically hurt him. For a moment the bubble spun wildly out of control, but then steadied.

"I'm not going to make it." Carter's eyes had a foggy look, and he swayed back and forth, the bubble matching his motion.

"Get us as close as you can and out of the lava field." Doug shifted, locking an elbow under Carter's armpit. "I'll carry you the rest of the way."

Behind them, the heart of the city was gone, just a few nubs of buildings remained. Doug saw only the tip of the sun as it sunk lower into the earth. The cavern ceiling bent downward, touching the magma below.

Carter fainted.

The bubble crashed into the side of the tower.

Doug kept his grip on Carter, cradling the boy, so that when Doug landed on the stone bridge, he took the brunt of the impact.

"We have to move!" Alex ran toward the gate.

Doug slung Carter over his shoulder.

"Step it up!" Alex was already halfway across the bridge.

"You want to carry him? I did just wake from a coma, but if you think you can do a better job, by all means take him."

"Hurry, I'll get the gate."

The gate was wide enough for several carts and tall enough that a dragon could pass underneath without ducking. No visible chains, ropes, gears, or any kind of opening mechanisms were attached to the gate or wall.

An ember landed on Doug's chest, and he patted it out, but not before it left a hole in his shirt and burned the skin beneath.

Doug shifted Carter, wrapping the boy in his travel cloak and holding him with both hands as he leaned forward to protect Carter's body as much as possible. Embers kissed Doug's back, and he did his best to ignore them. There was nothing he could do but keep walking.

Blood dribbled from Doug's burned back, running down his side and collecting in his boots so that, with every step, there was a wet suction sound.

Although the distance across the bridge was a fraction of what he had run earlier, it felt ten times farther. Each step required him to summon his last reserves of strength. Already the pain in his sides had returned, and he breathed so hard that he could feel his lungs pressing against his ribs.

"Open the gate." Doug chose not to set Carter down. He feared that, if he did, he wouldn't have the energy or will to pick him back up.

"I don't know how," Alex said. "There is nothing here. Not even a keyhole."

The metal gate was smooth. Nothing was painted or etched into it. The rock walls to the side of the gate were equally polished.

"It must be magic of some sort," Doug said.

"Well I don't know any magic."

"Neither do I."

"Can we wake Carter?" Alex asked.

Doug shook his head. There was no way they would get him awake.

"Then what do we do?" Alex said. "My father, my people, everyone is counting on us."

The expanding magma reached the round tower. It tilted, and its base shrank like a sand castle devoured by water.

The stone bridge groaned and shook beneath Alex's and Doug's feet.

"I think it's over kid."

"There has to be another way." Alex half hung over the bridge's railing looking down. "Maybe another exit or way out."

"It's done. There comes a time when all your effort isn't enough."

"No!" Alex made a fist and pounded on the gate.

"You think I want to die as a human, or die at all? This is the only way out. If we can't open it, that's it."

"Then we break the gate down." She knocked on the gate with both fists, kicking it between each hit. "I will not die here!"

Doug wanted to live. He wanted to be a dragon again and to feel the sunlight, real sunlight from a real sun, on his scales. He wanted to go back home to his cave and live in peace without drama, people, or noise. He knew there was no way out.

He leaned against the gate. The cold metal felt comforting against the wounds on his back. If they were going to die, then he wanted to take in the sights. It wasn't every day you got to see an ancient city swallowed by fire.

The sound of gears and whirling came from below their feet. The gate creaked and fell away, retracting into the ground.

Doug lost his balance, falling backward.

Blinking and confused, he saw a long shaft of light, and at its other end was blue sky.

"Get up, get up, get up!" Alex lifted Carter off Doug's chest. "We gotta go."

"Why did it open?" Doug crawled and then stood.

"I don't know, but let's not risk its closing again." Alex passed Carter back to Doug, and they ran toward sunlight.

32

HER SWORD

ULESDAY, 7TH OF WINEWEN, 1162.111

When Kane's eyes opened and she saw that everything was cast in that puke-green light, she knew she was back in Agnar. After what felt like months, she was out of Yorndrak and back in the real world.

Forming her fingers into knives, she rolled onto her side and looked for Doug. She had to move fast, before he expected it. But to her surprise, he was nowhere in sight.

She lay on a bed. A frilly bed with a mattress that was too soft and sheets that were clean. The room around her was ornate with vases and other extravagant decorations.

Her legs wobbled as if the muscles had atrophied. How long had she and Doug been in Yorndrak? She shifted to add more muscle mass to her calves.

Opening the chamber door, she found Bova seated at a desk. The desk was covered in parchments and various quills and ink wells.

"By all that's holy, you are awake!" Bova set down a rubber stamper and clapped.

"Where is Doug?" Kane had to force the sound from her dry throat.

"Gone. He and the children left over two weeks ago."

Kane closed her eyes and reached out with her bond. It was true. Doug wasn't close. He was far off, but she did have a general direction for him. "Why didn't you wake me when he woke?"

"He wasn't awake. He was dying."

"He's alive. I feel him." Kane's stomach rumbled. She didn't need to eat. She gained no nutrition from it, though there were times she enjoyed doing so, and she thought maybe the hunger was something Doug felt wherever he was. She shrunk her stomach, removing it completely from her digestive track. "I have to find him."

"Of course, I will be happy to help, but as the new Arg'Natz, there are things that need your attention."

That's right. The whole blasted reason she ended up in Yorndrak was 'cause of the Arg'Natz, and now she was its bearer, well co-bearer, but the Grekers didn't need to know that. The Grekers would be a useful tool, but to take full advantage, she needed their loyalty, and there was only one way to get that.

"Summon your people," Kane said. "Tell them the Arg'Natz is awake and I wish to speak to them."

Word went out, and within an hour the entire population of Agnar gathered in the arena. From the arena's high vantage point, Kane saw lines of Grekers, like ants retreating to their hive, flowing toward the building where she waited. They left work, equipment in the fields, and dropped whatever else they were doing to head toward the heart of the city.

When the last Greker arrived, she stood up and took center stage. She boosted the size of her lungs and voice box so that she could speak loud enough for all to hear.

"I am your new emperor," Kane said.

Whispering and gasps trickled through the audience.

"I understand that is not how you have run things in the past." Kane crossed her arms. "Things are changing, and you will accept them. The Arg'Natz has always been a spiritual adviser while the Pontis ran your city, but now only my word is law."

A whole section of Grekers stood and turned their backs to her, as if to leave the arena. That was bad. She wanted to evoke fury, she wanted them to feel as if their way of life was threatened, but she didn't want them to leave.

"I understand why this causes you discomfort. I am an outsider. One who looks human and is telling you to change your ways." She held up a hand, and it shifted to become a blooming iris with bright red petals that continued to look red, even in the green light. "But here is the thing. I am not a mere outsider. I am something special."

Kane shrunk and took on Greker features, including their furry cheeks and coarse skin. "I can make myself look like you. Maybe that would ease your fears, but I'm not here to make things easy for you. I'm here because I'm destined to be here. I'm here because I am the Arg'Natz you have been waiting for."

She shifted again, but instead of taking human form, she kept her frame slimmer and allowed her ears to form points. She took on a bright orange skin tone that was perfectly unblemished. With every tweak of her features, the ruckus in the audience grew quieter and quieter. By the time she took on a fully Erediän form, not a single Greker yelled or heckled her.

"I am the one destined to bring back the Erediä," Kane said. "That will not happen today. It will not happen tomorrow. Nor is it something I can do in this city. I must return to the outer world. I have to seek the things that will allow me to bring them back."

Everything Kane said was total garbage. She had no intention of bringing back the Erediä, nor did she think it was possible in any kind of way, but the Grekers didn't know that. "So I ask you now. Resolve your differences. Fix this unrest between your factions and be strong. The day will come when I call upon you, and when I do, you need to be a strong nation. You need to be my mighty blade, for I will need your strength to return theŚlrediä to this world."

The crowd broke into a roar.

Cheers. Shouting.

It was exactly what Kane wanted. She hadn't lied about wanting them to be strong. They would be a powerful weapon, and if she swung them at the Sisters or Doug, then so be it. They wouldn't be any the wiser.

33

THE CHAMBER

ELDSDAY, 9TH OF WINEWEN, 1162.111

Owen, Edgar, and Gideon stood on the ramparts to the palace, overlooking Elene. The city was eerily quiet. Usually at dusk, there was a chorus of noise as people shuffled through the streets or went about preparing for evening activities.

"Well?" Edgar asked. "Is the city clear?"

Owen opened his eyes. "I sense no one but your soldiers."

"The last caravan?" Edger said.

"I put Conner and Cynthia on it myself before it left for Compitum," Gideon said. "I did another walkthrough of the city. It's deserted."

"You are sure?" Edgar asked.

Owen looked to Edgar. He paused for a moment and then knocked Edgar in the head with his walking staff. "It may have been awhile, but I still don't like stupid questions. We both told you it's empty."

"You going to do something about this?" Edgar looked at Gideon while rubbing the back of his skull. "You're my protector."

Gideon shrugged.

"I fear another whacking, but I have to ask," Edgar said. "Do you think we stand a chance?"

"Maybe." Owen looked across the city and then turned northwest as if seeing something they couldn't. "I don't see the branching paths. I never have, but I know we have faced worse, and yet here we still stand."

"It's different this time." Edgar sighed and followed Owen's gaze to the horizon. "We no longer have the weight of the world on our shoulders. For once, we have to rely on others to save us."

"They are good kids," Owen said.

"I remember being that age." Edgar ran a hand along his stubbled chin. "I'm not sure if they think of themselves as kids."

"I got a few years on them." Owen chuckled. "They will always be kids to me."

"I spent so long trying to protect Alex," Edgar said.

"You spent?" Gideon smirked.

"You know what I mean," Edgar said. "We did our best to keep her out of this for as long as we could. I wish she didn't have to face these responsibilities."

"Carter is the closest thing I have ever had to a child of my own." Owen shook his head. "No, that's not right. Carter is my son. Maybe not by blood, but he is my son, and I know how you feel. We raise them and guide them as best we can, but in the end, they must make their own paths."

"Most parents don't have the Sisters meddling with their children's fates," Gideon said. "So you two can't blame yourselves entirely."

Owen and Edgar nodded, and silence overcame the three men as they stared at the abandoned city.

At last count, Gideon determined they had roughly six thousand soldiers to defend Elene. With Elene's fortification, the water reserve, and overall design, six thousand could outlast a siege for years. Six thousand would be meaningless against an army of dragons.

"It will never be the same," Edgar said. "These are Elene's final days."

Gideon followed Edgar's gaze. The king was looking west across the inner ward and the deserted streets.

"Oh posh." Owen thwapped Edgar again with his cane. "You think I'd be here if I didn't have a trick or two up my sleeves?"

"No," Gideon said in protest. He saw where things were going, and he didn't like it. "Don't even think about it."

"You got a better option?" Owen gave Gideon a cold stare. "We need to stall, and I can't think of a better way to hold the dragons at bay."

"The last time you did it, you almost killed everyone in the city."

"It's different. There aren't hundreds of people crowding inside. We won't go through the air as fast."

"What are you two talking about?" Edgar asked.

"I'll show you." Owen said.

Entering the palace, Owen led Edgar and Gideon up a staircase to the main residence. Their footsteps sounded extra loud without the other usual noises radiating through the building.

"The passage Alex used to sneak out of the castle, you knew of it, correct?" Owen asked.

"Of course," Edgar said. "I've been using it since I was younger than she is."

"It's not the only secret your home has." Owen paused at the top of the stairs to catch his breath.

"I know about the one in the left wing too." Edgar offered his arm for Owen to use as support, but the magician ignored it.

"Oh do you?" Owen said. "What about the one in the great hall or the front courtyard?"

Edgar narrowed his eyes and glanced from Owen to Gideon.

Gideon laughed.

"Sure, give it away." Owen threw up his hands, acting as if he were annoyed, but Gideon knew he wasn't. He was enjoying this as much as they all were. Sometimes, specially when facing something bad it's nice to have those you consider family by your side.

"There is more to the place than the two exits," Owen said. "I built several safe rooms, a secret vault, and the chamber we will be visiting today."

"You built?" Edgar said.

"You think a place like this organically evolves?" Owen said. "I designed Elene and named it."

"I thought by now I knew all your secrets," Edgar said. "I'm impressed."

"Elene was an impressive woman." Owen's cane clanked on the palace's marble floors. "Honoring her memory was the least I could do."

Gideon felt that was an understatement. She was by far Owen's better half, and Gideon missed her. There were lots of people he missed, but he especially missed Elene.

As they reached a long corridor, Owen turned to enter the palace libraries. It was dark, and Owen spoke something softly. Instantly the lamps in the ceiling sprung to life. Gideon knew the library was small. Smaller than the records house in the city, smaller than the great library in Compitum. Smaller than Owen's personal library, its high ceiling made the room feel open. Books covered the outer walls, and the golden-rust tones of the shelves and furniture gave the library a welcoming feeling.

Owen walked to the dead-center point of the library. He muttered something, and a set of chairs and reading table hovered then scooted out of the way before gently landing again. Etched into the stone floor was an old Dunder saying, and below it was a symbol that looked like a circle with a triangle in it. Owen placed his palm over the triangle. The etchings shone with a brilliant silver light, and then the stone shifted, revealing a narrow staircase.

"What did you say to open it?" Edgar asked.

"Nothing," Owen said. "It recognized me by my blood."

Only once had Gideon visited the hidden chamber. He did not like the idea of visiting it again.

The stairs descended less than thirty steps and opened into a round room that was no bigger than a wagon. It was such a tight fit that Gideon stood on the stairs so Edgar and Owen could enter without having to stand pressed against each other.

"This is the secret to Elene's defense," Owen brushed his hands on the curved walls. The stone was black and smooth.

"I know your love for showmanship," Edgar said. "But for once, can you give me a real explanation?"

Owen flicked his wrists at the walls. They buzzed with energy and then came alive, offering a perfect view of Elene from the highest tower of the palace.

"What is it?" Edgar asked.

"It's an amplifier in a sense," Owen said. "It will allow me to convert my own magic and strength into a barrier. Once up it won't let anything in or out of Elene."

"Including air!" Gideon hoped that Owen remembered how important breathing was. "The last blasted time he had it going, half of the city's population fainted from lack of air, including Owen! Then no one could turn it off."

"I woke up before anyone died," Owen said defensively.

"You sound like Carter," Gideon said.

A proud smile slipped across Owen's face.

"How much time can you buy us with this thing?" Edgar ran a hand along the smooth reflective wall.

"Depends on the dragons and how many people we have inside the city," Owen said. "The last time, we had the walls packed with people, and it took us over a week to run out of air."

"A week, that's it?" Edgar let out a long sigh.

"It will be far less this time," Owen said. "Every time a dragon tests the barrier, I'll feel it, and it will weaken me. At best, I'll buy us a few days."

~

Gideon lay in bed wearing only his skivvies with the window shutters tied open. Sweat ran down his temples. It was as if summer was refusing to let go of its hold on the southern lands, proving it could stay for a bit longer. Not that the seasons were living personifications like other beings he had come across.

The door to Gideon's chamber creaked. A warm orb of light floated in. Behind it, staggered a tired looking Owen. Gone was his cane. Instead, he held a bottle and two glasses.

"Time for a drink." Owen held up the bottle

The light was too dim for Gideon to be able to read it.

"Depends," Gideon said. "What are we drinking."

"Have I taught you nothing? It's never the what that matters. It's always the why."

Gideon climbed out of bed. For a moment, he thought of throwing on more clothes, but ultimately it was hot, and he knew Owen cared little about nudity.

"What's the why this time?" Gideon cleared his lute from a table and pulled out a seat for Owen.

"I'm thirsty, and it's been awhile since we had a chance to sit and talk."

"And?"

"And..." Owen sat slumped over in the chair, letting out a deep breath. "And I'm worried. Worried about things that only you and I can talk about."

"Time?"

"No, the Weird Sisters." Owen snapped his fingers, and the

bottle's cork popped. The bottle then lifted of its own accord and filled the two glasses.

Gideon lifted his drink and smelled it. Honey bourbon. He took a sip, and caramel with cinnamon ran across his tongue. There could be no mistake. It was a Lockhaven vintage. His favorite. One he hadn't tasted for a long time.

"What about them?" Gideon asked.

"They are playing both sides."

"They always do."

"So which side is in the right? Medrayt and his army or ours?"

Gideon swished his glass and took another swill.

Gideon knew how the Sisters thought. They dealt with the big picture, and often the little things meant nothing to them. They did not care who they had to hurt or what the consequences of their actions were as long as the possible outcomes became more favorable. Because of this, there was no way of knowing which of the pawns in motion would create the outcome they desired.

"I don't know," Gideon said.

"That's what I feared. We could be the side they want to lose. The children could be hurdles that are merely meant to make Medrayt stronger for overcoming them."

"They could."

"So what do we do?"

"We do what we've always done." Gideon finished his bourbon and poured himself another glass. "We put up a fight. We do what we believe is right, and we hope for the best."

34

THE CRIMSON PLAINS

ULESDAY, 12TH OF WINEWEN, 1162.111

Carter felt the cold before he felt anything else. Not a chill or a breeze, but an aching freeze that caused his whole body to shiver. With each twinge, small hard things bit into his sides. He suspected they were wrents, but the only way to know for sure was to sit up.

"Hey sunshine." Alex sat on a stone eating something he couldn't identify. It sounded wet, but the sky was so dark that he had trouble making it out.

"We made it," Carter said.

The last bit of dusk, hovered over the mountains in the distance while the stars above shone brightly. Seeing them for the first time in weeks brought a sense of comfort that Carter hadn't known he had missed.

"We made it." Doug also sat on a rock, a different rock than Alex. Why were there so many rocks, and why was he on the ground shivering? "Where are we, and why is it so blasted cold?"

"Urmon is somewhere that way." Alex pointed to the mountain range. "We are on the Crimson Plains. It's always cold here."

"How is that possible?" He knew the Grekers had kept them drugged and then there was the time on the raft, but could that account for their being so far from Compitum? After he fainted, he didn't know what had happened. There was a chance he had been out for an extended time.

"It just is." Alex finished what she was eating. She reached into a bag and tossed something apple-sized to Carter. It was long and gave way to squeezing.

He bit into it.

It was... he wasn't sure what it was. The waxiness of its skin coated his teeth while the tangy juices ran down his scratchy throat. The pulp inside was savory with a hint of sage. His stomach churned not out of protest, but in demand. He was starving. "Can I have another and why is it cold? Start a fire or we will freeze to death."

"Find us something that will burn, and we will burn it," Doug said.

Carter couldn't see a dang thing past the rings of stone, so he traced kölprufta.

Nothing happened.

He had drawn kölprufta thousands of times. He could do it in the dark and maybe in his sleep. He couldn't have messed up, could he?

He traced the agyl again, going more slowly and paying attention to each stroke. Again, nothing happened when he finished. Dropping his hands so as not to attract Doug's and Alex's attention, he proceeded to draw all eighteen of the main agyls, and not a one sprung to life.

Practically anyone could draw an agyl, whether they knew higher magic or not. All it took was time and determination. So why couldn't he draw one now?

"Prösenta," he said in a whisper so the others couldn't hear.

There was no buildup of energy within himself. There was no shaping the air to his will. There was only silence. His magic was gone.

"What did you say?" Doug asked. "I couldn't make it out."

"Just cursing," Carter said. He couldn't let the others know. Not now at least. Not until he figured out what was going on. "There's nothing out there to burn is there?"

"Nope," Alex said. "Just us, the stars, and too many rocks."

Owen had warned him over and over again about burning out. That wielding too much power could cut off a magician's connection to magic. Was his connection cut? He could feel it. He could sense the way of things. It taunted him. Maybe he needed more time to rest. More time to heal? "What time is it? I'm feeling wiped already."

"Less than two hours after sunset," Alex said. "We had to stop 'cause twinkle toes here has trouble walking in the dark."

"You try carrying a limp kid while walking in the dark through an endless field of rocks. Too much of a chance I'd drop him and do more damage."

"I'm just giving you a hard time," Alex said.

"Well don't." Doug grumbled.

Alex laughed.

"I'm going to lie down for a bit," Carter said.

"We got no beds, blankets, or anything," Doug said. "Tuck as close to the rocks as you can and whichever of us isn't on watch will put their back to yours."

Carter moved between the rocks that Doug and Alex sat on and lay down, bringing his knees to his chest.

Carter woke well before morning and offered to take the final watch to allow Doug to get some extra sleep. Doug wasn't willing at first, but upon reminding the former dragon how he had carried Carter for what turned out to be four days, he agreed to nap.

Once he was sure that Alex and Doug were fast asleep, Carter crept away from the camp. Not too far. He didn't want to get lost, but far enough so that he could speak without being heard. There he went through the training that Owen had taught him so long ago. He meditated, lowering his heart rate and slowing his breathing, and he focused on the power inside of himself.

Magic had always been easy for him. He could access it with a thought. It consisted of gathering his will, shaping it with words and intent, and then releasing it. That's it. Yet now, no matter what he did, he couldn't gather it. It was there, but it felt like a wall or doorway had locked it away.

Carter retrieved the spellstone that the Sisters had given him. It was flat, like a sand dollar, and small enough to fit in his palm with his fingers folded down to cover it. Words had been carved into it. He didn't know what they meant, nor did he know the language. The Sisters made him memorize the pronunciation, so even now, he could clearly say the words in his head.

He needed his magic not because of ego or self worth, but because without it, without the ability to cast the spell burned into the stone, all of this would be meaningless. Without magic, he couldn't free the dragons, and they would be powerless to stop Medrayt.

"What are you doing?" Alex stood on a rock, waving. In the golden light of the rising sun, she looked beautiful. He had grown to like her smile, and he couldn't help but think of how disappointed she would be when she learned he was powerless.

"I'm hungry." Carter slid the spellstone back into his travel pouch, hoping Alex hadn't noticed he had been looking at it. "I was looking for food."

"You won't find any. This place is a wasteland."

"You sure? I thought I saw a mouse or–"

"Trust me."

He stood and made his way back to the camp. The sun was barely over the horizon, but its light struck the bleached white plains around them. For as far as he could see, there was nothing but white earth speckled with rocks. "I know you said we were on the Crimson plains, but all I see is white. You sure you know where we are?"

"Don't," Doug said with a grumble in his voice. His eyes were puffy with big bags. "You know how much history she knows about this place? It's all she's talked about for days."

"I'm surprised Owen didn't cover it." Alex cocked her head sideways. "You messing with me?"

"No," Carter said, trying to sound sincere. "Owen is not a fan of human history. Says all it comes down to a list of people doing bad things. It's why I've spent so much time studying pre-Scourge history."

"You are in for a treat." Alex hopped off a rock and picked up her bags. "Today I'm going to tell you all about the fall of Lockhaven."

"Oh I know about Lockhaven," Carter said. "They used to be the kingdom north of Arwyn."

"Everything above the Nox River was part of Lockhaven till about five hundred years ago," Alex said. "See, back then–"

"Not again," Doug said. "You told it once. I listened. I know being human means being polite and considerate, but I can't handle it."

"Was the story that boring?" Carter asked.

"It was about humans who fought other humans, all of which are dead and don't matter. There was a big battle, and it was so nasty that it soured the earth and stained the ground." Doug lowered his voice and then cranked it up again in a dramatic way. "Hence the name, 'Crimson Plains.'"

"You prat!" Alex said. "You spoiled the ending."

"It was clear within the first ten minutes of you telling me about it. You really suck at telling stories." Doug grabbed his own gear and moved east, walking away from the mountains. "Let's go, day burning."

"If I'm so awful at telling stories, then let's see you do better." Alex hurried ahead to catch up with Doug. "If you don't like human history then awe us with something about dragon history or your own past."

"No," Doug said.

"She brings up a good point." Carter hopped over two rocks and took his place on Doug's other side so that he was sandwiched between the two of them. "Back in Agnar when you were in the arena–"

"Nope." Doug cut him off.

"Ohhh, I had forgotten about that." Alex clapped her hands. "You told Kane about a friend of yours, but we couldn't hear it all."

"I know we've been through a lot," Doug said. "I know that by Greker law you are my adopted wards, but I don't talk about the past, and I especially don't talk about her."

"Bellalyn," Alex said. "You say her name sometimes in your sleep. It's always sad or said in a panic. Who was she?"

"No."

"Let him have his secrets," Carter said. As much as he wanted to know about Bellalyn, for the moment he thought it was best if each of them were allowed to have their own secrets.

Doug sped up his pace, taking longer faster strides, making it impossible for them to catch up without running.

They walked in silence for the rest of the morning. At noon, they took a break, divvying up more of the weird Greker food, and in the afternoon, they walked some more.

The silence drove Carter mad because, without the distraction, he couldn't help but think of his own problems. Every fifteen minutes or so, he would breathe deeply, trying to gather his will to make an agyl, but every time he failed to connect.

When they made camp for the night, this time in an alcove

between two boulders, he did his best not to focus on himself but thought about Doug instead.

He had seen Doug's cave. It was modest, nothing fancy, or nothing like he'd expect a hermit's home to look like. It was clean and practical, but nothing too personal about it. He had no idea how long Doug had lived there, but it must have been awhile.

"Why don't you want to tell us about what happened with Bellalyn?" Carter asked. "You seem so sad and so lonely."

"I'm fine," Doug said. "In fact I can't wait to be a dragon again so I can be on my own and not pestered by a bunch of teenagers."

"I think you blame yourself," Alex said. "I know what it's like to feel responsible for people. I think you feel responsible for what happened to your friend."

"Of course I do!" Doug punched the sandy earth. "She was captured. We were somewhere we weren't allowed to be, and when I went for help, the other dragons refused to go save her. For years, I've asked myself, what if I had stood up to her so we never went there in the first place? What if I had been a little bit stronger, a little bit smarter? Maybe I could have taken the monster. There were a million things I could've done differently, and maybe one of them would have resulted in Bellalyn staying alive."

"You can play the 'what if' game for hours." Alex didn't use a soft voice, nor did it sound like she was trying to comfort Doug. "Shoot, you've played it for years, and look where it's gotten you, nowhere. Your friend died. That's sad, but there is nothing you can do about it now. You weren't the one who killed her. You tried to save her."

"But I didn't try hard enough," Doug said.

"Sometimes our best isn't enough, and there is nothing we can do about it." Alex rested a hand on Doug's knee. "You need to learn to forgive yourself. If not, your life will continue to be as empty and cold as it has been for all the years you've spent alone."

"I like being alone." Doug brushed away Alex's hand.

"I don't believe you–"

A howl ripped through the air, and all three of them turned to where it had come from. It wasn't deep like a dragon's roar, but still it was loud enough that Carter could feel it in his chest. On instinct, he went to gather his will, and, of course, nothing happened.

"Get low." Doug pointed at Carter while with his other hand he pulled Alex flat against the ground. "Don't move. Don't speak."

"What is it?" Carter whispered.

"What do you not understand about 'don't speak'?" Doug plopped his palm onto his forehead and drug it across his face. "I swear you are broken in the head."

A second howl shot through the air. This one was followed by a spire of flames. The light of the fire reflected off the white ground, illuminating the whole area. Before them stood a beast, as large as a dragon. It was feline with a violet coat of short fur. Along its back were yellow stripes, and protruding from its spine were quills.

The beast licked the charred ground. After a few minutes, it stretched and trundled fifteen parses to the north. It blew out another puff of fire and licked the ground again.

"It's a thylazine," Doug whispered.

Carter hadn't ever heard of one before. Of course, he hadn't known what a wrent was either, so sure, there were other creatures out here that wanted to kill and eat them. Maybe this one liked to drug its victims and then slurp out their brains. Or maybe it had no teeth and, instead of chewing, swallowed its food whole so it could slowly digest it in a super high concentrated stomach acid. The potential ways they could be killed were nearly infinite, and without his magic, there was nothing he could do to stop it.

"It's big, but I bet Carter could blast it," Alex said. "Hit it hard with a huge gust and send it flying. Then we run in the opposite direction."

"I don't think I can," Carter said. "I'm still running low from the wrents and fire."

Alex reached down for her knife. "Then we will have to fight it."

"We will do no such thing," Doug said. "Thylazine are harmless, and I think it's moving away from us."

The thylazine howled and unleashed another blast of fire, scorching the earth.

"Harmless?" Alex gave him a sideways glance.

"Mostly harmless," Doug said.

The thylazine licked the burned ground.

"See," Doug said. "If we don't provoke it, it should leave us alone."

A short flame, like a burp, slipped from the thylazine's mouth.

"It's like dragon fire," Carter said.

Doug rolled his eyes. "It's nothing like dragon fire."

"Carter's right," Alex said. "I've seen dragon fire, and that looks exactly like it."

"Thylazines eat weird things," Doug said. "The flames you see, well at least from what I've seen, they can partially control it, but they make the fire in their bellies or some other organ inside them."

"How is that different from dragons breathing fire?" Carter asked.

"Dragons don't breathe fire." Doug said. "The fire isn't from inside a dragon. It's magic."

"Dragons can do magic?" Carter hadn't considered that. Humans obviously could. He saw Grekers do something during the wedding, though that had been with the aid of the Erediän artifact.

"Why not?" Doug said. "Dragons can speak. Why wouldn't they be able to do magic."

"Can you do magic?" Carter asked.

"Me?" Doug laughed. "No, I left when I was a fledgling. I hadn't been taught. Besides, not all of our kind has a knack for it anyway."

"But how does it work?" Was it different from high magic? Maybe it was more like old magic. There were so many possibilities in how it could work, and the slightest bit of information could help Carter get his own powers back. "Is it different from my magic?"

"From what I know, a dragon can speak a bit of magic. It's all words, but they don't sound like words. More like clicks and noises. Sounds I don't think a human mouth could make, and when done right, fire appears in the place where the words were spoken."

"That's different." It could be like agyls, where any dragon had the knack to breathe fire. Whether they had an affinity to true magic or not. That would make sense, which meant Doug could learn to do it.

"The thylazine is a good sign," Doug said.

"Why?" Alex asked.

"Their diet is rocks and things high in minerals." Doug scooped a bit of sand and let it run through his fingers. "The Plains aren't diverse. It would never wander into the middle of the plains. That means we are at the edge of the plains."

They watched in silence as the thylazine grazed. It stayed for an hour and then dashed away to the north. They made camp, which Carter now knew meant they picked a random spot to sleep. Shifts went smoothly, and when it was his turn, he spent the whole time practicing all eighteen wards. Down the line, he did them the way he knew the town kids back in Hal memorized the names of the kingdoms. It did no good, though, and no matter how hard he focused, he couldn't connect with his power.

"I know we are going west, and Kale is west, but how is it you both know where it is?" Carter asked. By late morning, the white plains had turned to brown shrubs and then eventually green grass.

There were no rolling hills or mountains in the distance, only a flat land that stretched as far as he could see. It was a bit unnerving, not as bad as being lost underground, but that sense of not knowing where he was ate at him.

"We don't have a clue," Doug said.

"What?" Carter stopped in his tracks. "You mean, we are walking, and neither of you have any idea where we are going?"

"We have an idea." Alex pointed in front of them. "That's west. Kale is that way-ish."

"Didn't they teach you anything in princess school?" Carter asked. "We could be using the stars at night or timing the movement of the sun instead of blindly walking."

"I learned lots of things from all my tutors." Alex put one hand on the hilt of her sword and the other on her waist. "Want me to show you how to disable an unarmed man in a single hit? You can even try to stop me."

"I'm good." Carter stepped back, making it as clear as possible that he didn't want to see a demonstration.

"If you have a problem with where we are going then you take charge." Doug stretched and lay down. He let out a yawn and closed his eyes. "Which way do you want to go? Wake me once you have decided."

Carter looked back toward the Plains. The once-tall mountains were merely squiggles on the horizon, barely notable. With the nice weather and lack of incline, they were probably making eight to ten leagues a day. He wasn't sure how far the distance was between the Anber Mountains and East Reach Sea, but it couldn't be that much farther than it was from Hal to Compitum. Which meant they had, at worst, five more days of walking. They had to be close to the sea, and that would explain the flat land. Though they had been moving dead west. Chances are Kale was more southwest. "Where exactly is Kale?"

Alex snapped her fingers and pointed at him. "Therein lies the real problem."

"You don't know." Carter looked from Alex to Doug. "Neither of you?"

"No," Alex said. "Do you?"

Carter looked south-ish. "No, I don't."

"We were supposed to get a ship," Alex said. "We were supposed to sail there with people who knew how to get there. At this point we are estimating."

"It's gotta be more to the southwest," Carter said.

"I agree." Alex spun to match his gaze across the plains. "But let's say we hit the sea, how are we going to get to Kale?"

"We'll need a ship," Carter said.

Alex touched the side of her nose. "That's why we are going due west. The whole coast between the Caerkaldor Islands and Yemto is lined with small fishing villages. As long as we don't end up too far south, we will be able to find a place to get a ship."

"Alright," Carter said. "Makes sense."

"It's a good thing they taught sense at mage-school? Medic-school? I'm not sure which thing I should make fun of you for." Alex tapped Doug's side with her foot. "Come on big guy, it's time to get walking again."

"I hate walking." Doug let out a low groan. "Walking is the least efficient way to get anywhere, and all it does is make me more tired and more hungry, not to mention that the three of us stink. I need to bathe."

"The closer we get to the coast, the more streams and rivers we should run into," Alex said. "I'll make you a deal. You up your pace, and not only will I agree to bathe, but I'll scrub down Carter while you hold him. As a princess, it is my duty to do charity work."

"I'm not that dirty." Carter leaned down and sniffed his shirt. At one point, it had been a cream color, but now it had not only brown smudges, but dark bits where ash from the under city had gotten on him. He smelled smoky, like a campfire. It was a nice smell that brought back memories of sleeping in the woods with Dale and Allison.

What would happen to him if his magic didn't come back. Dale was destined to take over his family business, and Allison was already skilled in running her family's farm. By that train of thought, he guessed he would finish his medical training with Owen and be the town healer. It wasn't glamorous, but at least he could still help people.

"Let's go, stinky." Doug patted Carter on the back and pushed him forward.

"You smell too!" Carter sniffed, catching a not-quite-citrus scent. "What is that?"

"I've been smearing the juices from those weird fruits under my armpits."

"Why?" Carter asked.

"It helps neutralize the funk," Doug said.

Carter disagreed. To him it smelled way worse.

Doug skirted ahead and both Carter and Alex fell in behind him. They walked side by side, and Carter watched the way Alex took her steps. She moved like a hunter with a quiet grace, her hand always near her sword. He had seen time and time again that she could handle herself, but for the first time, he thought about what it must mean to be a princess. Being a princess was her defining trait. A month ago, he thought that meant snobbery and royalty stuff, but he knew her well enough now to know that it had more to do with a weight on her shoulders. Being a princess to her meant responsibility, and if that title was taken away from her, she wouldn't change. She would still care as much about her people, and she had the skills and knowledge to be anything she wanted.

Who was he without his magic?

35

PROMISE OF REVENGE

ORNSDAY, 6TH OF WINEWEN, 1162.111

Cooke heard Medrayt talking, but when she walked into the temple chamber, he was seated alone on the stone dais. "Only you freaks can see the future," he said. "I only meant, I expected one last attempt where you tell me the error of my ways."

It had to be the Sisters Three. They had done this before. Visited and not allowed themselves to be seen by her.

"Then that is your mistake," he said. "I do what I feel I must. Now begone."

Medrayt slouched forward, releasing a long sigh. Whatever they had been doing, they must have left.

"The Sisters?" Cooke sat down beside Medrayt.

He nodded. The simple act made him sway left and right as if dizzy.

"What did they want?" Cooke guessed they wanted him to cease his plans of attack, but knowing what she did of them, it could be something completely random, like to eat more meat.

"They want me to not attack Elene."

"But you are doing this because of what they showed you!"

"And they said that was an error on their part," he said. "They miscalculated, and paths diverged in ways they didn't intend."

"What do we do?" Cooke laid her hand on his knee. Knobby bones nearly poked through his skin.

Medrayt looked at her with bloodshot eyes. The whites were so red that she had trouble making out the veins. His cheeks were sunken. "We need a united front."

"Is there a chance that they are right and that attacking is a mistake?" she asked.

"They do not see the future, only possibilities," he said. "They misjudged the attempt on my life. They could be doing the same here. Or this is a game. It might be that they want me to attack and are goading me into it by telling me not to do so. They have a skewed perception, and we have no way of knowing their true intentions."

"There are the Red Hounds," Cooke said. "I have over three hundred active members across Majerä. We could send them instead."

"Against an army of thousands in a fortress that has never fallen?"

"A single Red Hound is worth ten ordinary soldiers."

"I know, but let's hold them back for now. Gather them. Prepare them, but we will save them for the final fight." Medrayt put his weight on her, leaning hard into her shoulder. "If we want humanity to survive, I need to follow through with the dragons."

"Can you handle it?" Cooke asked before she had time to process the words, and she regretted them the moment they passed her lips. Angering or offending Medrayt was not productive.

He met her eyes. The wrinkles around them were deep, and a milkiness clouded his pupils. He took in a deep breath and then dropped his gaze. "I don't know if I can, but I have to try. There is no one else who can do this for me."

Cooke didn't like that. She didn't want to fly south. She wanted to care for him, now, when he would be pushing his skills to their max and would need her the most. The toll the magic was taking on him was brutal. She wished she could have a do-over, and instead of allowing Medrayt to sacrifice himself to take over the dragons, she would do it. Of course, she might not have been strong enough, but it would have been worth trying. Now she had no choice. She had to go and be his voice, his public face. "How long will it take to reach Elene?"

"A bit longer than we planned," he said. "I will send you back to Stobnyk Kol to make preparations and then to stall the shoel. Neither will be much out of your way."

"You promise to care for yourself while I am gone?" She narrowed her eyes at him.

"I will."

She ran a hand across his cheek. He was young enough to be her grandson, and because of the magic, he now looked older than she did. It tore at her heart. "Please do. We all need you."

She stood, not willing to say any more than what was already spoken.

Before leaving the temple, she double-checked the dried supplies and jugs of water. There were several months' worth. As long as he took the time to care for himself, he should survive.

When Cooke exited the temple, the dragons stirred from their hibernation state. They shook off the sleep, and their bones cracked and popped, some moving for the first time in over a year.

Cooke made her way to the black and silver female that regularly carried her. It was stocked with a decent saddle as well as supplies. Every dragon she passed sat on its haunches with its head raised to the sky, awaiting orders.

"I'm ready," Cooke said after securing her harness on the dragon's back. Medrayt must have heard, because a moment later, her dragon and all the other dragons moved in unison, stretching their wings and leaping into the air.

Like clockwork toys timed perfectly, the dragons moved as one, circling and rising higher above Dras. The sound of their wings and the rushing wind was deafening.

From the compartment on her side saddle, Cooke withdrew a scarf. She wrapped it tightly around her face and ears, protecting herself not only from the noise, but also the cold.

Medrayt kept back a group of twenty-five adult dragons. They were his protection, and she had insisted. The rest of the dragons, including the adolescents were in the air heading to war.

~

Cooke debated whether it was right to allow four hundred dragons to descend upon Stobnyk Kol. The snowy foothills around the villa had enough space, but they did overlook Demral, the largest harbor in Caerkaldor.

She could keep her students in line, but was not confident that a swarm of dragons wouldn't cause sheer panic in the port city. Maybe that's what they needed, a wake-up call and warning of what was to come.

The downside of the dragons not landing near the villa was that Cooke would have to trek through the snow, and that seemed like an awful lot of work to spare the emotions of the locals.

"Take them down here." Cooke leaned in close to her dragon's neck, knowing Medrayt could hear her through the beast's ears.

Cooke's dragon landed outside Stobnyk Kol's walls, and all the others followed suit. Their array of colors and scales reflected off the fresh white snow.

"Headmaster!" Devina's voice rang across the snowfield before Cooke managed to get her feet on the ground.

"What is it this time, girl?" Cooke slid off her saddle and down the side of the dragon's neck. She sunk knee-deep in the snow.

"The dragons!" Devina said with panic in her voice.

"There are dragons?"

"Headmaster!"

Cooke chuckled and looked back to assess the dragons. Each had settled down, like a dog in front of a fire, as if to take a nap.

"The dragons won't harm anyone," Cooke said. "But the city folk won't like it. Have a squad of fourth years set up on Demral's outskirts in case anyone feels inspired to do something stupid."

"I'll send word right away," Devina said. "Anything else?"

"Recall the Red Hounds. All of them."

"Are you sure?"

"It's time."

"Letters, messages, travel..." Devina wiggled her fingers as if doing complex math. "They can all be back within five months."

"Do it."

Devina bowed and turned to head back into the villa.

"Devina!" Cooke didn't try to hide her annoyance.

"Yes?" Devina paused and looked back with with pang of irritation, as if the simple act of waiting caused her physical pain.

"Help me inside," Cooke said.

"Of course! I'm sorry for not thinking." Devina bent her arm in a hook shape and offered it to Cooke.

"Thank you." Cooke took Devina's arm. "Although unlikely, I may not return from Elene."

"Don't say that!"

"I expect to. I will not be in the heat of battle. That is not the service I am to supply, but things can happen in war, and you need to be prepared."

"I don't like to think of such things." Devina held her lips together tightly and frowned.

"We have that in common."

They hit a deeper patch of snow, the bank that students had created when clearing the road to Stobnyk Kol. Devina walked backward and, with both hands, lifted Cooke over the snow and set her down on the icy stone road.

"I prefer to think that I will live forever," Cooke said. "But that may not happen, and if it doesn't, this school and you are my legacy."

"The students would not listen to me if something happened to you."

"That's not true. You are of House Cooke as much as I am." Cooke pointed to the gates leading into the villa. "This home is as much yours as it is mine. You are the last heir to the family. It belongs to you."

"But–"

"No buts. When your father died, I did my best to raise you, and if anyone can handle this school it's you."

"Yes, Headmaster."

"About that," Cooke said. "It's clear you run things here day to day. I think it's time that you keep the title."

"Oh no, I couldn't, I mean–"

"You have earned it."

"But there..." Devina did the thing where she crossed her eyes so it appeared that her brain had broken. "What would I call you?"

"How about Natalia or Aunt Natalia?"

"I think I can do that."

"Good." Cooke patted Devina's elbow and let go. "Now go. I know there is a list of fifty things you want to get done."

"It's only twenty-three..." Devina bit her bottom lip. "You were joking, weren't you?"

"Go." Cooke laughed. "I have my own things to arrange before I must head off again."

"Of course, yes head–" Devina took a deep breath. "Yes, Aunt Natalia."

In a flash, Devina was gone, and Cooke hobbled toward the infirmary. There was a slight chance she could end up facing Carter or Owen in Elene. She couldn't do that unprepared.

Both magicians had her beat in raw power, but neither could handle her mastery of alteration magic. If she had possessed the proper supplies when meeting Carter in the woods, he would have left the altercation powerless or more deformed and broken than Mogul.

Cooke did not have faith in The Silver Lady, nor did she think such things mattered, but she had left the wooden infirmary intact because of what lay beneath it. A maze of crypts and tunnels that had once been used for rituals and storing offerings.

The secret labyrinth was where Cooke had her agyltorium and workshop. It was where she created her wind burs and other devices. Only a trusted few knew how to reach it, and none knew all its secrets.

From her office in the infirmary, Cooke traced fögzrupta onto the fat timbers that formed the floor. The wood in a four head radius blurred. She drew prösprufta, and the wood turned intangible, revealing a staircase.

Cooke moved down the stairs, taking her time and moving slow, for the last thing she needed was to fall and break a hip. At the bottom, she reached up and pulled on the threads forming the agyls she had drawn. They flashed, and the wooden floor returned to its usual state, sealing her in.

From the time she could walk, the tunnels had been her playground. In total darkness, she was able to find her way, but fools do foolish things, and she was no fool. She traced Kölprufta and used its light to finish climbing down the stairs.

To her surprise, Mogul was at the bottom waiting for her.

"I take it that there is a reason you are intruding upon my personal space?" Cooke demanded.

"Where is it?" Mogul's lips were cracked, and an unusual raspiness hung in his voice.

"I've spent half a day on the back of a dragon freezing my ass off." Cooke jiggled a leather cord strung along hallway's wall. It stirred, bringing to life a series of agyl lamps. "You need to be a bit more direct. I'm a tad worn out."

"The clear concoction. The one you used on me and on Bash."

He moved in close, so close that she could smell the zewik juice on his breath. "Where is it?"

That's what he was after. A quick fix for his missing arm, even though she had told him there was no such thing.

There were three ways into the tunnels. Two required magic. That meant Mogul had entered through the pantry in the main house. How long had he been down here? Since she had first left for Gwen?

"The mixture you refer to is not stable," Cooke said. "I do not keep it around. Even if I did, I would not allow you to take it again. It would kill you or turn you into something less than human."

"I don't care." Mogul swung his one fist at her.

Cooke didn't flinch.

At the last second, Mogul diverted the blow and struck the hallway wall.

"I don't want to live," he said in a low tone.

She couldn't leave him here like this. He would end up hurting himself or one of the students. Did she dare bring him on the attack to Elene? At least there he would have a place to direct his anger. Maybe that was the answer. There would be no fixing him. He was broken, but maybe she could at least use him one last time.

"Dragons have been flying reconnaissance over Elene," she said. "We wanted to keep watch to know what kind of war machines they might use to defend against our attack."

"I do not care about Elene and your meaningless plans–"

"Be mad. Grieve for your loss. There is nothing wrong with that." Cooke bent so that her nose was level with his. "Do not belittle me or what the Red Hounds stand for. Do not throw away the thing your life has been dedicated to. Sure, you may not have an arm, but the one thing you will never lose is your family here."

Mogul pushed against Cooke's chest as if to move her aside, but she knocked his hand away and slapped him across the face. Grabbing his jaw, she squished in his cheeks and jerked his face to hers so that he couldn't look away.

"Gideon, the one who took your arm, is leading the defenses at Elene." Cooke paused long enough for the words to sink in. "If you want to be angry, if you want to direct that anger in a meaningful place, direct it at him."

"I thought the Red Hounds were to stay put, that this was only you and the dragons?"

"It is," she said. "But I can always make an exception."

He straightened his posture. "I want to go."

"Why should I let you?"

"I am a Red Hound."

"Are you?" She stuck her chin up, looking away from him. "This behavior of yours does not reflect that."

"I'm sorry." Mogul pounded his chest. "Please let me come."

"Then I ask again," Cooke said, "why should I let you?"

"Because if you allow me to, I swear by The Devourer that I will kill Gideon."

36

TAVERN TALK

ORNSDAY, 21ST OF WINEWEN, 1162.111

Alex wanted warm food. Maybe a nice bisque or hot tea. It didn't have to be fancy. Though with every step, the streets of Yemto mocked her because, no matter which way they turned, she caught the smell of leek stew. She did not want to see or smell leeks ever again in her life.

It had been late at night when they arrived at the city gates, and the only places open were the kind of unsavory places where one shouldn't go. She had never been to Yemto, but it was one of the more important cities in Arwyn and the largest port on the east coast.

"I don't like this," Doug said. He had a foul look on his face.

"You don't like anything." Carter jabbed him in the ribs.

"I don't like people, 'specially people who stink." Doug held the back of his hand to his nose to block the smell. "It's fishy and sweaty mixed with the salty sea. It's disgusting."

"The harbor isn't far." Alex wasn't sure how far the harbor was, but she knew it couldn't be that far. "Suck it up."

Instead of cobblestone streets, like Compitum had, or dirt streets, like she encountered in Hal, Yemto's roads were littered with shells from oysters, clams, and drocs. It meant that every step they took involved a crunching or grinding, like walking on gravel, which gave the city a dingier vibe.

"You sure we can't just go to the big house?" Carter looked down the block, and Alex followed his gaze. In the distance was a small hill, and on it was a fort with a manor house at its crest. "You can do the princess thing, and they will give us a ship."

"Duke Kelsworth runs Yemto," Alex said.

Carter shrugged.

"I know you don't get politics," she said. "Especially the subtle nature of them, but I can't ask Kelsworth for help."

"You are a princess, can't you order him?" Carter asked.

"Technically yes," Alex said, "but it doesn't work like that."

Carter poked his nose repeatedly and squinted at her. "And if you can't ask for help when your kingdom is about to go to war, I don't know when you could. At that point what's the point of being princess?"

"Trust me," she said. "My plan is faster."

"I think you have a problem with asking for help," Carter said.

She shook her head, brushing off the comment, and continued past a pub. The buildings gradually changed from stone to wood as they reached the poorer section of the city, and by the time they got to the harbor, everything was made of wood. If it weren't for the near-constant rain and high humidity of the region, it surely would have been a fire hazard.

Jetties and a seawall formed the harbor in a perfect circle. The only egress was on its far side between two lighthouses. Each penetrated the fog with a series of glowing agyls that legend says could be seen from more than twenty leagues away. The lighthouses were for more than navigation. They also housed archers armed with long bows that could deal with any invading or pirate ships.

"I still think if we want a ship we need to find a pub or inn and locate a captain there." Carter walked backward eyeing the unnatural number of drinking establishments along the harbor. "They seem to like alcohol around here."

"You want a captain who has been drinking since Ulesday to get us out of here?" Alex said.

"What's today?" Carter asked.

"Ornsday."

"Yeah, ok, but there has to be a more sensible way to go about this."

"Look at all these boats. We will easily find someone who will ferry us to Kale."

"Are they boats or ships?" Carter tilted his head to the side.

"I don't know the difference," Alex said.

Carter scratched his chin. "I think there is a difference."

"It doesn't matter does it?" Doug made a low grumbling sound, like a baby roar. The closer they got to Kale the crankier he got.

Alex took the lead, walking along the docks. She skipped the larger vessels. Most were for transporting goods and the rest were meant for a large group of passengers.

A sloop caught Alex's eye. Its narrowness meant it was built for speed, and it looked like the crew was on board, which meant setting off shouldn't be too hard.

A man stood near the gangway, drinking from a brown jug. His clothing was dirty, but instead of the common linen of the region, he wore dyed cotton, a sign that his boat was profitable.

"Excuse me," she said. "Is your captain about?"

"About what?" He ran the back of his hand across his lips and wiped it against his maroon shirt.

"May I speak with him?" Alex asked.

The man eyed her, stopping for too long at her chest. He cocked his head over his shoulder, looking back toward the ship. "Fulton! A woman is here requesting if you are about."

Three other sailors popped their heads above the deck, staring at Alex and her companions.

"Get back to work you lazy crots," a man said. He had curly blonde hair and a dark face covered in sunspots. He stopped at the top of the gangway, keeping his distance. "What do you want?"

"My friends,"–Alex spun, acknowledging Doug and Carter–"and I are looking to procure transportation."

"And my mates and I are looking to be dukes," he said. "Why should I care?"

Alex patted her pouch, making sure to jingle the coins inside. "We need passage to Kale."

"No one goes to Kale." The captain turned his back to them.

"Wait! I can pay." Alex pulled her purse from her belt and untied it. She didn't have many coins on her. Not after helping as many travelers as she could when making her way to Hal. She did have one thing, though, a ring given to her by her father for her sixteenth birthday. The Eos crest was stamped on a sapphire embedded in a silver band. "This should cover it."

The captain limped down the gangway and took the ring. His eyes narrowed and then widened before he handed it back to her. "Begone. I will not deal with thieves."

"We aren't thieves." Alex raised her voice.

"No way a ragamuffin like you came across this without it being in an unsavory way." The captain stomped his good foot on the gangway. "This is Yemto. Maybe if we were in Breen, but I'll not risk the law here. Go."

Before Alex could argue further, the captain turned and re-boarded the ship.

"Great plan," Carter said.

"You're not helping," Alex said.

"Can we go to the duke and ask for a ship now?" Carter looked at her with big eyes. Tired eyes. It had been a long day for them all. "Please?"

Alex had been betting on the ring being perfect payment. She hadn't thought anyone would accuse her of stealing it. Yemto's books still fell under Lockhaven's old system. Here, theft was worse than murder.

"A moment, miss?" The man with the jug leaned in close so no one else could hear. "If you are looking for a ride. Try Tamryn at the Bearded Stag. Please make sure to say that Kendall sent you."

The Bearded Stag sat northwest on the fringe of the harbor. It was no different from any of the other pubs they passed. Once inside, Alex recognized the establishment for what it was, a run-down hole-in-the-wall. Trash and spilled drinks littered the floor. Dim lamps were spread too sparsely throughout the room, and the patrons didn't care enough to look away from their drinks to see who had entered.

"No," Doug said. "This place smells like ogre piss. I'm going back outside."

Alex didn't know if Doug literally meant ogre piss or if it was an odd dragon saying.

"We'll call if we need you," Carter said.

"I'll be listening." Doug waved a hand in front of his nose and slipped back through the pub's entrance.

Alex asked the bar keep if he knew who Tamryn was. He shrugged, but a crotchety guy who smelled like sour whisky grunted and pointed to a corner booth. In it sat a woman with fiery hair, though silver streaks wound through it. Her skin was dark, but less wrinkled than many of the men in the room.

"Tamryn?" Alex asked as she approached the woman.

The woman cleared a stein, and then peered into it as if looking for more. She held it up as if to make a toast. "I may be, but can't know for sure till I get some more of this."

Alex waited for the woman to get up, but she didn't budge.

"You going to fill it or what?" The woman pushed the glass toward Alex.

Understanding, Alex took the mug to get it refilled at the bar.

The woman cupped her hands around her mouth. "Caerkaldor ale. The good stuff."

Alex dug out two copper rounds from her purse and placed them on the oak bar.

The bartender held up three gnarled fingers. Alex added another copper and took the mug. She carried it carried it back to the woman, who took it, handling the mug like she would a baby. In one fell swoop, she chugged the entire thing.

"You Tamryn or not?" Alex said, her annoyance clear in her voice.

The woman smiled at Alex and slid the stein across the table.

Alex slid it back, and the woman broke into a cackling laugh. Then she scooted over to make room in the round booth. "Sit. We will talk."

Carter sat on the opposite side of the booth so that, when Alex sat, the woman was trapped between them.

"What is it you want with me?" Tamryn said. "Green John send you? You don't look like skinners, too young, but John does have a thing for the young ones."

Carter caught Alex's eyes, but she waved him off. "We have need of a vessel, and Kendall said you might be able to help."

"Kendall sent ya?" Tamryn's voice was a mix of accents. At times she spoke slow as if from Kelsam, and then there were certain words that were cut short, as if she was from Ralk. "Kendall's a decent gus. He owes me one or two. Nice to see he's finally giving me some of the please and thank-yous, if you know what I mean?"

Alex did not know what she meant. The woman was clearly

drunk out of her mind and was the last person to carry them to Kale.

"Never mind." Alex slid sideways as if to stand, but Tamryn reached out and put a hand on her shoulder.

"I ain't conventional. Never pretend to be. But I got a ship, and if you need going, I can get you there." Tamryn lifted her hand and leaned back. "For a price."

"How much to get to Kale?" Carter asked.

Tamryn lowered her mouth and narrowed her eyes. She leaned out, scanning the booths near them. "We don't say its name around here. Folk are superstitious about"–she paused as if thinking–"that place."

"Can you get us there or not?" Alex had seen enough. She didn't have time for this, and if the woman had a boat, then worse-case scenario she could get them in the right direction and pass out in a drunken stupor.

"I can." Tamryn smiled. "For a price."

"You said that." Carter leaned forward and mouthed, "I think she's drunk."

Alex shook her head. It had been a long day and was only getting longer. "We are in a hurry," Alex said. "Stop haggling and tell us what you'd want."

"How many?" Tamryn asked.

"Three of us," Carter said.

"That won't be cheap." Tamryn mimed rolling a coin between two fingers. "A risky place, multiple heads, and an expedited rush. I think..."

Alex pulled out her purse and laid the ring on the table. Tamryn put her nose close to it, as if smelling it, but Alex guessed the woman was attempting to focus her eyes.

"This reminds me of a story..." Tamryn leaned back, slouching in the booth.

Alex gritted her teeth. "We don't have time–"

"You will make time," Tamryn said. "This is one you'd want to hear..."

~

The Shifter and The Devourer met at a local tavern. Neither drank, for neither needed to drink.

"I want you gone from this place," The Shifter said.

"And what can you do to stop me?" The Devourer smiled, for he always wore a smile on his face.

"I can do things."

"So can I."

"But, should we face each other," The Shifter said. "It could damage the world in a way I do not wish to see happen."

"True, but I am willing to risk that."

"I'm not, so I propose a deal." The Shifter revealed a parchment. "We hold a wager. If I win, you leave this place, and if you win, I leave."

"What is the wager?"

"We prove who is the most powerful."

"I can eat souls," The Devourer said. "Can you?"

"I can be anything I want. Can you?"

They sat in silence, neither knowing how to prove who was the most powerful. Then finally The Shifter raised an arm and pointed across the pub. "See that man, his name is Pwarthen. He is a carpenter with a wife he loves and three children."

"His soul smells young. It would be nothing more than an appetizer."

"I do not want you to prove your power by eating him. I want you to convince him to leave his family."

The Devourer watched Pwarthen like a farmer sizing up a boar before sending it to the market. Then he nodded. "I can do that."

They debated the rules, but after a time, they agreed that The Devourer had one hour to convince Pwarthen to leave his family. If he succeeded, then he won the bet. If that hour ran out with no result then, The Shifter had a half hour to convince Pwarthen. If neither were able, then both would leave the world and never return to it.

The Devourer took his time, speaking with Pwarthen, getting to know his quarry. After fifteen minutes, he decided that Pwarthen was not particularly smart, nor was he very dumb. He lacked ambitions, and what made him happy was building furniture in his shop and returning home to his family at night.

The Devourer offered Pwarthen money, fame, magic, and women. Pwarthen turned them all down, one after the other. He had no interest in such things. He had all that he wanted in the world. He was content.

The Devourer offered more, saying he would get Pwarthen a new family, and he could get him magical tools that would make him the best carpenter in the world. He could get the wood from trees that didn't exist in this place, making his creations one of a kind and powerful.

Pwarthen turned down every offer, and when the hour ran out, The Devourer was frustrated, but knew there was nothing that The Shifter could do to win the bet.

The Shifter ignored Pwarthen and left the bar.

The Devourer laughed, counting the clock.

Ten minutes later, Pwarthen's wife entered with their three children. She held the youngest in her arms and dragged the other two behind her. Pwarthen smiled in delight, for seeing his family was enough to remind him of his happiness.

Pwarthen's wife handed her husband the baby and then stepped back. Her body bubbled and oozed. It warped and grew taller and more muscular. When done, she had become a horrible creature with bones on the outside of her body and a face that was all teeth and slime.

Pwarthen was so horrified he almost dropped the child and didn't notice that all three of his offspring were crying in fear.

"This is the real me," Pwarthen's wife said. "I thought I could live this lie, pretending to be something I'm not, but it's time you know the truth. I'm The Shifter, but I still love you and think we can still be together, raising our children."

The blood drained from Pwarthen's face, and he handed back his youngest child to The Shifter. He spoke no words, but ran from the pub. No one ever saw him in that town again.

"You cheated." The Devourer sounded angry, but he still wore a smile.

"I did no such thing," The Shifter said. "I did what we agreed. I proved that I was the most powerful by getting Pwarthen to abandon his family."

"We agreed to not harm or threaten his wife."

"I didn't. I am his wife. We have been married for more than four years."

"Then this was a ruse, a trap?"

"I am The Shifter."

"It doesn't matter. I will not leave this place, and you cannot make me."

The Devourer did not understand the full extent of The Shifter's power, for it had been many years since The Shifter had visited this world. To The Devourer's horror, he discovered that not only could The Shifter be anything it wanted, but there was power in The Shifter's words. When The Shifter made a deal, it was unbreakable.

Thus The Devourer was forced from Majerä and could never return.

"What does that have to do with my ring?" Alex asked.

"The moral is, don't make a deal unless you are the one with the secrets." Tamryn tapped the tabletop. "I recognized the crest on the ring."

"So?" Alex said.

"So, I want more." Tamryn mimed rolling a coin again.

"This ring is worth more money than you could make in a lifetime!" Alex made a fist, but released it. This wasn't an argument she would win with violence.

"The ring is stolen," Tamryn said. "I'd have to fence it as well as risk my own limbs. If you want me to take such a high risk, you'll have to pay me more."

"It's not stolen!" Alex let out a long groan.

"What else you got?" Tamryn asked.

Alex was not going to be outplayed by a drunk sailor. "How about this, you take it and be happy with it, or we will be the ones going to the guards. I'm sure the constable would love to hear about how you tried to sell us a stolen ring!"

"I did no such thing!" Tamryn slammed her palm on the table, drawing the eyes of the barkeep.

"And who are they going to believe?" Alex said. "You or me?"

Tamryn picked up her stein, giving it one final shake apparently to free the last few drops. Then she looked at Carter and back to Alex. "I knew I liked you. Let's do this."

37

PIRATES

ORNSDAY, 21ST OF WINEWEN, 1162.111

After exiting the Bearded Stag, Tamryn stopped dead in her tracks upon seeing Doug approach them. Her hands flittered to her waist where Alex was sure a weapon of some kind was hidden.

"He's with us," Alex said.

"You are a big guy." Tamryn poked Doug in the chest.

"You smell like a boar that rolled around in its own vomit," Doug said.

Tamryn clapped and laughed. "You don't know how close you are to being right."

Doug groaned and fell in line at the back of the group.

Tamryn led them through the harbor and to the pier where her ship was docked. They made their way past a bunch of fishing vessels and other rigs, but finally stopped in front of a boat with a single sail. It was small, smaller than the one they had approached earlier, and it hung low in the water with barely two parses from the deck and the creeping waves. Written on the side of the vessel was "Saundra."

"Don't dawdle, hop on board." Tamryn looked about the pier, untying the rope that kept the boat in place. "Big man, take the capstan. Girly, unhook the boom, and boyo man the wheel."

Alex, Carter, and Doug all climbed aboard.

Tamryn finished untying the boat from the pier and climbed the gangway. Once on deck, she stared at them. "Why aren't you doing what I ordered?"

"None of us know what those things are," Carter said.

The humor was gone from Tamryn's eyes. She pointed to a horizontal bar. "Capstan." She pointed to the horizontal shaft protruding from the mast. "Boom." She then pointed to the back of the boat. "Wheel."

They took their places. From Doug's grunting, Alex guessed that he had the hardest job, while Carter's was the easiest, steering the ship while the drift of the harbor pulled it away from the pier.

The rig was a mess of knots, ropes, and pulleys. Alex wasn't sure which she should untie. "What do I do here?"

Tamryn ran to the other side of the vessel, messing with the pulleys there. "Untie the boom so I can unfurl the sail. The second you do, drop to the deck because it will swing fast."

Alex found the ropes holding the boom in place and uncoiled them from the front of the deck. The moment she finished, Tamryn hit something, and the sail flopped out, snagging in the wind. The ship lurched forward, and if Alex hadn't already been sitting low, to stay beneath the swinging boom, she would have been knocked off her feet.

Tamryn tied off the rigging, locking the sail. "Good easterly winds tonight. We can probably make it to Kale before noon."

As they sailed for the center of the harbor, Alex heard shouting and looked back to the pier they had left. A big man in leather was waving his arms and stomping as if having a temper tantrum. Other people were running toward him, and he pointed at the *Saundra.*

There was a flash of tinder and a red firework shot straight into the air. It exploded leaving a lingering cloud of glitter. A heartbeat later, a second firework exploded, this one green.

Alex followed the trail of the second firework and realized it must have been fired from one of the lighthouses at the harbor's entrance. There was movement on the seawall, and she could see a group of archers silhouetted by the bright agyl towers.

"Tamryn." Alex said the woman's name slowly, drawing it out. "Is this your ship?"

"It is now," Tamryn said.

"We are not stealing a ship." Carter turned the wheel, as if to head back to the pier.

Tamryn pushed him out of the way and aimed the *Saundra's* bow for the gap between the two lighthouses. "No good now, boyo. This ship has sailed." She broke into laughter. "If they catch us, we will all lose more than our thumbs. They don't take kindly to pirating here."

"We aren't pirates!" Carter said.

"If you aren't pirates," Tamryn said, "then why did you help me steal a ship?"

"Carter is right." Alex used a stern tone, trying to assert her authority. "Turn us around."

"I'm not going to hang because you have a weep of a conscious." Tamryn cut the wheel so that the ship turned a few degrees, allowing the sails to get maximum wind.

"They won't hang us," Alex said. "I have connections with the Duke."

"Duke ain't here," Tamryn said. "He and a battalion of ships were called west to Elene."

That was a bit of news Alex wished she had known sooner. Using her authority without Duke Kelsworth around would have been easy. Not only could they have gotten a boat in a more legal way, but they probably could have gotten a more reliable captain and a much faster vessel. Though at the same time, without anyone to vouch for who she was, they might have run into the same trouble as they did in Compitum. If they turned around, what was to stop a mob of angry sailors or the local authorities from locking them up?

"Are we stealing the ship or not?" Doug asked. "If we aren't, then I'll throw her overboard, and you two steer the ship."

Tamryn dipped a hand into the front of her jacket and removed iron knuckles with jagged teeth. "Touch me, and you'll pay for it."

"She's right," Alex said. "It's too late now. Going back will only slow us down and might put us in more trouble."

"You sure?" Carter asked.

Alex nodded.

Looking over each of them, Tamryn lowered her hand. She then glanced back at Doug as if she still didn't trust him. "This is going to get a bit hairy. I had hoped we'd at least make it past the towers before word got out. Never thought Jetsam would notice. I janked his ship so quickly."

"Why did we steal Jetsam's boat?" Carter asked.

"Ship," Tamryn tapped the wheel. "She ain't got paddles. This is a ship."

"Ok, why did we steal this ship?" Carter said.

"Jetsam doesn't treat his wife right," Tamryn said.

"Like he's mean to her?" Carter asked.

"Like he beats her, which for a Garan ain't too uncommon. There have been plenty of times she gave him a beating too, but this last time, he walked in on us. He nearly beat her to death." Tamryn pulled open her shirt revealing a scar on her shoulder. "He thought he had killed me, and well, you can't blame a man for beating his wife's lover, that's natural, but what he did to her was wrong."

"He had to have seen you," Alex said. "What's to stop him from taking this out on her?"

"Saundra, such a lovely sounding name, ain't it?" Tamryn

smiled. "Saundra's brother was going to get her away from him. You met him earlier, Kendall."

And now it all clicked in place for Alex. They were messengers sent to let Tamryn know that Saundra was safe; and they were extra hands to help her steal the ship. It was smooth, and if Alex wasn't annoyed at being the one played, she would have thought it was impressive. "You realize that if we live through this, I'm voiding our payment. We never agreed to help you steal a ship."

"Fine by me," Tamryn said. "Course, nothing to stop me from taking you somewhere other than Kale. Lund should be nice this time of year."

"I can still throw you overboard," Doug said.

"And if you do, you'll have a few holes in you." Tamryn clenched her fist. "But now is not the time to haggle or argue. We have a bigger problem to deal with. We have to make it past the lighthouses."

They weren't halfway across the harbor yet, but they would soon be in arrow range.

"Carter," Alex said, "we will need you to shield us. A blanket of wind should do, enough to divert any arrows."

"I'm not sure I can," he said.

"It will be easy for you." Alex pointed to the top and bottom of the towers. "They will be firing from both the tops and bases, so you'll have to keep the wind barrier pretty close to us to make sure they can't shoot below it."

"That's not what I mean."

Alex noticed a hint of worry that stuck out in his voice, and she looked at him. His cheeks were flushed, and he looked down, not meeting her eyes. "I'm still recovering from the wrents incident."

"Recovering how?" Alex asked.

"I'm weak," he said. "I probably can't muster more than a breeze."

"Summon it, and we'll make do."

"Ok, by weak, I mean I might not be able to use magic at all."

"Why didn't you say something?" Alex groaned, mimicking the long, gritty ones that Doug commonly let loose when dealing with Carter.

"I hoped it would come back." Carter traced an agyl in the air, but when he finished, nothing happened.

That was a massive problem. A problem that Carter should have told them about the second he knew. To be fair, he had warned her that magicians could burn out their power.

It also wasn't Carter's fault. He'd had no choice. If he hadn't acted, they all would have died, killed by the wrents or the melting cavern. The bigger concern of course was, without his magic, how would they undo the spell controlling all the dragons? No, she couldn't worry about that now. She had to prioritize. The next thing they faced was a volley of arrows meant to kill them.

"Carter's magic is out," Alex said, "which we will deal with later. What else we got to stop arrows? Anything?"

"Who are you people?" Tamryn took a step back from the wheel.

"I'm Alexendra Eos, daughter of Edgar Eos. This is Carter, apprentice to Owen the Magician, and that's Doug. He's a dragon. Stuck as a human. It's a long story."

Tamryn opened her mouth to speak and let out a long, drawn-out burp. "How much did I drink back there? Did I try zewik? I've sworn never to touch the stuff. Please say I didn't."

"You didn't," Carter said. "We have important business in Kale. Life-or-death type stuff. We need you to take us there."

"You lot are either the best liars I've ever met, or you are telling me the truth." Tamryn seized the wheel. "And so you know, I've known many amazing liars."

"I could try catching the arrows," Doug said.

"Too fast, even with your abilities," Carter said.

"What kind of ship is this?" Alex asked. "Is Jetsam a smuggler or something? Maybe he has some weapons or–"

"It's a fishing ship" Tamryn said. "I was going to take his current load to Lund and sell it with the ship. I could live off it for a year. Like, really live."

"We got company," Doug pointed to the gap between the lighthouses. In the bay, on the other side, were two cutters. They turned in place, forming a barricade.

"Damn it to the abyss and back." Tamryn looked toward the harbor. "You think Jetsam saw me?"

"Yes," Carter said.

"I can't jump ship if he can identify me," Tamryn said. "But you lot are welcome to make a swim for it. No reason for all of us to lose our faces to the axe."

A single archer raised his bow and shot up at an angle.

The arrow splashed into the water ten parses ahead of the *Saundra*. In less than a minute, they would be in firing range. They needed to act fast, but Alex had no idea what to do.

"The things they shot into the air that flashed with light, what were those?" Doug asked.

"Fireworks," Carter said.

"How do they work?" Doug said. "Is it magic?"

Carter shook his head. "Not real magic. They are agyls of fire and air set to explode with special metallic shavings that burn."

"Do we have any fireworks?" Doug glanced around the fishing vessel.

"All ships are required to have them," Tamryn said. "Should be in the dry hold."

"Get it for me." Without waiting for a response, Doug pulled a harpoon out of a bin. He balanced it in his palm, as if judging the weight. "If there is more than one of the fireworks, bring them all."

Tamryn found three fireworks. Two red and one green. Doug tied one to a harpoon. "Once ignited, how long before it launches?"

"Thirty seconds at best," Tamryn said.

"Light it." Doug held out the harpoon.

Tamryn drew a small agyl, which caused the bottom of the firework's tube to spark.

Doug's lips moved as if he were talking to himself.

"You want to be a taintson at the bottom of the sea?" Tamaryn slid away. "That will explode and if it doesn't kill us, it will light this ship on fire."

"Quiet," Doug said, "I'm counting."

After what seemed like too long, Doug threw the harpoon.

It sailed through the air, too fast for Alex to track. Seconds later, an explosion shook the lighthouse on the right.

Dazzling light reflected across the water.

The archers in the tower screamed, jumping out windows.

Before all could escape, the lighthouse shook and collapsed.

"By Edimear's tit, what did you do?" Tamryn asked.

"Light the second," Doug said.

Tamryn did as told, and Doug threw it. A moment later, the second tower flared with light, but the explosion caused no physical damage. "Damn. Missed."

"Missed what?" Alex asked.

"The window," Doug said. "They have crates inside with fireworks written on the side. That's what I hit with my first throw."

Doug wrapped the third and final firework around a harpoon. Tamryn lit it, and he threw it.

They waited.

"Well?" Carter asked.

The whistling sounded across the water followed by a storm of light. Glittering sparkles and flares shone brighter than the agyl beams at the lighthouse's top.

The tower shook, but this time didn't fall, though it was enough of a ruckus that the archers bolted, fleeing down the seawall.

Carter cheered.

Alex gave him a cold stare. Those were innocent men and women doing their jobs. Lots were hurt. Some might be dead. It was nothing to cheer about.

"Don't be celebrating yet, boyo." Tamryn once again lined up the bow of the ship with the gap between the lighthouses. "There is the royal navy to deal with."

"Can we get past them?" Carter asked.

"Getting past them is easy," Tamryn said. "The fun will begin once we hit open water. It will be a test to see whose ship is faster."

38

OPEN SEA

ORNSDAY, 21ST OF WINEWEN, 1162.111

As much as Doug didn't like Tamryn, she had been right. Slipping their fishing ship past the navy cutters was simple. The two ships had been trying to make a barricade and were relying more on intimidation than anything else. So, when the *Saundra* squeezed between them, it took their crew time to lower the sails and pull up anchors.

The excitement quickly wore off, though, because once they were out to sea... they were out to sea. There was nothing to see but an endless blue that stretched to the stars.

Sure, there were two armed ships in pursuit, but they all were slaves to the wind, and although they constantly shrunk the gap between them and the *Saundra*, the shrinking was minimal. Three hours later, the *Saundra* was still ahead by more than a nautical league.

"How long before they catch up?" Alex stood at the stern of the ship. Carter was at the bow. It was as if the two of them were keeping as much distance from each other as they could.

"Way I see it?" Tamryn bit her lip. "They should catch up about the time we get to Kale. If they follow that long."

"We wrecked the lighthouses and stole a ship, you really think they'll give up like that?" Doug said.

"Kale is a creepy place." Tamryn rummaged through the compartments on the side of the ship. "Those that go there tend to not return."

"No chance to outrun them?" Alex said. "What if we ditch the cargo?"

"Not going to happen." Tamryn swung open a cabinet and grinned. Inside were jugs of water secured with netting. She popped one open, took a long sip, and smacked her lips. "Those fish in our hold are my easy ticket."

"What if I re-offer my ring?" Alex caressed the pouch tied to her belt.

Doug suspected that Alex didn't want to let the ring go, but was willing to do what she must.

"No," Tamryn lay down on the deck, crossing her legs and looking up at the stars. "Now that I know who you folk are, I want no one to know. Could hurt my reputation, and that's all a girl has."

Doug kept quiet. He knew nothing of sailing or swimming, and thought the matter was best left to those who at least appeared to know what they were talking about.

The conversation lulled, and the night ticked by. When the sun rose the next morning, the clouds were a deep periwinkle with streaks of pink that rose from the water to fluffy cloud banks. By midmorning, the sky went fully grey, and they faced a constant drizzle. The winds picked up, which increased their speed, but it also meant they had to deal with choppy waters.

Carter, who had been keeping away from the others, perked up and knocked on the deck to get their attention. "What's that?"

At first, Doug thought Carter was pointing at the navy ships, which were now so close that Doug could count the number of women and men on the deck. Then he looked up and saw what had caught Carter's attention.

Dragons.

Hundreds of dragons dropped from the grey clouds.

The dragons moved in an unnatural pattern, banking and rising together. It was eerie, like ghosts from his past returning to haunt him.

Dragons from all the clans were present, including elders and fledglings. They came in all shapes and sizes, and the vibrance of their scales outshone the sunrise.

"Toothless bark-chewing twit!" Tamryn turned the wheel, pointing the sloop to face southwest. "I can't outrun that."

"Kale," Alex said. "They are going to Kale!"

The dragons reached the navy ships, and still they moved not like a flock with a shared goal, but as a single body. No dragon should move in such a way. It was disturbing, against the nature of what it meant to be a dragon.

"Those taintson idiots." Tamryn swore.

Sailors on the navy vessels scrambled. A moment later, a wave of arrows launched from the deck.

Aided with agyls, there was a chance the long bows could provide the force needed for the arrows to penetrate a dragon's underscales. It would take dozens of wounds to cause any real damage.

Arrows tinked against dragon bellies and fell back to the sea. The act of violence drew the attention of the dragons.

The dragons split into two groups. Each dove for a different cutter.

Bands of fire swept across the water, creating scalding clouds of water vapor. The hot, damp air steamed the archers before the flames had a chance to reach them.

Death screams carried across the still sea, and in too quick a manner, they stopped as both navy ships were eaten by dragon fire.

The attack happened so swiftly that the humans didn't have time to react. Not a one managed to jump ship to escape the smoldering inferno. The wind shifted, and Doug caught whiffs of sulfur and burned flesh.

Dragons were not a weapon, and it hurt to see his kin used this way. Medrayt needed to be stopped. This was wrong.

"No!" Carter kneeled by the mast, tracing invisible things in the air. "I still don't have my magic. I can't do anything."

The two squads of dragons merged into a single group again and continued on their path toward the *Saundra.*

"Doug?" Alex's eyes pleaded with him.

Dying by dragons as a human would be a fitting way to go. The kind of thing Carter would read in some story. A tragic thing. "They aren't acting like dragons or moving like dragons. Medrayt is in full control. The question is whether he will let us be."

"Everyone overboard!" Tamryn swung open the same compartment she retrieved the water jug from. She reached under the netting and pulled out what looked like flattened hides. She traced an agyl on one and handed it to Doug.

The hide expanded with air to form a ball at the base. The top looped into a hoop that was big enough for a hand. "What is it?" he asked.

"Ollip bladder." Tamryn inflated two more and passed them to Carter and Alex. "It will keep you afloat."

"What about you?" Alex asked.

"I'm not leaving my easy ticket." Tamryn pointed. "Kale is two to three leagues due south. If you are lucky, the current will take you most of the way."

"We can't leave you like this," Alex said.

"I'll be fine." Tamryn gave Alex a hug. Then she pushed the girl backward and over the rail of the ship.

"Alex!" Carter dove in after her.

"Well big guy, do I need to push you too?" Tamryn winked at

Doug, and he didn't like the feeling it gave him. It was the same kind of feeling that Kane gave him, and it didn't feel right.

Holding the ollip bladder with both hands, Doug jumped overboard.

He managed to clamp his mouth shut, but that did nothing to stop the water from surging into his nostrils.

He coughed, taking a full mouthful of the salty brine. It was warm and strange, like being in an oversized stewpot that had cooled down. For his first experience with the sea, he was pretty sure that he didn't like it.

The ollip bladder kept him from sinking, and by the time he stopped coughing, Carter and Alex had swam over to him. Alex took off her cloak, wound it through the bladder handles, and tied it off so they were all linked together.

Doug kept one hand on his bladder, but with the other he held the back of Carter's shirt. He felt selfish, as if he were playing favorites, being Carter's safety net instead of Alex's, but between the two of them, he thought Alex stood a better chance of taking care of herself.

A beating roar filled the air.

Shadows dropped from the sky. Swift blurs, mixed with the flare of dragon fire. Something forcefully struck the *Saundra* and Doug heard the sound of wood breaking. The water churned and a wave rolled over their heads, dragging them further from the ship.

White water and a humid mist protected them from the scalding vapors, and when they resurfaced, the *Saundra* was gone. No shrapnel from the boat or signs of wreckage remained, it was as if the entire ship had been pulled under to never to be seen again.

Alex laughed.

Doug gave her a cold stare.

"I know. She's dead, but..." Alex straightened her face. "I just realized that when Tamryn hugged me, she stole my ring."

Doug laughed. He didn't mean to. It slipped out.

"That's not right. She saved us," Carter said. "She's gone. You can't laugh at her. That's wrong."

Doug and Alex laughed harder.

The stress. The weeks of running. The constant dance with death. It all seemed to boil out and even though Doug knew it wasn't funny, he couldn't help but laugh. There was something to be said about dying doing what you loved, and in the short time he had known her, he suspected that Tamryn truly loved swindling people.

"You're right," Alex said. "Besides, we better get moving. We may not be able to beat the dragons to Kale, but we shouldn't give them extra lead time."

Doug scanned the sky. The dragons were already back in the clouds heading south. The entire sea was flat in that direction, and he could make out the outline of an island.

39

KALENDOR

ULESDAY, 22ND OF WINEWEN, 1162.111

Not for the first time, Alex was grateful for Doug. His enhanced strength and powerful kicks kept them on track, making their swim to Kale twice as fast as it otherwise would have been.

The horrible thing was watching the island burn as they approached.

The dragons circled Kale, bathing it in fire.

They did so for twenty minutes, and when they were done, there was nothing left.

By the time Alex put her soggy boots on the rocky shore, all she could see were rolling hills of ash.

What only hours ago had been forest or meadow was now blackened earth. The fire had burned so quickly only glowing embers remained. If there had been Dragon Lotuses on the island, they were now destroyed.

"Let's check the other side of the ridge," Doug said. "They may have missed something."

"Let's get dry first," Alex said. "It shouldn't take long, and we will regret it if we don't."

They cleared away ash, unearthing a bed of hot stones, and laid out their boots and socks. Doug got fully naked, throwing his clothes onto the rocks, clearly not caring. She thought it must be a dragon thing.

Carter left on his britches but removed his shirt. It was the first time she had seen him topless, and she was surprised that he had some muscles on his arms. Nothing like Gideon or the soldiers in her father's army, but when you expect soup and get bread, it does make you do a double take.

"We can head around the beach a bit and give you some privacy," Carter said.

"Privacy?" Doug said. "You need to use the bathroom? I gotta go too."

"I don't need to go to the bathroom, and I'm fine here." She unbuttoned her shirt and threw both it and her pants onto the rocks. She felt no shame standing in her undergarments. To prove her point, she undid her cloak from the ollip bladders and spread it out to dry. She could have easily used it to cover up and hoped Carter saw that she chose not to, that she had nothing to hide.

"Well I gotta go," Doug said. "Give me five minutes. No. Make that ten."

Doug headed over a low hill and while he was gone, Alex took the time to survey the island. Kale had a bean shape with a ridge running along its outer edge. The center of the island formed a valley that was hidden from view. There was a slight chance something remained there, but she and Doug both knew that the dragons hadn't missed a thing. But what else could they do? They had no ship. They had zero supplies. They were screwed. Might as well investigate anyway.

When Doug returned, they got dressed, and not only were her

pants and shirt dry, but they were warm and cozy, a sensation she hadn't felt in a long time.

They hiked single file up the outer ridge of the island. The climb was gradual, but high. She estimated the zenith was at least a thousand parses above the beach. The smoke and soot were more distracting than the exercise, and by the end of it, she was sweating so bad that ash clung to her damp neck and cheeks.

The valley on the other side sunk below sea level. There must not have been much vegetation before the dragon assault because, although burned, there weren't any ash drifts blanketing the ground. Scattered across the basin were structures that might have been a city once or some otherworldly temple. Centuries of weather had torn the place apart.

"About time," a cold voice said. "We were getting bored."

Alex turned and saw the Sisters. All three floated above the ground in their white dresses. The ash floated through them, and Alex chuckled at the idea of its leaving them dirty, though she knew it would never happen.

"Do we get bored?" Clothu said.

"No." Lachesis shook her head.

"Then why did you say it?" Atropos asked.

Clothu shrugged. "So we would appear more relatable."

"I don't like it," Atropos said.

"Neither do I." Lachesis turned to look at Alex. "We aren't bored. We knew exactly when you would get here, and we popped over the second you arrived."

"Now we sound less mysterious," Clothu said. "Should've stuck with the bored angle."

"What do you want?" Alex said. She hadn't meant it to sound so blunt, but the island's destruction and her failure to recover a Dragon Lotus had worn her patience thin.

"We want what we always have wanted. To guide you, and right now you need guidance."

"Get out of here," Doug said. "You three have done nothing but cause trouble."

"Doug!" Alex said.

"Think about it." Doug leveled a finger at the Sisters. "We already know they manipulated us into traveling here. I left the dragon clans because of them. Carter changed me into a dragon, and they helped you sneak away from home. Where would we be if they hadn't gotten us involved?"

"If Carter hadn't turned you into a human," Alex said. "Kane would have killed you."

"And who pissed off Kane in the first place to make her so vengeful and angry?" Doug growled, showing teeth.

The Sisters turned to each other and shared a knowing look.

Atropos took a deep breath as if to calm herself. "We understand that you and Kane are linked now, and your opinion may be biased, but we assure you the actions we have taken have only been for the good. Kane has never been open-minded enough to see that."

"I don't see it," Alex said. "Think about what Doug said. None of us would be here on this island if it weren't for you three. Even Medrayt's actions and what he is doing can be traced back to you."

"Medrayt was meant to be a savior." Clothu crossed her hands as if praying.

"But you screwed up," Doug said. "You pushed him too far, like you did with Kane. Instead of serving your needs, they retaliated against you."

"Doug is right," Alex said. "All of this is your fault. If you hadn't messed with Kane or Medrayt, my father, Gideon, and Elene wouldn't be in danger. You created this situation."

Atropos laughed. "We see what you cannot."

"We see all paths," Clothu said. "And we–"

"You see what you want to see," Alex said. "You manipulate lives with no care for how your actions hurt or affect people."

"We also do not like to be interrupted," Lachesis said.

"What are you going to do about it?" Doug waved his arms

through Lachesis' non-corporeal body.

"We are powerful beings." Atropos motioned a hand toward her sisters.

"Born in a time before this world existed." Lachesis tilted her head sideways. "Before many worlds existed."

"We will still be here after your deaths," Clothu said.

"You are will-o'-the-wisps," Alex said. "Unable to exist anywhere outside of your abode in Compitum."

"We have caused genocide. We have destroyed worlds. We have saved races from extinction. Few hold the power we have."

"What has your power gotten you?" Alex asked. "You stand here belittling a dragon stuck in human form and badger two teenagers. If you are so powerful, then why are we all in this situation? You created this mess and you are powerless to stop it."

"We are not escape goats for your sins," Lachesis said.

"We have manipulated things." Clothu made a pretend coughing sound. "But we have left free will to you."

"The only people you have to blame for being here are yourselves." Atropos said.

"Ollip pratter," Alex said.

"They are right." Carter shuffled past Alex to stand beside the Sisters. "You chose to run away from your daddy and your kingdom. They may have helped you, but it was all you. Just like I was the one who chose to attack Doug. That is on me and no one else."

"Wait a bleeding minute!" Alex shoved him in the shoulder. "You don't get to act like you are all grown up and have learned the error of your ways. You are as immature as that day I saw you standing on a table in the Square Boulder."

"Who are you to judge?" Carter raised the pitch of his voice, making it sound three times more feminine. "You act all better than me because you are older and more worldly, but when push comes to shove, who does asinine things like refuse help from Bova, who sincerely wanted to help us, or gets in a sword fight with her own guards?"

"You hid that your magic is gone." Alex felt her cheeks flush with anger. If Carter wanted to fight with words, she was going to win.

"I burned it out saving our lives!" Carter yelled.

"Not telling us about it being gone almost got us killed," Alex said. "You are a child playing at adult things."

"You are lucky I can't do my magic or–"

"Or what?" Alex slammed her chest into his knocking him backwards. "You'd use the one of two spells that you know?"

"Enough!" Doug stepped between Alex and Carter. He placed a hand on each of their shoulders and pinched the pressure points at the base of their necks.

Alex squirmed, but Doug's grip held.

"You both are brats," Doug said. "Cut out the fighting. We got more important stuff to deal with, like stopping an army of mind-controlled dragons from destroying your home."

"Finally, a sensible thing to say!" Atropos clapped.

"Is it though?" Clothu asked. "His perspective is marred by his own selfishness."

"True." Lachesis nodded her head.

"What about my magic?" Carter asked. The heat in his voice diminished, replaced with a weariness. "Is there a way for me to get it back?"

"Bad question." Atropos crossed her arms.

"Stick to Doug's topic," Lachesis said.

"It was much more on point." Clothu floated forward till she hovered above Carter.

"Please?" Carter clasped his hands, begging. "I need it."

"You don't," Clothu said. "We are not fortune tellers here at your whim. We tell you only what we need to tell you, and we only came to say one thing..."

Lachesis coughed into her fist, clearing her throat. "Never get in a l—"

"Lachesis!" Atropos clapped a hand across her sister's mouth.

"Sorry," Lachesis said. "I thought we shifted from intimidation back to humor."

"What my sister meant," Clothu said. "Is that the dragons did not scorch this island to hinder you or to destroy the Dragon Lotus. Medrayt knows of the power in the blossoms and he would never risk losing access to that power. In the heart of Kalendor, in the ruins below, you will find what you seek."

"Why did Medrayt burn the island then?" Alex asked.

Diverting the dragons here and having them use fire could have been a test run for his attack on Elene, but there were other places not so far out of the way that would have been more suitable options.

"He did it to slow down the shoel," Atropos said.

"What is a shull?" Doug asked.

"Shoel," Clothu said. "You will find out."

Without speaking another word, the three ghostly beings vanished.

Alex took the lead as they made their way into the valley. Neither Carter nor Doug acted as if they wished to speak about the encounter with the Sisters. Alex for sure had no desire to rehash the fight with Carter. Her feelings hadn't changed, and she didn't expect them to.

The three walked in silence.

The deeper they went, the more the smoke and ash faded, giving their watering eyes a reprieve. Erosion had left few standing structures of whatever had once existed in this place. They followed a dry creek bed that had been baked into hard dirt by the dragon fire. The creek had flowed into a lake that still had a mark or two of standing water, and in its center was a bent steeple.

These ruins were the largest around, and the only ones that looked like they could be entered, but Alex saw no doors or windows, other than a balcony thirty or so parses off the ground. The entire structure appeared to be made of a dark metal though not a single speck of rust appeared on it.

Carter placed a hand on the wall of the structure. A moment passed, and he whisked it to the right. There was a grating sound and then a rounded section popped open that was barely big enough for Doug.

"Your magic is back?" She didn't mean for it to come off as hopeful as it did.

"Etriä." Carter's fingers ran across worn symbols that she didn't recognize. "It had instructions for opening a door."

Alex pulled out her small agyl orb and held it out to see inside the opening. Inside the structure, she found metal ribs running along the walls and a ladder that dropped down to an unknown depth. The air was funky, like stale water, and the instant she climbed in, the humidity increased.

"Let me go first," Doug said.

"I got it," she said.

"Maybe." Doug scooted passed her. "But if I slip, do you want me to fall and land on you?"

Alex wanted to argue for the sake of arguing. She had hoped their trek into the valley would calm her nerves, but she felt more angry and feisty.

Doug disappeared into the hatch and Alex followed.

The rungs of the ladder were covered with some sort of black goo. It clung to Alex's fingers and was not quite skin temperature. She wiped her hands on her cloak and slowed her pace. Twice she lost her grip, but luckily neither Doug nor Carter noticed.

The shaft ended in a room shaped like an oval with hallways branching to both left and right. The walls were mostly smooth and with patches that appeared to have been painted with a dusty, rough coating. In some places roots had burrowed through the walls, and webbed outwards, blocking some of the doorways.

"Not a flashy place, is it?" Carter said.

"What did you expect? Alex said. "Gold lace curtains?"

"I thought it would be prettier. Curved archways, designs sculpted into the walls... The other ruins where we faced the wrent were nicer looking than this. This place is so bland."

Alex ran her hand across the grey wall. It was smooth, and brittle. She thumped it with her palm, and it cracked. Prying a section off with her finger revealed metal beneath it and more of the Etriä scribblings.

"That's what I'm talking about!" Carter cleared away a chunk of the grey substance. "That's classy. It's not rusted a bit."

"The grey stuff looks like a dried liquid," Alex said. "Maybe tree sap?"

"Doesn't smell like tree sap." Doug winced. "I wouldn't touch it if I were you. It smells wrong."

"Wrong like what?" Carter asked.

Doug took a long sniff. "Like sickness. Like an infected cut."

A hard mass struck Alex in the chest and knocked her backward. She smashed against the wall, causing sheets of the grey gunk to shatter and fall to the ground. With both arms, she pushed against the weight on her chest and recoiled upon feeling something moist and slimy.

Doug acted before Carter could. He kicked the thing off her chest, and it bounced down the hallway. With a single hand, he grasped Alex and jerked her to her feet.

"What was it?" Alex waved the agyl lamp over her chest, revealing a dark grey sludge.

"I don't think that stuff on the wall is tree sap." Carter picked up a thin plate of the broken substance and used it to scrape the gunk off Alex's chest.

"Must be a shoel, the thing the Sisters mentioned." Doug said. "Did either of you get a good look at it?"

Alex and Carter shook their heads.

A blur shot past Alex, missing her face by only a single mark. She followed its movements, swinging around to see that it landed on Doug's stomach. The shoel was worm-like, stretching a parse long. Its head was fat, and it had no visible eyes or noticeable features. Its flesh was squishy like a caterpillar's, and yet when Doug wrapped his fist around its tail, it flinched, revealing an under mass of pure muscle.

Doug jerked the thing off his chest. He swung it like a club, and threw it down the hall. It struck the floor, skittered and snagged on dried tree roots before coming to a stop.

"I think you hurt it." Carter stepped toward it.

The shoel scrunched up like an markworm and sprung forward.

A circular mouth, hidden on the creature's belly, cocked open, revealing two rows of angular teeth.

Carter belly flopped. The shoel shot over him and stuck to the wall. It crunched, shrinking down and leapt again.

Doug caught it by the tail and slammed it as hard as he could against the ceiling. A clattering sounded as more sheets of the dried ooze fell then shattered on the floor.

The shoel wrapped its tail around Doug's neck and lashed out, trying to bite Doug in the face.

Doug pounded the shoel with both fists. Again and again he beat it on the left and right side of its purulent body, and still it didn't stop. It acted unaffected, as if it couldn't feel the punches.

"Sword!" Doug said.

Alex tossed the agyl lamp to Carter and jerked out her sword.

She swung, aiming not to slice, but to stab the shoel. She had perfect aim, but instead of sliding into the gunky creature, the blade bounced off its skin.

Alex tried cutting the creature with a side swipe. Nothing. She then raised the sword above her head and brought it down with all her strength. Still the blade couldn't penetrate the shoel's flesh. "It's not working. Any other ideas?"

"Try your sparker," Carter said.

She didn't see why that would work, but didn't know what else to try. She pulled the sparker out of her pouch. She pressed on it, feeling the usual grinding sensation, and then embers shot from its tip and landed on the shoel's back.

Like oil on hot coals, a fire flared.

The shoel let go of Doug. It made a wet farting sound, and thrashed from side to side on the floor.

Fully on fire, the shoel screeched, but Alex didn't hear it through her ears. She heard it directly in her head. "It's yelling in my brain."

"Me too," Doug said. "I think you only made it madder."

The flaming shoel sprung at them. Doug shoved Alex out of the way and backhanded the shoel. It crashed the grey wall. There was a sizzling sound and then the entire wall caught on fire.

The tree roots caught fire, and Alex saw what was about to happen.

"It's all going to go. We gotta get out of here!" Alex jumped for the ladder, scrambling up as fast as she could. She hoped that Carter and Doug followed.

She hadn't climbed fifteen parses when the screeching in her head shifted to a high-pitched whistle. The noise was so loud that she lost focus. Not wanting to fall, she slumped forward, sitting on a rung. Still the sound ate at her, making it so that the simple act of sitting was too much.

She rolled backward.

"Got ya." Doug caught her, using his chest and stomach to pin her against the ladder.

They hung there for three minutes, and finally the noise in her brain ceased. Wiping water from her cheeks, she looked behind her to see that Carter had been as incapacitated and lay thrown over Doug's shoulder.

"I've seen some strange things these past few months," she said. "But that has to be the strangest."

"At least we know they can be killed." Carter rolled off Doug's shoulder, climbing onto the ladder above Alex.

"Oh dunggrubber." Alex rubbed her temples while looking

down into the flaming inferno of the hallway. "Do you think there are more of them or that there was only one?"

"There has to be more," Doug said.

"Maybe not," Carter said. "Medrayt must have had the dragons torch the island to kill those things. This might have been one that he missed."

“Doug is probably right,” Alex said. "This would be too easy if there weren't, and none of this has been easy."

"If we are going back in, we should do it armed," Doug said.

Carter mumbled something under his breath.

"What was that?" Alex asked.

"Just that if one of you knew how to do agyls, all it would take is learning two to make fire."

"I had classes and some of the finest tutors," she said. "But it wasn't my thing, and maybe instead of giving us a hard time 'cause you can't access your magic right now, you can try and be productive?"

There were no trees or anything burnable above ground. The dragons had seen to that. Judging by the fact that the fire was still flickering in the hallway below them, there probably wouldn't be anything flammable below them either.

"We can use my cloak and your sword," Carter said. "At this point I don't need it, and it should burn. It won't burn long, but it's better than nothing."

When the fires finally faded, they climbed back down the ladder. Where a funky humidity had clung to her before, now the air had an itchy smokiness that made her scrunch her nose up in an attempt not to sneeze.

They knotted strips of cloth around Alex's sword and then lit it on fire. The Greker fabric burned, but did so slowly, making it a much more practical torch than she would have suspected.

"Which way?" Carter asked.

Doug sniffed, leaning back and forth, and then motioned.

"There is burned shoel that way. I don't smell any down the other halls."

"That's good enough for me." Alex led with the torch. The hallway snaked around, descending into the ground, and after several hundred parses, it opened up to a round stadium-like room. Along the way, they didn't see another living shoel, though they passed several clusters of dead bodies.

The room was big, more like a cavern, and the ceiling was high with a narrow shaft at its apex. Light streamed down the shaft. Like spokes on a wheel, other tunnels branched off the main room.

At the center was a dark pit. It was perfectly round like a well and easily twenty parses wide. But what caught their immediate attention was a small platform on the other side of the well. On that platform they saw a patch of dirt, green grass, and purple flowers. Dragon Lotuses.

"There!" Doug broke into a run and just as quickly skidded to a stop.

A black blob rose out of the patch of dirt. At first Alex thought it was an extra large shoel, but then her heart sank. The blob took on the human form of Kane.

"Hello, husband. It took you long enough to get here." She pretended a yawn. "We've been waiting a week."

"Why are you here?" Doug said.

"Doing what I set out to do from the start." She bent over and picked up a thin object. She ran it over the hard surface of the wall, and it sparked a flame. "Funny thing about these flowers, if you dump oil onto them..."

Kane dropped the match. It landed in the patch of Dragon Lotus.

"No!" Doug yelled.

"...they burn." Kane laughed.

The flowers, glistening with oil, burst into flames.

Alex felt the air leave her chest. Her head spun. This was their last chance to save her kingdom, and now it was over. It was all over.

40

THE BARRIER

ISLEDAY, 25TH OF WINEWEN, 1162.111

Gideon watched Owen. The old man sat comfortably in the center of the hidden chamber. His eyes were closed, though they darted back and forth beneath the lids. "The dragons will be here soon."

"Can we wait a bit longer?" Gideon asked.

"You know what to do?"

"I have it covered." Gideon grunted. For as long as they had known each other, Owen should have realized that things were under control, or at least as under control as they could be.

"This isn't easy," Owen said. "It will take time. Better to have it up early than late."

"Be safe."

"I always am."

"That's not true."

"No, I guess it isn't." Owen's lips curved into a smile.

No other words were needed. Gideon watched as Owen muttered a mix of Etriä with Alderish.

The mirror black walls of the chamber sprung to life, displaying the vista of Elene. The sky was cloudy, and heavy rain fell upon the city.

Gideon left.

There was nothing more he could do in the chamber.

It took some searching, but Gideon found Edgar standing on the city ramparts. The sun was setting. Not in a beautiful way. There were too many clouds in the sky, so the transition from day to twilight was more like a greying that shifted to darkness.

"It's begun." Edgar pointed to a starburst of light floating far above them. It was bright and steady.

The longer Gideon stared at the light, the more he could tell that it was expanding, forming the top of the dome that would protect the city. "How long before it's fully up?"

"Half a day," Gideon said. "That should give us enough time for the barrier to be in place before the dragons arrive."

"He mention Alex or Carter?" Worry hung in Edgar's voice.

"No, only that the dragons were on their way."

"It's so much for her shoulders to bear."

"For the light, do you not remember when we met?"

"The thing with kryrkonal. I remember."

"You were two years younger than Alex when that happened."

"But I had you and Owen by my side, and both of you made up for lack of experience."

"And Owen and I were useless for that fight. It was all you."

Edgar let out a long sigh and then put his back to the stone so that he could look Gideon directly in the face. "Can Owen handle this?"

"I don't know."

"He's not what he used to be."

"No," Gideon said. "Not since he came back from Flint with Carter."

"What can we do, anything?"

"Keep his body hydrated and nourished. This will be as much about physical endurance as it will be about magic."

"I'll oversee that, personally," Edgar said.

"I was going to handle it."

"I want you to handle the men. We have a grace period, but it won't last. You put them where you see fit and have them do whatever you think best."

There was no point in being strategic with the placement of the soldiers, but Gideon couldn't tell Edgar that. The stress of his daughter missing, his brother returning, and his kingdom under attack, it would be too much. Best to let Edgar hold on to his hope, so at least one of them had some.

41

DRAGON LOTUS

ULESDAY, 22ND OF WINEWEN, 1162.111

The patch of Dragon Lotus burned. The blossoms curled inward. Their tips browned, blackened, and then turned to ash. They were gone and so was Doug's last chance of ever being a dragon again.

"I will kill you!" Doug felt fire in his cheeks. A raw anger unlike anything he had ever felt as a human surged through his body.

Kane pranced to the edge of the deep pit and took a bow.

Doug knew then that he would kill her. He didn't like death. He didn't like the idea of killing, even in defense, but there was nothing in the world that would make him happier than killing Kane.

"You've tried. I doubt it will go any better this time." Kane's facial features where hidden in shadows and her tone plain. He couldn't tell if she was mocking him or meant it sincerely.

Not since their walk across the Crimson Plains had he focused on their mutual bond. At that point, she had been in the east, far behind them. He felt like a fool for not reaching out to test it before now. He should have known she was this close.

"I'm feeling rage." Kane tilted her head from side to side as if cracking the joints in her neck. She bent over, and then pops rippled down her back. "That's new. Didn't know you had it in you."

Doug charged her. With every step around the edge of the pit, he slammed his heels into the ground, pushing harder and moving faster. He hurled himself into the air, bringing up his fist. The aim was perfect, and Kane didn't have time to move out of the way.

She did have time to shape shift.

Instead of his knuckles breaking her nose, her face separated, leaving a gaping hole in its center. His momentum drove him elbow deep in her face. Her black gooey innards collapsed around him, and the two tumbled backward into the cavern wall.

"Doug!" Alex yelled. " Wait up. We're coming."

Kane formed a mouth in her stomach. "This is between mommy and daddy. Besides you two have your own problems to deal with."

From above, Doug heard a scratching sound and saw a slew of Greker soldiers enter from a side tunnel. There were too many for him to count, at least with his view obscured by Kane's twisting flesh. He could do nothing about them. Carter and Alex were on their own, just as he was.

"We've done this dance. You know who will win it," Kane said. "Why not be the better man and bow out gracefully?"

"Every time we've met, I've fought for my life. I've fought to protect others. This time I don't care about anyone else. I don't care about myself. I only want you dead." Like grabbing a ball of dough, Doug gripped the tendrils crawling across his face and squeezed them together. Using all his strength, he pulled. Kane's flesh stretched thin. She screamed, and he pulled harder.

Her skin snapped, whipping apart so that he held a black ball. The rest of her retracted and returned to human form.

"That was not nice." Her voice staggered, as if she were having trouble breathing. "Give me back to me."

"Then you won't like this." Doug flicked his wrist, and the ball soared into the air.

"No!"

The ball passed into the abyss in the center of room and dropped out of sight.

Through their bond, Doug felt a mix of emotions, including anger and frustration, but for the first time, he also felt sorrow. He had managed to hurt her. Something he didn't know was possible.

He needed to do it again.

Doug cleared the several-head distance between them. With one hand, he grabbed her neck. In the front of his mind and through the link, he focused on the idea of strangling her. She sensed it, and moved to defend herself, but with his free hand, he snatched at her side, plucking off a chunk of her abdomen. Where the skin broke, her flesh became black and blob-like. He did it again and again, a flurry of movement, ripping her to literal pieces.

The ground became littered with Kane. Some flecks were no bigger than a pebble, and others were as large as an apple. She tried to fight back, but every time she attempted to shift her form, he ripped out another chunk, which reset her shape and slowed her down.

Kane countered by shrinking so small that she slipped from his grip. A heartbeat later, she popped back to her full size, on the other side of the pit. Her usually gorgeous hair was matted, and her skin looked feverish. Bags swelled under her eyes. "This is a whole new side of you."

Through the bond, he didn't feel hatred or repulsion. He felt something worse: attraction. She liked the fact that he was proving to be a challenge.

"It doesn't have to go down like this," she said. "Maybe I made a mistake. Maybe I should have never tried to kill you, but instead should have recruited you."

"You are sick."

"Possibly." She shrugged. "But I see something in you I can respect. I see a drive and passion you've never shown. We both know you don't care about the dragons. Me and Medrayt are not the bad guys here. It's the Sisters that need to be stopped."

If there was anyone Doug disliked more than Kane it was them.

"You know how it goes?" She stood, her breathing returning to normal. The sweat on her brow sinking back into her. "The enemy of my enemy is my friend. I could help you get revenge on the Sisters."

"Maybe if you had offered a day ago, when I still had hope of being a dragon again, but not now. Now you and Medrayt have stolen the last bit of my identity."

"I can see why you'd say that." She straightened. Her chest split open to reveal a cavity. A single Dragon Lotus perched on a black pedestal inside. "But you're wrong. There is still one more lotus. It could be yours."

"What's to stop me from killing you and taking it?"

"I am the Arg'Natz."

"Half of the Arg'Natz."

"Half is enough. Already I can feel my body mass returning to normal. Once it would have taken days to recover fully from that."

She was telling the truth. The Dragon Lotus was real and not a trick. He could feel it through their bond. With her ability to heal herself, killing her could be impossible. Though if he severely hurt her again, he might be able to steal the lotus.

"Do you think you can disable me before I can destroy this one?" Her chest closed, sealing the blossom inside. "Your only chance of ever becoming a dragon again is by joining me."

This was it. This was what he wanted. All he had to do was say yes. It would mean turning his back on Carter and Alex and the dragons. If it was truly the last blossom left, they would need it.

He toyed with the idea of saying yes and killing her anyway. He needed to convince her to give him the blossom, but she would sense that through their link. There could be no lying. He could eat the blossom and then turn on her, but again she might sense that too.

He could agree to it.

What did the dragons mean to him? He felt horrible that they were slaves to a monster. It made him feel sick seeing them move in that mindless way, mere drones without the grace and beauty a dragon truly possesses when flying. Yet he left the dragons a long time ago. Their problems were not his.

Or were they? Carter and Alex, though, he cared for them. Something he had not done for anyone in a long time. Not only that, he cared what they thought of him. If being a dragon meant betraying them, then he didn't want to be a dragon again.

"That's a shame," Kane said. "I thought we could work together on this."

"I want to be a dragon. I do. I want to tell the Sisters that they can shove an entire ollip up their asses, but..." he trailed off looking to the teens. Alex held one of the Greker's spears and was using its butt to knock a Greker off Carter's chest.

"I get it. I had a family once too." She whipped her arms outward and everything from her elbows to hand become gleaming blades. "Let's finish this."

She didn't say it as a threat or in a melodramatic way. She said it with a hint of disappointment. She had hoped he would betray his friends and join her. It was odd, but at the same time, there was no one who understood better than him what it was like to be lonely.

Kane formed wings and crossed the abyss.

Like titans, they collided.

He didn't try to defend her attack. He had been there and seen that. Doing so was an endless loop. His only hope was to go on the offensive himself.

Her arms drove into his shoulders. He felt pain and the warmth of his blood running not only down his front, but down his back.

He drove his fingers into her face. Stretching and pulling her skin apart. She fought back, reshaping her head into a single mouth with jagged teeth. He pulled back, but wasn't fast enough. His left pinky got caught, and she bit through it.

He screamed.

Blood ran down Kane's neck

The pain was so sharp that he couldn't think. He saw flashes of white, and the sides of his vision quivered. Through the bond, he saw Kane stagger, stunned by the pain.

Reforming her human head, Kane swished her tongue around the inside of her cheeks and spit. Doug's finger landed on the ground between them. The cut was clean, straight through the skin and bone. "Doesn't feel good to have a bit of yourself torn away, does it?"

Doug's mouth felt cottony, unable to form words.

"It's ok. You don't need to say a thing." She raised a blade arm and stepped closer. "Now is when the last free dragon dies."

The ground shook, and Doug looked toward the teens. They were no longer fighting the Grekers. Instead the Grekers and kids stood shoulder to shoulder facing the pit.

The rumbling grew so loud that Kane looked away from Doug and toward the Grekers. "What is it?"

A Greker said something to her, and her eyes narrowed.

"We cleared out those slugs," she said.

He responded.

Kane's brows curled upward. "What do you mean there are more and that they are bigger?"

A mass of sludge spooled out of the pit. It was larger than a Greker, but smaller than Alex. Where the small shoel had squishy flesh, this thing had a jointed shell covering it from tip to end. With every wiggle, the armor plating grinded.

A Greker threw a spear at the thing. The weapon struck the shell and fell to the ground. The movement did draw the shoel's attention, however. Tentacles unraveled from its front and reached out to wrap around the Greker. Carter and Alex backed away, but the other Grekers fought, trying to cut their comrade free.

The trapped Greker's head popped. Blood and brain matter spattered the cavern floor. The remaing Grekers fled, shrieking.

The shoel forced all its tentacles into the dead Greker's dangling esophagus. There was a wet, pouring sound, followed by slurping.

The tentacles detached itself from the shoel. They flipped and flopped, spinning around the neck hole.

Alex turned away, as did Carter, but Doug didn't.

Neither did Kane. He could feel through the bond that she was intrigued. This was new to her.

The silky tentacles wound together, congealing into a single mass. When done, the dead Greker had a baby shoel for a head.

Like a fish out of water, the Greker, twitched uncontrollably. Doug heard a buzzing in his head. It was like the screams from earlier, only not as vibrant or painful.

The shoel slinked to its feet, shuffling toward the Grekers with its arms outstretched, as if wanting to give a hug.

Kane ran, getting in front of the shelled shoel. She shifted to three times her size. Using a roundhouse kick, she knocked it and the shambling Greker back into the pit.

With blade arms ready, Kane waited on the pit's edge.

Nothing happened.

Through their bond, Doug could feel Kane shift from panic to easement. Whatever the shoel were, they were enough of a threat that even Kane was worried about them.

With a sigh of what could only be relief, Kane looked back at Doug. "Should we finish what we started before we were so rudely interrupted?"

The ground shook again, this time far worse than before. A moment later, a swarm of shoel exploded from the pit. There were dozens of the worm creatures as well as the big, shelled things.

Fear screamed through their bond and Kane retreated to Doug's side. "We are all going to die here," she said.

42

THE BLACKNESS

ULESDAY, 22ND OF WINEWEN, 1162.111

The sight of the shoel caused the hair on the back of Alex's neck to stand on end. A horrible chill ran down her spine.

The shoels' moist bodies slunk across the cavern floor. Their pulpy forms radiated a noxious smell that turned Alex's stomach sour. Primal terror set in. She didn't want to run. She needed to run. She needed to run and keep running for the rest of her life, never looking back.

Alex forced her eyes away, and the second she did, she was able to think again. Her pulse reverted to normal, a bit too quickly. She dared another glance at one of the shelled shoel, and the moment it entered her vision, she had trouble thinking.

"Move it!" Carter pushed her to the ground.

A worm flicked past her head, landing on a Greker. Razor teeth shredded the Greker's nose. It screamed, and the shadow thing ate the rest of its face.

"Fire." Alex kept her gaze down, and by doing so, her brain took control again. There couldn't be any doubt. The sight of the larger shoel caused an irresistible terror. Neither Carter nor Doug seemed to be as hit as hard as she was, and she wondered if magic might be at play. "We need fire!"

Alex pulled the sparker out of her pouch and struck it, sprinkling sparks onto the nearest shoel worm. The creature ignited, bellowing in her mind.

"We need to regroup," Carter said as jerked her away from the mob and toward Doug.

The pair slid under the tentacles of a shelled shoel and broke free of the chaos. Behind them they heard more screaming Grekers.

"How you doing, big guy?" Carter bent down, examining the nub where Doug's pinky used to be.

"What do you think?" Doug said.

"Keep pressure on it." Carter mimed how to hold the thumb to stop the bleeding. "If we are lucky, it will clot fast."

"What about the beasties?" Doug asked.

"Don't know," Carter said. "Alex?"

"We don't have a choice." Alex winced. The walls of the cave, the floor, all were devolving into a blood-soaked mess. "We need to run."

The Grekers had seen Alex use fire on a worm and were lighting torches, but the flames were useless against the shelled shoel, and the monstrosities tore through the Grekers' lines. Limp bodies were torn to bits, others thrown against the cavern wall.

"We can't run," Doug said. "Kane has one more Dragon Lotus. We need it."

Kane struggled to hold her own. She had shifted into an Ollip so big that her back scraped against the ceiling. Wormlings clung to her calves. Their tails wiggled like black flames.

The size advantage meant Kane had no problem tossing the shelled shoels back into the pit, but it was a stall tactic at best because, a few seconds later, they would crawl back out.

"We get the Dragon Lotus from Kane and then somehow get out of here alive, agreed?" Alex said. She looked them over. Carter was bruised and bleeding down the side of his abdomen from his run-in with the Grekers. Doug, who was extra pale, breathed heavily as if worn out.

"We will do it like before." Doug rose to his feet, using the wall for support. "I'll deal with Kane. You two secure an exit route."

"You can barely stand, and you are still loosing blood." Carter reached out to help Doug, but the former dragon pushed him away.

"I'm already healing thanks to the Arg'Natz. Give me another minute and... well, I won't be up to full strength, but I'll be able to throw a punch."

A yell, higher than any Alex had heard, erupted inside her mind. She covered her ears by instinct, but it did nothing to quell the scream.

Kane had grown two hands out of the side of her ollip's chest and was using them to rip the shell off one of the armored shoels. Like shedding a corn husk, the shell came off. Beneath it were dozens of nesting worms. They swarmed Kane, biting her hands, and crawling across her body.

Kane shrunk, drawing the shoel in, and then ejected sharpened quills that tore through the worms and caught the shelled shoel.

The mind yells increased ten fold, and Alex staggered to her knees. She didn't know how the others were bearing it. It was bad enough facing Kane, but to have to deal with the shoel made this a losing fight. There were too many sides. "That's it."

"What?" Doug let go of the wall, standing on his own.

"We are going to listen to some advice that Kane gave you. She said that the enemy of my enemy is my friend."

"So you want us to work with her to stop the shoel?" Doug asked.

"No." Alex smiled. "Do the opposite."

Doug's eyes widened, and a grin stretched across his face. "I can work with that."

"Good." Alex handed Carter her sparker. "You can't fight worth crap without your magic. I'm going to drop the shambling Grekers. I need you to burn them. Got it?"

Carter shot a series of sparks into the air.

"Any questions?" She looked to them both. Neither protested. "Let's do this."

They formed a triangle formation with Doug as the point. The first shambler ignored Doug completely and dodged Alex's leg sweep. It grabbed for Carter, its circular mouth bending in the direction of his face.

Alex stomped the heel of her boot at the back of the shambler's knee. Bones popped. It tumbled over and continued to crawl, still trying to reach Carter. She kicked it in the side and felt ribs splinter. It didn't seem to register pain or notice.

Carter lit the thing's head on fire.

The mind-cries rang in her brain.

The other Greker shamblers turned to them. There were sixteen in all. With arms clawing at the air, they charged.

The first two ran past Doug and dove for Carter.

Alex kicked one, sending it flailing into the pit, while Carter dodged the other and lit it on fire.

"Doug, go!" Alex said. "They don't want you. They are after Carter."

"What did I do to them?" Carter drove his boot heel into the flaming shoel.

"You are the one lighting them on fire," Doug said. His color was back to normal, and the blood had stopped gushing from his finger nub.

"They know a real threat when they see it!" Carter let out a squeal as a shambler he hadn't seen grabbed him from behind.

"Real threat?" Doug ripped the worm out of the shambler's neck. The headless Greker body fell to the ground.

"You heard Alex." Carter gave Doug a glaring stare. "Go get the Dragon Lotus."

Doug tossed the worm into the pit and leapt over the remaining shamblers, running toward Kane and the horde of armored shoels.

"Carter, back away from the pit and toward the cavern walls," Alex said. "Try to space out the shoel so I have enough time to deal with each individually."

He crept sideways, spreading the distance between the shamblers. It didn't work as well as Alex had hoped. The possessed Grekers hadn't all been in perfect shape. Some had wounds on their legs and were limping, others were missing arms. One didn't have a torso and moved by clawing its fingers in the dirt. Five were capable of running and proved it by charging Alex and Carter.

"Alex, they are coming!'

"Shhhhh." She was counting in her head. Timing their movements. She couldn't take out all five. Not at once, but she had to remember she wasn't fighting regular folk. These things kept coming, no matter what, but they weren't exactly fighting with swords or focus.

Gideon had taught her that there was a rhythm to fighting, an art to being on a battlefield. One had to listen to the music and adapt to its beats and flows. So she listened, taking in every sound, shuffle, and movement. She struck low at the first Greker, using her sword to slice the tendon on the back of its leg. On a human, there is too much muscle in this spot, but on a Greker she managed it easily.

For the second shambler, she wanted to take a stab at its neck, but its neck was gone, replace by a shoel. So instead, she grabbed it by the back of its arm and tugged it down, slamming it so that it landed on its back. She rolled out of the way of its teeth and brought her sword down where she thought the Greker's heart was. She struck rib and settled for leaving a gash along its chest, slowing it down enough so that Carter could finish it off.

He was on her heels lighting it on fire.

"Watch your back!" She sprung to her feet then kicked the third shoel. She reached Carter in time to swing him out of the way as the fourth and fifth were about to grab him.

"Thanks."

Across the way, she could see Doug. He held a segment of shell and was using it as a shield, still fighting his way to Kane. He seemed to be having as much trouble as they were.

"They want you." Alex directed her attention back to the three functioning Grekers. It was as if the longer the shoel controlled the bodies the more control they gained.

"It's 'cause I'm so sweet." He winked at her.

She laughed. Not because it was funny. It wasn't. She laughed because it was so awfully bad. The kind of bad joke that Gideon would have loved to hear. "We are fighting for our lives."

"They keep coming, and they keep coming for me."

Carter was right. They needed to change tactics. She needed to focus on crowd control and her sword wasn't good for that... but one of the Greker's spears would be perfect. She eyed the carnage across the cavern floor and spotted one. It was twice the height of a Greker and designed for thrusting. It would be perfect.

"Come on." Alex patted Carter on the back and then ran to circle around the pit in the other direction. The route brought them dangerously close to Doug and Kane's fight with the shelled shoel. Looking in its direction caused terror to reform in her gut. Not mere fear, but a physical repulsion.

Alex picked up a spear.

Bracing her feet, she took a strong stance and leveled the spear so that it pointed toward the closest Greker. She moved forward, thrusting the spear into the shambler's knee. It was meant to be a feint to get the shambler to react, but it didn't. It merely took the wound and continued moving toward Carter.

Alex lowered the point of the spear and swung it upward rotating her shoulders and allowing her hands to follow the movement. This left her shoulder exposed, but since the shamblers weren't after her, she felt it was worth the risk.

She struck the shambler in the groin and jerked the spear sideways so that the weapon ate into the shambler's inner thigh. She felt the tip hit bone then pulled back.

The shambler tipped over, and Carter lit it on fire.

The last two shamblers attacked together, and on instinct, Alex threw all of her weight into the thrust. She managed to drive the spear through the chest of the first and into the side of the second.

Alex drew her sword again and dismembered the first shambler's leg. Stuck together, both possessed Grekers toppled over and Carter subjected them to the wrath of his sparker.

"Let's finish this up." Carter pointed to the limping and crawling shamblers still trying to reach them. Methodically, one by one, they cleaned up, being careful not to miss any and making sure every shambler was burned to a crisp.

A chorus of screeches sounded from the other side of the pit.

Kane was human but giant-sized again. At her feet, Doug stood on an armored shoel that had been deshelled. From the creature's moist back, he drew out worms and threw them at Kane. The shapeshifter tried to block them, but they bit into her and held on. Already, there were too many for Alex to count.

"Nothing can stop me," Kane yelled. "Not even these things."

"Don't forget our bond, dear wife. I can tell when you are lying, and you are terrified."

Alex felt sympathy. Actual sympathy for Kane.

Kane was a monster. She deserved to die a thousand times. But Alex understood fear. Being on the other side of the pit, fifteen parses away, she still didn't feel safe and wanted to run.

Doug threw more and more of the shoel at Kane. For every one she blocked, two more attached themselves to her. Sheets of her black flesh billowed out, flowing into the mouths of the shoels. Her mass decreased.

"You will regret this," Kane said in a voice so low that Alex had to strain to hear.

"I regret nothing." Doug jammed his fist into Kane's chest. She gasped, closing her eyes.

She whispered something into Doug's ear.

Her chest opened, releasing Doug's arm. In his palm was the Dragon Lotus.

Kane's body ballooned outward, slamming Doug against the wall. Her thin flesh formed into ribbons, entangling any shoel not already feeding on her. They become a knot of shadow and horror, and it was impossible to tell where one ended and the next began.

Kane made a groaning sound.

The ball that was Kane's body rolled, slowly at first, but then it picked up speed, falling into the pit. She took all the shoel with her.

Alex gasped.

"Gorph," Carter said.

Doug, limping, stayed as far away from the pit as possible and followed the wall until he reached Cater and Alex's side.

"What did Kane whisper?" Alex asked.

"Nothing that matters," Doug said.

Feeling too tired and hurt to run, the companions fled the sunken chamber as fast as they could. When they exited the steeple, a light rain was falling across the island, stilling the last wisps of smoke and ash.

Only a few black clouds dotted the sky. Past the island's ridges, Alex could see specks of blue. The rain would pass, and after being trapped underground with the foul creatures, the water felt refreshing on her skin.

"We did it." Carter faced Doug. "I can't believe we did it. Can we see the Dragon Lotus?"

"Take it." Doug pushed the blossom into Alex's hands. "This is yours. Not mine."

The blossom was heavy, like a full grapefruit, and smelled of warm memories. The folds of the petals looped in on themselves as if forming an infinite pattern. Beads of water from the rain pooled in the folds of the blossom, and no matter which way the light caught the petals, they glistened as if caked in a thin layer of ice.

"We are stuck on an island, hundreds of leagues from Elene." Alex held out the blossom for Doug to take. "This does me no good. I think you have earned it."

"What about the dragons?" Doug asked. "How can we free them without the lotus?"

Alex plucked a single petal from the blossom. It came free with no resistance.

Carter gasped.

Doug snatched the blossom back as if he feared Alex would harm it further.

"The Sisters said all we need is a single petal to undo Medrayt's spell." Alex wrapped the petal in a strip of cloth and stored it in her belt pouch. "That means you have practically a whole blossom to chomp on. I don't know if it will fix you, but it's worth a try."

"That's crazy," Doug said.

"Eat. The. Gorphing. Flower!" Not waiting for Doug to protest again, Alex snatched the Dragon Lotus from Doug's palm and shoved it into his mouth.

Once it was in his mouth, Doug didn't resist. He chewed and swallowed. With a worried look, he glanced from Carter to Alex. "Is it working?"

"That was a waste." Carter threw his arms in the air. "Not only are we stuck here in the rain, but you force fed him our chance to stop the dragon army."

"We don't know that," Alex snapped.

"I know magic," Carter said. "Unless these are pure magic they won't have the power to do what we need. It's all over. And look, it didn't even work. He's still human."

"You don't feel any different at all?" Alex asked, hoping for anything.

"My stomach aches a bit, like I ate something bad." Doug shrugged. "I'm sorry, but I don't feel any different."

Alex had been so sure she was right. She had thought it out. The Sisters had set all of this in motion. They wouldn't let things move forward if there wasn't a solution. There had to be. Otherwise they would be meddling right now.

The breeze picked up, and the rain fell harder. Alex crossed her arms in front of her. Night was coming. The last thing she wanted was to be near the steeple when it got dark. She needed to be as far away from the shoel as possible.

Something snapped.

Doug hunched over, holding his gut. His face was scarlet, as if something were strangling him.

"Doug?" Carter said.

Doug twitched, and when he did, a gnarly mound of flesh poked through his back, ripping through his shirt. His body continued to bend and twist in unnatural ways. His arms popped and rotated out of their sockets, and his head went bald, not from his hair falling out, but from its becoming matted and sucked into his scalp.

Doug's human form wasn't breaking or mutating. It was shifting, differently from how Kane shifted, but still shifting. It took less than a minute, and when done, Alex found herself standing in front of a fat red dragon.

Like a dog trying to dry off, Doug shook and let out a long sigh. His wings flapped. "It's like coming home." Doug's voice reverberated several octaves deeper than Alex was used to hearing.

"It's been a while," Alex asked. "But you think you're up for flying?"

"I'm more ready than you know." Doug flapped his wings, holding them open. The wind struck him, billowing out the saggy bits. "It won't be quick. We will have to stop for breaks, and it will take four to six days."

"I'm fine with that," she said. "Carter?"

"I'm all for getting off this island and rushing to save the day."

"Hop on." Doug leaned down, or at least attempted to, his pudgy gut was so round that leaning down for him was like a regular dragon standing.

Alex grabbed a spike protruding from Doug's back and hoisted herself up. She then leaned down and offered Carter a hand. He climbed up in front of her, and they sat between the ridges above the middle of his back.

"You good?" Doug said.

"I think so," she said.

"We are going to have to do a test run." Doug stretched, arching his back. "Get to mainland and then stop. If I fly at full speed, you two might freeze to death. We will need to get you better clothes."

Doug leapt into the sky.

His wings moved in a rhythmic, controlled way, drumming the air.

Less than ten parses off the ground, the wind nipped at Alex, and she pressed into Carter, using him for warmth.

"We are flying!" Carter shook his hands cheering.

Alex thumped him on the side. "Hold on with both your hands."

"I'm not going to fall," Carter said.

The higher they went, the harder the rain felt. East, from where the winds blew, she saw clear skies. They would have to endure the rain for only a bit longer.

Doug rose out of the shadow of the ridgeline and into direct sunlight. The view was spectacular. Never in her life had Alex been so high in the air. And the way the sun sank into the sea on the horizon–

Doug's body snapped.

His wings retracted and were sucked into his shoulders. Between her thighs, Alex felt the scale ridges soften and shift from reptilian to a warm skin.

They fell.

The moment Doug dropped back into the shadows of the ridge, he changed back into a dragon.

Carter landed on Doug's back, but Alex didn't.

Doug caught her with his hind claws. Gliding toward the earth, he set her back on the ground and landed. "Sorry, I don't know what happened."

"I think it might be the consequences of not eating the whole blossom," Carter said. "Seems sunlight makes you human."

"That's stupid," Doug said.

"Any stupider than a flower turning you back into a dragon?" Carter asked. "This is magic that follows no rules I've seen."

"Let's try again," Doug said. "This time, I'll stay clear of sunlight."

43

WAR

ELDSDAY, 29TH OF WINEWEN, 1162.111

When Gideon heard the horns sound, he knew the dragons had been spotted. He arrived at the ramparts in time to see them make their approach.

The colors of their scales in the high sun and the way their bodies moved were beautiful. They were ancient and rare. Something he hadn't seen in a long time. They were also the enemy.

The first death was a green dragon with yellow coloring along its spine. It flew into the invisible barrier surrounding Elene. Its body made a thud as its neck snapped then it went limp.

Two more dragons crashed into the barrier before the rest managed to divert their path. They settled on the mountain peaks above the city and the plains to the east and west.

From there, the hours blurred. The dragons took turns rising into the sky, forming a single line, and blasting the barrier with fire. Their attacks were clunky at first, but after the initial attempts, their timing was perfect so that there was a constant stream of dragon fire. As the flames licked the barrier, it shimmered with pulses of amber light.

At noon on the third day of the siege, the dragons changed their pattern so that instead of one constant stream of fire eating at the barrier, there were three. It meant that the dragons had less downtime, but fatigue was still a long way off for them.

Gideon began to worry on the fifth day. He entered the chamber to check on Owen, and the mage was dripping with sweat, so much so that if he hadn't known better, he would have thought that the old man had just stepped out of a bath.

Gideon barked orders at the men keeping watch. Several minutes later, they returned with towels and fresh clothing. Edgar, who looked as if he hadn't slept in days, followed them into the room.

"A runner warned me," Edgar said. "What happened? He was fine ten minutes ago. I only went to use the privy."

"It's the cost of the magic." Gideon knelt by Owen's side. "Take off his britches. I'll get his shirt."

Edgar did as told, unbuttoning the pants and sliding them down while Gideon opened Owen's shirt. The old man's skin was a greyish hue, and it felt cold to the touch. "I don't think he can last much longer."

"This didn't happen last time?"

"There wasn't an army of dragons pounding on the dome."

"What do we do?"

"Dry him and keep him warm." Gideon winced at a dank smell.

The watch brought agyl-heated water. Edgar and Gideon washed Owen and dried him. When done, they wrapped him in blankets.

"Can we wake him?" Edgar asked.

"Only he can do that."

"So why doesn't he?"

"Because he would die if it meant buying us more time."

"Then what do we do?"

"Prepare for the barrier failing. It won't last."

"You sure?"

"Yes, and at this point, we don't know if the kids are coming. We have to be ready for the worst. I'm going to have the men prepare the catapults and weapons."

"We can't fend off those dragons."

"I agree. We can't, but it won't stop us from trying."

On the sixth day, the barrier above Elene flickered, and after one final surge, it faded out of existence.

Gideon was ready for it. He stood on the walls of the inner ward, waiting. The instant the barrier fell, catapults launched metal spheres with spiked teeth.

The dragons weren't ready. They, or at least Medrayt, had no way of knowing when the dome would fail, or if it would fail. So they were unprepared for the barrage.

The spheres found their targets, snagging the necks, limbs, and wings of the dragons. They were like Cooke's wind burs, but more volatile. Each of the soldiers, including Gideon wore a smaller set of them attached to their belts.

Explosions rocketed through the dragons. Blood and entrails rained upon the city. Dozens of dragons fell from the sky.

The soldiers along the wall cheered.

"Don't be stupid," Gideon yelled. "They will regroup and attack."

The dragons did. They retreated, flying above the grey clouds, and then they came in waves of four.

The range of dragon fire was limited. At most, it could hit ten parses, which was well within catapult range.

With only four attacking at a time, the dragons had room to maneuver and they knew to be aware of the explosive barbs. But they didn't know about the arrows.

"Archers!" Gideon yelled. The soldiers on the wall shuffled, notching long bows. "Fire!"

Like the barbs, the arrows were agyls assisted. They flew straight, and instead of pointed arrowheads, they were capped with small versions of the explosive barbs. A single arrow, unless perfectly shot, couldn't kill a dragon, but it could do some serious damage.

The arrows ripped through the wings of the lead dragon. It tumbled and crashed into the outer wall of the city.

Two more dragons were downed by arrows. A third one, in attempting to fly out of arrow range, got blasted by the catapults. Its neck ripped in half, but didn't fully separate, so it dangled in the wind as it crashed on to the eastern plains.

Another wave came and then fell.

The soldiers continued to cheer, and Gideon feared they were growing cocky. All it would take was Medrayt deciding to do a full-out assault, and there would be nothing they could do to stop him.

A single dragon appeared, dropping below the clouds. On its back was a rider. Gideon couldn't mistake the rider's monkey form. It was Mogul of the Red Hounds.

Mogul's dragon brought its wings in close and dove toward the city. Its underside became so filled with arrows that it looked like an upside-down porcupine. Still it didn't divert from its path.

The dragon opened its wings, slowing.

Mogul jumped off it, and the dragon crashed into the eastern outer wall.

Stone and men flew in all directions. All five catapults that had been anchored to the wall were destroyed or buried under rock.

Mogul had landed on the roof of a building on the outside of the city. With his one arm, he drove his bo staff into the slate tiles and skidded to a stop. Flipping, he hopped down the building's side using molding and ledges to slow his descent.

A new wave of four dragons approached, and the archers turned their focus skyward. Only Gideon continued to watch Mogul. "Watch from below!"

The monkey-man, skittered up the broken wall, and before the archers knew what was happening, he tore through their ranks.

The bows were too cumbersome for close range, and the trained assassin had no problem dismantling the entire squad of archers on the east wall.

Removable wooden platforms spanned the wards of the city. Mogul scampered across one, heading for the catapults nearest the palace.

Gideon drew his long sword and readied himself to block Mogul's attack.

"I hoped to meet you again!" Mogul's pupils were dilated so big that the blacks filled his entire eye. "I owe you for what you did to me."

Gideon couldn't be taunted or provoked. He squared his stance at the end of the platform and readied himself.

Mogul swung his staff, fast, too fast. Something was off.

The bo staff smacked Gideon in the wrist. A bone broke. He suspected his left thumb, but he ignored it, pushing back the pain.

"Playing tough?" Mogul cackled, showing teal-stained teeth. Zewik juice or some other similar concoction. It meant the monkey-man was pumped up.

Mogul jabbed with the staff. Gideon deflected it. It thudded against the platform, which shook.

As if for fun, Mogul jammed the butt of the staff against the platform, creating a drumming sound. He laughed, swaying with the beat. "I know something you don't know."

"What?"

"I don't want to live, and I'm happy to take you with me."

Ten dragons fell upon the city. They came in low and from the unprotected eastern side of Elene, sweeping the walls with fire.

"Goodbye meatbag." Mogul threw himself at Gideon. He wrapped his legs around Gideon's waist and hooked his one arm around Gideon's neck.

Gideon hacked at the monkey-man with his sword. Chunks of

fur, flesh, and blood, filled his vision. Mogul didn't let go. The zewik juice clearly protecting him from the pain.

It took a head butt and jamming the sword pommel into Mogul's temple before his grip loosened. By then though, the dragon fire had reached the platform.

Gideon drove his sword into Mogul's gut and jumped.

Mogul laughed.

They dropped three stories and out of range of the flames.

Midair, Gideon flicked his wrist and twisted his arm, splitting Mogul in two.

Gideon hit the cobblestone street. He rolled. Pain ripped through his shins. Fractured. That was fine. He could push through it.

There was nothing he could do about the dragons above. He'd have to trust that the remaining archers and catapults could handle the onslaught. The city's biggest vulnerability was the east wall. He'd serve best there.

He made his way past the burning shops and homes.

The destruction of the outer wall was worse when viewed from the ground. Stone blocks, bigger than a barn, had crushed the surrounding buildings, and he knew of no masons or agyl masters that would be able to repair it.

Gideon climbed the wall in time to see two new dragons approach. They either didn't see him or didn't care about him. That was good. He could use that.

Timing it as best he could, Gideon jumped off the wall. He missed one dragon's wing, but snagged its tail spike.

The dragon thrashed, trying to shake him off. When it didn't work, the dragon increased its speed and rose vertically, shooting into the sky.

Using the dragon's ridges like rungs, Gideon scaled its back.

The dragon broke into a cloud bank and burst through the other side.

Gideon squinted.

Golden sunlight shone down and reflected off the tops of the clouds. Here, he saw, the reserve dragons flew, waiting to be activated by Medrayt. Had they all been sent in at once, Elene would already have fallen. Medrayt, it seemed, truly did want the city as whole as possible. Thank goodness for human pride.

Gideon pulled a cluster of burs from his belt. Strung together with metal threads, like weights on a fishing net, he twirled the metal spheres. He should have worn more, but he never expected to have an opportunity like this.

He threw the burs. They spun upward, and streaks of light darted between the spheres.

A silver dragon with indigo markings on its face caught the baubles with its front claws.

The air pressure changed.

Gideon felt it in his ears.

A spider web of lighting erupted from the baubles. The electricity spread, leaping from one dragon to the next.

It wasn't enough to kill them, but it was enough to stun them.

Not all the dragons were in range, but at least forty or so were.

Those hit with the electricity lost control. Vomit, urine, and feces poured from them and their bodies convulsed. Falling, the dragons became tangles of wings and limbs, dropping into the clouds.

The dragon Gideon rode snarled.

Gideon wedged his sword in the dragon's neck. The scales were so tight that he could fit it only a few marks deep, but that was all he needed. He jiggered the blade, working it into the perfect position. He knew he had paralyzed the dragon when it stopped struggling and went flaccid.

The dragon plunged into the clouds, flipping head over tail.

Gideon held tight.

He waited till they were fifteen parses off the ground then removed his sword from the dragon's neck.

The dragon hissed. It stretched its wings to right itself, but it was moving too fast to stop itself from crashing into the ground.

Dirt and dust flew into the air.

The impact threw Gideon off the dragon's back. He hit the ground. More bones broke. His body rolled, and when he came to stop, he knew from his shallow breathing and wheezing that at least one of his lungs had been punctured.

He was more than five leagues to the east of Elene. It would be a brutal hike, but he could make it. He just needed–

The dragon roared.

Gideon had forgotten about the dragon. That was a mistake.

Teeth slashed at him. He rolled away, springing to his feet.

The dragon dropped a claw on him, pinning him to the dirt.

With both front claws, it scooped up Gideon and held him like a child would a captured firefly. The dragon opened its mouth, clearly intending to eat Gideon.

Gideon thrust his sword upward. Not in a killing blow, but one timed so perfectly that when the dragon bit down, the sword sunk into the soft flesh inside the roof of its mouth.

The dragon opened and closed its mouth. The pommel of the sword jutted past its lips, and no matter how it moved its tongue or shook its head, it couldn't remove the blade.

Gideon tumbled to the ground. The pain of all his injuries reverberating with each bounce.

Dropping to all fours, the dragon spoke. The words were soft, too quiet to hear, and yet Gideon recognized the cadence. He rolled out of the way, barely in time, as a blast of fire surged from the dragon's mouth.

The pommel of the sword melted in the fire, and the heat traveled up the blade and into the Dragon's maw. Liquid metal boiled out of the dragon's nostrils, and it yelped in pain.

The dragon wasn't going to survive, and there was nothing Gideon could do to ease its passing.

"This is not right, Medrayt." Gideon yelled. "I know you are there. End this. Put this poor creature out of its misery."

The dragon curled into a ball, tucking its head into its belly. It spoke the words for fire. Flames tore through its gut, filling the air with a charcoaled stench.

Gideon didn't have the stomach to watch the beast suffer. He let out a long groan and limped, turning to start the long walk back to Elene. Every step hurt. Though surprisingly, he had no open wounds. The blood splattered on the front of his armor wasn't his.

Black and blue bruises covered his chest, streaking down both arms. He could no longer form a fist with his right hand. The bubbling he felt in his chest was without a doubt a punctured lung. He hoped he wasn't bleeding internally, but the chance of that was impossible.

Gideon heard flapping wings and looked up. Another dragon approached with a rider on its back. He blinked and then squinted, brushing dirt and sweat from his brow. It was Cooke.

"You took out a whole dragon. That makes you a hero, right?" She looked toward the city. "Or does it make you a failure, 'cause what is one dragon among hundreds?"

Gideon brought up his left fist.

"That's right, you aren't one for talking, are you?" She smiled. "I like that. It's an attractive quality."

Gideon grunted.

"This is war," Cooke said. "As much as I respect your ingenuity, I can't let it happen again."

Cooke shoved both her pinkies into her mouth and whistled.

Gideon heard more wings. Six dragons landed, forming a ring around him and Cooke's dragon.

"You want to make this easy or fun?" Cooke asked. "I'm ok with either."

A salty, metallic taste ran across the back of Gideon's mouth. He spit. A wad of blood stained the ground.

"I'm not in much shape for a fight," Gideon said.

"I don't care."

"I wasn't talking to you. I was talking to Medrayt."

"He doesn't care."

"He does," Gideon said. "He and I go back, much further than you."

"The dragons are his. Let's see what difference your history makes. Will he spare you? I doubt it."

Three dragons sprung on Gideon.

Gideon's thoughts shifted to Edgar and how he had failed. Elene would fall. The palace, which had stood for hundreds of years, would be destroyed. Gideon's collection of art, slices of history, would be ruined. And his precious instruments would never be played by anyone.

His thoughts blurred as his mind filled with nothing but pain. Teeth and claws tore at him. His sense of awareness faded.

Death took him.

44

DRAGON FLIGHT

ULESDAY, 22ND OF WINEWEN, 1162.111

Carter was cold. Again. This was after he had put on an extra pair of pants, a jacket, and wrapped a blanket around himself. He didn't complain, though, because Alex wasn't complaining. On the plus side, his butt was hurting less than it had been.

The flight from Kale to the mainland had been horrendous. They arrived before dawn and stopped in a small town where Alex traded in the last of her coins for blankets and supplies. Doug spent the entire day sleeping while Carter and Alex converted an ollip saddle to fit Doug.

Before dusk, they woke Doug, fed him, and as soon as the sun set, they were in the air again. That first night flying in the comfy seat had been exciting and magical. Now, seven nights later, he shivered, and his teeth clanked.

"Do you think we will make it before dawn?" Carter leaned back so that Alex could hear him. She still insisted sitting behind him, even though they both had safety belts in case they slipped.

Alex peered at the world below. Although dark, they could make out the tops of trees and the reflection of stars in the Nox River. "At worst, I think we have less than fifty leagues. We might be closer. Everything looks different up here."

They didn't know what they would be flying into. Medrayt's dragons had left Kale hours before the companions had arrived on the island. Unlike Doug, the dragons didn't need to stop during the day, though they would have to break at least for an hour or two. Still, it was impossible for Carter and his friends to catch up and it meant that by the time they got to Elene it could be too late.

"Are you ready?" Alex asked.

"I don't know." Carter was pleased that she couldn't see his face. "I'm still blocked off from my magic."

"The Sisters said you didn't need it."

"The Sisters said a lot of crap."

"Not all of it was crap." Alex laughed.

"I said a lot of crap too." He risked turning enough to see her face. "I'm sorry about what I said."

"I'm sorry too," she said. "I think it hurt that after these past few months you didn't trust me enough to tell me about your magic."

"I was embarrassed."

"I didn't know great magicians had such emotions."

Carter opened his mouth to reply with something snarky, but decided to let it go. He deserved it. He deserved more.

"I need your help Carter." Alex said it in her real voice. Not the one she used when being tough or bossy, or when she was trying to sound smart. She said it as herself. "I need you to free the dragons. Can you do that, for me?"

Carter thumbed the pouch on his side. In it was the stone with the spell the Sisters had given him and rolled up with it was the Dragon Lotus petal. "It's not that easy. You can't understand."

"Try me," she said.

"You ever make stew?"

"I loathe stew."

"I hate stew too, but I still know how to stew a stew."

"I get the basics. You throw stuff into a pot of hot water and let it sit there."

"Right," Carter said. "With stew, you put whatever you have on hand into it. There is no finesse or skill. So, let's say you are skilled at making pierogies and–"

"That's the food they had at the Square Boulder in Hal?"

"It's questions like that one that make us common folk think royalty are all unpoxed. No one should ever be unsure about what a pierogi is."

"What does any of this food have to do with you freeing the dragons?" She smacked him lightly on the waist. "I don't need to know how to cook. I need you to free the dragons. Can you do it? Will you do it for me, please?"

"I got it covered," he said. "I'll free them."

For the rest of the night, they flew in silence. In his head, Carter practiced the spell the Sisters gave him. He repeated it over and over again. Each time, he tried to clear his mind to gather his will. It never came, and he had to trust that eventually it would.

Carter knew they had reached Elene when he saw smoke sprouting from the mountains on the horizon. The city looked like a smoldering hive, but instead of bees, dragons swarmed it. Dozens of smoke tendrils backlit by fire leaked into the sky, twirling, mixing, and forming a black cloud.

"We are too late." Alex buried her head between Carter's shoulder blades.

"No," Doug yelled back to them. "They are still fighting. I can see movement on the walls. Humans."

"Do it." Alex prodded Carter. "Cast the spell."

"I can't," Carter said. "Not from the air like this, moving so fast and maybe not from so far away."

"Bring us in perpendicular to the mountains," Alex yelled to Doug. "There are low plains, but enough foliage that in this light we will be impossible to see."

Doug banked left and descended, dropping hundreds of parses over the course of a league. They skirted a forest, and its top branches made a light brushing sound while rubbing against Doug's scales.

Across the grassland were farms and other outbuildings. None were damaged or showed signs of being burned. That was good. At least the local people weren't paying directly for their failure to get here sooner.

As they got closer, bits of ash fell from the sky like snow, and the foul, sulfurous smell was twice as strong as what had plagued them on Kale.

Doug opened his wings, slowing himself so he could land, but abruptly flapped them again, jerking into the sky so hard that Carter had to hold on with both hands to keep from falling out of the saddle.

"What was that?" Carter asked.

Doug curved west, moving away from the city.

"Doug?" Alex yelled.

"There was a body ahead," Doug said. "It was on the plains. It was too dark for you to see, but I couldn't miss it."

"I expect there to be more," Alex said.

Doug slowed again, as if to land. "I think this might have been Gideon."

Carter felt Alex's knuckles jam into his waist. "Take us back," she ordered.

"I don't think that's–"

"Take us back."

Slowly, as if reluctant, Doug tilted his wings and looped around. He settled on the ground, his feet crunching on the dry earth.

"Where?" Alex jumped off Doug's back. She had her agyl orb ignited before she hit the ground.

"Ahead, that way." Doug tilted his long neck to the right.

Carter unhooked his safety belt and chased after Alex. He had known Gideon for only a short time, but one thing that had been clear was that Gideon was family to Alex. If this was Gideon, it could break her. He hoped for Alex's sake that Doug was wrong.

Rivets scarred the ground, deep gashes where something big and powerful had sliced away the dirt as if it were soft sand.

"Alex wait," Carter said. "You don't need to do this."

"I need to know." She pressed on.

Blood stained the earth. Not a pool, like Carter would have expected, but strings of splatter, dotting and weaving across the ground.

Alex gasped and put a hand to her mouth.

The body, or what was left of it, didn't look human.

Raw flesh, pulled apart. Clumps of hair, skin, and muscle thrown about, haphazardly as if the dead person had been shucked like a cob of corn.

The mess and tangles of flesh were so unruly that Carter couldn't identify the body parts. The vulgarness of it overwhelmed him, and he tasted bile in his mouth. Why would Doug think that this carrion had been Gideon?

Alex dropped the agyl orb.

It hit the ground and bounced.

Light flickered against the still-wet meatpile, and the orb chinged, stopping as it hit a large rock.

An oblong chunk of sandstone, two parses high, stood upright. Gideon's decapitated head lay jammed onto the rock's peak. Scraps of skin flapped where his neck should have been and trails of crusty blood ran down the stone, seeping into the earth.

Alex hadn't moved since dropping the orb, and Carter wasn't sure how he should react. Was he supposed to offer her comfort, or would that make her angry? He didn't know what she needed.

"I didn't want you to see this," Doug said.

"What is this?" Alex's breathing took on a gasping quality. "This wasn't a death done in battle. This isn't how a person dies in war. This is murder. Flat-out murder."

Intestines lay sprawled ten parses from clumps of hair. Bones in a heap were piled on top of shredded leather. The ferocity of the death suggested that it had been quick. This was not a slow, drawn-out torture. At the same time it was overkill.

Gideon hadn't merely been murdered. He had been torn to pieces and then played with as a cat might throw a mouse into the air, not realizing it was dead.

"He didn't suffer long." Carter reached out and put a hand on Alex's shoulder.

Whipping around, she knocked his arm away. "Is that supposed to be comforting?"

"I..." Carter looked to Doug for help, but Doug was looking at the sky toward Elene. "I don't think there is anything I can say to comfort you. This is a terrible vile thing, and no matter how many times I try to tell you I'm sorry, it won't fix it. All I can say is that we will find Medrayt and make him pay."

Alex sniffed, sucking a glob of snot back into her left nostril. She wiped her cheeks, but within seconds, fresh tears rewetted them.

"I failed him," she said. "I didn't get here fast enough."

"We did the best we could," Carter said.

"Did we?"

"It's not over." Carter pointed to the city. "The fight is still going. It might be too late for Gideon, but your father..."

Alex inhaled a wobbly breath. "You need to make him pay. You need to cast the spell. Right now. Stop Medrayt. Stop the killing!"

Carter wanted to. He wanted to be able to snap his fingers, to let loose some magic and end this madness. That wasn't how magic worked. For starters, other than Doug, he couldn't see any other dragons. The night hid the land, and they were still leagues away from Elene.

"I can't," Carter said. "We have to be closer."

"How close?" Doug asked.

"In the city."

Doug swore in dragon tongue. "I can outfly a few dragons, but I've been pushing all night to get us here. There is a chance with them being controlled that they can't maneuver or fly as well as I can. If that's the case, I'll get you into the city, but once in the air above the city, there will be too many of them for me to dodge."

Carter didn't know how large the radius of the spell would be. He might need to cast it once for every dragon, or once for all of them.

He had been arrogant when the Sisters gave him the spell. It was magic. He was a magician. It would be simple. He should've thought it through. He should've asked questions instead of assuming he could handle whatever was thrown at him.

"We will have to get closer," Carter said. "It should be in a place where I can see as many dragons as possible."

"The reservoir." Alex held one hand notably higher than the other. "It's on the peaks above the city. It should be untouched from the battle and offers the best view of Elene."

"If I land with that many dragons, they will rip us to..." Doug's glare shifted to Gideon's head, still resting upon the sandstone slab. "We won't survive."

Alex followed Doug's look. Her lips drew together, tightening.

She crossed the broken ground and stopped at the rock. New tears ran down her cheeks. She kissed her fingers and used them to close Gideon's eyes. Reaching behind Gideon's head, she grasped his dreadlocks.

"Alex," Carter said. "Let me–"

"No." Alex jerked the head off the rock. Stinky cords of blood spun, wetting her travel cloak.

Alex sobbed.

Carter's own eyes watered. He had never lost someone close and seeing the pain... the way Alex's bottom lip quivered, the way her hands shook, or the way she struggled to keep her breath. It hurt.

Alex took off her cloak. As if swaddling a baby, she wrapped

Gideon's head in it. She tied the top in a neat bow and laid it on the ground. "No one will tear us apart like they did to Gideon. We are going to fight, and we are going to end this."

"I understand your determination, but I am one dragon," Doug said. "I cannot fight off hundreds of other dragons."

"You don't need to," Alex said. "You and I are going to be a distraction."

"How is that going to work?" Carter asked.

"We are going to leave you at the reservoir." Alex kicked over the bloodied sandstone slab. "As much as I want to be a part of the action and to be there when you end this, Doug and I can do more good, keeping the other dragons from noticing you. We already know Medrayt wants me. So, I'm going to tempt him and give him what he wants."

"No, if anything..." Carter was going to say that she should wait here, but he knew her well enough to know that would never happen. She would be a part of the fight, even if she was there only to distract Medrayt's attention from him. He had no choice in the matter. "Alright."

"Alright?" Alex's eyes went wide with confusion.

"If this is what you think is best," Carter said. "Let's go save your city."

"Doug?" Alex asked.

"I'll fly. I'll fly faster than I ever have. Tell me where to go. I'm with you."

Alex used the back of her hand to clear snot from her upper lip. "Let's kick some ass."

45

HIGH MAGIC

ELDSDAY, 29TH OF WINEWEN, 1162.111

Less than a league away from Elene's walls the companions passed dozens of dead dragons. Their bodies lay broken with the fire of the burning city reflecting off their scales.

"They didn't deserve this," Doug said.

Carter was amazed that those defending the city had managed to bring down so many dragons, and he wondered what the price they had paid for those deaths. How many human lives had been spent in a pointless war?

"I think we are spotted." Alex kicked Doug's right side.

Carter looked to see an orange dragon with a peach-speckled underbelly. It was flying parallel to them. Watching, but not reacting. Surrounding its head was a purple aura that matched the color of the Dragon Lotus. Vibrant, like a band of lightning.

"What is it doing?" Alex asked.

The aura shifted to a darker hue, and the dragon suddenly snarled.

"Medrayt knows we are here," Carter said. "I think he took full control of the dragon."

Doug shot straight up, giving them no warning. If it weren't for the safety strap, Carter would have fallen off.

Doug's wings flapped hard, outpacing the other dragon. Carter thought they were free, but then he saw ten or so dragons that had been circling over the city turn their way.

"So much for stealthily getting Carter to the reservoir," Doug said.

The reservoir was twice the size of the lake around Owen's cottage. It had an oval shape that was too perfect to be natural, and as they got closer, he could see aqueducts flowing from it, down to the city.

"We can make this work." Alex tapped Carter on his side. "As Doug flies past, you jump."

"I'll break my neck," Carter said.

"I can get you low." Doug brought in his wings, preparing to dive. "It will be less of a fall than when we jumped off the *Saundra*."

Doug broke into a spin, almost throwing Carter off his back a second time. Doug pulled up, dodging a blue dragon and then a green one.

"I don't think I can do this," Carter whispered.

"Then we will all die, and Gideon will have died for nothing." Alex put a hand on his shoulder. He thought it was for comfort, but then she jerked him backward, undoing his safety strap.

She kissed him on the cheek and pushed him.

Carter fell stomach up. He saw her face. Red eyes and lips parting to speak.

"Save my city," she mouthed.

Then she and Doug were gone.

Cold water slammed into Carter's back, knocking the air from his lungs.

He sunk, struggling to right himself.

When he surfaced, he scanned the sky for Doug and Alex, but in the chaos, he couldn't find them or the two dragons that had been chasing them.

Carter crawled onto the rocky shore. The raining ash clung to his skin and clothes, and when he tried to wipe it off, it smeared, leaving streaks.

Standing on the cliff at the edge of the reservoir was like being in the heart of a storm. Layers of mindless dragons flew in a circular pattern above the city, seemingly waiting for Medrayt's commands. He could see faint auras around each of their heads.

The dragons walking the walls of Elene and fighting the soldiers had darker auras. They moved in erratic ways and breathed fire, scorching stone.

Enough stalling. He had to try and end it.

Carter unhooked the pouch from his belt. He had left it sealed shut after the last time he read the spell. He had the thing memorized, but he didn't want to risk screwing it up.

Days old, the Dragon Lotus petal still looked fresh, not showing any sign of wilting. Carter had avoided touching it, for fear of harming it, but now he was surprised to find that it felt velvety between his fingers.

In his other hand, he held the spell.

He could feel his magic. It was there. It hadn't gone away, yet it still felt muffled, as if a wall was keeping it at bay. He focused on that wall. He focused on tearing that wall down and allowing his magic to rush free.

The Dragon Lotus petal called to him. Like a beacon in fog it demanded his attention. The amount of power it contained was overwhelming. With it he could do anything. He could turn Elene into a crater. He could summon the sun. He could kill every single dragon with only a thought.

His magic might be gone, but the Dragon Lotus's magic could be his.

Carter pushed the thoughts away.

He was here to free the dragons. That was it.

Carter read the spell.

The Dragon Lotus grew warm.

He glanced to the sky, hoping it had worked.

Nothing. The auras still clouded the dragons.

Over the wreckage of the east wall, Carter spotted Doug. His plump form with Alex on his back was impossible to miss. Three dragons flanked his sides and rear, while two others soared below and above.

Carter was sure Doug and Alex were only seconds away from death, but then Doug pulled his wings in close, falling into the dragon beneath him.

Doug and the dragon grappled with each other, or at least it looked that way. After a moment of falling, Carter realized Doug was pulling the other dragon down, using his superior weight to keep it trapped. The other dragon fumbled, trying not to break free, but to claw at Doug's face.

Waiting, till they were less than ten parses off the ground, Doug kicked off the dragon, propelling himself and Alex back into the air. The dragon struck the ground. It didn't get back up.

It was another unnecessary death that was Carter's fault.

Carter took in a deep breath, slowing his heartbeat. He cleared his mind and focused on the Dragon Lotus and its link with the dragons.

He repeated the spell, this time saying it from memory.

Nothing.

He was about to try a third time when he heard splashing.

A black and silver dragon skimmed the surface of the reservoir. It landed on the shore. Perched on its back was Cooke. "Now why would you be up here all alone?"

He opened his mouth to speak, but she held up a finger, stopping him.

"Don't say a word," Cooke said. "I've seen what you can do and have you covered. If you so much as use an ounce of magic, there are six dragons that are going to drench this entire cliff with fire. Not even you and your magic can stop that."

He pointed to his lips and held up an open palm.

"Go ahead," Cooke said. "But remember we are not alone."

"I don't want to fight you." Carter said. He meant it too.

"Good, I don't feel like fighting you either. This would be much easier if you don't resist."

"If you are going to kill me, then why bother talking to me? Why not have the dragons do your dirty work like you did with Gideon."

Cooke squinted as if trying to read Carter.

"That was you, wasn't it?" Carter asked.

"Not me. We aren't alone." Cooke motioned to the dragon's head.

Carter wondered if she could see the aura or if she only meant the gesture figuratively.

"I wouldn't care if you died," Cooke said. "But Medrayt has other plans for you."

"What?"

"Plans."

"And if I refuse?"

Cooke tilted her head up. Circling over them in a holding pattern were six big dragons. "Will you submit and allow me to restrain you, or are you going to fight?"

"Can Medrayt hear us?"

"Yes and no. If he is actively controlling this dragon, then yes. It depends." Her dragon's aura was a dark purple. The same color of the aura of the orange and peach dragon he had seen earlier. Carter bet Medrayt was listening.

"I demand an audience," Carter said. "Let me speak to Medrayt, and once I have said what I have to say, you can do whatever you wish with me."

"And how am I supposed to–" Cooke's dragon leaned its head

down, forcing her to grip its spine to keep from falling off. "I guess Medrayt is listening."

Carter's instinct was to tell Medrayt to go suck an ollip's tit and then to try and take out Cooke before the watching dragons had time to use their fire. That seemed stupid though. He knew if Alex were here, she would tell him it was stupid. He needed to play this a different way. "I was on Kale, and I saw the shoel."

"Lies." Cooke rolled her eyes. "We cleared Kale. It will be months before they return."

"We were deep in the island. At a great pit. There we saw not only the wormlings, but shelled monsters impervious to fire. The mere sight of them made my skin crawl and caused an unnatural sense of terror. It took all my will to not run from them."

Cooke's dragon snarled.

"It was there that we found this." Carter opened his fist, revealing the Dragon Lotus petal.

"What is that?" Cooke asked.

"A very special flower filled with more magic than you could ever imagine. This is the same kind of flower that Medrayt used to put the dragons under his control."

"Why do you have it?"

"I was going to use the same spell Medrayt used and take the dragons for myself. I was going to be the new dragon lord. It is what the Sisters want." Carter opened his other hand revealing the spell stone.

The dragon took a catlike stance. Its knees bent, ready to spring and attack. "Why haven't you used the spell?"

"Too much. It's all too much. The things I saw on Kale. The things I saw before getting there. I don't want any of it. I want to go home to Master Owen. I want to see my friends, Allison and Dale. I don't want to be a hero. I don't want to risk my life. I want to go home." Carter placed the spell and the Dragon Lotus on the ground. He then backed away from them with his arms raised. "Can I please go home?"

The dragon relaxed. Carter took it as a sign that Medrayt had agreed to the deal. Cooke must have come to the same conclusion because she threw down a pair of manacles. "Put those on and bring me the stone and petal. If what you are saying is true, I'm sure Medrayt will let you go home."

Carter clanked the cold iron around both his wrists. He picked up the Dragon Lotus and stone, carrying them to Cooke. "Please make him understand, I didn't know what I was getting into. I was foolish. I let the idea of controlling my own army of dragons blind me. I don't want that much power. The power to destroy islands and cities on a whim. The one who controls that much power would be unstoppable, and I couldn't handle it."

"The power has a price beyond that." Cooke stared at the blossom. "Medrayt has paid it tenfold."

"He is strong then," Carter said.

"He was strong." Her voice quivered. There was regret and pain there. She cared for Medrayt. That could be a problem.

Cooke flipped the petal between two fingers. "The spell. Is it for real? It would have let you take control of the dragons?"

"Yes."

"What do you want to do with the boy?" Cooke leaned forward speaking to the dragon's aura. Carter was sure then that she could see it.

The dragon turned its back to Carter. At first Carter was terrified, thinking it meant he was supposed to come with them, but then he realized it was a pass. Medrayt was letting him go.

"Are you sure?" Cooke asked the dragon. Her high tone suggested she was as shocked as Carter.

The dragon flapped its wings and leapt into the air.

This was it. It all came down to this.

Carter watched, refusing to blink.

Magic erupted from Cooke.

She had done it! She had taken the bait and tried to take control of the dragons. Though from the way she had acted, Carter thought maybe it hadn't been to betray Medrayt, but done in some way to help him.

Beams of power, shot through the air and struck the dragons. On impact, the auras splintered, exploding like fireworks. Glittering bursts of light filled the sky, merging and mixing.

Through closed eyelids, the brightness of the energy burned Carter's pupils.

When it faded, he opened his eyes again.

Across the city, he saw the dragons snap out of their mechanical movements. Many shook their heads or reared back, retreating confused. Some lashed out at nearby soldiers as if they were the ones to blame.

A big black dragon, with scales the color of midnight and tiny clusters of red, landed in front of Carter. It had no aura, and it looked at him with its head tilted.

"Woah," Carter held up his shackled hands. "I mean no trouble. I'm sure you are confused, and I'd be happy to explain. See–"

The dragon whipped its tail at Carter.

His ribs crunched.

Pain shot through his chest, and he flew backward.

Carter hit the ground hard, dislocating his shoulder and cracking his head on a rock. Everything went black.

46

BURNED OUT

ALLSDAY, 33RD OF WINEWEN, 1162.111

Carter awoke in a warm bed. Not his own, but still, it was a bed, and it had been months since he had slept in a real bed. Blinking, he looked around the room and did not recognize it. The walls were stone, though heavy tapestries covered most of them. One, he was sure, was of The Silver Lady.

"'Bout time," Owen said. He sat in a chair, no not a chair. Carter wasn't sure what it was. It was as if a chair and a couch had hooked up and made a baby. Owen seemed relaxed in it. In one hand, he held a cup of tea, and in the other a book. Setting the book down, he looked to Carter. "Don't move fast. You took a nasty blow to the head."

Carter touched the back of his head and felt pain. He also felt no hair and a long line of stitches. "Did you have to shave it?"

"It's superficial and will grow back. Better to be bald for a time, though you don't pull it off like I do." Owen fluffed his shoulder as if clearing away invisible locks of hair.

"It's over?" Carter asked.

"For now."

"Doug and Alex?"

"They are safe," Owen said. "I was told Doug was pretty rough, bleeding from fighting off dragons, but at dawn when he changed into a human his wounds healed. Fascinating magic there. I've since observed the change myself. In all the years I've lived, I've not seen anything like it."

"How bad is the city? How many people died."

"Too many."

"I'm sorry," Carter said. "I'm sorry we didn't save more lives."

"You did the best you could, and in the end, you still freed the dragons."

"I didn't," Carter said.

"What?" Owen sounded taken back, surprising him wasn't something Carter ever found easy to do.

"We had..." Carter trailed off. "There was this thing and creatures and a flaming sun. I used my magic, and we escaped, but I burned it out. I can't do a basic agyl anymore."

"Then how did you free the dragons from Medrayt's control?"

"I didn't do it. I tricked a woman, Cooke, into doing it. She is the one who broke the spell."

Owen took a sip of his tea.

Carter lowered his head.

"See the lamp in the corner?" Owen asked.

"Yeah."

"When you look at it, what do you see?"

"An agyl emitting light."

"You can see the actual thread?"

"Yes."

"Then your magic is not burned out. Merely blocked."

"For how long?"

"I don't know. Could be a week. Could be a century. Depends. I once had a block for ten years." Owen shivered. "Worst ten years of my life."

"How do you know it means I'm blocked and not burned out?"

"Because when I look at the lamp, I can't see the agyl."

"Master Owen!" Carter's mouth hung open. "Are you sure?"

"I've been able to see magic my whole life. I know when I can't see it anymore."

"But–"

"I've led a long life, you know that, right?"

"I've assumed, but you've never told me the details."

"There is only so much one man can do to change the world. I've put in my dues and paid prices more horrible than you can imagine." Owen leaned back and let out a long, slow breath. "I'm tired. This isn't a bad thing. It is my reward."

"I'm sorry." Carter said, not knowing what else to say.

~

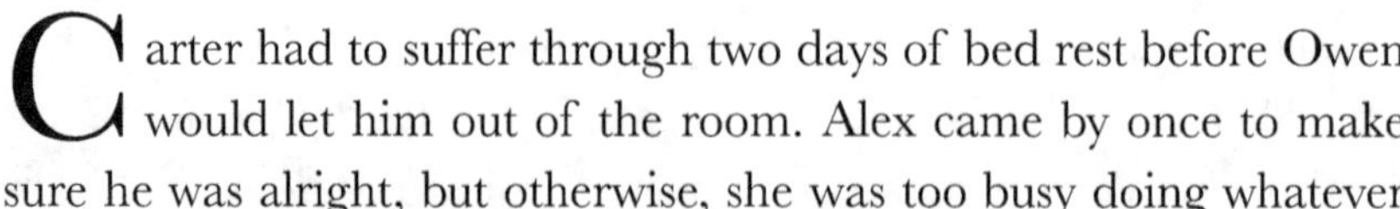

Carter had to suffer through two days of bed rest before Owen would let him out of the room. Alex came by once to make sure he was alright, but otherwise, she was too busy doing whatever things a princess had to do.

It's not that Carter was mad or felt slighted by her. It was that he felt guilty. He had never seen Elene, so he had no idea what the city looked like when in full splendor, but he had seen the destruction. He knew how much rebuilding and how much help the people would need to put their lives back together. He wished he could be by Alex's side or down on the streets doing whatever he could to make things better.

On release, Carter went to the palace stables. They had been emptied of animals to give Doug a place to stay. It was the only place big enough for him to transform without risking structural damage.

The sun shone brightly without a cloud in the sky, but it was cool. Fall was on its way out, and already a winter breeze swept through the city.

Entering the stable yard, Carter smelled citrus, which was a comfort since he had been expecting the musk of animals. If Doug had been living there for a week or so, it shouldn't have been a surprise.

"Doug?" Carter called out.

A clanking sound came from inside one of the three barns. The double doors flew open, and Doug walked out. He wiped his hands on a floral apron and set down a metal bucket.

"Carter!"

Doug smiled. An actual smile.

"What are you doing?" Carter asked.

"Making use of my reward for saving the kingdom."

Carter shielded his eyes from the bright sunlight and peered into the barn. It was mostly empty, with high windows keeping it well lit. The only thing in the whole place was a goat wearing a leash tied to a post.

"About time." Carter clapped his hands. "This whole vegetarian thing is stupid."

"Nester isn't for eating!" Doug slapped Carter in the back of the head. "I'm milking it. The kitchen staff is teaching me how to make five kinds of cheese."

Carter couldn't tell if the goat was the reward, or if it was the cheese-making lessons.

"I need to head down to the market, if you want to come. I've been thinking that a bit of herbs, maybe parsley or sage, could really boost the cheese's flavor."

"I'll walk for a bit," Carter said. "Master Owen only gave me a limited release. I'm supposed to be back in an hour. Though I gotta say you have the strangest priorities."

"You make do with what you got." Doug held up his fat hands and wiggled his fingers. "I figure if I'm going to be human for half the day, I should at least get something out of it."

"How is the whole, dragon by night, human by day thing going?"

"I keep ruining clothes," Doug said. "It would be much easier if I could go about naked, but people keep getting upset. Indirect sunlight is enough to keep me human, but if I'm in a dark, enclosed space, I'll revert to being a dragon. That was a weird day when we figured that out."

Doug would be alright. At least that wouldn't weigh on Carter's conscious.

"I'm sorry," Carter said. "I'm sorry for that day in the cave. I dragged you into this whole mess. Alex and I got ourselves into it, but it was forced upon you because of my stupidity, and I'm sorry."

"It's what it is." Doug said. "No hard feelings."

Carter and Doug passed through the palace gates. Sweaty workers, who were making repairs, stared at Doug for a moment before gathering their things and walking away.

"What was that?" Carter asked.

"Word is out about me. They know I'm a dragon."

"Don't they know you helped save the city?"

"No one cares. They know I'm a dragon. It is all that matters."

"You know, with this all over, you can go home."

"That's the idea," Doug said. "Once you are better and once the memorial happens, I plan to fly you and Owen back to Hal. I can't wait to get back to my cave."

Carter hadn't meant the cave in Hal. He had meant home to the other dragons, and he was pretty sure Doug knew that was what he had meant, but Carter let it go. "I've not seen Alex much. How is she doing about Gideon?"

Doug shrugged. "We don't talk about those kinds of things."

"What was the last thing you talked about?"

"Poop."

"Like the stuff that comes from your butt?"

"If humans poop from somewhere else, I've been doing it wrong."

"Why were you and Alex talking about poop?"

"There were hundreds of dragons here," Doug said. "They were here for over a week. Usually a dragon is aware of where it poops. Dragon poops can be acidic and often solidify, becoming impossible to remove once it melds with an object. So there is a lot of dragon poop all over the city, and they are struggling to clean it up."

Carter thought back to their journey from Kale to Elene. Whenever Doug had to go to the bathroom, he did land, leave, and come back for them when done. Carter hadn't thought to ask about the details.

"Alex wanted me to tell you the soldiers searched the city and the refugee camp," Doug said. "No one matching Cooke's description has been spotted. I still think she must have died casting the spell, or the dragon she had been riding killed her.

"I guess," Carter said. "I just don't like knowing she might still be out there."

Doug looked west, toward Kale. "I know how you feel."

47

REQUIEM

ISLEDAY, 5TH OF REPARE, 1162.111

"You don't have to do this," Alex's father said as he adjusted the right pauldron of her ceremonial armor.

"I disagree." Alex buffed a smudge from her azure breastplate. Utterly impractical, Arwyn's crest had been burned in its center with a glowing band of white light. If she ever wore something so silly in a real battle, it would do nothing but make her a target. Yet today was about image. The breastplate conveyed strength to her people, which they badly needed now.

"I'll be right beside you." He kissed her forehead.

"I know."

Her father walked through the curtain first. He announced her, and a rumble of cheers and stomping followed. She waited, hoping it would die down, but when it didn't, she parted the curtains and passed through them.

Alex took her place at the front of the pulpit. Below her, people filled the streets of the city. She saw men and woman of all ages. She saw kids sitting on adults' shoulders and elders being supported by their families. These people. They were why she had left Elene. It was for them, and now she got to tell them it was over.

"People of Elene." Alex spoke, and the crowd grew quiet. "What you have experienced has been unfair and unjust. It has been tragic. Every one of you has experienced loss, but the time of fear and of hiding is over. I am pleased to say the dragon threat has ended."

Screams of joy erupted from the crowd.

"This will not be easy," she said. "But in time, we will heal. We are Arwynians, after all. We are strong. Proud. Maybe a bit too proud, but we are survivors."

Laughter sounded in the streets.

"Never forget those who gave their lives, not only for our city, but for our kingdom." Alex took a deep breath and spun, taking in the monument for the first time. The smooth stone forming the obelisk was white, reaching higher than the inner walls of the city and was as wide as a full city block.

Doug and Carter entered from behind the curtain. Both were dressed finer than she'd ever seen them. Oddly, it didn't fit. Lace and embroidery did not suit them ,and yet Carter had an extra bounce in his step. For some reason, he was a fan of frilly clothes.

Carter stopped in front of her, holding a leather bound book open, while Doug stood beside him holding a single inkwell with a quill resting within it.

"We will write the names of those we have lost in this book so they will be remembered." Alex shook excess ink off the quill. In clear plain text, she wrote *Gideon of Elene*. As she formed the letters, the walls of the monument illuminated, and Gideon's name appeared, carved in elegant letters in the stone.

Alex didn't know how the monument worked, only that her kingdom's agyl masters, under Owen's guidance, had created it. In multiple ways, it was a work of art.

"This memorial does not bring back our loved ones." Alex's eyes watered as she thought of Gideon. "It doesn't make the pain of losing them hurt any less, but it ensures that, for generations, their sacrifice and valor will never be forgotten."

Alex didn't fight back the tears. She allowed them to fall and didn't bother wiping them away.

EPILOGUE

"Turned out better than we thought."

"Did it?"

"The major players lived, even Kane."

"Can you call what she is experiencing living?"

"She can only blame herself. We didn't want this path. We didn't want the shoel to awaken yet. She and Medrayt brought this course early."

"Should we warn them?"

"They will know soon enough."

"Besides, on Kale they made it clear they want nothing to do with us."

"But we can't let them proceed without guidance."

"Of course not."

"I say we send an emissary."

"Medrayt lives. There are paths in which his way could still bring us what we want."

"He still has a small contingent of the dragons under his control. He could aid our ducklings."

"Can't trust him. I'd much rather send Friday."

"He is too busy."

"Then who?"

"Look down the paths, sisters. Look at the horrors to come. We need someone who can offer guidance, even when they are out of our reach."

"Stop being coy. Who do you suggest?"

"The Destroyer."

"It is no longer indebted to us. It most likely hates us."

"For now, but things have a way of changing."

NOTE TO THE READER

Thank you for reading ***Wrath of Dragons***. If you enjoyed the book, I hope you'll consider **leaving a review**. They're the lifeblood of indie authors and the most important factor when others decide if they will pick it up.

Want More Elderealm?

Want to know the story of how a fledging Doug left the dragon clans? Join Scott's mailing list and get DRAGON FLIGHT, an exclusive bonus story!

He'll also send word whenever he release a new book, and you'll get updates with behind-the-scenes sneak peeks!

GET IT NOW!

http://www.scottking.info/blog/bellalyn/

The adventures in Elderealm continue in...

AUTHOR'S NOTE

I was a freshman in college when I stumbled upon the idea of a fat dragon. Dragons are always big and scary, but never fat. You never hear of an obese dragon. Dragons would be top tier predators. They could eat as much as they wanted. I've seen plenty of fat dogs, cats, and other animals. So why not dragons?

I wrote a short script called "Doug the Obese Dragon" for one of my media classes. It was horrible. But it was in that story that Doug was born. His personality was pretty much there from the start. He was cranky. He didn't like the other dragons, and he wanted to be left alone.

That was seventeen years ago.

Since that time, I half-attempted to write a novel and wrote a screenplay. Neither were bad, but neither felt right. It wasn't that the story wasn't good enough or the characters weren't fun enough. It was that I wasn't there yet as a writer. I hadn't honed my craft enough yet to be able yet to tell the story that I wanted to tell.

Fingers crossed I'm finally there and that you enjoyed this book. Sixteen years is a long time to have a story in your head. I am not the same person I was back then. Sure, I'm still sarcastic, and humor is my default coping mechanism, but I've grown. My perspective on the world and life isn't the same, and in that time, things like 9/11 and other horrible events have happened.

Fantasy fiction has gotten grim and dark. Those kinds of stories have a place, and when I'm in the mood, I enjoy them. But when sitting down to create the current version of *Wrath of Dragons*, I knew that's not what I wanted it to be.

I'm alright with characters dying. I'm alright with them suffering or having terrible things to face. I'm not alright with the lack of hope. I'm not alright with things being so dark that there are no jokes or places for happiness.

My background in college, grad school, and post-education focused on film and photography. One of the most important things in photography is contrast. A photo needs dark darks and light lights. When the whole image is the same tone, it feels bland.

My hope with *Wrath of Dragons* is that it has a nice contrast. The lighter moments matter because, by comparison, they make the darker stuff seem darker, just as those low moments help make the nice ones more fun.

Some absolutely gut-wrenching things will happen to our heroes in the next several books. I can't help that. It's what has to happen, but I can promise you that there will always be laughter.

The real world is already a dark place. The news at night is so depressing that many people simply avoid it. I don't want this series to be that way. I want it to be a place where, sure, it might pull at your heart, but at the same time it offers an escape.

That's what books did for me when I was growing up and facing the harshness of life. Hopefully, this book is me giving back and doing the same for others.

ABOUT THE AUTHOR

Scott King is a writer, photographer, and educator. He was born in Washington, D.C. and raised in Ocean City, Maryland. He received his undergraduate degree in film from Towson University, and his M.F.A. in film from American University.

Until moving to follow his wife's career, King worked as a college professor, teaching photography, digital arts, and writing-related classes. He now works full time as a game photographer and author.

As a board game photographer, King shoots games for websites, online stores, and for other marketing needs. He also produces an annual calendar that highlights board and other hobby games.

To learn more about Scott and his work, visit his website at www.ScottKing.info. You can also follow him on Twitter via @ScottKing.